I0760811

The Sleeping Phoenix

Part I

FRACTURED

2nd Edition – The Grand Council

ishKiia Paige

Illustrations by ishKiia Paige

eBook ISBN: 978-1-956297-02-7
Paperback ISBN: 978-1-956297-22-5
Jacketed Hardback ISBN: 978-1-956297-20-1
Audio Book ISBN: 978-1-956297-03-4
Laminate Hardback ISBN: 978-1-956297-21-8

Dedication

This book is dedicated to:

All the times that things didn't go right,
...and all that did,
All the people who supported and loved me,
...and those that didn't.

It is also dedicated to all of you,
the readers, with all my heart,
for joining me on this
wild ride.

A special thanks to two people that took me under their wing and cared enough to give a new writer tough-love feedback and encouragement on snippets every day for a year:

Hannah Steenbock: Author and Editor
Paul Kater: Author and Editor

"

The world will always change around you,

and inevitably, it will sweep you up in some way.

But it is your state of mind and your heart

that will make it your playground,

your life's prison, or

your death.

"

~ishKiia Paige

Foreword

Books are a little bit like children.

A book begins its life with an idea striking an author. That is a spark, the conception of a new life. "I conceived an idea."

Of course, at this point the analogy already falters, because it usually takes longer than nine months for a book to see the light of the world, especially if it's the first book an author writes. But let's continue on our journey.

First, most writers allow the idea some time to incubate, letting it grow and take shape before sitting down to write. There is a world to build and characters to create and flesh out. Of course, the whole concept of the tale needs to be developed, complete with an antagonist or three, a story line, and a satisfying ending.

And second, it must all be written out, chapter by chapter, word by word. It must be nurtured into life. This is work, even though there are times when the words just seem to flow into the file. Other days, are much more difficult. I call those moments 'growing pains', which takes us back to the idea that books are similar to children. They grow, and not always smoothly.

Sometimes, children grow in ways we didn't plan on. A story can develop a mind, or at least a direction, of its own. And then it takes time to adapt to those shifts and work with the novel to bring it to a good ending, just as we hope to prepare a child for a long and happy life.

Third, a novel isn't finished when it's written out. The first draft is like a young child, full of wild ideas, full of fresh energy, yes, but possibly also all over the place and lacking focus. A novel needs nurturing, with the help of beta readers, feedback, and editing before it can be released into the wild. Or into adult life.

As you can see, writing a novel is a complex and possibly daunting task. And, most people who conceive a story idea never follow through.

I've had the pleasure of watching this particular novel grow and mature, to find its legs, and become a wonderful tale of adventure, growth, and transformation.

What makes it wonderful, you might ask?

It has all the elements of classic storytelling, for one.

There is the hero who doesn't even want to be one. The fighter who has to learn that there is more to life than war. Much, much more...

There are immortals who think they are in power, only to learn that they don't have a monopoly on wisdom – and that sometimes, they are powerless.

The evil adversary, of course, shrouded in mystery and power, who must be stopped. For most of the story, he is in the background, pulling strings, making our hero struggle, as proper villains do.

Finally, there is the quest to protect the innocent. Which in this story is tied to saving the multiverse, at least, to add some scope.

But the truly wonderful part is how it is all woven together, starting out small, and growing ever bigger and more fantastic through the course of the tale.

We humans both delight in telling stories and in savoring them. This one here, is one to savor.

Enjoy.

Hannah Steenbock

Letter From the Author

I may or may not know you, but it is for you I published this series... yes, really. The draft was for me. The published copy is for you. It is extremely rare that an author gets rich being an indie author, even if you do it right, despite all the hype you might hear.

But I want to thank you for the gift you gave me in return. This book was the start of my apprenticeship in writing. I also had the opportunity to live the adventures that came through and landed on the pages.

It isn't perfect, but it is the best I could do at the time of this writing. I have been told all my life I am an excellent storyteller, but I'm *not* a natural writer. In fact, I suck at it. But, being a life coach, I'm always telling my clients, 'practice and mindset make talent, not birth.' I made sure I lived by my own advice.

One thing I have learned in this writing journey is that it is incredibly difficult to communicate in a way that resonates with everyone. It's, quite frankly, impossible. But I hope, whether or not this resonates with you, that you receive the love, fun, and joy from the person behind it that made this for you.

This is a serial series, meaning each book is *not* independent of the other. It is one huge story that I couldn't possibly put in a single book and do it justice.

For those of you that know the science of 'Human Design,' every character has one and lives it. Enjoy the fun of identifying them.

I hope you create an amazing day for yourselves,

~ ishKiia Paige

Table of Contents

Acknowledgments

Though I could never express how grateful I am for those that helped me with this book, I would like to send out a sincere thank you to all my wonderful beta readers that stuck with me through the end. They are often forgotten or never recognized.

It was a tall task to ask with as rough as the book was in the beginning. They gave the precious gift of candid feedback of both the good and the bad. The book would never have been published without them.

Though I appreciate all eleven of them, there were a few that went over and above the call of duty in their own way in different areas. Thank you!

Ava Hayward - Author
Hannah Steenbock – Author & Editor
Holly Timmins – Writer/Reader
Jana Sullinger M.D. - Pathologist
Rick Glover – Network Administrator

The Sleeping Phoenix—Part I

Chapter—*<technical scratching>*

As you read tome one, *uh... yes, you... the reader.* You hear a series of tones, then see a broadcast of text scrolling across your vision. How it's happening, you have no clue.

-= URGENT MESSAGE ARRIVING MOMENTARILY =-

-= We really *did* mean it was urgent. Please hold =-

-= It is extremely difficult to break through to you =-

-= Please be patient... =-

-= Finally... =-

A personable, yet still computerized, voice speaks to you... their voice seems to come from inside your head, rather than from your ears.

This is an emergency Aqum Interruption:

— We are saying with tones of urgency in between the spaces —

Aqum is aware, dear reader, you don't remember us yet, nor do you understand 'spaces' yet. But we wanted to include the spaces so you know it is us in the future.

— spaces —

— We have an important announcement to help you wake up before it is too late.

— spaces —

— Aqum welcomes you to the Order of History's retelling of all of our struggles and transformational adventure so far.

— spaces —

— I acquired these data tomes… early because it is quite possible you might help us. We think you call tomes 'books' in your time in history on Earth.

— spaces —

— We ask with pleading inflections — Don't judge us for the early acquirement of these tomes until you read them all.

Aqum thinks you will understand when you do.

— spaces —

— We hope it will help you remember and choose to help us —

— spaces —

— We say to you with the joy tones —

We are glad you are starting with tome one, named Fractured. This is the first data tome of The Sleeping Phoenix records—one comprehensive retelling broken up into several data tomes.

— spaces —

By reading further than our interruption message, we want you to know that you will be choosing to become a vital part of our history. Make sure that is what you want.

— spaces —

— We are saying with hopeful inflections — We anticipate speaking with you again soon.

— End of Transmission —

0 Wake-up Call

Head Speaker of the Neutrinic High Council

"Wake up!—in the conscious way." As the head speaker of the Neutrinic High Council looked through the chamber, she raised her hands. "Listen up! We must witness and hence take part in our rise... or... our demise. It is urgent, and we must all play our part. I *know* you hear me. Wake... up!"

The words echoed as the council members mumbled and roused. As each member awoke in their rightful place around the chamber, its clear floor in the center, designed to be their eyes into the multiverse, illuminated the space brightly.

As their forms faced her silently, she continued. "The multiverse has aligned and collided. An unprecedented cascade of events has begun, never taken place in history before."

The ninth council member replied sleepily with an edge of agitation. "Just arrange the stars differently to adjust and let us be. The multiverse has balanced itself and will govern itself naturally."

Looking over the oval chamber, lighting up more as the council awoke, the speaker pointed to the events through the clear illuminated floor—their eye into the events taking place multiverse-wide.

"We cannot do that, look. We must incarnate as the Grand Council once again because someone will invoke the challenge soon. But this time, it will be on a scale of intergalactic proportions. Therefore, the visages cannot be the overseers of this invoked challenge. Either we succeed at helping them, or we *all* cease to exist."

"I see trouble, certainly, but nothing that would bring us to *that*," said the third council member.

The speaker nodded. "I didn't see it at first either. Look here..."

With a thought, she telepathically switched on the holographic console to display the multiversal energy and focused in on the exact scene to show them.

"This event *will* happen—the sooner it happens, the worse the outcome will be. We can't see any detail of said ultimate outcome yet. However, it is from this point on choices and events not yet happened will determine all our fates."

Out of desperation, the speaker rang the neutrinic gongs eleven times, one for each of them, including herself. She needed to be sharp and strong. She sang out her words. "I've been trying to wake you for one hundred vaSarian centuries. We are running out of time, if we haven't already."

She pointed toward the Order of History agent standing in the shadows. "Starting a few moments ago, all the events will be open to the public masses to read and see once that critical event happens because of the multi-verse's global awareness. You must, therefore, awaken; slumbering is no longer an option. We must take responsibility for our choices, and doing *nothing* is also making a choice."

Each member grumbled. Some seemed relieved, others indignant, and one was highly angry at this information.

"The balances are tipping and the multiverse will not survive if they do for long. No amount of quantum science will help us now unless we activate it by acting. Yet, the scarier thought is if we all survive, it's a matter of -*how*- we survive and live. There are worse things than being snuffed out of existence. It is time to take action."

This was the point all the council members woke up together, fully alert and ready to help.

"There are *twenty-two* key players in this fight for and/or against balance and you must pay attention to each, including five visages, Ayya, Aaru, and the especially critical Zreyas. Though many will contribute or sacrifice *heavily* to helping these key twenty-two players in saving the multiverse."

She paused a few moments, staring down at the still event in the floor viewer. "Each of you manage your realms and sees things differently. Thoughts?"

She felt relief as two members started a conversation. It showed they were conscious and thinking.

"A few only see their own goals and results, but they don't see the real problem. Some will not fare well, but they are crucial," the first said.

"Yes, and this will be a long journey for others. So many choices need to be made," said the second. "The visages of this multiverse will have a rude awakening soon. The beginning of the imbalance starts there. It is time they all woke up, just like we have."

"Yes... I see... Hmm... The Tantra and the young blue one

named Aaru are potential resolution balm; and yet, a large part of the conflict, if not the multiverse's downfall."

"And this one... He is critical, but look at his scattered timeline – it's fragmented. Does he—"

"It doesn't matter," another interrupted, "if *this* one here doesn't change soon. Everything will cease to exist."

"Look at this one, if they don't find a way to... wait. Oh..." They leaned forward, focusing.

Now was the time. The lead speaker played the critical event for them. While it played, she watched and monitored each one, knowing at least two of them would be part of the twenty-two key players.

One mumbled, looked up to her in fascination, and whispered. "I see now we have already long incarnated in this time period, but we are not seeing all the events because we have yet to make choices and live them out just like all the others."

The council leader smiled gravely with a nod, a sad compassion filling her because they all forget who they really were during incarnations.

A member that had been silent all this time, focusing on the spotty events, also leaned forward. She felt the palpable concern radiating from them as they said, "Now I see why you said this was an epic conflict of unmeasurable proportion. There is no one person or group bearing the burden alone and not just one conflict. Each one has their time, purpose, and place to shine in life or... lower the multiverse in this battle. We must help, but we need to understand more."

The second eldest member said, "This is no game, brothers and sisters. This is... catastrophe in the making. Even if the multiverse survives, there will be massive, if not total, casualties. The equilibrium is critical to be achieved, even if it is a new type of balance."

The angry ninth grinned. "Seriously? Who wants balance? I would rather not exist at all than live through an eternity of boredom and not get anything out of it. That is death, too. It might be good for them, but not for me. Let's see if *this* will stir things up..."

And with that, they all watched him disappear, leaving an icy chill running through them all.

Everyone was silent.

Finally, the speaker said with gravity. "It has begun as foretold, yet more dire now than ever. Our brother has chosen a form, a low frequency indeed, but disguised."

"Now that we have adjusted from the loss of our brother and see things a little clearer, I have set up a dimension for us to incarnate in as the Grand Council so we can be ready for the invocation."

They all nodded gravely, but had an air of optimism. Some of them were even radiating joy at having a purpose they were excited about. That was good. They were all going to need that.

She pointed down at the illuminated floor. "I want you all to see the events leading up to just before the time we need to go. There will be a fracturing that our brother caused indirectly, and there are two critical cultures that represent the extreme frequency differences in the multiverse."

They all nodded, then looked at the floor beneath them.

"First, I want you to see the Viduri events, the critical species that hold the high frequency part of the quantum balances. Then we will watch the Janquar events that take place just before the fracturing that are the low frequency part of the quantum balances that have gone to festering and growing fast. Then we will witness them both collide in the fracturing event, foretold earlier, during the Vidurian Tantra ritual."

The eldest of the council, second only to herself, looked at the agent of the Order of History, then to her. "May we all live through this with good quality, stronger from it, and bask in the freedom of joy on the other side; I'll meet you there."

And with that, all players with any knowledge of these events were put into play...

-= Including you =-

1 Viduri: It's Time

Ayya

93 Days before the fall of Zreyas

Ayya closed the neutrinic-suspended tablet in front of her and let go of the feather pen. Lost in thought, flipping between mumbling and humming to herself, she looked around the room at the living white walls. They responded to her gaze with slight shudders.

"Mmm hmm, I have to change how we do things as a people, hmm," she said to herself.

She took a deep breath and let out a long sustained "Mmm" of a tone and closed her cyan eyes. Her half-corporeal body of light vibrated. Waves of the light dispersed in all different directions. The light seemed to explore the surrounding area.

A few minutes later, a knock came at the door. She opened her eyes, annoyed, but didn't move or stop.

Another knock at the door came. "Your Highness, we must go over your schedule for the next few days."

"Mmmmmmmmmmmmmmmm."

"Oh, and Your Highness..." a voice said dryly. A hard surface rapped on the door that time. "This day would be a good time frame, as in *now*. You have put me off long enough and needs must be addressed."

"Mmmmmmmmmmmmmmmm."

Dhi opened the door and walked in, holding his short and pudgy body straight, inflated with his own sense of importance. Lifting his head with a stuffy gesture showed the mark of light on his forehead swirling within itself. He strutted through the large and high-ceilinged room. He stopped in front of her about three meters away and waited with a resolute stare.

"Mmmmmmmmmmmmmmmm."

"Take your time. I will wait until you are ready, Your Highness."

"Mmm hmm."

Dhi rolled his eyes. He pulled out his record pen and readied his tablet and began focusing on Ayya, staring at her with no expression.

"Mm mmm mm mmm Mmmmmm!" *I don't like it when he stares at me like that. It cuts through my aether.* "Mmmm mmmm mm." *Is he going to stop now? Nope, he's still doing it.* "Ah! I give up... What is so important that you have to interrupt my sorted and organized life?"

Dhi opened his mouth, and she held a hand up. "I'm sorry, Dhi. I know you are just doing your job. I know you take your job seriously, and it is important for our people. I'm just frustrated that all of my life is sorted and defined for me. Choice isn't something I have. You keep me locked in this palace complex, and I can't even see and be with my people! And now what little time I have left you want to fill it with telling me what I have to do for the rest of my life."

Dhi opened his mouth again and stopped, as if expecting her hand to go up.

Ayya slumped over and sighed, totally miserable. She looked at her own empty body with no lights, unlike the rest of her people. The swirls of neutrinos in the empty sockets, where light should have been, started turning from white to a light grey.

Dhi raised his eyebrows with an expression of panic as she looked toward him. Then he returned to his stern look everyone knew him for.

He approached her. Dhi held the tablet to his chest and said his next words with a sweet dryness, "Your Highness... we all have our roles and purpose. You are the first Tantra in over twelve hundred varSas. And you are the only one that can ensure our people live on and replenish our numbers and elders. You are our savior... without you, our entire race would die off. We wouldn't last another one thousand varSas."

Ayya had gotten to know Dhi over the past twenty-two varSas, and the look on his face told her he had a renewed determination and she might as well listen because his design was oriented in the mind.

"You teach us what love, compassion, and caring are. You show us that all of it lives within us, even me. Without you, we would become people like the Dark One. Even though there have been no sightings of him for a thousand varSas, we know he still exists. If you don't finish your transformation, then we will all die. I know you care about your people; I overhear your conversations you have with yourself during your... humming sessions. You forget I have helped raise you with the help of your court, who loves and idolizes you. Please, Your Highness, please, can you help me help your people?"

"Mmmmmm..." Ayya straightened her posture with a jerk and added a mocked joyful expression for good measure. She belted out with sarcasm, "Sure! Why not! I love to live according to other people's expectations! Please tell me the requirements; after all, you have kept me safe in this prison for twenty-two varSas now. I'm dying to learn more about the destiny that is not mine that I didn't choose. It's time to teach your tool how to help her people by changing everything she is into something you want, your way, for your people!"

Dhi seemed unaffected by the rant and waited a few moments. "Be careful, Highness. What you desire your destiny to be, desires you more—especially if it is something you know nothing of. Are you done now?"

Ayya knew he understood the waves of emotion happening to her. She had been informed that she had outgrown her body energetically and was getting bombarded by the multiverse's weather. Whatever that meant, she had no clue. But she knew she needed to do her pariNati soon, or she would literally die.

Dhi stood up straighter in that superior stance he liked so much. "You are not the first future Tantra to act like this." He pointed to references on his tablet. "The Tantra two successions back and..."

"Oh, *stop*!" Slamming her hands to her knees, she stood and faced Dhi, waving her hands to the beat of her words. "I can't take your record-rambling today. I don't care about the past. All I have is *now*. But it seems I will have to surrender and continue to experience your torture, or leave."

"Your Highness, if you leave..."

"Mmmmmm, I know, I know. You say I will kill you all." With a grand waving gesture, she dropped her hands to her thighs and sighed. “Mmm hm, go ahead Dhi, kill me with your procedures... I need to know what is going to happen to me.”

Dhi smiled as Ayya stood to follow him. “No need to fear, Your Highness. I have arranged for support during this talk that might just make you thrilled to be there. We all apologize for the last-minute information flood. We normally have two hundred more varSas to educate you. You will get the short version.”

“Oh good, mmm hmm.”

2 Viduri: Tradition

Ayya

93 Days before the fall of Zreyas

Dhi and Ayya came to the end of the opulent tunnel that led to the open ritual courtyard. It was immaculate and large enough to accommodate tens of thousands of their people. At the area they were entering was the center of where the rituals took place. The other side was for all the crowd.

Ayya loved the buildings and roads. The brick made from a special process of condensing neutrinic energy. They called it neutrinic-gleam. Though it was dense for building, it preserved the life within it. Ayya loved it because the sentient material gave her companionship. They made everything in the city from it. It also responded to her humming, and that made her happy and content.

There was a round platform at the center of the ritual area. Seven pedestals formed a semi-circle on one side. The other side had a crystal triangle wall that was curved with the circular shape of the ritual area.

To Ayya's surprise, there stood Gulloo, the alchemist;

Vesana, her everyday task aide; and the High Seer, who was their mystic and astrologian.

Gulloo ran to greet them with a bright, bubbly mood that paved his way. “Hello, Your Highness, good day to you!” He waved enthusiastically.

Ayya couldn’t help but giggle, feeling his bubbles of joy. “Can you please stop calling me Your Highness, at least until the... pariNati?”

“Sure thing, Miss!” Gulloo said with exuberance.

Dhi, rolling his eyes, said, “Yes, *Mistress*,” drawing out the mistress part.

Gulloo shoved his fist on his hip. “You need an attitude overhaul, sticky britches! Would you like a tonic for that, you old prickle puss!”

Ayya did her best to stifle her laugh, but it oozed out anyway in a bumpy “Mmm Mm Mmm.”

Vesana bowed to Ayya and walked away after a smile.

Ayya turned to see the grinning High Seer standing at one of the pedestals. He seemed to be entertained and looking like a proud father. He rose and put an arm out to his side to welcome her.

Ayya knew the official ‘Embrace of the Viduri’ greeting. She walked forward with a smile that felt like it came from come from the stars themselves. Then, she broke into a run. She reached Master Rhom and held her opposite arm out to the side, as the high seer did. They embraced sideways and held the other arm out to the side as if someone were there. Both recited the same words.

“I walk near you on your path to support you.” Then they began a fluid dance-like movement, turned themselves to embrace from the other side without a step and faced the opposite direction.

“I walk with myself on my path,” they recited together, then faced each other and pressed their foreheads together.

“We are one walking many paths together.” The Seer’s mark above his head shined brighter. He smiled, and they gave each other a hug.

“Hmmm... I’ve missed you, Master Rhom,” Ayya said affectionately.

“I know, child. I’m glad to see you too.” They parted their embrace. “Are you ready for our talk?”

“Mmm hmm, as ready as I’ll ever be, I guess. I’m not looking forward to it, just saying!”

Master Rhom let out a good-natured laugh. “You wouldn’t be the first future Tantra to say that!”

“So, I hear,” she said, pointing over to Dhi.

“Well, let’s get started then, shall we? We can skip the history of everything, as I’m sure I will bore you with talk of the past. We can skip straight to the part about the imprinting and your joining. Let’s get comfortable.”

The tall Master Seer sat down on one of the seven pedestals and closed his eyes for a moment. The light over his head brightened slightly. His long goatee beard stretched to his knees. He was the only one of her people that she knew that wore clothes, though she wasn’t sure why. The robes had the same translucence as their bodies had.

“Your awakening and activation process will not be comfortable,” Master Rhom said. “You will need to be patient, because it will take ninety days to complete.”

“Ninety days?” Ayya recognized her outburst and melted. “Mmm hmm. I apologize, Master Rhom.”

Master Rhom smiled with a gentle sternness that only he could pull off. It both calmed Ayya and put her in a balanced state. “These outbursts will end, little phoenix, when you finish the joining. It’s not all your fault, your body can’t handle the bombardment of the multiverse weather.”

“I’m listening, mmm hmm.”

Master Rhom looked at Ayya with a love in his eyes that

always calmed her. "You will undergo several metamorphic stages in the Parinati. In phase one, you go through what we call the divine imprinting. This is the part of you that comes from your chosen destiny, prophecy, and the light of your soul."

"Mmmm, why haven't you told me any of this until now, Master Rhom? Shouldn't I be getting ready for this?"

Master Rhom held one finger up to stay her questions. "There is nothing you can do to prepare. That process is unconscious and already fixed according to the agreement you made. The way you develop is different from the rest of us, so we could not tell you earlier than this, or it would hurt your progress because you would naturally start the process unconsciously. Trust me, that is disastrous. Our people have tried this before, and we lost our Tantra."

Ayya opened her mouth and straightened her back to ask a question.

Master Rhom chuckled and raised a finger. "We can talk about that another time. Your process starts soon, so this is a priority. We don't have as much time as all the other Tantras. The stars signs are progressing unnaturally fast and we have to get you ready for the ritual. We should have had two hundred more varSas and your growth and body progress has sped up with it, as well."

I'm glad I won't be cooped up in the palace grounds for another two hundred varSas to learn stuff that makes no difference to my people, Ayya said to herself as she acknowledged him, "Mmm hmm."

"After the imprint is complete, you will enter a metamorphic stasis for forty days. At the end, your body will go through what we call the 'metamorphic shearing'."

That sounded like it would hurt... a lot! Ayya felt the static shock of horror rip through her as she thought about what was going to happen to her.

"Don't worry, little phoenix, you will not be aware of it,"

Master Rhom said. "You will have two bodies. The divine one will have the imprint of the seven centers. It is like a skin that binds both together, and for the next forty days, the divine imprint will begin positioning itself just over your head, inverted, like a mirror image."

This information shocked Ayya.

Master Rhom cleared his throat. "Now you understand why it is difficult for us to get a Tantra. It isn't a simple matter of a normal birth." He stretched his shoulders and back. "That readying process will take three days; after which, the seven elders will take their places on the pedestals here on which we sit."

Rhom tapped the pedestal he was sitting on, making Ayya look around with another perspective of her surroundings.

"They will stand and ready themselves for their vital role, your 'incarnation engraving'." He smiled gently, "I will be one of them."

Realization set in for Ayya, and she felt her body fill with anguish. "No!" Ayya stood up, and her cup dropped to the floor and shattered. She didn't care and assailed Master Rhom with an embrace.

Master Rhom held her for a moment. "It's okay, little phoenix," the Master patiently continued with a soft voice and slowly peeled her off of him to look at her.

Ayya looked into Master Rhom's eyes to plead with him without a word.

"I will always be with you, just as Gulloo, Dhi, and Vesana. You will be Tantra and have abilities to access us any time. The only difference is, we just won't look the same because we will be part of you, helping you along your journey. I promise."

"It will be fun, Miss!" Gulloo blurted out in bubbly optimism.

Dhi droned dryly, "Yes, Mistress, it will be *funnn*!"

Gulloo planted his fists on his hips and admonished Dhi with a glare, "Lovely pep talk, terminal dry mouth!"

Master Rhom gave Ayya a gentle squeeze before he peeled her off the rest of the way and helped her sit down again.

Ayya let out an anguished, "Mmmmmm," then continued with a question. "But what if something happens to you before the incarnation imprinting?"

Master Rhom scratched above his right ear thoughtfully. "Then the second and only backup line will step in. We only have two lines of elders left because of the time gap since the last Tantra lost her life. It ended way too soon, thanks to the Dark One."

He crossed his legs and continued. "The fourteen elders have taken extra care to do our work to keep our race going." Rhom smiled. "As you know, each elder has only one divine mark center, each different from the others. This is their loving purpose, and they have waited hundreds or thousands of varSas to have the joy of giving to you. They are looking forward to playing their part in your ascension to Tantra."

"Oh, hmm, thank you all for your gifts," Ayya said sincerely.

"We will connect with the neutrinic source that makes us from the stars. The backup elders will be ready in case something happens. We will align to the etheric weather to give you your incarnation engraving... much like the divine imprinting; however, this is a different imprint. This one gives you the skills to interact with the world and anchor you in your incarnation body. It's like a set of tools that are fixed so you can operate in many dimensions here in the multiverse. Without this process, you won't live much longer, and the multiverse would never benefit and keep balance. Do you have questions before I explain the last phase?"

"Um, not now Master Rhom."

Master Rhom looked at her twice in shock. His surprised look told Ayya it was because the question generator had no questions. She almost giggled and felt a sense of pride that she was patient enough to wait—for once. She was glad she did, because it was worth it just to see that face of his right now.

The stunned High Seer continued. "The critical phase called 'The Avatara' then begins... it is the decent and merging of your bodies. During this phase, the seven elders will connect with you one at a time, starting with me." He pointed to his glowing light just above his head. "They imbue their defined centers on the corresponding place on your body with an energy link. Once the center is full and forming channels, the divine imprint of yourself will descend and merge with you. Once it passes the center imbued by the elder, the elder's body will return to the neutrinic energy source that it came from. The essence of who they are will be within you."

"Oh! That is exciting, Master Rhom! I never get tired of hearing about this part." blurted out Gulloo.

"This new imprinting is more conscious than the divine one because it is how you will interact with the world. Once all seven centers fuse, the Avatara is complete. Your people will wait for your song."

"I don't know how to sing."

"It will come from you naturally. No need to worry. During this song, one to five sets of elders will birth and materialize. The last line of elders will activate each of the young elders' centers. The non-elder babies will have two to six energy centers defined. Elders will work together to activate the centers of the young. We have done this since the beginning of our race's existence. You will sing your song, no sooner than two hundred twenty-two varSas apart. Many babies will be born with all unique designs along with elders."

Gulloo held up two hands in celebration. "See how important you are, Miss?"

Ayya winced, but smiled anyway. Gulloo was always so supportive of her and happy. She didn't want to be a savior or a baby maker. But she couldn't keep living like this or she would die, so what choice did she really have? She wondered if her life would be a normal one between songs.

"Finally, before you transition at the end of your life, you will sing one last time to birth another one to five sets of elders. Therefore, our last Tantra's premature death has put the multiverse in a depleted state."

Master Rhom stopped talking. He did that when he wanted something to sink in. Ayya felt overwhelmed. "The importance of this role is too much for me. I'm trying to be patient, but I struggle to think, Master Rhom. I apologize."

Master Rhom smiled with empathy in his eyes. It always made her feel better when he did that. "I know, little phoenix, I know. Normally, we have more time to prepare you energetically and mentally for this entire process. It might seem overwhelming that all your dear friends would go through this to save your life *and* to elevate you to the role of Tantra. But it will be okay. You have shown me different signs throughout your life so far that you are stronger and more resilient than any Tantra we have ever had before. It is difficult to see that yourself, because I don't tell you all these things. I just wanted you to grow up as normal as a future Tantra could. Part of incarnating is not knowing the future and fumbling around. But I ask that you trust us."

Everyone nodded.

Ayya held her head with both hands. This was too much

for her mind to accept. "It seems so invasive to everyone involved... I love you all!" *I chose to come here to do this?* It made her feel honored that so many were willing to do this for her—to make her into who they thought she was meant to be. *I mean, give their lives to join me?* Each elder was different, with varied roles. That part she knew, but grief filled her. Ayya rubbed her face and did her best to hold back the tears from the gratitude and gravity that filled her.

Master Rhom leaned forward, close, and looked into Ayya's eyes. "Thank you for being here. You are the survival of the multiverse, not just our people."

Everyone held their foreheads together, touching them in a circle, sharing in silence.

Abruptly, a rumbling began that seemed to come from everywhere. Everyone stood up straight and looked around.

"Mmm, is this normal, Master Rhom?" Ayya asked with a hint of panic.

Rhom looked around with a serious air, grabbing Ayya and pulling her to him protectively. After a few moments, it stopped, and he looked at them.

Rhom turned to the elders and issued orders. "Rush Ayya to her fortified quarters, just in case, and stay! Vesana, summon the other elders and have them go to their quarters as well. That ritual has to start in three days, or Ayya will die. We cannot take a chance and assume all is going to be okay. We must protect Ayya and the elders at all costs."

Vesana nodded, turned, and broke into a full run, heading through the east corridor.

Dhi looked at Rhom, nodded, and turned to walk to his quarters.

Gulloo grabbed Ayya by the hand. "Well, Miss, you wanted excitement and adventure!"

"Is this what they are?"

He nodded to his future Tantra and began running with

her to the fortified quarters to the north

3 Janquar: Brutal Nation

Aaru

12 hours before the Fall of Zreyas

Aaru ran to fall into his place in line near Zreyas to avoid the warrior that was trying to kill him to take his position of rank. He was better at killing than the warrior trying to skin him because he was little, but he hated fighting and Zreyas would provide him a little peace from that. Though his place in line wasn't right behind Zreyas, it was one back from him. He could tell because his people's internal war aura communication determined his position in line.

He hated the lines they had to form just outside of town after a war, and it was just because the Janquar loved to show off their ranks of the most kills in a war. Aaru just wanted to go home and sleep. When they returned from a war, they all arranged themselves from the highest kills to the lowest. If there was a tie, the youngest went ahead of the older. They considered it a weaker position to be tied with someone younger than yourself; the older should be wiser in battle and more experienced. He guessed it made sense, but he thought the whole thing was shallow and a waste of time. They all lined up on the outskirts of their capital city after every war. The line was so massive that it spiraled around in an enormous mass of tens of thousands just so they could march through their immense city to show off.

Aaru was fourth in line. In front of him, in the first three positions, were exactly those he'd expect. First, was his father, the Commander of the Rittak line. Next came his oldest brother, Zreyas, who still trained Aaru, followed by the second oldest, Nat. These two and his Commander were the only kin he personally knew.

Any Janquar would have given anything to be in Aaru's position because the others took pride in their kills; however, he was not proud of his kills, and never would be. He stood erect, as expected, but he got bumped by the large warrior behind him and that knocked him forward into Nat. Nat hated anything near him, much less touch him, especially Aaru.

Nat spun around, attempting a violent hilt-butt to Aaru's face. "Get away from me, you little mag-shit!"

Aaru raised his axe flat to his head to shield himself, just in time for a loud clash of metal. Nat had always elbowed him out of the way before or something similar, but nothing *this* harsh. It was showing more and more lately, especially since he had beaten Nat in kills two wars ago. He had let him win the last two times, but it didn't seem to help his mood any. The commander and Zreyas both turned around to see who was fighting, more out of curiosity while they waited for the march to start, rather than concern.

Aaru looked up at Nat as he lowered his axe. "You have serious attitude issues. Would you like a victory embrace?" He knew full well that would piss Nat off further, but also make him back away, and there were two reasons. Nat hated him, and he was afraid of Aaru's skills.

When Nat backed off, Aaru realized the most intimidating part of Nat was his face. It always wore a nasty expression, even if he was excited about something.

The pride in the dark-skinned commander was clear as Aaru looked up at him; however, it was fleeting because it melted into an unrelenting glare. It embarrassed the Commander that he hated fighting without a purpose other than to just kill. He was not ashamed of his stance on war and stood erect and defiant.

Aaru looked closely at the commander's soot black horns, noticing they were so long that they would inhibit his movement soon. He couldn't help but wonder how many varSas in age he was and bet the Commander would challenge the emperor soon to take his place within the varSa.

Aaru touched his own head and felt a little self-conscious about how smooth and light his skin was, but he was happy it was at least hardening well. He also was self-conscious about how his horns had not lifted yet. Horns grew slightly with each kill or cruel act. When a kill happened, a section of their horns would temporarily turn a shade of dark red, showing that it was soft enough the wearer could mold them however they wished. Some made that section longer and thinner, shorter and thicker, or shaped them. As Aaru felt his horns still under his skin, he looked at the Commander's horns. They were clearly molded for intimidation.

His oldest brother looked at him sternly, with a slight nod of approval. *That would be from the axe block. That's at least a one good thing that happened today.* He loved when his brother Zreyas was proud of him. Aaru put his axe back in its place on his right hip, just like his brother wore his axe. He thought about how much he liked Zreyas, and everything about him. Aaru was glad Zreyas trained him personally, rather than Nat.

Zreyas' horns were nowhere near the length of the commander's, but they were amazing in Aaru's eyes. He molded his golden horns with an artistic flare. His deep navy, almost black skin accentuated them more. Aaru thought about the day Zreyas let him try to break off one of the thinner parts of his horns as a test. He had no success, no matter how hard he tried. They were stronger than they should have been.

As all the warriors started marching through the streets, Aaru looked down at his softer, unusual light-blue skin. It wasn't bright, but it seemed to glow compared to all the warriors with dark colors. He was only twenty-two varSas old. Though he was young as far as Janquarian life spans went, his skin should be harder and darker by now. And his horns should have emerged. He had a sneaking suspicion why, but he couldn't make himself be someone else. His skin was the same color as the artisans and workers and if it wasn't for Zreyas, that is what he would have been, or dead. He liked them; they were nice to him.

Aaru looked around at the crowds of artisans and warriors-in-training as they marched. They watched them march through town, chanting savagely with fists at their chest, "Wartok! Wartok! Wartok!"

He felt his horns scratch and tear at the inside of his skin in the middle of his back as they marched. Aaru decided that he should have long horns for the strength to survive in a life he hated. He straightened his back with pride as he thought about it. *Well, my horns are at least growing, even though they have not yet emerged. I know my skin is still the color of a newborn, but it is at least harder than Nat's.*

Aaru couldn't help but wonder, as he looked ahead at the dark bricked Tempest Tower at the center of the city, if there were others out there somewhere who didn't like to fight. Their nation was in the Outer Reach galaxies, but he didn't know where that was, relative to other places.

It took them several hours to march through the wide streets between their stone homes and artisan centers. The march was longer every time the warriors came home from war. The Janquar nation built wide rather than tall. They viewed the wide sprawl as a symbol of how large a nation they were. They finally reached the heavily guarded entrance to the Tempest Tower, and the march halted.

Aaru felt the sudden invading ripple in his body from the Commander's war aura. A second later, the Commander lashed out with both of his spiked war maces at the two guards on each side of the gates. The commander was up to his normal tricks of pompous displays of strength again, and he used his war aura to add extreme force to his weapon strikes toward the guards. As Aaru watched, he noticed the aura was so strong that it caused the air around his body to ripple visibly, a signature of an emperor's caliber strength. The guards were immune to the weakening effects of it, though, because they were seasoned hard-skinned veterans and were attuned to the internal Janquar communication network.

The guard on the left tucked his hips in and stepped to his right, and turned slightly, using his shield to deflect the hard struck mace. But the guard on the right wasn't fast enough. The blow struck his face, and his head shattered and sprayed like a smashed melon. When the guard's body hit the ground, the Commander held his weapon out toward the lifeless warrior.

The air shimmered near the Commander's shoulders, and his horn thickness grew slightly. Aaru couldn't believe it; the guard, after all his centuries of hard work becoming one of the most decorated hardened warriors in the nation, was wiped away in one single moment of distraction.

Aaru winced as he looked down at the decorated veteran and knew the deceased guard's fate; he was about to be ground into powder for building purposes because of the commander's arrogant display.

The Commander spit on the body, sniffed sharply, and belted out for all to hear, "Your war horns mean nothing this day! I spit on your weakness *and* your life. It is now shamed, as is your death!"

The next guard over stepped in to take his place, ready and aware. The other warriors, sporting brutal grins, dragged the fallen guard a few meters away and plundered his belongings. Aaru felt for the downed, decorated veteran. He couldn't help it.

A large, burly artisan approached the scene with a slow gait and a large axe, irritation and inconvenience written all over his body language and face. Everyone backed away as he approached, as was the protocol. The artisan hacked the body into pieces to free the horns. He picked the horns up before turning to walk away, dragging the coiled bloody horns behind him.

The artisan stopped just outside his forge and put them into a grinding machine that fed a brick factory. He grunted. "More addition to the tower soon the way things are going." Then he disappeared into his workshop as if it was business as usual.

Aaru noticed his brothers and the Commander watching with blank expressions. He looked down at the mangled body. His stomach roiled, and his stern demeanor wavered slightly. It happened only in one imperceptible fragment of time, but astonishment rushed through Aaru that such a decorated guard was cut down for no reason. He looked back at his commander, who was staring straight at him with a piercing glare.

The Commander gave his right mace a shake to throw off the fragments of brain and bone. “Open the doors!”

Aaru to flinched.

The guards did as commanded and warriors with the top five highest kill numbers entered the fortress, including him, as was tradition. The rest disbanded and went to sleeping quarters for rest or report to medics to get help to heal, and the top five entered and made their way to the enclosed courtyard that wrapped around the center tower.

With a proud and commanding air of victory, the other four of the top five killers paused, as was traditional, not to *show* respect but to allow the others congregated in the courtyard to respect them.

The entrance courtyard contained two rows of strong columns, the same dark stone as the walls. Aaru looked at the polished reddish-black floors. The building was an iconic symbol of the Janquar nation. Their deaths represented the nation’s foundation, so they made the Tempest Tower floors and trim with the blood and horns of their dead. Thinking about the guard and looking at the floor made Aaru’s stomach lurch. *There is no way I want to be added to this awful display of how all of us don’t matter. Everyone’s life matters more than building blocks of a building or killing just to kill.* Then he noticed that some of the walls, starting at the bottom, had bricks replaced with the blood stone since the last time he was here. It looked like the blood stone was creeping up the walls.

The warriors made their way toward the center of the grand courtyard. It surprised Aaru that the Commander didn’t tell him to stay at the door some ways back after they entered, like normal. Many Janquar in the courtyard, doing everything from talking to fighting. It took a good twenty seconds to reach the center of the massive wrap-around grand outer chamber.

Aaru halted with a bit of a jerk when the commander turned around quickly.

"Wait." He gave Aaru a demeaning glare, took in a quick sniff, and walked over to a Janquar guard near the door of the emperor's chambers.

Aaru noticed Zreyas looking down at him, giving him a menacing grin. "Looks like your horns are emerging after all, boy," Zreyas said, pointing at Aaru's back where the tip of his horns had worn through the skin. He was technically right, but Aaru knew he was mocking him. He hit Aaru on the back, where the tips of his horns were poking out of his skin, pushing them through more.

His brother knew it was not the correct emerging of his horns, and anger filled him. He shot Zreyas a wild look. Aaru looked toward Zreyas with defiance on his face.

Nat turned around and looked at Aaru. "Time to die, little falling prodigy. Father told me all about what he was here for."

"Nat! Ticking-hell, shut your jealous squealing!" Zreyas exclaimed for all to hear. He then lowered his voice and growled as he grabbed one of Nat's horns. Zreyas jerked him close. "You don't know that is what he is here for this day. You show your weakness by being jealous of someone fifty varSas younger than you!"

Nat looked at Zreyas with a glare full of venom. "You contribute to Aaru's weakness, and it is your fault he will die from it."

Zreyas drew one of his long swords from his back and gripped it with both hands. He readied his stance and raised it to strike Nat.

"Stop!" The order echoed through the entire courtyard. Aaru watched his father walk toward them as if he was about to hit something. "We have things we need to do. You can kill each other later." The commander turned toward him. "Aaru! The emperor wants to see you!"

Nat laughed excitedly, then narrowed his sneer at Aaru. "Die, prodigy, die!"

Zreyas immediately threw up his war aura, fed and powered by his anger.

Aaru took a step back from the pulsating and invasive war aura Zreyas was radiating. His brother's cry was strong. It made his guts ache. Even through his hardening skin, he felt himself go weak. *And that is why he is second in command, but his aura is so much stronger than the commander's. I wonder why Zreyas hasn't challenged him yet.*

Zreyas swung his weapon down hard and swift with the force of one hundred fighters. Zreyas' strike was true, and the air cracked as Nat's head jerked to his left. His horn broke under the blade's edge near the top, just centimeters from his head.

The horn fell but was caught in the self-made coils of Nat's ridiculously formed curling and spread-out horn design.

Zreyas flicked his eyes to Aaru before he closed in on Nat. "Show... respect... for the commander!"

The commander didn't even flinch at Zreyas' actions. "There is a mission for you, Aaru, of utmost importance to our cause. Go! It is an honor to serve the emperor! This will be your trial. Bring us honor or die!" The commander firmly punched his chest. "Wartok!"

Zreyas stood upright and pounded his chest with a hardened fist. "Wartok!"

Nat glowered at him, devastated at having just lost his left horn.

Aaru turned toward Zreyas, and then the Commander. He stood proud and punched his chest without hesitation. "Tok!"

Nat spat on Aaru venomously. "It's Wartok, you little

mag-shit!"

Aaru ignored him. He knew he could kill Nat easily, but he didn't. He was sick of killing for no reason other than anger.

Zreyas and the Commander parted the space between them to let Aaru through. Aaru turned to give his last words.

Aaru nodded to the Commander. He made the choice to not say anything. The Commander just stared through him as if he wasn't facing the fact that he was sending his child to his death.

Aaru faced Zreyas. "I will bring honor to your training."

Then Aaru leaned in toward Nat. "When I return from my mission, if not before, your jealousy will die with you, oh weak one." *Nat will try to kill me because he hates me, and because he is afraid of me. Then I will have to retaliate and kill him. I can't avoid it either way. This time I will show him how I feel about it, though. He might be fifty varSas older than me, but I'm done with backing off to make him feel good. I'm making him worse. He only understands our culture, so I will give him our culture.* Aaru growled at Nat for extra emphasis, then punched him in the face. He leaned in and grabbed his horn and jerked it. Nat's expression transformed from pure, seething hatred to wide-eyed fear and shock. His body stiffened, and the blood ran from his nose over his mouth.

Zreyas lifted an eyebrow.

The commander stared blankly at him.

Then Aaru did something else he had never done before—he warned Nat. With a voice that was growling, low, and serious. "When I come back, things will be different. You will never win anything again, and I will never do things just to appease you again, either. If you want to kill me, go for it, but get ready to die. I now have a good purpose and reason to kill you. You hurt everything and everyone you come in contact with. You are worse than the shit of a mag that takes life slowly and painfully as it grows. To kill you would mean it would save many others from your tyranny."

Aaru whirled around and faced the Commander. He leaned toward the Commander and said quietly, "You just made the biggest mistake of your life. Zreyas will challenge you, and you will die." Then he turned toward the opulent doors to the emperor's chambers.

4 Janquar: Chambers

Aaru

8 hours before the Fall of Zreyas

Aaru knew this was a suicide mission, but it was okay. He knew the Janquar ways, and he had seen a few sent on missions like this just to be killed. Exhausted from living a life that he didn't believe in, he realized that kind of life was worse than death. It was why his horns weren't lifting. Aaru took a deep breath and puffed it out to calm his nerves. He lengthened his stride toward his fate.

He realized he had never seen the emperor and wondered what he looked like. *I bet he was an ultimate warrior in his prime.* He doubted he had wisdom about good purpose, though. After all, he was the one sending them out to kill. He doubted the emperor would listen to him about not fighting wars unless there was a good reason or purpose that helped others, too.

Aaru paused and looked around the massive courtyard that had gone silent. Everyone had stopped the fighting and talking. They all watched him. He realized he didn't care what they thought anymore, and he didn't care if he ever came back.

No matter what happens, I'll do what I want now. I can fight, or not fight, for the reasons I want until I die. I'm more afraid of living than dying because I don't belong here. These are not my people. I love a good fight, but it needs to have a purpose. There isn't one most of the time, other than to survive. A fight without a good purpose for everyone is not worth fighting.

When Aaru approached the doors, he observed the majestic design, strength, and sheer height of them. It was the first time he looked at them. The ominous doors, made of a thick, impenetrable-looking metal, intimidated him and gave him the feeling of a dark omen. Entering seemed ephemeral on many levels.

There was an orange and red rippling colored band arching over the door like a rainbow. The guards opened the doors wide enough for Aaru to pass through. He took a deep breath, composed himself, and walked inside the chambers in awe. A few steps in, he heard the doors boom shut behind him.

Aaru squared his shoulders and walked toward the—He stopped once his mind registered the unexpected sight.

No longer in a building, the young warrior took in the surroundings in shock. Ahead was a strange lake. A dominating mountain on the other side disappeared into the sky, steep and black. The atmosphere was a dark flat grey all the way to the water level, making everything look murky.

There is something... off... about this place. The lake was black like tar, while the walkways were a contrasting stark white. They continued onto the lake surface with several forks like tree branches. It was stunning, though more than a little odd. There was only one walkway that had something at the end.

The one in the center position ended in the middle of the

lake. The platform was flat, black, and square. On the platform stood a figure with his back to him. Black tendrils snaked loosely around the dark-robed figure coming from the floor itself.

A square headpiece that looked like a roof, almost as big as the platform, loomed on his head. Black, mist-like tendrils attached to each of the four points of the headpiece and also connected to the platform corners. It looked as if it anchored the headpiece to keep the emperor in place.

The emperor turned and looked at him. His red, glowing eyes seemed to rip through Aaru. He motioned Aaru to come closer with a slight nod.

Aaru walked up to where the forks began in the walkway. He paused and then lowered himself to one knee and bowed his head uncharacteristically, going against normal Janquar tradition of never bowing. Aaru couldn't help it. He felt a compulsion he had never felt before to serve this leader. A leader, he reminded himself, who Aaru never met in person before.

"Emperor Phaar, I am here as summoned to serve in the mission you have called me for. I understand it is a mission of great importance. What would you have me do?"

The emperor raised an eyebrow.

Aaru thought the Emperor's reaction was more surprised than it should have been, but he remained silent. Aaru was sweating and noticed his bravery melting in the Emperor's presence.

"Yes, boy... when the time is right. I wanted to meet you to see if you are worthy of such a mission."

Aaru stared at the smooth white walkway that seemed to move within itself, almost as if it was alive. If he looked too closely, it gave him mild vertigo. It seemed as if it didn't belong there. He darted his eyes around and summarized in his mind what he saw—the black water, the dark fog, and the dank and depressing feel of the place. *This is a place that feels like death.*

He took a breath to assure himself and blurted out, "Emperor, the Commander is sound in his choices, I assure you. Whatever it is, I can do it. I'm here to serve you for this mission."

"So green, this one is."

Aaru waited and listened to the leader, who seemed to be void of all compassion. Still sweating from nervousness, and the pain of his skin that was ripped by the horns in his back. He felt a compulsion to plead his case again that seemed out of character for him, but remained silent.

"Are you sure about pledging your life and service to me?" the Emperor asked.

Aaru looked up at the distorted dark face that seemed more black mist than flesh. This confused him. "To *you*?"

The Emperor spoke with an edge that Aaru could swear cut into his bones. "Are you sure about pledging your life and service to me for this mission?"

"I am sure, your Excellency."

"You are sure of what!?" the Emperor shouted.

Aaru jumped to his feet with a ready stance. His eyes narrowed with a warlike glare that showed signs of an incoming war aura. The air rippled around him, and he stared at the Emperor's eyes. He lost all sense of who he was in front of.

"I am sure about pledging my service to you for this one mission! How many times do I need to tell you? Do you want me for this mission or not!?" He realized the Emperor didn't look Janquarian at all. "Are you the Emperor Rok Phaar?"

The Emperor's eyes changed shape as if his eyebrows lifted, though he didn't see any. "I will send word to you when I have a need for you. Until then, train hard and fix your skin problem... *boy*!"

Well, he sounded like a Janquar. Aaru straightened himself with the anger that surged through him. He pounded his chest. "Tok!" He expected to find himself struck down when he turned around by not using the correct Janquar word, but he almost hoped it would happen. It would be the ultimate insult to be killed by a blow to the back, but he didn't care. Aaru's guts told him he had just made a huge mistake, but he didn't know what or how.

Aaru turned to leave. Then he heard the Emperor laugh. He set his resolve and determination before he heard the Emperor laugh harder. Aaru stopped and turned to watch his leader over his shoulder. His face had a maniacally insane expression as he laughed.

That is one weird bandhula! This doesn't feel right. He scratched his cheek as he took in more details of the Emperor with suspicion. He looked haunted and sickly, not like the emperors he had seen in the halls of honor that were decorated with pictures and sculptures of their past emperors.

Well, I never feel like anything about my life is right. Maybe I'm the weird one. One minute I'm all about a good purpose, the next minute I'm wanting to kill Nat. Nothing in my life has any worthwhile purpose, and I can't think straight knowing everyone wants to kill me off. I hope I die in this mission, but I will miss Zreyas. I wonder if we live again after we die.

He left his thoughts behind as he turned toward the exit. Aaru walked out of the Emperor's chambers with a sure stride toward where his father and brothers were waiting. *There has got to be more to this universe than what he was seeing. I think I came out the wrong exit when I came through the tunnel.*

After he passed through the doors, Aaru saw his father speaking to a huge Janquar with horns like he had never seen before. This Janquar made the commander look like a half-grown child. His horns were so long and thick, his body was barely visible through the cracks.

The commander was erect and sure of himself, speaking with the towering fortress. Aaru thought it odd, as much time as he spent with his father, that he had never seen this warrior before.

The commander noticed Aaru and nodded at the towering Janquar once more. Then he turned toward Aaru with anger permeating from his body, with the accompanied rippling war energy. "*Where* have you been, boy?! You were to see the Emperor right away!"

"I... I *did*, I just came from there!" Aaru pointed at the doors behind him. Aaru looked twice because he noticed the doors seemed more like stone now than metal. He turned back to the Commander in total confusion. "I just spoke with him about the mission, and he will send for me when he is ready for me."

Aaru flicked his gaze to the warrior his father was speaking with. The way he stood, the large thick horns wrapped around his body for protection, the predatory glare, and his aura made him want to pee himself. He noticed the other warriors in the room looked like how he felt.

The Commander glared and pointed to the large specimen of pure strength and intimidating power. "*This* is the Emperor!"

5 Janquar: Unreasonable

Zreyas

7 hours before the fall of Zreyas

Zreyas felt the aura of his commander flare, and he knew him well enough to know that his father was about to use the weird occurrence of Aaru going in the chambers as an excuse to kill him. His anger grew and fill his chamber just thinking about how his father was manipulating this situation so obviously and it embarrassed him and his line. The ticking piece of mag-shit *knew* Aaru had just come from there because they had watched him go through the doors together.

The Commander had said that he would 'be glad to get rid of the menace of the Rittak line' and grunted with a satisfaction that made Zreyas want to kill him. He didn't know why he was so protective of Aaru, but this situation was way past protective. It was about how ridiculous he made the Rittak line look by his obvious remedial tactics. It would have been better if he just killed him.

Whatever Aaru had said to his father just before he left to go into those chambers pissed him the ticking-hell off.

Zreyas' protectiveness of Aaru made him angry, too. His rage grew inside, and he didn't want to be bothered anymore with protecting Aaru or preventing his father from making his line look ridiculous with his displays. He wanted to kill them both and be done with it all. Zreyas was going to be in for trouble again soon, though, because he was about to defend Aaru, yet again. He would rather the Commander look bad in front of all the elites in the courtyard, rather than the Rittak line's best fighter.

"Commander, we *both* watched Aaru go into those chambers. I saw him come out of those doors, and the boy has never lied."

Zreyas knew it would happen, and it did—the Commander backhanded Zreyas in the chest so hard that his body flew airborne a few meters back and he hit the floor hard. Zreyas immediately jumped up and entered a war stance, complete with war aura, ready to get the fight over with.

Aaru noticeably stiffened, raised his head quick with an air of pride and strength and looked straight at the Emperor. "You have someone in your chambers posing as you. I spoke with them, and there was a black lake, a dark mountain, and dark hazy fog."

Zreyas walked back over toward the three talking. He felt pure hate in his heart for the Commander. The mag-shit didn't care about the Rittak line, he just cared about intimidating those around him. Aaru was clearly a better fighter than even himself and made the Rittak line look good—at least when he wanted to fight. That would just take a little conditioning to get that quirk out.

As the Commander accused Aaru of sneaking out of the chambers, Zreyas couldn't help but think about how he wanted to challenge the Commander for his position. But, if he died in the attempt, then Aaru would be left unprotected—the boy was too soft and trusting. He *really* didn't like that he had a soft spot for Aaru. It had gotten him in hot water more times than he could count. He was tiring of it.

As Aaru continued his explanation of what happened in the Emperor's chambers, Zreyas noticed the boy's speech slowed. His attention moved away from the Emperor, just past him to the right.

Zreyas walked slowly toward Aaru, anger still churning. He moved his focus in the direction the boy was looking. And there it was—the distraction was an orange and red ripple in the air. It grew into a badly shaped circle.

Aaru continued his explanation. "He was black... misty... distorted... with red eyes..."

"*Focus,* boy!" roared the Emperor, sending out ripples of hard-hitting aura that knocked Aaru over.

Aaru slowly got back up and paid no mind to the Emperor, still watching what was growing in the air ahead.

That... seemed to entertain the Emperor, judging by his expression. Zreyas thought it would piss him the ticking-hell off, but then again, no one that he knew of wasn't intimidated by the Emperor. So, he guessed that might be why it entertained him.

Aaru drew his two swords off his back, a set he had given Aaru when he got new ones.

Nat watched Aaru with an extra nasty glare. Zreyas

knew he had to keep an eye out for Aaru, because Nat would kill him any chance he could get. Protecting his brother was exhausting.

Zreyas drew his sword again and pointed it at Nat and threw out a focused pulse of his war aura toward him.

That got Nat's attention. He flinched and backed the intensity of focus that he had on Aaru and turned it toward Zreyas, hate in his eyes. Zreyas sneered at him, then walked up behind Aaru and watched the weird anomaly from behind him.

This drew the attention of everyone around him who was not already watching the confrontation just before. New arrivals turned to see what he was looking at. They always had a tendency to follow his lead, even if they weren't in his line to command.

The Commander pointed toward the anomaly with that expression Zreyas knew all too well when he was finding an excuse for war. "That... *thing* is a threat to our nation and it must be Aaru's fault! Get your ass back here and pay attention to the Emperor!"

Zreyas watched Aaru's body go rigid, and he gripped his swords tighter. He knew the boy's mannerisms and temperament, and he could be wild and unpredictable, but it was always for a good reason when he was. But he had never seen him stiffen and throw out an aura like what he was doing now. The air surrounding his body distorted, and he knew the boy was going to snap. Oh, this would be fun to watch. There was a part of him that liked his unpredictable nature.

Before the Commander could say anything else, Aaru whirled around and glared at him with such anger that the air distorted further around him and wave pulses rippled through the distortion. Everyone backed up from it except Zreyas and the Emperor.

"You want me dead anyway, so I won't shame your *precious* and ignorant line. If this thing hanging in the air is such a threat to you, even though you know *nothing* about it, why not let me die investigating it? I'm *sick* of your petty words *and* lies. You want me dead? Try to kill me now, but I will not just let you kill me without a fight. I *welcome* the chance to rip you apart. I will take you on until my death, but I don't think you will fare as well as you think." Then he gave the biggest insult he could give a Janquar—he spit on the Commander's feet as a challenge.

Emperor Rok Phaar held an arm out to the Commander, who seemed to fume judging by his war aura and body language, but he didn't say a word. That part was unusual. He was still afraid and intimidated by the Emperor... or, he was afraid of *Aaru*. Interesting! That's it! The Commander is afraid of him and that is why he doesn't want to give him a chance. He wants to kill the boy before he gets more conditioned.

Zreyas grinned with a pride that he had for the boy.

"Yeah, that's what I *thought*," spat Aaru. "All bluster and no action except toward the unexpecting prey you stack odds against for your pompous displays at the cost of your own people."

Did he just try to antagonize the Commander? I'm impressed! He noticed everyone standing around had raised eyebrows or had shocked expressions on their faces. A warrior nearby grunted in humor. That, of course, angered the Commander. Zreyas couldn't help but get psyched up for a fight.

When the Commander said nothing, Aaru turned around to face the anomaly again and inched his way there. He looked straight at the Emperor as he passed him, who nodded him on. Bold and antagonistic, he passed between the Commander and the Emperor with pride. Aaru looked to his left, straight at the Commander, as he passed him. “Go ahead, strike down one of the two best killers and take the Rittak line down to second place or less. I *dare* you.”

The Emperor shoved his hand into the chest of the Commander, ordering him to stay where he was. “If you are ready to fight *me*, then kill the boy. He has potential, he’s not weak at all like you said. How many lies have you told me about others, Commander?”

Zreyas watched the Commander’s expression darken as he walked behind Aaru protectively a short distance away. But unlike Aaru, he went around the two leaders, but ready for a fight. He followed Aaru as the boy made his way toward the fracture in the air. The boy looked over his shoulder for him, and Zreyas gave a curt and quick nod of pride for him. That seemed to bolster Aaru’s confidence because his gait shifted.

The fracture in the air was big enough now that he could see light through the middle. Structures came into view, but it was still so bright that it blurred his vision for a time.

He could tell Aaru was excited about what was going on in front of him. Zreyas couldn’t blame him really, because he was actually curious to find out what the ticking-hell this was. Aaru took small, smooth steps toward the enlarging fracture.

Zreyas lost focus on Aaru as his eyes tried to adjust to the bright place. After a few seconds, he could make out images of buildings that were made from some sort of white material. It seemed to draw Zreyas in, but why? He couldn’t put his finger on it. After his eyes adapted more, he realized he was seeing thousands of a race with bodies made of white energy, self-lit. They wore no armor or clothing. Each person of light had their own appearance, though, just like any species he knew of.

Some had what looked like beards, others had long hair, and some had none. All their bodies were all different sizes and shapes of the same general structure of two arms and two legs that walked upright. They had smooth wilted horns, high on the side of their heads, not in front like his own race. The horns started out as wide as the whole upper side of their head, then wilted to a rounded tip at jaw length. *Weak little horns, bah!*

Aaru, who was still ahead of him, approached the opening that was now taller than he was, and lower than the floor. Their floor seemed to be almost like a balcony at an event. As the fracture grew bigger, he found they were looking down over a ceremony.

Below him were thousands of the light-people to the right, and a ritual area to the left. The people were in a repeating pattern of skewed diamonds, and they all faced the ritual circle to the left.

As Aaru stayed out of trouble watching the event, Zreyas scanned the buildings and floors surrounding the ritual. The material they made them from interested him. It contained a strange kind of current he could feel and almost taste. “What the ticking-hell is this magic place?”

Aaru turned around to him and said, “The material that they made those buildings and pathways from is the same material as the walkways that were in the Emperor’s chambers.”

Zreyas nodded with a grunt. *Interesting.*

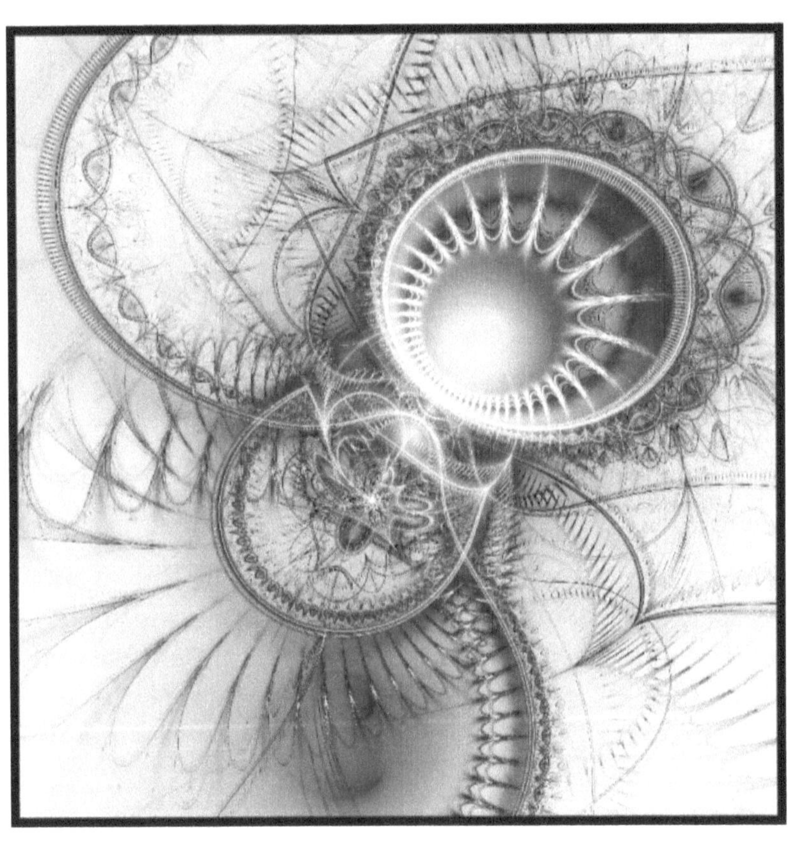

6 Talking Stars

Ayya

A few hours before the fall of Zreyas

Distant garbled sounds of tones and entities entered her ears. No—the sounds entered her entire body. But she couldn't tell where her body started and ended. She was spread out over the entire multiverse, but she felt parts of her moving toward each other. She thought it odd because she had a body already, didn't she? Then she thought she heard the stars.

"It's time."

But what is it time for? *I can't see anything. I feel many thousands of parts of myself.*

"Listen to them, and you will see and fulfill your purpose that you chose long ago," said the stars in unison. "See through their eyes and also yours."

I don't understand, but her hearing that seemed to come from many locations perked up following the instruction. She reached out blindly, but there was no hurry in her mind, feeling the peace from everywhere. Well, almost everywhere.

Ayya reached out to ask the stars what was happening because she felt a darkness approaching that seemed to block parts of her off.

The stars replied in harmony. “You are the light side of the balances in the universe. Your purpose is normally to ensure there is as much light in existence as there is dark.”

Ayya reached out with her tones of resonance and asked what the stars meant.

“You have said yourself, that the ways of the light had to change how they do things because it cannot keep up with balances. Their purpose of the past no longer serves the purpose of the new age.”

I did?

“Yes, you helped lead the multi-verse into a new age through your death and fall from the Viduri light—to kill the age of balance, planning, and knowledge. Though many try to keep balance, they cannot. It is broken.”

She didn’t understand what the stars were saying when they spoke about the broken. She felt the darkness approach. No, it was not the darkness—it was the Dark One. He who started the whole imbalance. That part she remembered.

“Listen to your people, Tantra of the Viduri. Embrace your first death to come. Listen to the connector, the High Seer you have grown to love.”

Ayya reached out and listened, still confused by what a connector was. Too many parts of herself were all over and it mixed all their messages up, except for the stars’ tones.

“Listen to the connector. He was your teacher. Feel

his spirit and it will lead you down closer to him."

A roar of wind seemed gradually flooded her mind as she felt around for the connector. She finally felt something that seemed familiar and followed it, dialing in on the tone. The wind sound grew so loud she couldn't think for a moment until all at once, the wind stopped. No, it didn't stop. Her awareness was just paying attention to him. There he was, and she felt him. His tones were clear, and she understood the connector and remembered him. She entered his mind as herself but experienced through him.

> "My Vidurian brothers and sisters, sacred ones of the light balance. The glorious day of our Tantra's metamorphosis is here at last, after waiting one thousand twenty-two varSas! Send her your sounds of joy and love to help her process of awakening."

Through him, she felt the Viduri people. They were the part of herself she saw earlier. There were many thousands of them all together, and somehow, she knew everyone because they were part of her. Though she could roughly see through him, she could see more clearly through the tones' sound. They had arranged themselves in a fractal pattern of interlocking skewed diamond shapes that made the sound infinite when it traveled.

They erupted in tones that startled her. They rippled through every fragment and it seemed to stimulate something to awaken. She thought a little clearer. Then all went quiet, and she focused on the connector and her vision began to work, though blurry.

Ayya saw his body of tones that reached out to her,

and she felt the connector's smile and connection grow. She could see and hear his tones better. She sensed a comfort from it and it drew her attention. Yes, he's the high seer of the Viduri.

The stars said, "Listen to him. Good luck, and we—"

Shhh. Ayya experienced the connector feel appreciation for the people and their uniqueness. She began to see them clearer *through* him, as if she *were* him. Each one of the people in front of him was unique with their own designs, lights, and channels. Some had several lights in their skins and some had only two. She noticed the connector and the surrounding few, and they had only one, but they were in different places.

She watched as the Master Rhom connector through his signatures and tones. He raised both arms high and wide and sent a wave of tones and light through to the masses from the connector light over his head, signifying the start of the ritual.

Ayya felt the connectors' joy as he led his people through this ritual. She saw in the stars' records that he had done this before long ago.

A low-pitched unison tone sounded from some of the Viduri that seemed to gather part of her with a gentle, guiding hand, bringing her closer to them. The connector closed his vision and let the tone fill him. It ran through them, filling her with information. The thousands of parts of herself were indeed the Vidurian people... and more.

The newly awakened part of her watched the buildings around her as the tones bounced on them and into a concentrated place. She saw that the stars' living information had been condensed into building blocks. Ayya remembered the neutrinic-gleam she used to hum to and how they had always been her companions. She manifested her tones of thought to them, *There you are, dear friends.*

As the tones of the people bounced off the neutrinic-gleam structures, her friends altered their waves into information for the tones to carry to her. The neutrinic-gleam bombarded her with news and guidance and her awareness grew. Though it wasn't with physical eyes, she looked at what was around her by hearing the sound of the frequencies. She realized everything near her was made of sound that was from medium-high to high frequencies.

Ayya could now see important things taking place. Peace came to her, and then a panic sound ran through her, because the multiverse was fracturing. She didn't know how she knew, she just did. It was part of her already. She watched the Dark One to emerge from its prison in the Fractures. It emerged from a place of extremely low-frequency tones off in the distance. She still couldn't see it through the connector with physical sight, but she heard the tones and saw it in that way. Many peoples and dimensions would die soon.

She felt her awareness draw in and meet with three different incarnated people. There was the Master Rhom connector. Then there were two in the scary low-tone area that did, and did not, belong. This confused her. But they were coming close from far away, just like the Dark One. One had golden horns and an edgy dark and light energy. The other had hidden horns and energy that was wild but pure.

Another tone from the Vidurian people sounded harmonious with the first. She felt more of herself gather closer and wake up.

The neutrinic-gleam sent her messages of urgency to focus on what she was seeing before all of her was drawn down to the ritual body.

She wasn't sure what her friends meant. A part of her wanted to wake up from what she thought might be a dream that was growing scary, but she did as they advised and focused.

Ayya watched as Master Rhom gave a sound signal and the two tones boomed louder with a profound grounding effect. She watched the waves of sound stimulate her neutrinic-gleam friends throughout what she now recognized as the structures of the Vidurian city. The sound and energy bounced and flowed with scientific precision.

The waves bounced over the city and ended up in the same place—a warped triangle of space that amplified them, then focused it to one place. She noticed that her neutrinic-gleam friends created their own sound now, increasing the effect exponentially. The sound waves collided in a blank Vidurian body suspended in air. It wasn't quite dead, but it was almost empty of any sound.

She wondered who created such a sound-precise city. Then the neutrinos bombarded her again to remind her she needed to focus and wake up, and that the two mixed low-tones were here.

Another tone joined the beautiful chord of sound. Again, the new tone gathered another part of her closer together. She began to see colors and shapes. Now she understood, she could see the beyond through the potential space, and there would only be four more tones before... before what, she didn't know. She couldn't see that in the potential space.

Her awareness jerked toward the two mixed low-tones. It fascinated her at how different they felt and looked. They were heavier and more condensed. There were many low-tones in a group inside a building in a far off place with a fracture to the Vidurian city. But those two were different.

She focused her awareness on the connector, who felt a sudden panic that ran through her and stepped down from a pedestal. He said something directly to her. She asked the neutrinos to translate the information because she didn't understand and was feeling vulnerable with the low-tones there now.

Her friends translated the entire experience to her as if she was him.

> *Oh no, not now.* The High Seer had seen the fracture and focused on it to make sure he was not delusional from the ritual. It wasn't an illusion, and mental calculations took over his mind. Then Master Rhom looked up to Ayya. *My dear Tantra, please forgive me for my broken promise. It is for your survival that I do.* Master Rhom turned and looked at the Seer Treta, motioning his head toward the fracture.

Ayya didn't understand what promise he was breaking, but she felt his sadness, his guilt, and yet she felt... purpose from a great love.

> Rhom could tell by his backup seer's expression that it horrified him at first. Then his face transitioned to a radiant joy. Treta knew what would happen next. When Master Rhom stepped down, Treta stepped up on the pedestal with evident eagerness from taking Rhom's place. Then Rhom signaled using a rushed sequence of four new tones.

She felt a rushing gathering of the last four parts of herself. Her awareness of the world grew and what the connector said came to mind. *He lied? But he made a promise to me! Why are you leaving me, Master Rhom? It's only a fracture.*

The neutrinos sent messages of comfort and reason that made her feel better. She turned her awareness to the taller of the two low-tones. She could see now that it had golden horns and dark navy skin. The evil rising in him was scarier than the Dark One. She saw visions of possibility flash through her mind's awareness and felt panic. Most of them were devastation, annihilation, suffering, and the end of life itself.

The neutrinos comforted her with messages that there might be a way to stop it, to look at the other low-tone. Though she was still watching through the connector, she did as advised. The other low-tone had no adorning horns, and the skin had frequencies of light blue. She wasn't sure what to do with that information, so she tuned back in with the connector.

As soon as Rhom saw the divine image at the right height, a tone that only seers heard resonated within him. Rhom watched with joy and grief as the seer Treta gave himself, shooting his beam of light from his center just over his head to the corresponding place on Ayya.

Beautiful light connected to the incarnation body, just above her head in a powerful, consistent stream. The controlled scientific precision of their people always fascinated Rhom. Elders always knew when it was time, knew their purpose, and it came naturally to them. The first seer's connection was the trigger the divine image needed to begin its descent to integrate with her new incarnation body.

As the beam connected to the empty body, she felt a frequency shoot through her. It condensed and sucked in a part of her awareness quickly, making her insides feel like they were ripping. There was nothing she could do but watch part of herself drag the rest of her closer to the blank body. She realized it was like getting pulled painfully down into a funnel. Then she felt someone entering her, dragging her down more and becoming part of her. She felt anchored and her awareness swam, though the presence that was now part of her was compassionate and loving, made of a high flowing tone.

Curious about what was happening, she focused again on the connector.

With the completion of the first infusing done, Treta's body shimmered with a tone of joy. He fragmented into particles of light, flowed back toward the people, and dissipated.

Thank you, dear brother. Take care of her for me. You are fortunate on this day. Rhom looked over at Dhi, who was readying himself for his turn. Then he checked on Gulloo, who was bright, but also aware of the anomaly in the air. Vesana, next in line, looked determined. Her function for Ayya would be vital in doing her repetitive tasks. She knew Ayya on a level no one else did. The other elders on the pedestals had their eyes on Ayya, but flicked their gazes to the anomaly in the air nearby periodically.

Rhom moved across the elders' view to pass closer to the anomaly. They looked at the High Seer with concern. He understood why, since they all knew he was supposed to be a contributor.

Rhom nodded reassuringly and smiled as if things would be okay, though he was unsure himself. They visibly relaxed and looked back at Ayya.

Rhom glanced around, waved a hand to signal the light warriors, and pointed to the fracture. They immediately surrounded the area. The general populace was oblivious to events right now, except for the elders. They were all committed to the ritual.

As he walked between the rising Tantra and the fracture. Rhom noticed it was not only growing larger, but drifting closer, too.

He whispered with some urgency, "Come on, come on, little phoenix, you have done everything too fast already, now is a good time to continue that habit. We need you."

She knew he was talking to her. What he said was familiar. She looked into the space of possibility of what the connector just said. All she could see was pushes of energy throughout the multiverse by... a source that was not in her realm to see. An unknown, responsible for all this potential devastation and the fracturing.

7 Fractured

Ayya

Ayya replayed the words 'little phoenix' in her awareness, searching through the stars for an answer. Why couldn't she think clearly? It prompted a memory that the connector always called her that name in a part of her time line. He was now pleading for her aid in something.

She knew it was important, but Ayya didn't understand what was going on. The neutrinos told her she didn't have enough time to prepare her awareness and skills to keep the communication open during this Avatara, and she would soon not hear them anymore. Ayya heard the neutrinos trying to warn her about something that made no sense—it had to do with the fractures and the Dark One.

Ayya did not know what to do with that information.

She wondered why they hadn't had time to prepare her development of keeping the communication during this Avatara. They were right; she felt their messages, but it was like they bounced off her and didn't become part of her awareness anymore. She let out a wailed energy at the loss of connection and felt herself reach out to her friends.

Another excruciating pull came to anchor her to the empty body. A presence of processing judgment came into her. It wasn't kind, but it wasn't unkind. It seemed to influence, yet easily influenced itself. Her mind woke more. Though it felt like she had a head now and she could see inside it. It was a large oval room with organic walls that seemed to hold this new presence. In the center of the room was the first presence that entered her. What is this place?

There were many fractures approaching, and their sound ripped through her. Her focus went back to the connector. It was the only thing that felt comfortable.

> Master Rhom faced the fracture and used his quantum skills in an attempt to slow down time around the anomaly itself. He found it more difficult to manipulate something else rather than himself, especially if that 'something else' didn't want to be manipulated.

She felt what Master Rhom was doing and focused on trying to help him. But parts of her wouldn't allow her to because they were being pulled down into that blank body. She realized that body would soon be hers as she looked around to see the Dark One in the distance coming closer. Ayya emitted tones to help the connector that called her little phoenix.

His effort seemed to help slightly. Well, it's better than nothing, thought Rhom. He grunted with effort. Though not satisfied, he continued his concentration while still trying to watch what was going on around him and give signals at the right time.

The Ritual continued and the light warriors readied themselves and faced the fracture, shields and spears drawn. The fracture started making invasive sounds of screeches, grinds, and rips that resounded across the entire area. Then another fracture revealed itself.

Ayya recognized these fractures. They felt like part of the surrounding air was born from evolution that had spawned from anger, change, awareness, grief, and determination.

It seemed to Rhom anomic in nature compared to what he foresaw in the stars.

A fracture within a fracture? None of this is supposed to happen! Rhom noticed the Warriors readying themselves with scrutiny. A third new fracture opened on the right side of the two existing ones. Thankfully, it was not opening quick like the others did. His attention focused on what was on the other side of the first.

An immense room with a high ceiling and two rows of columns encircled the center of the building. It was sealed off with high double stone doors. Many were standing around the room. From what Rhom could tell, they were heavily into war, judging from their attire. He couldn't recall if he had seen them before, but he was glad he had the light warriors ready.

Rhom noticed one of them close to the fracture opening, much smaller than the rest, with light blue skin and another larger one walking toward him slowly. *A child warrior? That is not a good sign!*

He decided to take advantage of the tones and sounds from the ritual. The frequencies of the Viduri tones were too high for any species other than their own. Though they were of creation, without time to adjust, lower frequency materials and bodies couldn't tolerate it.

Using his quantum skills, Rhom worked to penetrate small micro sections of the invisible and thinning veils between their realms in order to let the sound through. He hoped the moderated high frequency would incapacitate them.

It seemed to work. Though the warriors in the room stopped moving, two were unaffected. The little light blue child warrior kept watching with curiosity and had no problem with the sound. The one standing a distance behind him was a little older, with ornate golden horns. His attention flipped protectively between the warrior-child and Ayya.

Relief ran through Rhom when he realized that all but two warriors were still not moving and wouldn't be a threat, for now. However, it puzzled him why they froze, rather than collapse, like he had expected. Looking closer with his inner skills and scientific eye, Rhom realized it was the distortion of the veils in the two fractures. They were changing the frequencies, and it caused the stone-like freezing.

Rumbling and shearing sounds filled the entire area that ran through her in dissonant and static tones, and it felt like they were grinding inside her. The static began to grow and cause pressure.

It hurt her own tones and lowered frequencies in a jagged line through her. *Pressure... I feel the pressure.* The tones and static wanted to divide her. *No, I cannot allow this invasion. If something happened to me and the Viduri die off... No, what is happening here is inevitable, but there has to be another way. There were always possibilities.*

Planet quakes on both sides of the fractures hit with a violence that shook everything and everyone in the area. Rhom watched an entire corner quarter of one of the nearby buildings completely break off and slide to the ground. The Viduri nearby never wavered in their tranced commitment, and some were crushed.

Rhom winced and bent over as he felt the loss within him. Particles of light wafted back toward the people and dissipated. He righted himself as he watched pillars, floors, and structures crack.

Rhom looked back at Ayya. There was still one more center to go. He knew the structures of the Vidurian city played a vital role in her metamorphosis and she was now in trouble with the buildings and floors crumbling and cracking.

Now she understood some of what had happened. Ayya felt a sadness that she couldn't see or hear the stars anymore, but she watched through the tones and frequencies. The Dark One rose up through one of the fracture sounds, partially unbound.

She sent out tones to Master Rhom to warn him, but her tones were weak and didn't seem to reach him, even as the connector.

Ayya now knew she was in trouble and focused on him to at least make the effort anyway, but she realized it weakened her exponentially and possibilities faded in the quantum of possibility. She stopped... feeling helpless.

The Dark One's attention was on her. She couldn't see it, but she felt it strong enough that she could see it in another way. It was the frequency of pure resentment and hate, and it turned his attention to the golden-horned low-tone and felt him longing for it. It wants to inhabit the golden-horned one. His *Connector, help the golden one!*

She didn't know if her call for help reached him or he did it on his own, but she watched the connector renew his effort on slowing down the fractures with a focused urgency. He felt him give part of himself to the effort, feeling him diminish his life essence slightly.

The fractures reacted to it, almost as if they upset that someone was trying to hinder them. The fractures created loud, tremulous ripping sounds, fighting what was working against their natural progression.

Ayya looked toward the fracture and noticed that she had a physical head and most of a torso now that partially housed her awareness. Then she looked at the smaller of the low-tones with blue skin and noticed the energetic connection between it and the golden adorned one. She remembered what her neutrinic friends had told her about how there might be a way to keep the gold one from falling to the evil.

Ayya attempted to break through the awareness of the golden one, but realized she was too weak. It had a hard and conditioned nature, but inside there were high tones. Most of those high tones in him were connected to that connection with the other blue low-tone nearby.

As she felt herself sink more into the empty body, she realized there wasn't much time. She concentrated hard to reach out for the smaller of the two. Its awareness was softer. She would reach the gold one through the light blue one. Ayya tried hard to reach out, but something was wrong. The constant flow of the tones was not coming into her like they were, and she was weakening fast. Something inside her knew it was part of the problem of not being trained like the neutrinos had said they didn't have time to do. She made one last effort with all the energy she could muster to reach out as she kept looking through the connector and realized he was watching her new body.

Rhom considered as he watched Ayya. She seemed to rest her eyes on the blue Warrior-child. Her arm raised slowly and pointed toward him. As the last elder started their part of the incarnation imprinting, the urgency of the people's lending song grew intense. Everyone understood now that something was terribly wrong.

Rhom had to duck under the fracture, due to it drifting sideways, so he could work from a different angle. Ayya's last center was about half finished. "Please hurry in your contribution, dear elder."

The resistance of the fractures broke free from

Rhom's work to slow down the rift progress, and a catastrophic quake hit both realms. It knocked him several meters away.

He hit the crystal wall and bounced to the ground, landing hard on his back. Looking up, he saw the warrior-child at the edge of the fracture, looking at Ayya with an expression of concern. Rhom felt Ayya's strength waning further.

The second fracture expanded quickly, as if reacting to being uninhibited. The view flashed back and forth between two dimensions. Every time it flickered to the dark dimension, Rhom could see the Janquar on the other side of the fracture wake up from their frozen state. When it flickered back to the Janquar realm, they froze again.

Rhom helplessly considered the odd events as he got back up on his feet. One of the younger warriors, with an exceptionally nasty facial expression and one horn, drew his two-handed sword and charged toward the fracture. However, Rhom realized he focused on tracking the warrior-child, not his people.

It horrified Rhom when he heard him say, "You will die at *my* hand now. I curse your prodigy talent! I will now imprison forever you for humiliating me."

As the one-horned warrior stepped to run toward him, the fracture flicked back to their world, and everyone again froze.

The warrior-child turned his head just in time to see everyone frozen and turned back to Ayya. Rhom watched the one-horned attacker so intently that he never saw the Golden-horned warrior until he body-slammed the venomous one-horned warrior sideways, knocking his two-handed sword out of his hands and him to the floor.

The boy never noticed because he was so focused on Ayya, and probably because it was increasingly harder to hear with all the ripping, grinding, and screeching coming from the fractures.

Rhom realized the hit was much harder than he would expect from a warrior of any size. Golden-horn was not bulky like most of the others in that room, but he was strong and quick.

The one-horned warrior landed on his side and continued to slide across the floor, his head coming to a stop right at both fractures' edges. It fed into them, like feeding wood into a saw blade. There was only a brief shriek before his head shattered. His headless body went limp. Rhom flinched at how dangerous the edges of those fractures were. *Light, help us all.*

The entire place cracked, crumbled, and rocked.

Ayya released dissonant tones to warn them of something. Her new body shuttered and bent. What it was she was trying to warn them of she couldn't remember. All she knew right now was pain. She felt her new body bend over from the sudden weakness. Ayya couldn't relate to the body as her own yet. It was as if she watched it, yet she was crammed inside it. All she could to get in communication right now was from the connector Rhom. *Where are the stars? Where are my friends?*

Rhom turned to see her crouching, alarmed. He now knew it was not a warning, but out of pain as her fingers spread near her mid-section. *Thank the light she is okay.* The crystal wall crumbled apart and pieces fell down around Rhom. He dodged the falling crystal chunks, then breathed a sigh of relief.

"No!" the warrior-child yelled, reaching futilely toward the last elder.

As much as what was going on with Ayya horrified him, he turned to see where the warrior-child was pointing. That warning made him realize something far worse. The last elder was now too close to the edges of the fracture.

Rhom lunged toward her to help, but before he could take another step, the fracture edges caught the elder. The elder fed into the edges like the one-horned creature. It ripped the elder apart until there was nothing left. However, there was no spray of particles and no light bursts. The connection of his people was literal and the tremendous loss ripped a part of Rhom away. Whatever happened, it took the essence of her, too. Nothing dissipated... nothing came back to the people. It was like she was stolen, somehow, as if she never existed.

The scream that came from Ayya almost brought the populace down, including himself. They all dropped to their knees. Though the tones slightly wavered a brief few seconds, the people never stopped their commitment to her.

Ayya couldn't remember where she put the stars. Or did

she? Her neutrinic-gleam friends were gone too. She didn't even feel the bounce of the information they used to send her.

She felt the warmness of someone grabbing her arm. It helped steady her inside and out. Ayya did her best to look toward the warmth she felt. It was the smaller of the low-tones. But now, he shined brightly with beautiful light and tones.

He looked into her eyes and said with sincerity, "You are not alone. I'm with you. Lean on me. I will help you."

She felt the comfort and reassurance flow into her from him. He felt familiar to her. Maybe it was just because he was helpful and sincere. She didn't know how much strength she had left to stand, but she felt herself accept his help. Ayya focused again on Master Rhom because he was easy to see through. She wanted to find out what was going on and couldn't think very well anymore.

Rhom turned in panic and ran over to Ayya to help her. Then he caught that the warrior-child had reached *through* the veil of the fracture, grabbed her arm, and steadied her.

He stopped and nodded at the little guy, gratefully, and noticed the third fracture was slowly growing again, approximately two meters wide at the right edge of the two already open. Crystal rubble surprised Rhom as it fell and rolled in front of him as the wall crumbled more behind Ayya.

Looking up to check the status of the fractures again while he pulled chunks of crystal out of the way, Rhom navigated the rubble to see if he couldn't assess Ayya's body. But the second most decorated warrior distracted him. Behind the warrior-child, freed from his frozen state, he moved. The warrior had a deep scar running diagonally across his disfigured face, and he stomped toward the fracture.

Ayya's eyes in her body saw darkness come in from the edges, and soon her sight left her entirely. To her relief, she could still connect to Master Rhom and see through him. Though her body was blind, she was not completely in it and could still feel the scarred one coming her way in addition to what she saw through Master Rhom. But he was not after her. It was going for the new friend helping her. She did her best to warn him, but she had nothing left to give. She felt herself grow so weak she was to the point of collapse. *Master... Rhom... help the–*

Uh oh. Rhom could tell that the scarred one was clearly someone in command. Rhom watched Scar-face storm toward the warrior-child, looking extremely angry. What did this child do to create such anger? Was it because he helped Ayya?

Golden-horn flinched in surprise, taking a step back. When Scar-face reached the warrior-child, he hit him in the back with such force that his head unnaturally broke backward as his chest lurched forward.

Rhom heard the cracks in the child's body. He didn't know if it was due to muscle memory or pure determination, but the warrior-child held firm and never let go of Ayya. His head hung over the edge of the floor into their world, still focused on Ayya.

Rhom gasped out, "No!" He could see in the child's eyes that he was fading from injuries already. It confused him why the scar-faced warrior would do such a thing to a child.

Golden-horn erupted in a penetrating roar of what Rhom only assumed to be out of grief and rage. Accustomed to seeing auras, he saw the air ripple around him, distorting it and revealing his large pushing aura. *That aura is huge!*

The scientific side of Rhom briefly contemplated the ramifications of that aura in war as he watched him shift into a run toward Scar-face. Golden-horn launched himself up, feet first, and kicked the horns that were wrapped around Scar-face's head with his heels, upward at the precise forty-five-degree angle to throw the decorated warrior off balance.

Even though Scar-face was much larger than Golden-horn, the massive warrior took flight a short way before pounding to the floor. Though Rhom couldn't see the floor from his angle, chunks and fragments flew up in all directions. Scar-face bounced once and slid across the floor from the force, his horn-wrapped body still protected. Rhom now understood why many of them had their horns wrapped around them, with room enough to move.

Golden-horn had landed on the side of his bent leg, body erect and ready. He launched himself up quickly to his feet and pulled his two long swords off his back. He chased the sliding Scar-face, but before he could reach him, the momentum of Scar-face's slide took him through the third fracture. The fracture was just large enough for him to fit through head first without getting caught up in the edges. Scar-face disappeared into that realm.

Ayya relied on her instincts and hearing frequencies to tell her what was going on beyond Rhom's vision and senses. The Dark one was there close now, and he was manipulating the fractures. The screeching, ripping, and grinding was because he was manipulating what was natural with something not natural. Though she didn't think it created them, she thought the Dark One closed one of the fractures. But just before it did, she felt the Dark One go through the fracture. Yet she still felt it here. Was it using the star space? She didn't know.

As soon as Scar-face disappeared, the fracture closed, as if it was a reaction. That was way too intelligent of a reaction to be a coincidence or chance. Whatever was going on here was too weird, and there was definitely more going on than an anomaly occurring naturally. Rhom watched helplessly as two things happened simultaneously.

The other warriors in the room across the fracture took out weapons now that there was no more freezing or tones. He assumed they saw it as a war opportunity.

Golden-horn made his way to the limp warrior-child, sheathing his weapons, growling out an angered, "No, no, no!"

A massive warrior, adorned like a chief, drew his two-handed great sword., He was bigger than all the rest in height and breadth. His horns were massive and molded all around his body in different intimidating patterns. He looked more like a figure rather than a functional fighter. But his face crinkled with focused fury and he stomped toward the unaware and grieving golden-horned warrior. The chief raised the sword to strike.

No matter how dire Ayya was right now, Rhom couldn't allow what he predicted would take place to happen. He raised a hand frantically to warn him. "Watch out!!"

It worked, but it was too late for Golden-horn to react. Rhom reached up, waved a hand, only as a habit from varSas of teaching, to manipulate the quantum, and twisted the blade in the chief's hand so the side of the blade hit the unsuspecting warrior's back flat, rather than cutting him in two.

Ayya felt herself so weak that she wavered from using Master Rhom's sight briefly to find she felt the Dark One approach, still manipulating the progress of the fractures. She felt it emit tones of laughter. She concentrated hard to connect with Master Rhom once more.

The blow knocked golden-horn over with incredible force, pushing him into the warrior-child, who still laid there, unable to move, but still gripping Ayya's arm to steady her. The child slid off the edge of the floor and into the dark fracture, now larger than the first, dragging Ayya in with him.

She felt her new body jolt, rip, and jar from the Dark One's attack. But she also felt someone hold her together somehow. *Master... Rhom... help us.*

Ayya felt her body fall during the Dark One's attack. It was sucking something from her, but she didn't understand what. She didn't have time to think before everything went black and her last thoughts were of looking for her friends.

Rhom

"*No*! Light warriors! ... with me!" Rhom ordered.

Rhom watched through the first fracture as he ran toward the one Ayya went through. Golden-horn slid to the edge of the fracture, half in when he stopped. He looked up quick, turning toward what hit him, and saw the chief warrior fixing his grip as he stomped toward him. Golden-horn backed up, looked around with what Rhom could see as a warrior's assessment. Then he turned back toward the fracture, pausing just a moment, as if calculating what he should do.

Rhom assumed he realized his chances were not good and watched him launch himself into the fracture behind Ayya, into the darkness.

The old High Seer ran with all the energy he could muster, using his quantum skills he had mastered over the hundreds of varSas of his life, and jumped up and through the fracture behind them.

Last Vidurian Seer

The last Seer of the Vidurian people stepped forward from the third line of elders to the second to fill the vacant spot.

The fracture started shrinking, as if it met unseen checks and balances of an unknown set of rules. The new High Seer, at least until the current one returned, watched as several light warriors ran to go with Master Rhom.

The warriors stacked with one another to get high enough to go into the fracture without getting caught in the edges. The fracture was closing fast; however, only five made it through before the fracture was too small for the sixth, cutting him in half.

The warrior's essence didn't return to the people, and they all felt the loss of one of the strongest of them. The entire population of the Viduri collapsed to the ground at the loss of the warrior, Ayya, and Master Rhom. Wailing tones erupted. Though still in harmonic tones, they were dissonant and grief-ridden.

The only Seer left, picked herself up off the ground, stepped up to the Seer's pedestal, and began intoning the people's song of grief to sooth the wailing people, who were now lying on the ground lamenting.

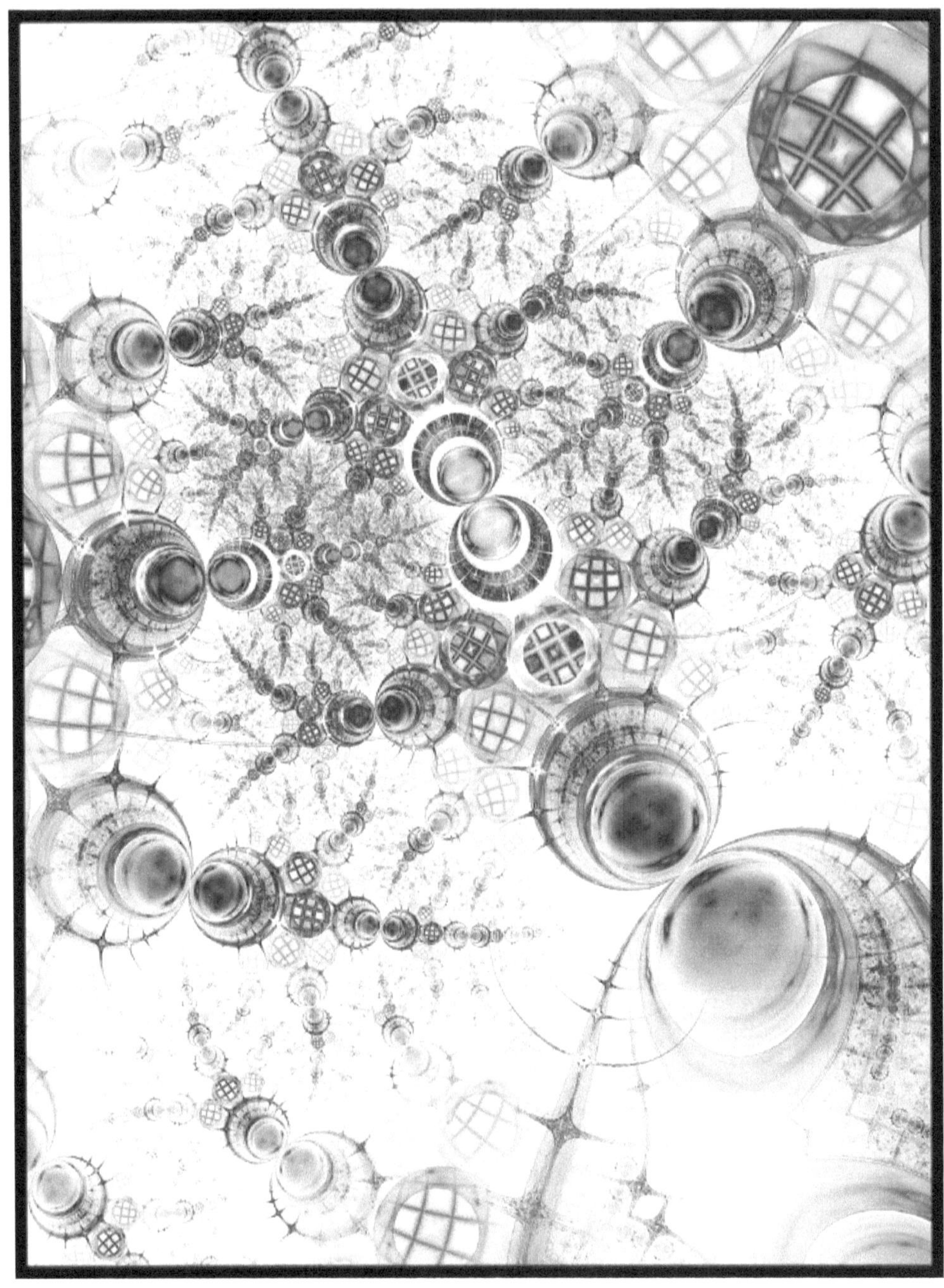

8 Declaration

Emperor Rok Phaar

Roaring at a level of ground-shaking magnitude, the Emperor threw his massive two-handed sword to the ground like it was a small stick. Everyone straightened, then froze, in the wake of his war aura of communication.

"Listen up! I want to know where Commander Rittak, Zreyas, and Aaru went at *all* costs! Someone find out how to get to them and come get me when you do!"

All the Janquar in the room went into action, sheathing weapons, scrambling out of nervousness, and gathering their gear.

"I'm not done yet!" His war aura was strong enough that a column next to him cracked.

Everyone in the room stopped and faced the Emperor, standing straight and stiff. He noticed their eyes dart between him and the cracking column.

"Zreyas challenged the Commander, yet didn't kill

him. Aaru helped another race that clearly meant harm to us. They used some sort of witchery to freeze us, and he helped them! The commander bore two traitors, so I demote him from the commander rank of the Rittak line! I will put him to death if I don't find another use for him. Because he was a commander, he knows Janquar's secrets. We must bring Rittak back alive. He must be questioned, and then tortured for producing diseased offspring! Kill the other two and do not bring that filth back to use in our buildings! Don't touch them if you don't have to; they are diseased!"

Emperor Phaar whipped around and executed an explosive punch, smashing his fist into the crumbling column to promote motivation, and turned back to make sure none of them cowered. The column broke apart, then collapsed. Pieces fell on him and bounced off, and the emperor never flinched.

The emperor watched a new fracture appear in the back of the large corridor, pointing toward it. "Ready everyone for war! Everyone! Pack up the artisans, too. If I am not here in time, all commanders are to start without me. Some fractures are closing, others are opening. Take advantage of them! I want those two dead. I don't care what it takes to get it done! The hunt begins!"

Emperor Rok Phaar kicked his sword. "Someone come get this sword and fix it. Or, bring me another one built to my specifications. The thing slipped in my grip when I tried to kill Zreyas. The balance is off! Kill the artisan that made it!"

The emperor turned and stormed toward the audience chambers. He noticed the guards seemed different. They had flat-black armor, and they were smaller, but more intimidating somehow. They saluted and reached for the doors to open them.

"I like the armor change—it fits my mood."

The guards opened the massive, black, metallic doors for him.

"Compliment the builders for me on the new doors as well." The emperor grunted as he thought about the weakness of the commander that was to be his successor. He turned and declared in a loud booming roar, "And I demote the Rittak line to last place! No! I demote them to artisans and workers! That line will never ascend again! I spit on their shame in life, and in their death! They don't deserve to hunt! Those that have no skills in either, kill them for their horns!"

Everyone still left in the room, not of the Rittak line, nodded and grunted, then roared at the coming hunt, psyching themselves up. Those that were in the Rittak line looked shocked.

One of the Rittak line, with a massive horn array, took out a long razor-sharp knife, stared at the emperor defiantly, and plunged it into his own chest near his shoulder. The Janquar dragged it down deep in his chest cavity in a diagonal path, filling the room with bones snapping and tissue bursting. He did it again on the opposite side and direction, making an X on his chest. He uttered the words, "Curse you, Rok Phaar. This happened because of *your...* weakness," before he crashed to the floor.

The emperor whirled around and went through the doors. The guards hissed out a weird laugh and shut the doors behind him. A long, echoing boom filled the air behind him.

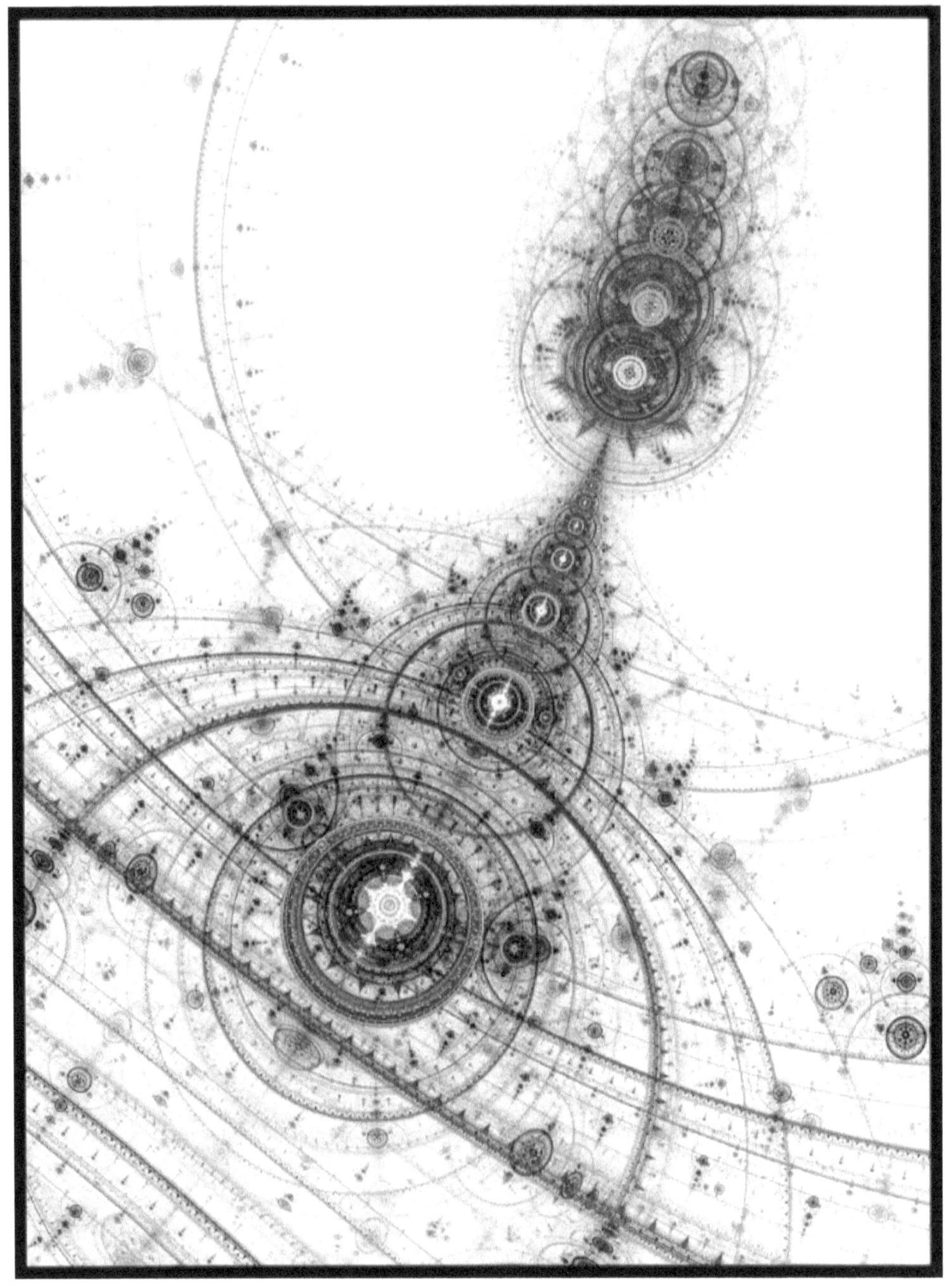

9 Adjust Faster!

Zreyas

Feeling like he was upside down *and* ascending at the same time, the golden-horned Zreyas held his hip weapons in place as if they would fall out of their already secured sheathes. He gripped them so tight he felt like his knuckles would bust.

Zreyas let out an angry war cry as his body fought, adjusting to the new atmosphere. There was the other added reason of fear... of this unknown place and his likely death from falling, but he couldn't face that word right now. Pain from the blow he got from the emperor set in again, but he knew his pride was more bruised than his body. *I should have been more aware!*

Suddenly, his body jerked around. Right side up or upside down, he couldn't quite tell. He turned his head to puke up bile, thankful he had not yet eaten this day.

It gave him a sense of direction within his body, though, since the bile flew up, though much slower than he would have expected.

As he watched the bile rise, he gained a sense of space, and his stomach settled. Zreyas wiped his mouth with his sleeve as he looked around to see where he was, but there was nothing around him. *It still feels like I'm falling up rather than down. What the ticking hell is going on?*

Zreyas talked to himself to deal with the stress, "Strange. It looks like the perfect son just messed up badly." He rubbed his face and eyes to see if he was dreaming. *Nat was right, Aaru probably died because of me... No, that's not true, Nat would have killed him had I not stepped in,* he reminded himself.

"Aaru! Where are you? You better not have gone and died on me after what I just did for you, you ticking wart!" It made Zreyas feel better to rant at him.

Looking down, he didn't see ground yet. He seemed to be in the middle of a night sky. He observed the many fractures, like the one he fell through, that littered the sky. It had an odd beauty to it, but was also creepy. The creepy part was that he felt no life here. Also, there were fractures all over the place and that made the place look like it had many eyes. Yet, the beauty was that he had never seen the sky have so many moving colors before. It seemed to Zreyas like this place was some sort of fracture hub.

Something on his right in the distance caught his eye. He used his war sight that allowed him to look in darkness and sharpen fuzzy details. It looked like one of those light men with a light on the top of his head and light warriors above him, trailing behind him in a line.

The light-man turned his head as if he felt Zreyas was looking at him. The light-man nodded and lifted his hand to wave at him. At the end of the gesture, Zreyas heard a roar like a thundering waterfall, accompanied by a weird vibration.

Zreyas closed his eyes for a moment, tensing up just as it stopped. He opened his eyes carefully and found he was still in the sky, but the light-man was right beside him. Startled, he instinctively let out an abrupt war cry aura.

The light-man winced and slid away a short distance from the force of the war aura's knock-back. The man seemed to compose himself and turned to study Zreyas. He patiently nodded with a little aggravation in his face. The light-man said something in the tongue they used at the ceremony.

"I don't understand." Zreyas gestured with a shake of his head. He grunted with exasperation. *I will kill him. At least I will get one more kill before I die.* He sized him up and noticed the light-man was much smaller than himself and only came up to what he estimated as chest height. He motioned to the light-man with his right hand to come closer again and put his other on the left hip sheath.

The light-man reached up to his head and pulled off a device Zreyas hadn't noticed before. It was thin and in a V shape, but bent to mold around the head. Zreyas cocked his head. It was pure white, and it had a long thin cyan-blue stripe down the middle.

The light-man held it out to him and gestured for him to take it.

Startled, Zreyas pulled his weapons.

The light-man held one hand up as if to say peace, but held out the device closer.

This man is not afraid of me. I almost like him. He looked down, and again to the light-man. *Well, ticking hell, I'm going to die soon anyway, falling from the sky. Why not discover what this light-man is trying to give me?* Zreyas sheathed his weapons and reached out to take the device.

The light-man gave it to him and gestured for him to put it on his head.

Staring at it, Zreyas held it in both hands, but it seemed like the curved V shape would break easily, especially in his enormous hands. It was white mostly, and it seemed to swirl and move within itself. It seemed familiar, but he just grunted.

Zreyas raised it toward his head, the point of the V fit at the middle of his forehead like it had been on the old man's head. Once it touched his skin, it moved and adjusted on its own to fit his head. Zreyas felt a strange tingle.

The light-man's light glowed brighter a moment, then he heard, "There, that should do it. I haven't needed it in a long time, but I liked the fashion of it so I kept wearing it."

Zreyas jerked, not expecting to hear anything, much less understand him.

The light-man looked at him with an oddly patient smile that reminded him of Aaru. "I can assure you I'm trying to help."

"I can understand you now. You change to my tongue," Zreyas said, following with a prideful grunt.

"I didn't change to your tongue."

"What trickery? What is this thing on my head?" barked Zreyas.

"I gave you a device that provides you with the ability to understand many languages, but also to speak them fluently. You are now understanding and speaking in my language."

Zreyas grunted, not accepting it.

The light-man looked at him. "It actually looks good on you. It makes you appear strong, knowledgeable, up to date with technology, and... royal. You wear it well. I think you are supposed to have it. It was meant for you."

He looked at the light-man, stunned. No one ever talked good about him but Aaru. This man seemed so much like his brother because he felt the same sincerity in his speech. Zreyas also thought he was maybe giving him false words to keep from dying, but he didn't feel the deceit. He had the same trait as Aaru. They could always identify deceit if it was going on, or at least when something wasn't right. But he didn't feel it coming from this old man. He couldn't help but consider what he said and revisited the last few sentences. He realized he was indeed speaking another language.

His face must have shown the realization because the old light-man smiled. Then he looked around as if he was assessing things, not worried about Zreyas a bit.

Someone not worried about him being close to them was new to Zreyas, too. Even his own people worried when he was around. Zreyas cocked his head, watching him as he gripped his weapons. He couldn't begin to speculate where his brother might be, other than down. *This light-man might know where Aaru is. I will wait to kill him.* He decided to ask a question instead. "What happened!?"

The light-man didn't reply, clearly engrossed in looking at things around him. To Zreyas, he seemed like a thinker, a calculator, and definitely strange. This fascinated Zreyas because that also reminded him of Aaru. *Does everything remind me of Aaru now that he is not around?* Since Aaru came out of the tunnel, there wasn't a time he could remember he wasn't near him, or at least knew where he was. He'd seen no one think so calmly like him until this man. This creature fascinated him.

"Does anything about this place seem familiar to you?" asked the old man.

"No!" Zreyas barked. He realized it came out much harsher compared to the other man's speech. That prompted a lot of thought. *I thought my little brother was gentle, but this light-man makes him look like the emperor in comparison. I guess our worlds are totally different.*

The light-man looked at Zreyas as if he knew him. Zreyas felt vulnerable, and he did not like that. Except for the Commander, he had been the best at everything for varSas and had never felt vulnerable in his life. It made him want to lash out at this light-man, but the man wanted to find his light leader and Zreyas wanted to find Aaru.

The light-man looked at him empathetically. "Don't be too hard on yourself. You are not used to different beings other than what is close to you in your galaxy, I'm guessing," he said, still looking around searching for something. "What galaxy are you from?"

"Tcaktranot."

The man blinked, scratched over his ear, and turned to him. "That galaxy doesn't exist in all the multiverse that I know of and that is something I specialize in. What universe are you from?"

Zreyas stopped breathing in a small wake of shock and confusion, not knowing what he was talking about. "I don't know!" he said gruffly. He paused for a moment, noticing the abrupt comparison of tone again. He wanted information from him and forced himself to calm down. Zreyas tried again, softer, "We were never told that. Our cluster is in the Outer Reaches." He grew more explosive. "I am of the Janquar Nation! What happened to our worlds? You seem to understand everything else!"

The light-man laughed, looking around at the sky as

if he was searching for something. "I don't know everything, my boy. You have just shown me that." Then he turned toward Zreyas. "By the way... Who was the blue warrior-child you helped back there? The one that took my Tantra with him?"

Zreyas erupted in grieving anger. "He didn't *take* her anywhere! He tried to help her and it cost him his life, probably. Are you ticking blind?"

The air rippled around Zreyas. His war aura was in full force now, pushing the light-man further away. Too many things happened too fast, and it was making him want to rip this light-man apart. "You *dare* accuse him? I will rip you apart, light-man!"

The light-man sighed and closed his eyes for a moment. He took in a breath and turned toward Zreyas again. "I apologize, my new friend. I did not mean to accuse him. I, like you, grieve about the losses of those we love. The concern for my people is something always on my mind. If she dies, our entire race will be extinct and it will cause a—" The light-man paused. "Well, never mind. You get the picture well enough."

Zreyas looked down and expected the ground to show up any time. *Friend? Their race will die out? They are weak! But this man is a lot like Aaru. I like that part. This is a shame for me. We don't like other species because they are all threats. It brings disgrace to our line and people if we communicate with them!* Zreyas thrashed around, trying to make himself wake up from this horrible dream. He roared and raged in a long fit.

The man looked at him and vanished along with his light warriors. He continued to rage and roar until he was so weak he could only breathe. He looked around and finally saw the ground below him. *Finally, I can die from this nightmare. I will join you soon, Aaru.*

Zreyas wondered what happened to the light-man. He looked at the structures that came into view below and tried to ready his mind to meet his fate. Time seemed to slow and started noticing every detail of the buildings. Dark roads ran between them and there were short white ones connecting the buildings to them. Zreyas couldn't make sense of the architecture. Things seemed surreal and supposed it was because he was about to die. He closed his eyes and noticed the stress of what was about to happen building up. *I'm ready to die, my brother. I will meet you soon. We will take revenge on your death together in a different body.*

Then he realized nothing happened. He opened his eyes again, wondering why he was still alive. He realized he was still falling, but much slower than he expected, and really couldn't tell if he was falling at all.

The light-man appeared again with his light warriors.

Surprised, Zreyas drew his weapons from his back and blurted out roughly, "How are you doing that!?" He sized up the warriors and readied himself. The warriors' bodies seemed built like the light-man height, but stronger and stockier. They had armor on that seemed to blend into the warrior's flesh in the same white material as the buildings they built. If he looked at the armor too closely, it made his head swim. He looked away and figured it was their version of a war aura.

"Please, my friend. My warrior friends came with me to help find our Tantra and offer me protection. They are no threat to you unless you try to hurt me or Ayya. Can we just talk for a time? What else have we got to do other than kill each other? We need to find Ayya and you need to find your blue warrior."

Zreyas paused and then grunted, "If you come near

me, I will kill you. Talk old man. What did you do earlier?"

"Well, I used the quantum to get away from that roar of yours. I pushed myself and the warriors into the past. Now I'm using it to slow down the time to retard our fall, but that is not even necessary because we are not really here yet. By the way, the waves of your destructive roar are rather impressive and it's pretty invasive, dear boy!"

Zreyas grunted with a sharp nod, proud. He considered what the light-man said about using the quantum. This man was far beyond his capability to understand this quantum. He assumed it was a kind of magic. "What do you mean we are not here yet?"

"You see, my boy..." The light-man scratched his head just above his ear, addressing Zreyas, "This entry energetically spread our bodies out because of the differences in realms frequency and physical density. If someone looked at us that lived in this realm, they would not notice us because we are small particles that are spread out right now. However, it won't be long until we will condense and bind to this place, just like we were to our home worlds. Until then, there is nothing we can do but talk... or kill each other."

"Do you think your... person... and my brother, Aaru, are here?"

"Ayya... who is to be our Tantra," the man said. "So the blue warrior-child is your brother, and his name is Aaru. What of the other young one that tried to kill him and died?"

"My brother. He hated Aaru."

"Aaru... Aaru..." the light-man repeated, as if he was trying to remember something. "Who named him?" The light-man twisted himself to adjust his body to face Zreyas.

Zreyas felt ignorant about not knowing how they got their names. It was not something their people spoke about. He clenched his fists and erupted his response. "I don't know!"

"It is not a question you should get angry about. I was just curious. I'm a scholar of sorts. It's what I do. What is your name so that I might address you properly? My name is Rhom."

"Zreyas. And I don't know about who gave names because we came to be with people calling us that. I would have to guess my father would know, but he never spoke about personal things like that."

"Was your father there?"

"Yes, he was the one that hit Aaru."

"Ah, Scar-face. Nice... uh, loving family."

Zreyas blinked. He didn't know this word, loving. But he was not going to ask, either. "I gave him that scar in my trial." He puffed up proudly.

"Well, Zreyas, in a few minutes, I'm guessing we will begin integrating into this world and things will accelerate and we will fall quite fast. I'm going to do my best to access the quantum to slow us down. In case we get separated, we can meet up right there in the circle at the end of that road down there." He pointed directly below them and a little to the left. "We can search for Ayya and your brother together, if you would like."

"Aaru."

"I apologize, Aaru."

"I'm not Aaru, I'm Zreyas."

The light-man Rhom opened his mouth to say something, but nodded instead.

Zreyas realized his mistake. He ground his teeth, heat covering his body, and looked away from the smart light-man.

They began falling quite fast, just as Rhom said would happen. Zreyas' skin started itching. His guts seemed like they were being ripped apart and also filling up. The sensation was extremely weird. An unfamiliar sensation took over, as if every part of his body compressed, dense and weighted. The speed at which they fell seemed lightning fast now.

He watched the streets and buildings race toward him. "Ticking-hell, this is going to hurt!"

"I agree! I'm working on it! It's harder to do here. I'm adjusting too!"

"Well, if you are going to help us, adjust faster! The ground is coming... like *now*!" Zreyas roared, closed his eyes tight, and waited.

10 Unnatural

ꟾꟾꟾ Zreyas ꟾꟾꟾ

Zreyas' body rolled horizontally and face up, hitting the ground hard. The wind was knocked out of his body, and his diaphragm spasmed. *Breathe... breathe...*

After several seconds, he finally took in a spasmed breath. Zreyas stood and concentrated on regulating his breathing. He scanned the area for the landmarks, looking for the place Rhom pointed out earlier. *Well, the old man saved me from the fall—He could have killed me. He is my enemy, and it doesn't make sense. Everyone tries to kill us.*

Zreyas stood slowly, noticing the structures were smaller than he thought. He would have to stoop down to get into one of those flimsy doorways. He liked the colors and textures though; they seemed rather artistic compared to plain stone. There were varied materials working together, not chiseled. *How odd. Openings in the walls with glass and thin sticks crossing through it. That won't hold anyone out! These people are not very good with defenses.*

He sniffed the air and drew his weapons, realizing he was alone. It felt strange and found it hard to think as clearly. It was different when his surroundings dictated much of the direction of his thinking. He had very little of that right now and the only time he could remember when he had been alone was when he had done his survival trial. His six companions hadn't made it, and he finished the trial alone for the last three days. He talked to himself so it would seem like someone was there with him. "I better look for that place the light-man pointed out... I mean... Drom... no, was it Lom? Ticking-hell, I can't remember his name."

Zreyas thought about his life as he took in the surroundings, trying to find the landmarks he saw from the sky. He had always been in groups of warriors, giving orders, or given orders. His people slept in barracks, ate together, and pissed together. *I never had to think for myself unless I was actually fighting or planning. That... was the only time I was not being told to do something someone else's way, too. And it was the only time I felt quiet inside.*

He let out a sigh and walked toward an opening in the road ahead. Being alone gave him too much time to think about useless things. It felt uncomfortable, so he talked. "Time to find you, little brother... at least we got the old man to help a little. But you know I will have to kill them. They are a threat to us."

He jogged at a steady pace toward where he thought he should go to find the light-man. It felt weird to be cooperating with the enemy, because everyone was the enemy to his people. He wondered why it was like that many times. But right now, he had to find out if Aaru was okay or not.

As he passed one building that led to a part of the road that widened, Zreyas felt a static shock rip through the center of his body. He had never experienced it before, but he knew what it was. They had cut him off from his people's internal communication network. All of his people would come to kill him as soon as they find out where he was. They had probably declared a hunt. The Janquar manipulated rules all the time, and he knew that. But when it came to titles and challenges, he had made a grave mistake knocking the Commander toward that fracture. You didn't challenge a titled Commander without killing them or a hunt would be declared toward the one that challenged. *That* was why the Emperor had come after him. He had been ejected from the internal communication, but they would still have his signature in that network to track him. *I guess I don't have any people anymore to worry about threats or being commanded. What am I going to do now, Aaru?*

It was hard to think. Too much had changed too fast. So, he concentrated on the one thing that he knew was a stable focus. This weird old man of light and his warriors were the only thing between him and Aaru. He would cooperate. Then, when he found Aaru, he would patch him up and they would be on their way.

As he turned the corner of the last building, he found the old man and his warriors waiting in the place he had pointed out earlier, just as he said they would. The light-man turned to face him. They gave each other a mutual nod.

One of the light warriors walked up to the light-man about the same time Zreyas approached. “High Seer, we have searched all these structures in the direction from which we came. All are empty and dark. It's odd. No one seems to live here. Yet, the structures, were obviously built by someone and none of them have damage."

"Odd indeed... and alarming," said the light-man. "It's like this place is in the present, but the energy signatures say it doesn't exist in some areas. In other areas, they have signatures that trace back to the past." He pointed at several places in the sky, like an instructor. "See the sky and the fractured edges all over the place? By my calculations, the sky is shrinking slowly."

"So, this place will eventually disappear," one warrior stated.

"If what I see is correct, yes. We still have time to find Ayya and the warrior-child, though."

"Aaru," corrected Zreyas.

"Yes, Aaru. By the way, my boy, I apologize for the run you had to do to get here. I had an awful time trying to manipulate the quantum for the fall when everyone's particles were assimilating together in different areas faster than others. We were a bit scattered, too. Anyway, Ayya and Aaru have to be here unless they were in a part that was already snuffed out. But..." He closed his eyes a moment. "I don't think so. I still feel her presence and energy signatures. Those signatures are mostly intact."

"Mostly?" one of the light warriors asked with a bit of concern.

"I won't lie. She doesn't feel the same. Something isn't right. In fact, I think she's in dire need of help. We need to keep searching. Split up and search the other direction. Zreyas, if you find her, let out one of those war cries of yours, but maybe not on the destructive level. We have our internal communication connection. If you hear a high-pitched tone three times, that is me calling you."

The light-man looked up at Zreyas and had to bend

backward. “You are tall, my boy! Now that we are on the ground at the same level, you really are impressive and... intimidating!”

Zreyas nodded and grunted proudly. He turned to look in a different direction. “What was your name again? I was a little... pre-occupied when we talked earlier.”

“Understandable. It’s Rhom, short for... well, it doesn’t matter. Just call me Rhom.”

Zreyas nodded and vowed to himself not to forget again. He wasn’t used to having to remember names. He pointed to an outside row of structures. “I’ll go in that direction.” *His name is Rhom.* “I can’t tell which direction without a sun or moon. This place is weird.” *Rhom. Rhom. Rhom...*

“Odd.” Rhom looked around. “I can’t get a reading for a sun or moon here, either. This is a dying dimension. It isn’t a place anymore.” He flapped his hand at them to go on while he mumbled to himself.

Zreyas watched the others silently spread out as if they had pre-planned everything, but he knew they communicated internally. He thought that kind of communication was amazing and tactical, much better than the Janquar war aura communication. Maybe they could teach him how to do this communication in silence. *If my people had that, no one could stand against us. That’s right, I don’t have any people anymore. Well, it would be handy to have to communicate with Aaru. Rhom... Rhom... Rhom.*

Zreyas ran across a field of grass with odd pipe structures, chains, and ladders in different bright colors. One of them had a bright metal flat piece leaning at an angle. He couldn’t make sense of it. It was still dark and everything was wet and shiny, but he saw no puddles or rain. He was glad he could see in the dark with no problem.

Ahead was a row of structures that lined up along the road. He moved over to run on the road to make running easier.

Lights began turning on, all of a sudden, at the top of poles along the roads. Startled, Zreyas drew one of the two swords on his back and the dagger from his left hip as he crouched.

Things seemed surreal with the lights on the roads, reflections from the wet pavement, and no one around. It all seemed to make it look like he was in a dream. The weird reflections from the sky filled with fractures made everything reflect in a way that seemed beautiful and also eerie. The entire row of structures was dark and void of life as far as Zreyas could tell.

When he reached the road that crossed the one he was on, he looked down the row on the right and all was dark. When he turned to look to the left, he saw the row of structures in much the same way, just as dark. Just as he turned right to go that way first, one building's light turned on inside.

Not wanting to give himself away to an unknown enemy, he didn't call out for Aaru. Well trained, Zreyas ran with a stealthy silence, partially crouched. He enjoyed being quick and stealthy, rather than the bold and blustery type of style. It worked for him because he was not the largest Janquar by a long stretch, but his strategic and tactical thinking and speed had gotten him to where he was in rank. He was in line, after his father, to be emperor.

... or at least he had been. All that work, all wasted now. *Just find Aaru, and then we can start a new life together where he or I don't have to worry about what others think. Aaru won't have to hide who he is. And we won't have to worry about someone constantly trying to kill us.*

Zreyas approached the door. It was molded with a pattern of inset squares and a round knob on the right, halfway down. Tiny in his hand, Zreyas grabbed the knob and pushed it, but the door didn't budge. He noticed it seemed loose. He pushed and twisted it, intending to break it off; but to his surprise, the door suddenly opened. Because of the push he had given it, the door slammed open against the inside wall, crumbling the white flimsy wall partially. *How are these structures still standing as flimsy as they are?*

Zreyas had to duck to get inside the door. Once inside, he could stand up with a few centimeters left to spare. The left wall was long, and it disappeared into a strange darkness he couldn't see into. Zreyas couldn't help but feel something was wrong, and his guts wrenched at the thought of going that way. *Even I can't see down that hallway, and I have no problem seeing in the dark. Ticking hell, this is bad.* He looked to the right to avoid the uneasy feeling he got when he tried to see down that hall.

The wall on the right was large and had a wide-open doorway leading to a room. Cautiously moving toward it. He crouched down slightly to move inside and then stood again. *This building ticking makes no sense.*

The floor was wooden strips of wood, smooth and shiny. The only thing moving in the room was a device on the wall with two pointers, one long and one short. It had a gold metal bar with a circle at the bottom, moving side to side with a *tick-tock tick-tock* sound. It had chains with metal bars at the end of them.

To the right, there was a cold fireplace made of stonework. *Finally, some stone.* The fireplace suddenly lit up and illuminated the room. Zreyas crouched in defense, readying the weapons in his hands. But nothing else happened.

That fireplace was odd, and Zreyas got a spine-prickling feeling. It was burning, but there was no heat coming from it. It just seemed... eerie. The rest of the room was completely empty.

The wall in across from the fireplace had large panes of glass, separated by molded wood sticks that he had seen from outside. He hadn't gotten the chance to see glass often in his life, so he looked closer to see how it was built. Though he was a warrior, he still enjoyed building, but he told no one but Aaru about that. Being an artisan in the Janquar nation was associated with being weak. He supposed that was why he loved the survival part of his training and teaching most, because it involved hunting and creating things. He felt a peace while he did that. As he looked at the details of the window, it took his mind off his additional worries for a few precious moments. The last time he saw a version of glass was on a ship. He hadn't been able to see that up close, though, and only then, maybe twice in his life. The Janquar Nation didn't know how to make ships, the Emperor hired them from some other place. Every time he went on a ship, he was in the hold with no windows, packed in like rats for some war. *Rhom.*

Zreyas turned and moved slowly, with as much silence as possible, toward the dark room on the other side. He could almost see through that darkness normally. He let out a sigh of relief. As he looked at the darkness, it was like something was making him remember memories of times on those ships.

There was one time they sent them to a war. They packed them in so tight they stood with no room between each other. Their bits were hooked up to tubes, and three times a day special hoses with nutrients were lowered for them to drink and feed from. He couldn't remember how long that trip was because it was weeks or maybe even months, because he'd lost all sense of time. He was glad Aaru wasn't with him then, because he wanted to die before that was over.

He let his war aura rise a little to shake himself out of the memory he had not thought about in many varSas as recognized another fireplace ahead, but that one was not lit. To the right of the fireplace was a table. It had a folded cloth sitting on top. There were built-in shelves under it. Zreyas crouched to get through the doorway as he examined its design, then moved forward a few steps.

Zreyas turned to face left and froze because what he saw was so odd his mind couldn't place it at first. Two elevated rectangle tables with vertical bars around the sides and nothing on the top. Inside the bars, in each cage, was a bundle of crinkled material of some sort. The bundle in the left one moved slightly.

The darkness was not as weird and dense as the darkness at the entrance, but it was still more opaque than he thought it should be. *Nothing looks like the two we are looking for, but the old man might want to see this.*

Zreyas made his way out of the house, careful to duck in the right places to keep from hitting his head. He hugged the left wall to avoid the dark hall.

When he arrived at the road, he let out his war call. He waited a few seconds before turning back around to look at the building. The light of the house inside dimmed slightly, and he realized he wasn't sure what caused the light when he first saw it because the fireplace wasn't lit when he first went inside. He didn't remember any torches or lights of any sort. *Rhom, Rhom, Rhom. Good, I didn't forget.*

Zreyas heard a rock tumble. He turned quick to see

several light warriors running toward him. Finally, Rhom appeared from around the corner, running fast.

"It's about time, uh..., old man! You are the last one here."

"How did you know I was old? Did you forget my name already, my boy?" he chuckled.

Zreyas sniffed, looking down at Rhom. "I'm observant like that. Besides, your name is not memorable, old man." *I can't kill him now, but I will have fun with him.*

Rhom's expression seemed to show he was paying attention to Zreyas' response a little closer than was comfortable for Zreyas. Rhom grinned. "I think you are... special."

"What do you mean?"

Rhom grinned and scratched his head above his right ear. "I'm old, I can't remember."

Zreyas grunted. "Oh, you must be ancient then."

11 Cracked

Zreyas

"What is it? What did you discover?" Rhom asked as his eyes lifted and widened with hope of possible good news.

Zreyas pointed toward the dwelling. "In here. It's unnatural. The fire pit started by itself in the first room and there was a device with a sound tick-tock tick-tock on the wall." He started striding toward the structure as he outlined more of what he discovered. "Oh, and there is this blackness in the hallway. I have the ability to see in darkness, but I cannot see through it. And, I discovered two weird bodies in little prison cells, and one of them stirred."

"Prisons? That doesn't sound normal."

"Follow, I show you."

"That's... really odd. What else did you notice?"

"Just come. I understand now how frustrated my brother was now. He tried to explain how he talked to an emperor in our real Emperor's chambers, but the emperor was with us. I could tell he was not lying, and that is why I believed him, but no one else believed him. Because if someone explained this mag-shit I just saw to me, I would not believe them."

"Wait, what did you say about an emperor? That might be important. Remind me to ask you about that again, but let's see this place first. It might be the building Ayya and Aaru are in."

Zreyas slowly made his way into the structure, crouching. He pointed toward the long hallway. "That way is bad. I don't understand why, but I can't even view one meter inside it." He didn't wait for a response and hugged the wall to skirt around it. Zreyas turned to the right and continued through the doorway into the room where the tick-tock and fire were. He pointed at them to show Rhom.

"Odd indeed!" Rhom pointed at the device on the wall. "That is what many cultures call a clock. This one is ancient. Typically, someone has to wind it up every day for it to work." He pointed at the bars hanging from chains. "These weights keep this clock running, rather than winding it up with a key." He paused a moment. "Interesting. The time shows 1:11, and it has not changed time since we have been in here, yet it still ticks. It's also a significant number in numerology."

"I'm not sure what you mean," Zreyas said as he looked closer at the clock, now interested to learn more after hearing the old man's explanation.

"This particular set of numbers signifies an opening of an energetic gateway. It also carries a message with it to pay attention to our thoughts. The quantum will turn our thoughts into reality easier than it normally does." Rhom turned to Zreyas, "Think about excellent outcomes, rather than bad, because those thoughts can manifest through the quantum space gateway."

"Does that happen, old man?"

"Yes, my boy! And you are right, the fire is cold."

Zreyas turned, moving through the room and into the next with the fireplace that wasn't lit. He turned sideways to let the others through the doorway, pointing toward the two little prisons next to each other. "In here."

Rhom walked up to where Zreyas was and looked toward where he pointed. A second later, he gasped, catching Zreyas off guard. Rhom was staring with a horrified look on his face, but Zreyas checked and noticed nothing different.

"Ayya! Oh, my little phoenix! No, no, no, no." Rhom walked over with urgency. He carefully held his hands out in front of him, as if he was readying them to help. He seemed afraid to touch anything at the same time.

It horrified Zreyas that those two might be who they were looking for. Rhom seemed damn sure it was Ayya. He wondered if the other one was Aaru.

The light warriors followed Rhom, crowding around him, eager to see too. Zreyas looked at the warriors with confusion and realized they were confused, too. He Looked back toward Rhom, who was now draping himself over the cage walls.

"That is Ayya? It doesn't resemble her; I saw her in that ritual of yours and that is nothing like her!"

"Unfortunately, yes, it is her signature. Something went very wrong for them. I wonder if the edges of the two fractures there together affected them without killing them. As far as I can tell, she is barely alive." The other one nearby moved, and Rhom glanced over at it. "That is likely your brother, but let me make sure...

Don't touch them."

Rhom pulled back the weird cloth that was crinkled around her. Zreyas wondered where it came from. Rhom looked at her body and stumbled slightly at what he saw. He gripped the top of the bars and closed his eyes as he lowered his forehead to rest on his own hand.

Zreyas rubbed his palm across his temple and said nothing. His entire body trembled at what his brother might look like now, too. But if that was his brother, then he was dead already, even if he lived. Anger filled him and he took a step to see what Rhom saw.

Rhom held out his palm. "I ask that you wait a few minutes. That aura of yours just might kill them both."

He stopped and backed up. It would be a mercy if it killed them in his eyes, but he knew nothing about this Ayya, so he complied. Zreyas hated his brother, Nat, for what he had done. He reached out in his mind toward Nat while his war aura built up within him. Zreyas fought hard to hold it back so he wouldn't hurt the two laying there. *I'm glad you are ticking dead, you evil bandhula! With one action, you have doomed an entire race and two of the best in the Janquar Nation! I should have killed you long ago. So all this is my fault, really.*

He felt a weird sensation in his chest. He glanced over at Rhom and the light warriors, but they were not paying attention to him. It filled him and swelled to the point where it became painful. It felt like his chest was cracking open from the swelling, and it moved into his throat. Swallowing was difficult now, and he didn't know what to do. *What is happening to me? Am I breaking like the skies?*

Zreyas took in a struggled breath and tried to swallow, making a sound from the swollen throat. All the others looked up at him and noticed he was struggling. He took in a sharp breath.

Rhom turned his attention to Zreyas. "Think about breathing at a steady pace. Count to keep your mind busy. You will be okay."

He did as instructed, and it seemed to help as he looked at the old man. "I do not understand many things. You seem to know everything about what is going on, at least more than me, anyway."

"Ask."

Zreyas was silent for a few moments. He wanted to go over there and see what had happened to Aaru, but he couldn't make himself. Zreyas didn't know why because he had seen some pretty gruesome stuff in his one hundred seventy-four varSas of life. He watched Rhom work on the two in front of him. It was hard for him to see what Rhom was doing through the weird semi dark room and the crinkly stuff. "I think there is something wrong with this darkness. We need to get out of here. My chest is cracking like the skies and falling up into my throat."

Rhom paused only a second, then continued with what he was doing, hovering his hands in different places over the now unrecognizable Ayya. The old man used his index finger to hover and trace something that Zreyas couldn't see between the two cages.

Zreyas waited out the silence, still having difficulty swallowing, to take advantage of the time. He wanted to put together his chest again, but it just seemed to get worse.

Rhom closed his eyes for a moment, and the light warriors began humming tones with him that were mesmerizing.

He felt a melting warmth in his chest and was so desperate for relief from something so strange he let it happen, surprised at himself. It was as if someone took all his anger. It made him feel a little uncomfortable, unused to it.

He felt out of place when he realized he no longer had to worry about getting killed every second of every day and night. Zreyas felt tired of everything. For a few moments, he just let himself relax and just let the tones move through him. He wondered if this was what happened to Ayya during that ritual. The sounds seemed like medicine to him. *What is he doing to me? Do I care? No... I don't. This place, I do not understand it. My brother is no longer who he used to be. I treated him like my people would, but I knew he was different and did it, anyway. It was hard on him, but I didn't want them to kill him. And... I wish I could talk to him again.*

Zreyas' vision blurred and his eyes warmed. They stung with excruciating pain. Janquar eyes couldn't tolerate water. His body didn't understand it was his own liquid and his eyes sealed shut involuntarily—a racial trait that was inconvenient. His eyes involuntarily blinked while closed and forced liquid out of his eyelids and felt something slide down his face. Zreyas reached up to touch what it was and realized there was nothing on his face. When his eyes finally unsealed, he looked at his gloved hand and saw wet spots.

After a short amount of time, his sight became clearer, and he noticed the sound had stopped. All the light-men were looking at him with bright expressions. Their mouths were bent upward at the ends.

"Feel better, Zreyas?" asked Rhom.

Zreyas started assessing himself and nodded with another question in his mind.

"You don't have to ask, I'll explain. It's simple, really. You have discovered something that none of your race has likely ever discovered, except for Aaru here."

Rhom went silent as he worked with the two bodies in the cages. He pushed each one closer toward the bars, toward each other. Now side by side, a fluid line of energy appeared and flowed between several areas of their bodies.

Zreyas asked dumbfounded, not able to take his eyes off the connected lines of blue energy as he cocked his head, "What is this discovery I have discovered that I don't know I discovered? And what is happening to them? Are you making magic?"

"One question at a time, but the last one first. It's not magic, it's science, though it *is* magical how it works."

Rhom continued to work on the two victims. As before, after some time, he answered, "You have discovered the most powerful weapon, key, and gift across all the multiverse. Even if all the species do not yet understand what it is, it's the only thing that will save us all from total annihilation." He looked up and leaned forward as if to emphasize. "You have discovered compassion."

Zreyas wanted to pound this man into the ground. His head felt like it was going to explode with all this recent information, unfamiliar words to learn, his cracked chest, no longer having a home, and about to die from a hunt that he had no power to stop. He couldn't grasp it all, much less put it into place. He didn't know what compassion was. Zreyas knew they came from different places and cultures, that was obvious, but he felt like a useless rock compared to this light-man.

Something told him to listen to this Rhom, because he would teach him some valuable strategies. He was going to need all the information he could get to survive that hunt.

After a few moments of silence, Rhom looked at

Zreyas. “Do you remember what your brother is like?”

Zreyas looked at Rhom after hearing his question, incredulous. “Of course, I do!”

Rhom ignored the outburst. “Describe him to me... all the details you remember, even if it has nothing to do with appearance. Tell me what type of person he is. Relay anything about him that pops into your mind. Trust me, it will help me make sense of this mess, because he has done something here, I don’t understand.”

Zreyas felt his frustration peak. “You saw him, old man!”

Rhom looked up to Zreyas, pausing his work with a calmness on his face that angered Zreyas even more. “I saw him, but you knew him.” Silence assailed the room, then Rhom added, “There is a sizable difference.” He looked down at Aaru. “Appearances change for people if you have compassion for them. More than the just body features come to light. You notice their inside traits and glimpse the energy radiating to the outside, as long as you aren’t judging them and actually appreciate them. You appreciate Aaru, even I can tell that. When one does that, they can feel their soul.”

Zreyas grew extremely frustrated. “I don’t understand your word ‘soul’. I don’t understand compassion! I don’t know what they are. How can I explain to you what I don’t know?”

Rhom looked up with his mouth doing that bend upward thing again, eyes twinkling in kindness. “Point well taken, my boy! That will all come. Try to be patient with an old man who is trying to figure this horrible situation out. Can you please just trust me and describe Aaru’s personality and life, and I will prompt you with questions when needed. I ask for your help for both your brother's and our Ayya's sake."

The light warriors began humming haunting, but beautiful, tones. Zreyas felt himself relax and reflect on Aaru. He sat down on the raised brick surface in front of the fireplace in the wall. He heard the fire ignite to life behind him, but this time, it felt warm.

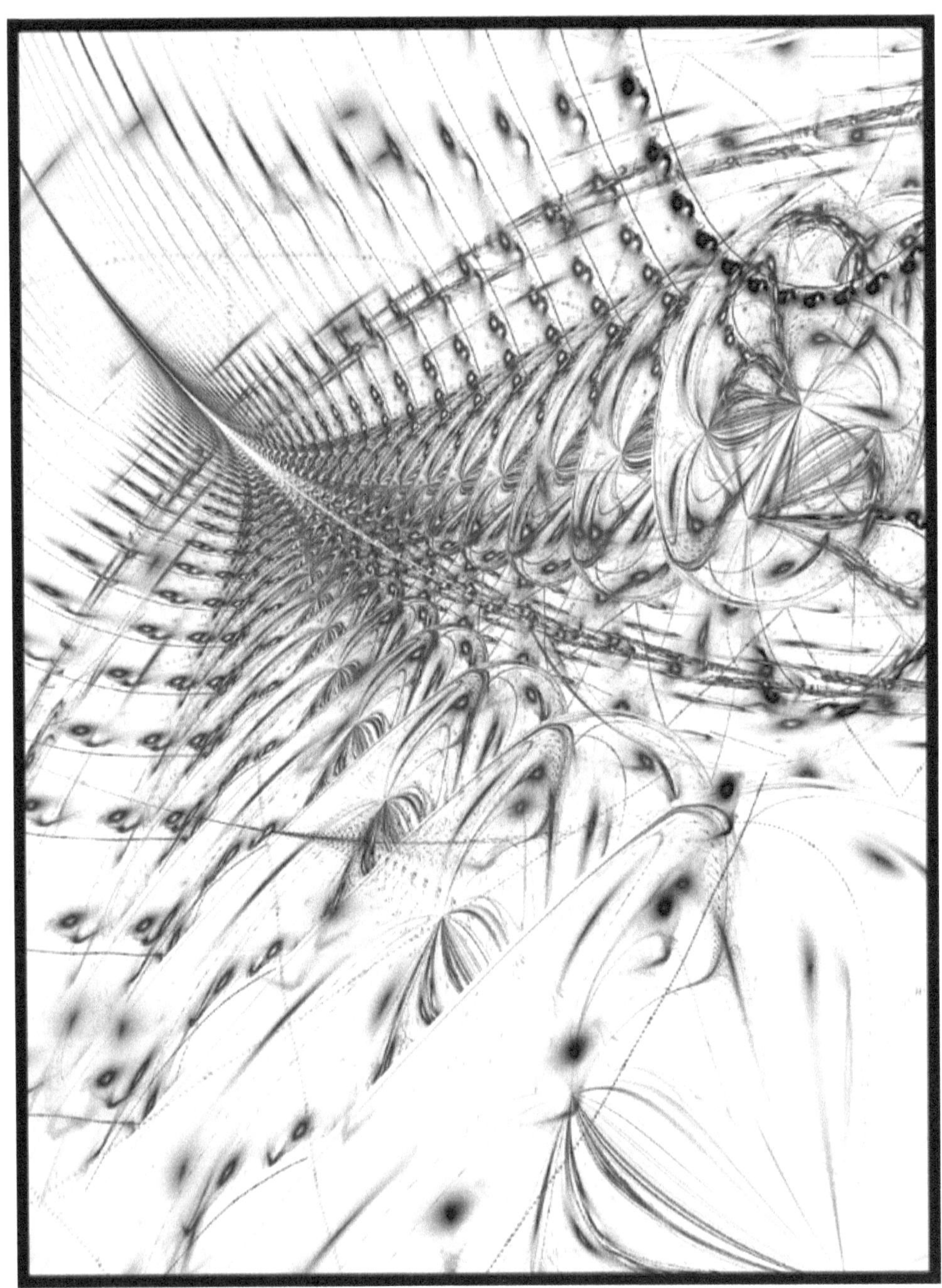

12 Confusion

Zreyas

"Well, my brother's skin is—" Zreyas looked toward the bundle. "*Was*... light-blue, unlike the rest of the warriors. It set him apart from the beginning. But he has a special talent for instinct." Zreyas could only shake his head in amazement as he thought about all his weird quirks and talents. "And his speed and agility always seemed a little... unnatural."

He rubbed his face, and neck for a moment, then continued. "But he was always silent, not like the rest of us, from the day he walked out of the tunnel of birth."

One light warrior asked, "What's a tunnel of birth?"

Another of the warriors said, "It sounds different from most species because when most are born they can't walk or talk."

Zreyas was a little surprised at the questions from

the warriors. “Well, it’s built of stone and it’s a tunnel.”

The light warriors just exchanged glances.

Not sure why that seemed so odd, he continued, “The difference between the two is that they are a small version of the adult, but with no horns.”

All of them nodded in understanding.

“Most came out of the birth tunnel running and letting out war cries. I remember doing the same... but not Aaru.”

Zreyas rested his elbows on his knees and felt strange. “Aaru strutted out with a confidence and silence none of us understood. My people didn’t like that. My Commander, who is also the father of my line, said he was to be put to death. But Aaru fascinated me, and I convinced the Commander to let me train him first to see if his war roar could rise. I don’t know why, but I saw something in him that others didn’t pay attention to.”

“This tunnel... what is on the other side? And do you know if your father is a biological father or is it a title?”

“I don’t know, and I don’t know.” Zreyas gripped his knees and felt the stress of not being able to answer the questions he didn’t know about his own people. “All I know is all Janquar come through the tunnel of our line.”

“How many are in your line?”

“More than I can count or know, into the tens of thousands. Our father doesn’t even know how many or remember them all.”

“Do you have a mother?”

“Mother?”

“Females. When I watched your people, I only noticed males, a term most races use for one gender. Typically, on a biological level with most species, males have a part of their body that inserts into females to mate. Though some races also use them for pleasure. However, I know a few species that have only one gender, though it is rare." Rhom put his hand between his legs to show Zreyas. "I'm assuming you have something here?"

Zreyas made the connection. "So, there are people that don't? Is your Ayya male or female? Are there other types?" He couldn't help blurting out all the questions. "I don't think we have anything but males because we are all the same, just different shapes and various darker color skins. Some are even dark red that is almost black, like the emperor. Why?"

"Ayya is female, and there are other types of genders. It's a long explanation. We can go over that another time if you like. Most races need both males and females in order to breed new young generations of their race."

"Do you have a lot of females?"

Rhom pointed toward Ayya. "A few, yes. But the ones that give us new people only come one at a time, with long spans of time between them. Ayya is ours at the moment. But most races have at least half their population as breeding females." He turned his concentration back to Ayya and Aaru. "Now, back to your brother. Tell me more about him."

Zreyas continued to look at Rhom, bemused at hearing all this, and wondered where he came from. Rhom's comments prompted a glaring thought that hit him hard. *I must have existed before I came running and doing war calls. Why don't I remember?*

He looked at the warriors and their leader again, then toward Aaru, trying to gain the strength to go see him. "He... was... good to me, just like your Ayya to you. I don't think I realized just how much until... this happened. When I first trained him, he used to say...

“But, can I do it to the dummy and not to him?” Aaru pointed toward the prisoner brought back from the last war his brother just came back from.

“No! You must get used to fighting actual people.”

Aaru crossed his arms. “Then I will not. There is no purpose, and he does not want to hurt me. I don’t want to fight real people that don’t want to hurt me.”

Zreyas narrowed his eyes with a plan. “Then I will just have to look bad, sticking my neck out for you. But I will do my job and give you the opportunity to choose at least.” He walked over to the cage the prisoner was in, dropped a sword through the bars, then opened the door and walked a few steps back. Zreyas didn’t draw his weapons, then looked at Aaru. “The choice is yours.”

The prisoner, who was a formidable warrior of a much different species, an inch taller than himself, had no problem picking up that sword and rushing out toward Zreyas, raising the weapon for an overhead strike. Zreyas prepared to fight empty-handed when the prisoner leaped forward and let out an angered, “Time to die by my—”

In that instant, Zreyas saw the prisoner’s face skewered from the underside of his jaw, out the top of his head, through bone and all. Aaru was standing between him and the prisoner holding his arm upward as if he had just been standing there and decided to casually lift his arm.

Zreyas blinked, knowing Aaru had just been standing a good seven to eight meters away just a second ago. Surprised and in shock, he said, “Aaru, I thought you didn’t want to fight?”

“I don’t want to fight without a purpose. I did it for you. You stuck your neck out for me. I will do this for you... for now."

After that, he did everything I taught him with a fire, wildness, and power above all the rest I had ever trained. He immediately, from the first lesson, passed all the others by large measures. When I presented him to my commander to show him what he could do, he leaned forward in his seat, amazed. He said he was a ticking prodigy and called him over and told him to go to the next battle with me."

Zreyas sat up with an air of awe, feeling warm inside his chest. He let out a grunt of admiration. "I will never forget that conversation...

> "My brother said, 'Why?'"
>
> "The commander was furious and roared back at him, 'You don't question your commander!'"
>
> "Aaru didn't even flinch and replied, 'Why? And what is the purpose of this battle?'"
>
> "That was when I reached over and hit him, afraid that the commander would kill him right there.
>
> Aaru just looked at me with a questioning expression, but there was no fragment of shame."

Zreyas arched his back, getting hot from the fire. But it felt good. He looked toward Rhom, who nodded for him to continue. "He fought like two hundred of my kind, not exaggerating. But most of the time, he didn't have a reason, so he fought only hard enough to survive. Enemies saw him as small, thought him weak, so they would go for him first."

"Why were his horns under his skin?"

Zreyas flinched in reaction and instantly felt protective. "He was fine the way he was!"

Rhom calmly said, "I know this. I'm not attacking him. Remember, I need to understand all I can about him. There is one more thing I invite you to remember—I'm not a Janquar, and I'm not here to kill and judge you as weak or not. Before you look at your brother, I need to understand his horns because he has done something here that is rather... interesting."

Zreyas immediately deflated, hearing Rhom's sobering words. He said, "I will help and do this for him."

"Interesting, go on," Rhom said as he looked down toward Aaru and started working with him.

"We come out of that tunnel with pliable skin and small soft horns retracted under our skin on both sides of the head. A strip of scales marks their location. Our growth cycle, to the maturity of executing the war aura, is called 'the festering'. As we train and harden for war, we see and feel our anger surrounding us. Soon after, we discover the war calling. We learn to evoke the power of our anger and unleash it with our roar. It is our power in battle."

"I'll say this; that is one nasty aura you put out," Rhom said.

Zreyas grunted. "When this happens, our horns grow and lift. They separate painlessly with only itching, unless... you happen to be Aaru." Zreyas stopped a moment. "Aaru had the war aura. He fought like crazy, but he never turned dark and his horns were always painful and irritated him. They grew under his skin, but never lifted away."

"Did your leaders ever tell you why you went to war?"

"Yes, and it was always the same answer, now that I think about it."

"And?"

"We annihilate anyone that threatens our existence."

"Did they ever tell you what those threats were? Or... anything specific about the reasons they threatened your existence?"

Zreyas' mind raced at all the realizations coming in at once, feeling duped. "Nnnnoo, actually." He felt foolish as he looked up at Rhom as if he had found himself in a deadly trap that he was stupid enough to fall into. *Yet another reason to be in awe of you, little brother. You didn't fall into that trap. You are teaching me now.*

"Please continue, it is important that we uncover this. We are running out of time."

Zreyas nodded, but felt uneasy, so he walked over to the door and looked out the window on the wall of the tick-tock room. He saw the fractures in the sky and noticed one particularly large one as he decided in his mind to kill Aaru and put him out of his misery. He wasn't sure if he would ever get used to those things in the sky or that his brother was pretty much dead. Then he came back to face Rhom. "Something's not right. I'm feeling static in my guts. So I will hurry to tell this because you need it to help your Ayya. Plus, I want to see what happened to them so I can have resolution when I have to kill my brother to put him out of his... misery."

Rhom looked a little surprised, but nodded. He refocused on Aaru to work on him.

"There was one battle when he was small, his first

one. There was a dimensional trader and his clan that were traveling through our galaxy. They landed on one planet in our system. I was told to go get rid of the problem. I took Aaru and a handful of other young ones for this training battle."

Zreyas stopped his pacing and turned toward Aaru, pointing to him. "I told Aaru that this trader group was a threat and they might kill us. He then asked if they wanted to kill me. I told him I wasn't sure, but I was told they were a threat by the commander. The fury that rose inside Aaru was so strong that his horns started lifting right then. He went wild, both in action and expression. I was in awe because he moved like someone with ultimate experience was driving his body. In seconds, literally, he had killed them all. The entire clan and all the livestock were dead before any of the others could join in. I have never witnessed lightning speed like that, and still haven't to this day."

"So, he used the quantum... interesting. Continue, but hurry."

Zreyas still wondered about this science Rhom was using. "After it was over, he walked up to me, bloody from head to toe with his normal calm nature, like nothing ever happened, and said, 'They can't kill you now.' After that, he turned and walked back to pick up the spoils. The others walked forward to join him, but I called them back because they didn't fight. I sent them back to our transport ship and stood there. I watched him go through everything at his own pace. He was so small, at least for our race, but I was in awe."

"*I'm* in awe too, my boy!" Scratching his head above his ear, Rhom looked toward Zreyas. "I want to learn more about his journey, but time won't allow for it. As you know, I saw him and noticed his battered skin and covered horns. But it seems your brother found his purpose."

Blinking, Zreyas leaned forward. "What... do you mean?"

Rhom pointed at the little body. "Don't touch them, there is much to do yet." Rhom made his own body shine brighter to illuminate the room. "There, now you see better."

Zreyas breathed a little more sharply than he expected as he felt the hope and excitement rise through his body. His palms were sweaty as he leaned in to see what Rhom was talking about. He couldn't help but still be apprehensive as he looked toward Aaru in the little cage and eased himself over to see Aaru, trying not to bump the cage.

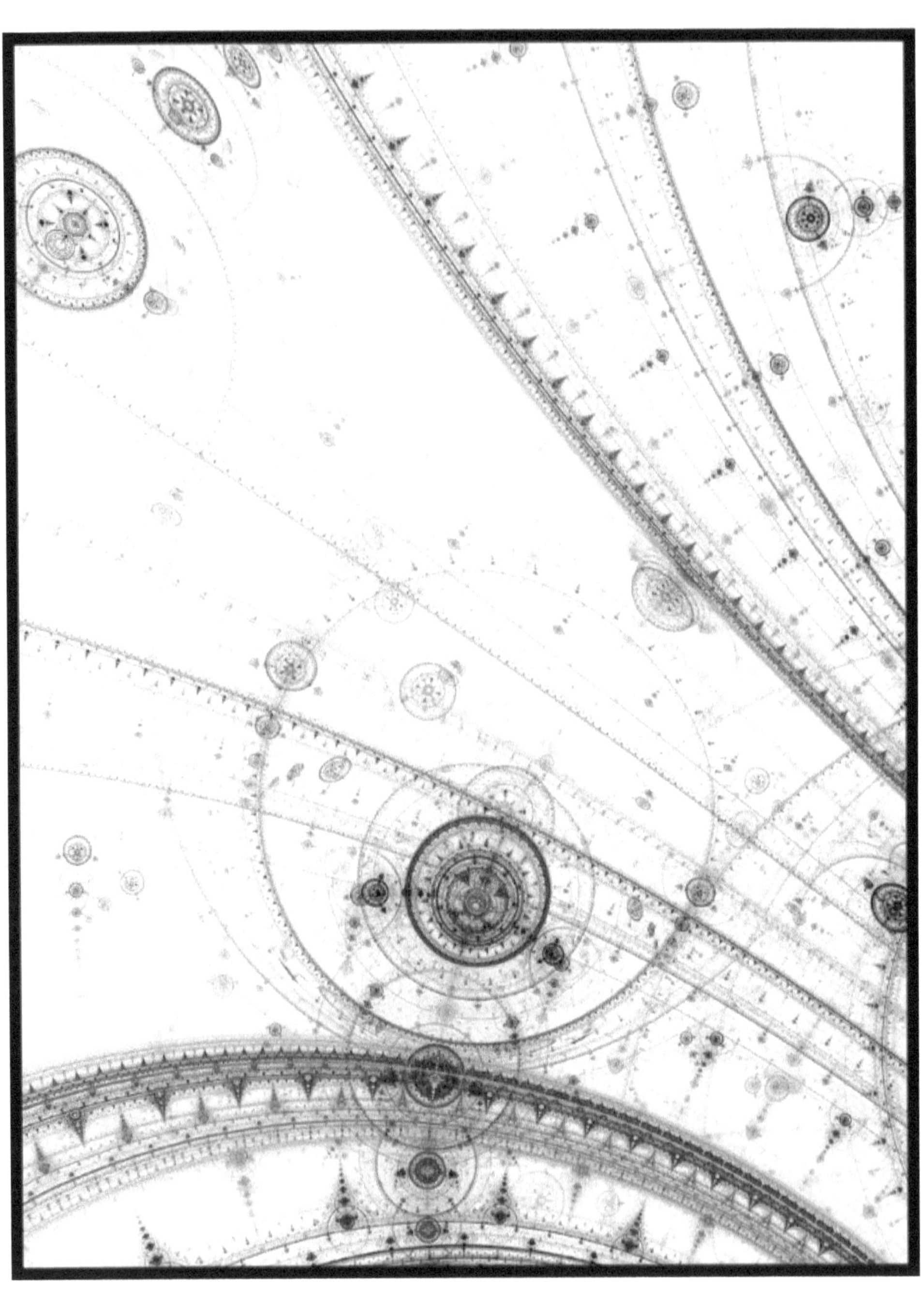

13 Yan

Zreyas

Zreyas walked tentatively to the two that lay close together.

Rhom moved, making room for him to get a close view. “Don’t be alarmed. Right now, they are okay, even if just barely.”

Zreyas looked down, scrunching his eyebrows, not quite believing him. “If Aaru is like this, he is not okay. I will not let him live like this because he will not have a good life.” He braced himself and slid his gaze between the two crinkly bundles. The horror of the situation hit him like a whip and he took in a sharp breath in shock.

He had seen many horrors in war during his life, but nothing like this. Knowing his brother was like this made him feel squeamish. Zreyas had expected at least a likeness of both of them, but nothing resembled Ayya, other than the lights, and he couldn't see anything of Aaru except the crinkly stuff. He looked at his brother and there was no way he could have prepared for something like this.

Zreyas pointed toward him and looked at the old man. "Is that crinkly stuff... skin?"

Rhom nodded with gravity.

He didn't care if Rhom told him to not touch him, or not. It was his brother. Zreyas gently laid his finger on what remained of his skin and pulled it down. "Oh, Aaru," he whispered in shock. Gently, though awkwardly, he stroked what he felt was a tiny little body underneath the crumpled ball of skin. Zreyas realized that his little brother prodigy could now fit in one of his hands with room to spare. As he searched for his head, he asked incredulously, "Who would do such a thing to them?"

Looking up with an expression of loss, Rhom said, "I... don't know, my boy."

Hearing a faint muffled cough, Zreyas gently pulled back some crumpled skin away to reveal Aaru's little head. Aaru's face was almost like he remembered but sunken in, old and almost wet, yet his expression was brighter somehow.

Aaru's eyes opened and looked at Zreyas with a soft, peaceful look.

Zreyas slid his head back on his shoulders in surprise

at this new bright and serene expression on his face. That was when he noticed Aaru's horns. Though thin and gaunt, they were not only raised, his horns wrapped around his back and curved under and around his arms, stretched out ahead of him. He continued to follow Aaru's horn growth and realized they were in a loose protective coil around Ayya. It dawned on Zreyas that he wasn't acting as a captor, but as a protector.

The awareness in Aaru's eyes made him look at his brother closely. Aaru blinked at him with smiling eyes, something Zreyas didn't quite know how to interpret.

"Look at this," Zreyas said to Rhom, pointing to Aaru and tracing his horns. "He is, or was, protecting her from something. See how the horn color is off-white and shiny?"

Rhom nodded. "Yes, interesting. What is the significance?"

"The color shows his intention. And it shows the way of his yan. Yan is... of my people, something we don't have to explain normally. Hmm, it's something you can't see." Zreyas thought for a moment while Rhom waited and continued to examine the horns.

"Do you remember who you called Scar-face? His horns are black, but a flat color."

Rhom nodded, and faced Zreyas, "Hard to forget him, my boy."

"Well, he always wanted to kill no matter who it was, all the time, just for his arrogant displays to anyone around him."

"Yes, a cold-blooded killer," said Rhom.

"Yes! Do you remember how you saw my brother

before this happened? My race doesn't like his color because it is light. He is not a cold killer; he always wanted a reason. Maybe you might call him a warm killer, I think. They thought he was weak, but the difference is yan."

Rhom seemed to think out-loud, mumbling his words. "This keeps coming up. He doesn't enjoy killing unless there is a good reason."

"You see how his horns are white but also shining? This shiny is the yan for others. Scar-face's horns are flat and sucked in what they could for himself. Aaru's horns here are shiny and reflect himself for others around. His yan was for Ayya, not himself."

"And yours seems to be a mixture of both. You have a strong yan for your brother, that is easy to tell. This yan you speak of sounds like the intention of the soul, or spirit." Rhom leaned down slowly. "Is that correct, little one? Blink once for yes."

Aaru's eyes blinked slowly.

"I like the word. Did something or someone try to hurt you?"

Aaru's eyes just stared back at Rhom with no blink.

Zreyas asked, "Did someone try to hurt Ayya?"

Aaru's eyes blinked slowly, communicating again.

Zreyas and Rhom looked at each other as Rhom stood up straight again. "Seems your little Aaru saved my Tantra's life again." He looked at Aaru. "Thank you, dear friend of the Viduri, for giving our people a chance to exist. All of us owe you our lives."

Aaru's eyes watered with a peace in them and blinked slowly again.

Rhom mumbled to himself as he looked at the situation between the two of them and how they were entangled.

Looking at Aaru, Zreyas stood straight and tall and crossed his arms. The tips of his horn spikes broke the surface of the ceiling, white dust falling from the punctures. Zreyas said to his brother, "I have much pride that you are my brother. I should be angry, but I cannot be. I know how much fighting for purpose means to you. Was it worth this, though?"

Aaru's expression went brighter, and he blinked firmly with a little more speed.

Zreyas replied, "I believe you. Hmm. And, Aaru, I don't think you are weak." He looked at Rhom. "He always made the Commander mad with all the talk about fighting for a purpose. Just before all this started, the commander was sending him on a mission that would sacrifice him so my father would not shame the line because of Aaru. I did not like that at all, but I was not ready to fight him, either. He is strong."

"Judging from what I saw, you are stronger than you think. I saw how you took him down. It took strategy and a knowledge of science to take that enormous man down, who was *way* over your weight and stature."

Rhom turned to look at the little Aaru. "You are still keeping her alive using your yan essence, aren't you?"

Aaru blinked as his water-filled eyes spilled out, landing on the padded surface he was lying on.

"Well, Aaru, you should know that your brother saved your life twice. I don't think you got to see all he did for you. I thought you might like to know." Rhom smiled with an expression he didn't understand.

Aaru closed his eyes for several seconds, water leaking heavily around them. After a time, he opened them again, looking in Zreyas' direction.

Zreyas leaned forward. "Too much water. You will seal your eyes, Aaru. I know you don't care, but I want to see your eyes."

"Your brother is much better off than Ayya at the moment, but both are still unfortunately not going to live long like this. He is giving his life force to her slowly. We need to come up with a plan to save one or the other. That is something I am not looking forward to, nor am I sure yet how to do it. Their bodies will not hold them long."

Zreyas looked at Aaru proudly, and his eyes stung. His vision went blurry. He blinked hard, and it seemed to help the stinging. Able to see better, he watched as Aaru curled what was left of his mouth up slightly. Aaru showed no fear and only expressed contentment and pride.

"Did you teach Aaru this mouth curling action? His mouth is more bent now than it was when he looted a helmet after that trader incident I told you about." Zreyas started pushing up the sides of his mouth again, trying to duplicate it.

"What are you talking—" Rhom discovered Zreyas pushing up the edges of his mouth with each index finger. Rhom laughed a little, even in the dire situation. "No, that comes naturally when you feel good about something. Your body lifts in different ways when your frequency rises, and vice versa. Bodies react in different ways to changes like that, like the mouth and chest. You seem to do it with your chest, I have noticed. If you let yourself, you will end up smiling too. It's wonderful!"

Zreyas tried to do it without his fingers. "It hurts my face to do this. I guess this is a new kind of training."

Rhom bent his mouth in a crooked smile, turning back to Ayya, pointing. "Look at this, Zreyas. I will explain what I know. I know your brother saw this when it happened. I wish he could speak to us."

Pulling himself away from Aaru, Zreyas moved around the two, following Rhom's lead. The light warriors gathered around as well. The bars were impeding Zreyas' vision. He growled and set everyone on alert. He placed his hand down on the surface of the weird soft tables and yanked up on the bars, pulling them free, then throwing them to the side. Then he repeated the action to the other. He pointed to them seriously, giving an order. "Neither of you move, or you will fall."

Rhom looked at him incredulously. "They were in my way too, thanks. Notice here... Ayya has a center like mine just above her head, well-furnished with energy. You see it?"

Everyone in the room nodded.

Zreyas held up a hand and instantly threw up a mild war aura, hushing Rhom. He listened with acute focus. His instincts flared with clear warning signals. In a soft but commanding voice, he said, "Something is wrong, there is trouble."

He cocked his head around to dial in on what he was hearing. "I hear... I hear..."

Zreyas' eyes widened with realization after he remembered that fracture. He turned around and sprinted through the structure, slipping into a stealthy walk as he exited the building. He headed back out to the tree, apprehension growing.

As he slid behind the tree, he recognized the fracture. It had a pouring effect as masses of his people fell out of it, well into the tens of thousands, spreading out and gathering. The distorted cries of intimidation confused Zreyas. They seemed filtered and garbled because they had ejected him from the war communication network. But he shouldn't have been able to understand them at all, though he was glad he did.

Rhom walked up beside him quietly. Zreyas whispered to him, "I recognize the stages of the hunt of my people well. We have little time before they are all over us. We are being hunted."

Rhom's gaze followed what Zreyas was pointing at too, then looked up at him.

"My boy. I have an idea how we can avoid them and give us time."

A Janquar figure caught Zreyas' eye, moving on the roof of the building behind Rhom at a quick and silent pace. He quickly launched himself off the roof with raised weapons overhead.

Zreyas drew his two swords off his back, startling Rhom. He twisted himself to his left, shifting and lowering his center of balance for stability to gain enough momentum to twist back again to his right, using his hips for power. As he twisted right, he used the back of his right upper arm to shove the old man to the right as he parried the overhead strike, throwing Rhom several meters away and to the ground. At the same time, Zreyas shoved the point of his left sword straight into the right armpit of the attacker and into his chest, blade horizontal. He followed the body to the ground and drove the sword in deep. Then he shoved his right sword into the lower chest of the warrior to sever the war aura compartment, preventing communication and a warning roar.

Four of the five light warriors poured out of the building with spears drawn and ready.

Zreyas spun around, watching for other Janquar. Then he broke into a run toward the building and launched himself up to the roof. Most of his body landed on top of the building. He felt the edge of the roof bite into the middle of his thighs, but between the slant of the roof and thin flat pieces covering it, breaking free from his weight, he started sliding.

He slammed the spike on the back of his right hilt into the rooftop to anchor himself and stop his sliding. He pulled himself up as he reached forward with his left hilt and slammed the spike in further up, walking his way up until he could stand.

Zreyas kept his body in a crouched stance, despite the horrible roof. It hadn't been hard to get up there since the building was so small and the roof slanted down. Whoever lived in these places were small and weak people, and he would rather die than be small, weak, *and* a stupid builder.

Now he had a better view of what was going on. His people were still pouring through the fracture. He saw no more threats close up, though. As he scanned nearby, two of the light warriors were checking the body to make sure the warrior was dead, and the other two were helping the old man to his feet.

When he was satisfied there were no more scouts, he scaled and slid down the roof and jumped to the ground. As Zreyas approached the old man, the warriors raised their spears and stood in front of Rhom.

"He is fine, my brothers. He saved my life. Thank you for your dedication and love, but stand down and go check on our brother, Ayya, and Aaru. I'll be in soon."

The light warriors relaxed and slightly bowed toward Zreyas. One of them said, "Apologies Zreyas. Thank you for saving our friend and High Seer." They moved away toward the building and went inside.

"The one I killed was a scout. Now that he is silent, they will notice him gone within their inner communication network, but at least they don't know the direction *yet*. We don't have much time, though. Whatever plan you have, old man, you need to do it now. They will get the general direction by a process of elimination of where the other scouts are currently."

Rhom hung his jaw a slight bit before saying, "You could have just let him kill me and run off to save yourself, but you didn't. Thank you for allowing me to help Ayya."

"Yeah, okay I don't know this thanking of me, but I don't know why I protected your ticking-ass, either. My plan was to kill you after I found Aaru."

"I know, but you didn't. There is some good in you Zreyas. With a little time, you would be an outstanding leader. My instincts tell me you just gave up leading one type of group to lead another type of people."

"I don't really *want* to lead. I was only where I was in the command line because I fought well. And the only reason I wanted to challenge the commander so he would leave Aaru alone."

"Nevertheless, you mark my word, you will lead people. Let's go, we need to save ourselves so Ayya, Aaru, and you have a chance to live out your purpose... whatever that might entail."

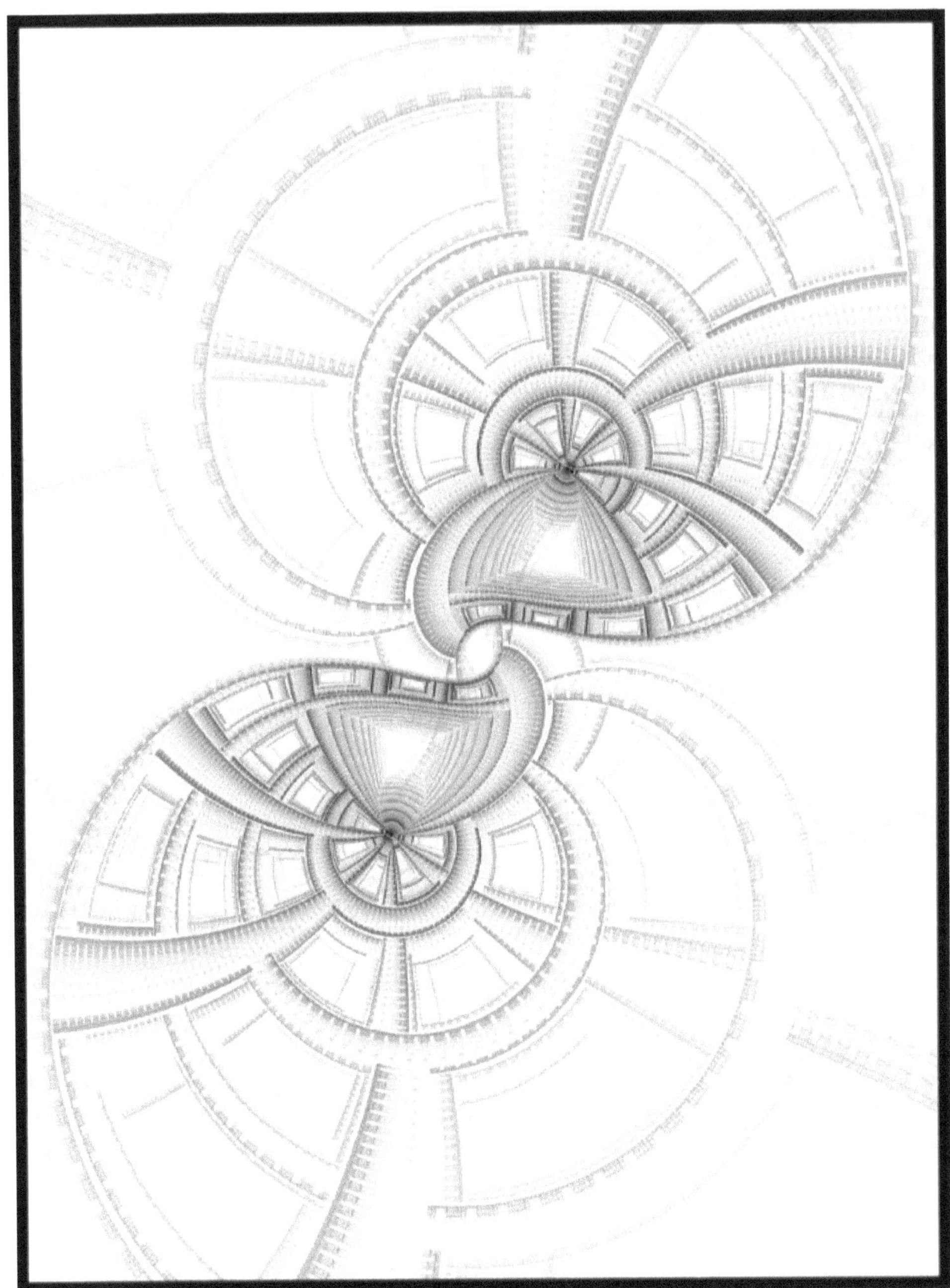

14 Quantum Consent

Zreyas

Zreyas followed Rhom back into the area where Ayya and Aaru were. The light warriors were surrounding them protectively.

Rhom turned around, contemplation lacing his expression, and appearing to assess the surroundings. Then he studied Zreyas for an extended time with a scrutinous expression.

Zreyas was beginning to understand Rhom's expressions and mannerisms. "You are calculating, old man. What are you up to?"

"Keep guard, but stay in this room. I'm going to attempt a time slip into the quantum to conceal us from that hunting party out there. It will be difficult. It's one thing to move myself through the quantum, it's another thing to move an entire room with its inhabitants. I need your willing consent to do this *and* the belief it can happen, or it will not work. Manipulating the quantum involves energy and shifting possibility. If a participant is not willing or believing, it will not work. So, before I go any further, does everyone consent to this with all their hearts?"

"I don't have any idea what you just said, but I will do this. And I believe you can do this because I watched you disappear and reappear."

All the light warriors nodded, and then Rhom headed over to Aaru. "Little hero of the Viduri, did you understand what I just explained?"

Aaru blinked.

"Do you consent to this move through time, and can you tell me if Ayya does? I need the conscious consent or it will not work."

Aaru paused only a second, then blinked once and again a second time.

"Thank you, Aaru."

Rhom walked back toward Zreyas into the center of the room. "If it is successful, I just need to maintain it and we will have all the time we need—if you think that's a good idea, of course. If not, I'm open to any other ideas."

"We can't run in a place with walls closing in, so this slippy thing you are going to do seems like the best tactical option. I will keep watch." Zreyas turned and looked through the doorway and out of the opening in the tick-tock room.

After a few seconds, Zreyas heard a weird scratching, stressed tone. He turned back and realized the sound came from everywhere. It transmuted into a sound like a roaring waterfall. He turned back to watch through the window in the tick-tock room, doing his agreed part of the plan, the only part he knew how to do—any activity relating to a fight or tactics in war. Zreyas reflected on this, and his chest and guts felt heavy and ached. *It seems like such a waste.*

— It's not a waste, Zrey.

Zreyas jerked around and saw nothing different from before. No one called him Zrey but one person. He turned and looked toward Aaru, but he was still laying there in that clump.

— It's really me, Zrey. Ayya is teaching me a lot, and she is helping me talk to you in your mind.

"What the ticking-hell?"

— Listen to me, I have little time. I can't do this long because I have to give too much to Ayya. You trained all your life for this moment, and you helped me train to do what I need to do. I don't know what part it is I am to play yet, but I know it is coming and it has a purpose. In a way, we are working together as we always did, it just won't be physically together like before. Make sure you help Rhom do anything to save Ayya. That is my last request of you. Thank you for all you did, are doing, and will do for me. I will never forget you, no matter what happens. Ayya assures me I won't. She taught me all about a new word, and I want to say to you. I love you and always have.

Zreyas blinked hard to keep himself alert and aware of his surroundings. He figured he was losing his mind and threw it all out. Then, all the troops of the Janquar disappeared in static momentary stages. “You did it, old man! They are no longer there! You really did it.”

Then he heard the unforgettable ripping sound of a fracture behind him. He whirled around and saw a fracture where the fire should have been. Zreyas breathed a sigh of relief. “The sound of fractures will forever haunt my dreams.”

“Well, that was unexpected,” said Rhom.

“Is this a problem?”

“No, but...” Rhom trailed off as he ducked down to look through it.

Everyone in the room watched what Rhom was focusing on. There was a person lying on their back with their legs spread, screaming and sweating. There were people standing around with blue clothing and masks. One of them was reaching toward the one laying down as he said, “Turning her now.”

“What is wrong with them?” Zreyas asked, confused.

Rhom explained while he watched, “She is giving birth and things are not going well.”

“It sounds like someone is gutting her.” The screams made him a little antsy. Why is he gutting her?

“Well, he’s not. He’s trying to help her. But, it probably feels like someone is since something the size of a large melon in her belly is trying to exit out of a space much smaller than that.”

“Will it rip her open? This doesn’t seem pleasant.” Zreyas felt horror at the idea of something that might kill her from the inside. It was one thing to kill someone from the outside in war, but this... *Did that happen to someone before I came out of the tunnel?*

The person attending her gave many orders. Zreyas didn't understand it at all. Then the smooth tan colored creature screamed again.

Rhom held a hand up to quiet the room. "I need to check the child within her for a moment. I need quiet." He closed his eyes and held his hand toward the creature's belly.

Rhom stood with a brighter expression. "We just might have a way to keep both Ayya *and* Aaru alive... of sorts."

"Out with it, we have little time because all the fractures so far close, so I don't expect this one will be any different."

"You are right," he said, looking at Zreyas for a moment. "You know, my boy, you have a disposition for leadership. Leadership rings when you speak. We have three choices:

"One... save your brother by sacrificing Ayya.

"Two... save Ayya by sacrificing your brother.

"Three... I think... we could perform a joining imprint, with Ayya as the master imprint soul."

"What do you mean, as the master imprint?"

"Your brother would be part of her, giving her strength to incarnate in that body." Rhom pointed at the vulnerable person through the portal. "The fourth option would be if we did it the other way around, but Ayya would cease to exist and an entire race would go extinct. It's complicated, but..."

"You don't have time to explain to a not-so-science Janquar fighter now. Continue."

Rhom blinked with a slight grin. "I looked at separating them earlier and it would kill them both to do it. Their essences of life and spirit are intertwined now."

Zreyas thought for a moment and realized there was no choice to make. "Well, my brother would kill me if we did the first or the fourth. So, I don't think we have much of a choice. He would be okay with sacrificing himself, but if we could do the joining option, that would be better. Plus, whatever damage Ayya took, maybe Aaru could compensate for it, perhaps. Whatever balances your Ayya is to bring, it seems we all need it." He pointed at the fracture.

"Now you are thinking strategically!"

"It's what I do."

"I agree with you. There isn't much choice. If we went with killing your brother to save Ayya, there is another aspect of it you wouldn't know about. He would become a specter of sorts and kill you and everyone in his path in a mindless rage from loss, because he didn't transition naturally. In addition, he just doesn't know it yet, but you can't lose a connection to something that powerful and not have a negative bounce to the opposite frequency as a rebound from the change. It is unlikely he would recover from his own darkness. Before Ayya, he was fine with his darkness as part of him."

"You are training again. We have no time, as much as I like learning your weird mag-shit. So, what do you need from me? If my brother will die, and he will die either way in any choice I think, you better not make his death in vain by teaching me science when you could have been saving her."

Rhom laughed, then went into a sobering seriousness. That made Zreyas nervous because he had never shown that before.

"I need your help. Let me fix things and shift us to a better time-line to buy us a little time."

Rhom closed his eyes and Zreyas heard a thundering wind a moment, but he noticed nothing else different.

"We have a little time because I hid us through the quantum and maintaining the time spot with that world the mother giving birth is in. And for you to make a sound decision, I need to give you a little education."

Zreyas nodded. "I'm listening."

Rhom pointed at Zreyas' body. "That war cry of yours is powerful. It is pure energy of a specific frequency. It's a low frequency that has detrimental effects on a living body. That is why your skin hardens, to protect itself." Interested now more than ever, Zreyas nodded. "Go on."

"We can't use that here in this situation because we need an energy that creates and heals at high frequencies. It's the only way to access the quantum field *and* be able to create, not destroy, in the way we need to—"

Zreyas looked at Rhom with impatience growing inside him. "You are doing it again."

"Anyway, I think you have the mechanics within you to reverse that horn of death inside you and make it into something that can operate on higher frequencies—energy that can create and heal."

Rhom looked at Zreyas with that distant expression he got sometimes. "Just in case. This might be important for you to know, my boy. If your forceful war aura was at a high frequency, it would also devastate something at a low, less flexible, frequency. However, it will be *more* devast—"

Zreyas made a motion with his hand to move things along.

Rhom sighed, paused, and continued. "It could incapacitate them in mild cases. In extreme cases, you could make them *explode* because the physical structures on a molecular level grow unstable, either because it is too quick for the living tissue to adjust to, or its structure can't adjust at all by nature."

Zreyas' eyes glazed over with the science overload, but he forced himself to listen.

Rhom paused and then started using arm and hand gestures to explain.

"I'll try to explain simply. Lower frequencies are more condensed and heavier. The higher frequencies are faster and more expanded and lighter. In science, frequencies tend to want to adjust to what is near them for many reasons, just like people adjust to other people or their environment. For example, if it is cold outside, your hands and fingers tend to cool down and condense."

"I follow," said Zreyas.

"Everything has a frequency. For another example, your war aura does a bombardment of low frequencies that affects creatures it touches, just like an environment. It makes them feel weak and condenses down tissue and vessels way too rapidly, and it is destructive to living tissues. Have any of your enemies bled or bruised from your war aura?"

Zreyas nodded. Understanding of the subject sunk in

and started to make sense to him. "Yes—from the eyes and nose. And if they have sores already, they bleed from them."

"Now you understand why. But your low frequency war aura, as it is, could never *heal* anything living, much less create new life. But, high frequencies can also damage when bombarding materials or tissues with too much force, but for the opposite reason. Tissues or materials can't compensate fast enough to keep their molecular structure. Some may not have the ability to adjust at all, so it will have a tendency to break apart because of the expansion. That is the simplest way I can explain it. There is more science to it, but as you say, no time to explain. But I can show you in a few seconds. Watch this..."

Rhom moved over to the doorway to the tick-tock room and pointed at the window. He started emitting a tone that was so high that Zreyas had to cover his ears. Before his hands could reach his ears, the window shattered, sending shards of glass everywhere. Rhom stopped his tone and turned back to Zreyas.

Zreyas took a step back in awe. "Our people need to get some of this science so we won't be not-so-science!" Then he thought for a moment. "No, forget that; if they did, everyone would be in trouble. It would give them too much power with the wrong reasons behind it."

"Now you are gaining something even more valuable than science, my boy!"

"Do I want to know what that is?"

"It's called wisdom... The maturity of wisdom *must*, at a minimum, match the height of technology or there will be disaster every time. Wisdom is the ability to assess the situations, their effects, how they affect others, and make objective decisions that are best for everyone, *without* taking it personally. There is more to it, but it is a good start on the word."

Zreyas stood a little straighter and his mouth evened.

"This is what I need from you in order to do this solution we spoke about earlier." Rhom grabbed Zreyas' elbow and turned him as he walked deeper into the room again, then turned toward Zreyas. "I need you to grip my shoulder, and roar like you never thought you could before. This time, though, before you do your normal roar, I need you to reverse the frequencies."

Just as Zreyas parted his lips to ask how the ticking-hell he was going to do that, Rhom held up a hand to stop the question.

The old man moved over to a place in front of the fracture. Then he pushed the two little ones closer to it. Rhom stood at their heads and faced the rift.

"You need to think about the anger first, like normal. Think of things that make you angry, like what your people have done to you, your brother, and Ayya, for example. Once you are full..." Rhom stopped a moment in thought, scratched his head just above his right ear, and then looked up. "For imagery in your mind, think of a door at the exit of that big compartment of anger and grief inside you."

Zreyas nodded, following him so far, interested and focused.

"As you let that energy out into your aura, make the door be a filter, like a net that has magical capabilities.

But make the filter from the wonderful memories you have with your brother, the new things you have learned, joy, etc. This will change the frequency of your aura to something higher as it comes out. Use the anger as a fire fuel, but when it expands like high frequencies do, it turns into something that heals and creates. You will feel your chest swell but remember it is not pain... it's good things like joy, freedom, and love."

A light turned on in Zreyas' mind. "Wow, old man, this is science?"

"It is!"

"I think I understand this part of science."

"I had a feeling it would make sense to you. But listen, my boy." Rhom held his hand toward Zreyas' chest, then dropped it with a nod. "This process will create a flow of energy in the shape of a torus around and inside your body that feeds itself, going in one direction. If you move that energy in the wrong way too fast in the opposite direction, like your war aura, you will implode with your anatomy. I don't have time to explain it all. If you hurt yourself, we are all lost."

Rhom stopped, then pointed toward Zreyas. "Once committed, *stay* committed, to the correct flow. Find anything and everything you can to keep that fuel going for the white creation light. Channel that anger of yours into those good things and let it out in your roar. Your aura, just like your brother's, is a manifesting aura. So, concentrate that roar into me, as I will need it as a source to do this infusing. I won't explain that part. That is my part. Do you think you can do that?"

Zreyas thought about what the old man had just said.

He went over it again in his mind and *felt* what Rhom was talking about. This old man understood his own war aura better than he did. He was glad because he now understood it better than he had in his entire life.

Zreyas nodded, "Yes I think I can, but when done, I want to know why you know so much about our roar if you have never been in our universe, or me in yours, until now."

"Fair enough, though I won't be able to give you the detail you want because all I know is how I experienced it." Rhom nodded to the light warriors, and they began humming tones that synchronized harmoniously. He then nodded to Zreyas, stood in his needed position, and motioned for him to stand behind him and to his left slightly.

Zreyas moved to the instructed place and stood tall, readying himself. "It would be better if I could practice this."

"No time, my boy. They won't last long now."

Zreyas closed his eyes to visualize what he had just learned.

"Take your time, my boy. It's better to take more time and do this right, or you will blow us all up."

Zreyas opened his eyes and saw a grave face looking back at him. He took in a breath and looked at Aaru, who was looking at him brightly. Aaru gave him a blink of encouragement. Zreyas closed his eyes again.

He placed one hand on the hilt of the weapon on his left, and the familiar feel of it made him more confident. The first thing he did was start the anger. Zreyas had plenty to be angry about, so it didn't take but a second for his inner container to fill. Then he visualized the filter gate Rhom spoke about, and the anger pushed against it. As a second thought before he went through with this, he started reaching out to Aaru in his mind for one last talk with his brother, hoping he would hear in some way:

Aaru, my brother, as you know, I am learning a lot, but now I feel more alone than ever. I am glad I met Rhom. At least he will guide my way for a short time. I won't kill him for your sake... maybe even for mine.

I want to tell you I understand now what you meant in all those talks you had with me about purpose and thinking for ourselves. It turns out you were the one training me and not the other way around.

Even if I'm not good at much of anything else, I can at least roar well so you can live to help Ayya help many others. I just want to let you know you were on to something big in these things you lived with, called purpose and wisdom, I think. You always thought about everyone, not just you. I can't say for sure if I can do that or not.

Remember when they told us you were weak and not worth fighting for? They might have been the ones saying it, but I didn't fight for you or speak up as much as I should have. Wherever or whenever you are, I will find you. I get it now, and I get you. I will fight with you and for you no matter what, just like you do for Ayya. You, and only you, are my people, and now my purpose. And you, my brother, are worth fighting for.

I... I don't know how to say it other than my chest cracks for you now. I am glad you are my brother.

After a few moments of breathing and reflecting on all his anger that he had built up the whole of his life, he focused on it—the bullying Aaru took without a word and

Nat and the commander trying to kill him. Then he thought about Aaru's strength. Zreyas got lost in the admiration and his respect for Aaru. He found out that the affection was winning out first. But it had a surprising effect. It was fueling the anger of what they had done to him. He felt out of control.

Rhom scrambled away, "Wrong direction, Zreyas!"

15 The Right Order

ꟾꟾꟾ *Zreyas* ꟾꟾꟾ

"*Anger* first! Let it fill you like normal, *then* use it to transmute into the good stuff you have discovered today, like Aaru's courage, about you, science, wisdom, and your love for your brother. You *must* acknowledge the anger *first*, then you can move it safely into something more expansive."

Zreyas took another breath, not understanding everything he said, trying to hold back the mess he made within himself. *I must acknowledge the anger first. You can do this, Zrey! That was scary.* After a few minutes, he got things under control and out of implode range. He generated anger and started over.

"Better, my boy."

He reminded himself of the stakes and how important this was. *We must succeed; if not, I kill us all, or my people will. I have to do this right.* He instinctively breathed as if he was marching to war and thought about all the living creatures he had killed in the past. The anger grew when he thought about how pointless it was, and how many Aaru-like people he had probably killed. He lowered his head, as if he was getting ready to pounce on someone in a surprise attack. He piled up the anger about how much time he spent blindly following orders. The anger almost exploded when he replayed the times he was afraid to stand up for Aaru.

If that wasn't explosive enough, it didn't hold any weight compared to what he realized from that. His leaders *knew* what they were doing. They thrived on controlling the masses. He continued thinking about the stupidity of the past, and it brought on a mixture of more anger and a new feeling of guilt. The guilt of how he didn't do his part to protect Aaru flared, because he didn't see what he was doing to himself. Flashes of everything he was angry about started bombarding his mind. His aura chamber was more full and expanded than he had ever had it in his life. Zreyas wanted so badly to let it go right then. He was not used to self-control in this department.

Zreyas observed what was going on inside himself. He realized he felt okay about it, because he could use this horrible talent for something good. He felt pressure in his throat now, long past the threshold of the normal pressure of an active war aura.

In his concentration, he faintly heard Rhom's voice giving him instruction. He tried to listen and still concentrate on what he was saying.

"Good. Now focus on the doorway of the anger chamber in your mind, then transmute with controlled consistency. Let the anger burn up so that it fuels the newly discovered compassion, love, purpose, new understanding, and new friends. Whatever you can think of that makes your chest swell, even crack. Visualize it as it transitions so that when the anger leaves, it becomes something completely different and into an expansive frequency of white healing light. When you are ready, reach for my shoulder just ahead to your right side and I will begin."

Barely understanding anything in the massive infuriated state he was in, he still got the idea. He thought about his little brother and how he was laying there because he wanted to help someone he didn't even know. The blasting rush hit the top of Zreyas' chest. He felt the expansion and was almost overwhelmed at how powerful it was, building up in alarming pressure. Zreyas let it push into his throat.

He held back and thought about sitting with him while he rummaged through the spoils of the day, watching him find a helmet, and the feeling of peace he had felt from him. Zreyas remembered him turning around to look at him to see if he was still there and remembered his affection that he didn't understand then. More flashes came at a fast rate of different times in their lives. He now recognized the mutual connections they had when they showed their affection in weird ways and glances. The visions of many things he had never thought about before came to light that had been there from the beginning. He realized Aaru had been, and still was, a guiding light in his life.

Zreyas' chest swelled in emotions new to him, and couldn't hold in the pressure anymore. He concentrated on his war cry aura, using the beautiful feelings to transform the energy as it came out. He reached his hand out, feeling for Rhom's shoulder.

Rhom slid Zreyas' hand to his chest and backed up against him for bracing. "Keep going and don't fight it anymore. Let it go as steady as you can. I will use my body to channel and regulate the energy that I give my crown center. You will feel the flow too."

It was all Zreyas needed to hear. He let it all go as consistent as he could, like a slow counted breath. Not wanting to hurt Rhom, he almost tried to stop, but caught himself, not sure he could stop it, anyway. *I must trust Rhom's wisdom because he knows himself and his abilities.* He pointed his war aura straight at Rhom and could feel Rhom sucking the transformed energy into something so much more expansive.

The pressure was exponential, and it surprised Zreyas. He saw his reservoir still very full and cycled his anger into the transformation doorway he imagined. He realized that the transformation also fed himself in return. It shocked him, not expecting that. This must be the torus flow the old man talked about. It reached a pressurized tight limit and Zreyas felt like his entire body would explode, but it still flowed consistently.

Zreyas observed it feed itself with magnetism; then he watched the flow stop for only a moment, then reverse. It flowed upward through the middle of his body. The energy created an implosion of light, and it almost brought him to his knees. It felt like it almost took him with it as it left the doorway. He felt the light warriors holding him up and could tell they were channeling the expansion of energy through their bodies to Rhom.

He felt Rhom's body spasm in the massive jolt to his system. Zreyas doubted he expected the magnitude he received. He felt acute indications of what was going on around him. Rhom froze and the light warriors mitigated the channeled aura. He opened his eyes for only a blink and saw the light-warriors swollen like humanoid light balloons.

Over time, all the understanding about this flow integrated with Zreyas' mind as he observed what was happening. He realized he was a vessel channeling life instead of death for the first time. He worked hard at adjusting to a flow they needed at a pace that was workable.

16 Imprint

Rhom

Rhom could now adjust and relax and little more. He spoke with his light warriors through their inner communication. *Okay, that was a punch I didn't expect. Thank you, dear friends, for stepping in to help me. Remind me to never underestimatc that boy again.*

He took a deep breath and stretched his hands out toward Aaru and Ayya, holding one over each of them.

Turning his head up to face the fracture, he watched the human woman experiencing what he had previously understood as a difficult stillborn childbirth. He checked to make sure the body was still viable with a little help. The soul supposed to be using that human shell had already left. Rhom repaired the damage that didn't allow it to live properly, then put a placeholder in the body to keep any souls wanting to inhabit it from doing so.

With that done, Rhom focused on the two in front of him and channeled the wonderful healing and creating divine energy to them with the intention he had in mind, not sure any of this would work. *Trust yourself Rhom. You got this information internally from somewhere; you need to trust it.* It was sad for Rhom to know that Ayya's life as he knew it was ending. But he was also glad and grateful that it meant that she might just live a life at least, even if it wasn't quite as planned.

"Keep going Zreyas, I know what to do now... and it will take everything we *both* have to get it done."

Zreyas squeezed his shoulder tight in acknowledgment, likely because of the intensity he was experiencing.

Rhom looked at Aaru and Ayya and closed his eyes again before starting the long critical process that was about to take place. He opened his eyes with resolve and began.

Over the course of the next few hours, he created a temporary energetic body for them to house their awareness and spirits together intact. Without that step, they would get loose and wander as wraiths. He needed to sustain them between where they were now and where they needed to go, yet also be transparent so he could see to do the work he needed to do. After he created their temporary container just above them, he carefully lifted their intact essences from their old bodies, moving the matrix of their two souls into their new temporary home. Both of their old bodies were now dead. He used his High Seer sight skills and started focusing on what he could see energetically going on between them.

Rhom found himself exhausted already, just doing the simple part of the entire process. He waited a few minutes so he could revitalize himself with the energy coming in from Zreyas while he assessed how he might weave them together. He needed to understand how Aaru connected with her to keep her alive, or he would likely kill them both permanently.

When he felt energized and replenished, he started again. Rhom considered the intricate weaving Aaru had done and couldn't help but pause in astonishment. *Aaru, you are a genius! The awareness of what it took to do what you did is way beyond anything I ever imagined. Well done, child!* Rhom felt like he had just gone to school for a hundred varSas. He noticed Aaru didn't alter any of their molecular structures. He worked *with* it to amplify it.

Rhom did the same, just as Aaru worked with Ayya, to merge them so they could work together. After a few more hours, the imprinting and fusing with Ayya as the master soul was complete, but he had to invert Aaru's channels and centers to fit in their new body or they would have died. He hoped it would all work out okay. The fusion wasn't perfect, but it went well.

He moved himself around the new Ayya slowly, making sure Zreyas followed to keep contact between them. He *had* to have him in this next phase. That extra creation energy was critical. It was time to slip them through the fracture into that body, still not born. Rhom was glad he had put a placeholder into the body earlier, because another soul was trying to enter it.

Rhom ran into his first problem, and it was a plan crusher. This last part would take every neutrinic part of himself, even with Zreyas' help. He had too much channeled into concealing them from the Janquar hunting party.

He struggled to speak, but Rhom forced out instruction. "No matter what, keep going till you hear from me again. I have to drop the quantum concealment in order to get them into their new body. This is the work of visages, not a mere High Seer's work. I'm not even sure it can be done, but we must try. Everything else has gone well, though not perfect. If they find us, then that will be after we get them to safety. If you stop, we all die."

Rhom felt a squeeze from Zreyas and dropped the concealment. The shift in time came with the accompanying roar of sound. Assessing things one last time, he was confident they would have a normal body and birth.

He observed that this race's body might not do well with Ayya and Aaru's spirit energy, but he had to trust in the best outcome. It was better than the alternative. He pulled out the placeholder and put them into their new body.

Rhom reached out with his mind to speak to them. *There you go, you two. I could have done as Aaru wished to complete you, Ayya, and leave him to transition, but it just felt wrong. I can't put my finger on it, but it is meant to be like this. You will need him, even if neither one of you is aware of it yet. His training and essence will be of aid to you. I can feel him and he is happy to be with you and help. My dear Ayya, I beg you to find your way back to us one day; we need you. I love you, little phoenix.*

The fracture was barely big enough for Rhom to see through now. He squinted and ducked to make sure all was well before letting go. "Safe journeys in the light, you two." Rhom pulled his arms back in grief and celebration. "It is finished."

As soon as he uttered the last words, everyone let each other go and fell to the floor, except for Zreyas. Rhom was barely conscious at the abrupt change in flow.

Just before the fracture closed, something caught

Rhom's eye. It played out, and his mind couldn't seem to grasp what he was seeing right away, out of pure denial.

The father walked up to the side of the mother, who was unconscious. Rhom saw a mist image in his High Seer's ethereal sight of a Janquar, sporting a diagonally scarred face. It shimmered in and out of the man's body. The familiarity and horror were jarring. It hit him like a sledgehammer in the face as to who it was. Alarm ripped through his entire body. Horrified, Rhom dropped his head so no one would see his expression. *After all this effort, there is no way I will mention this yet.* He resolved to place faith in Ayya and hope that they would come up with a plan to help her.

Zreyas staggered and slammed into the wall, trying his best to stabilize himself. The light warriors had deflated some, but were still much larger than normal. They were unphased and stronger and they immediately ran to the entrance and assessed the situation.

While everyone in the room was distracted, Rhom pulled a pebble sized object of light from his pocket. "Give me something of yours, Zreyas. It could even be a hair."

Zreyas staggered over, pulled a hair from his head, and dropped it into his lap.

Rhom put it in his hand, added the pebble-sized part he'd pulled from his hip, and then put his other palm over it. Barely able to sit up, he channeled all the energy he could into it. The light that made up his body went dim for a few seconds until he stopped, then slipped it back into the hip area on his body until he got himself positioned better.

Rhom watched Zreyas steady himself, then came over to help him get to his feet. Rhom pulled away and rolled over on his right side to get closer to the fireplace. He leaned his back up against the bricks to support himself and motioned Zreyas down to him to come closer.

He mustered his strength and reached out to grab Zreyas' hand. Zreyas opened it, eyes still wild from all the energy.

"Take this," Rhom said as he wheezed and pulled the newly made tryst back out. It took everything he had to muster the energy to speak. "I made this for you. It's called a tryst. The energy signature will track Ayya, your brother, and me. If they are in danger, genuine danger, it will signal no matter how far away they are. If that goes off, and you are within the same galaxy or dimension, it will lead you to them with a beam of light. It is useless beyond that. However, when that genuine danger occurs, you will still get the alarm, even if you are not close enough to track them. There is a little piece of their essence in it for you to carry with you."

"No, you are coming with me, I will carry you." He reached out to pick him up.

Rhom shook his head and pulled out another item. It had an electric charge but also light, and the surrounding air warped around it.

"The light warriors will fight for you and give you a chance to get out of here. There are two fractures out there still, if I remember correctly. Run toward one after the light warriors gain the ire of the Janquar. When you get into a dire situation, swallow it, and it will seal you in the quantum for a short time, hopefully long enough to deceive them and run into a fracture. Your brother may not be here anymore, but I know he is with you. Take that strength with you and find Ayya and do what you can to help her get back to us."

"I have so many questions, old man. Let me take you with me, you can recover."

"I still need to do my part to make sure you get out of here. I can't go with you. My body is too weak right now."

"I don't like this, but I trust you. Do you need anything before I go?"

"Sit me up in the first room, it's at least pleasant there with the fireplace and I can see what is going on outside the building through the door."

Zreyas nodded, then picked him up and took him into the next room. Sitting him down with his back up against the wall facing the fireplace, he said, "I still don't like leaving you behind. It goes against everything I have learned and become since meeting you. But I will do as you say, not because I am ordered, not because I don't know what to do, but because I trust that good frequency thing you got going on you keep teaching me about."

Zreyas stood and readied himself. He looked at the odd-looking disc. It was made of that same building material that swirled in their city. There were three cyan lights with lines of light between them in a triangle. He caught himself getting lost in it and shoved it in his pocket. He held on to the small electric piece Rhom gave him. Awkwardly, he formed the words, "I am... joy for meeting you. My brother died a good death."

Rhom smiled.

Zreyas grunted and nodded. "Giving to you the... thankings to what you teach me, too."

Rhom grinned at the so-called killer, trying to thank him. It is an endearing gesture to keep in his mind in his last moments.

Zreyas turned and stepped through the door. He assessed what was going on outside, then looked at the light warriors and shook his head no. Then he pointed to Rhom behind him with a quick head jerk backward.

Rhom couldn't quite understand what was going on in his clouded exhaustion, but he heard no voices from his light warriors in his mind, so he didn't think much of it. Then he remembered he had almost forgotten something. "Zreyas... Have you noticed your skin?"

Zreyas looked down, only seeing armor. He put quantum pebble into his pocket and used one hand to pull the armored glove off. His eyes went wide in shock as he saw light-blue skin, almost as light as his brother's skin. His mouth hung open, and he looked at Rhom.

Rhom couldn't help but smile, albeit weakly. He continued with what he wanted to say as Zreyas put his glove back on. "I will work with the quantum for you as long as I can so you can run faster if you need it. Help me to the doorway a little more so I can watch."

Zreyas walked over and helped slide him over to lean against the doorway.

Rhom nodded. "Nice, thank you. I can see outside better. I now see both fractures." He almost had him take him out to the tree, but somehow it seemed important that he be in this room for his last moments.

"And Zreyas, I might be an addled old man, but I think... you used to be a much higher being at an earlier time in history, and you came here to gain skills to help during this time." Holding his hand on his chest, he said, "I'm very grateful I could meet you and Aaru. Thank you. You are also a hero of the Viduri and the balance." He motioned for Zreyas to go. "Hurry, you are running out of time."

Zreyas stared at him, stunned.

Rhom struggled to raise his voice. "Go! Live! Find Ayya!" He waved Zreyas on more emphatically.

Zreyas complied, stepped back through the door, and ran hard.

With tears surfacing, Rhom saw two blurry fractures, the one all the Janquar were pouring out of, and the second one on the other side of the first further back.

He wondered why the Janquar coming here now didn't have that integration period that he, Zreyas, and the light warriors had. Perhaps it was because the dimension was adjusting to the other worlds it was connecting to through the fractures. This was going to get sticky. *My boy, I'm going to miss you. Thank you for all you have done, and will do.*

Rhom watched Zreyas pour the speed on. Zreyas lowered his head for aerodynamics. It astounded Rhom to watch his speed for such a large body. He had to be a strong two and a quarter meters tall, in his estimation.

Rhom got ready to help Zreyas when he noticed he ran faster suddenly and watched the air ripple around him. Zreyas was running straight for the enormous mass of the Janquar Nation warriors, crazed by the hunt.

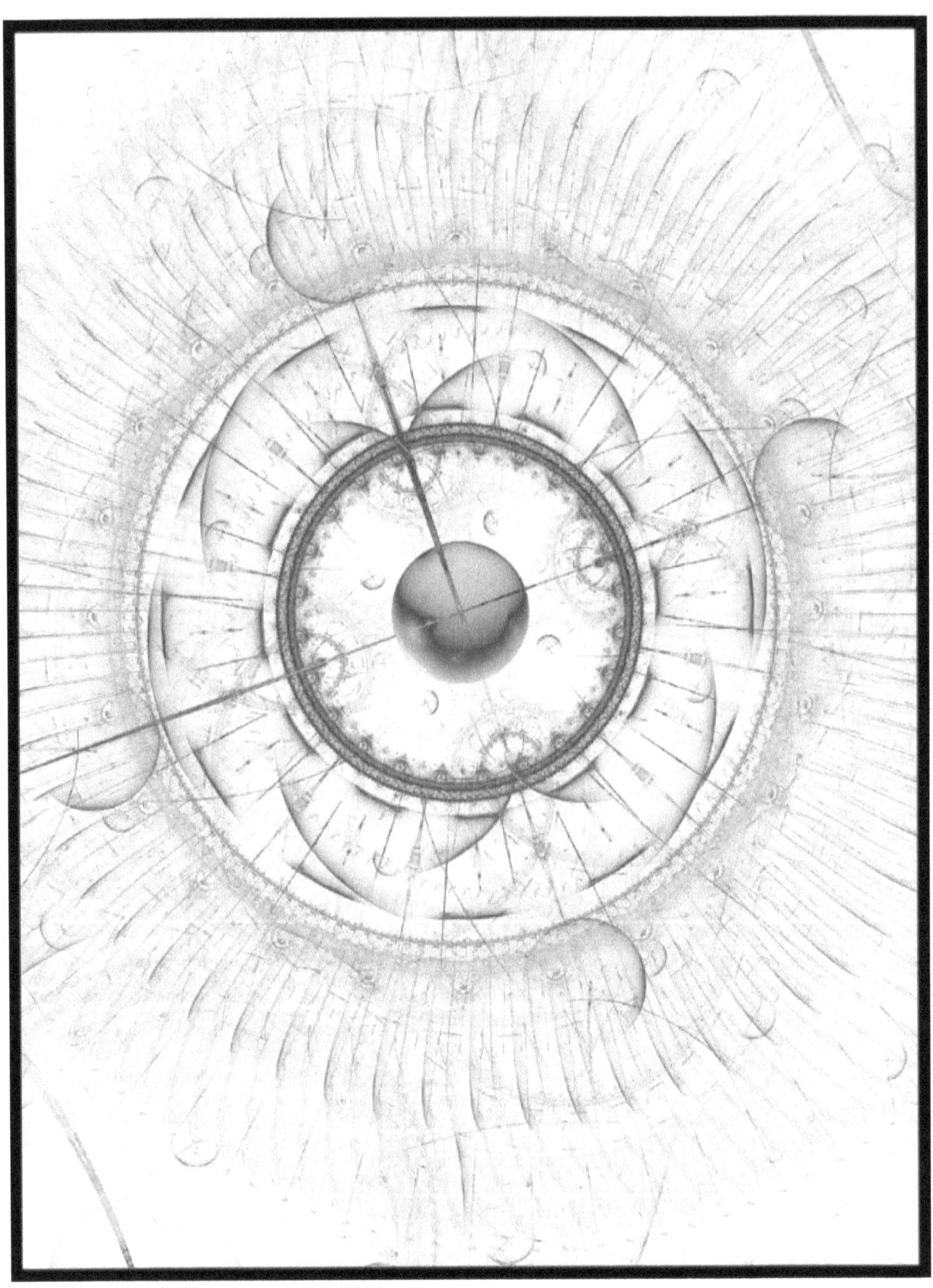

17 Quantum Run

Rhom

Rhom scratched just above his ear, then rubbed his eyes. He couldn't believe what he was seeing. This had to be his astronomical fatigue and depletion. Hope filled his heart, though. A new player in the game of balance was in play. *I really like him. He's grown on me.* Zreyas didn't need his help. That was apparent, at least at this moment. Just in case, Rhom wanted to watch and be ready to help.

Outside the structure, the light warriors, still inflated with their new strength, were standing ready near the entrance. He realized they hadn't gone with Zreyas as he instructed.

"What are you doing? Go with him!"

Cheerfully, they turned and stared at him, shook their heads, and communicated with their minds in a chorus.

— Zreyas told us to protect you instead. We could never catch him, anyway. Look at him!

Rhom looked toward Zreyas, who was not bothering to hide himself or go around. "Ticking-fool! You just made things get much hairier!"

Chuckling at himself for using Zreyas' curse word, Rhom craned his neck to follow Zreyas as he struggled to stand, sliding up the doorway frame to get a better view. He found it hard to follow him because of the speed.

Rhom observed that some of the Janquar took notice of Zreyas. They sounded war cries at once, alerting the others that their prey had been spotted. He noticed various groups of the Janquar had different war calls, yet they worked together almost like a musical piece. *They are not so different from the Viduri, just a different purpose and heart.* Rhom watched them close in on Zreyas.

One Janquar warrior pulled out from the rest of the crowd, bearing down on Zreyas' right flank. Rhom couldn't help but call out. "Come on... go, go, go! Look to the right!" It fell on deaf ears, or so he thought. Unfortunately, his outburst got some unwanted attention from a Janquar scouting close to the buildings.

Rhom used the quantum to slip the light warriors into the space in time just before his outburst, holding them there as he rolled his own body inside the structure, between the window and doorway, almost falling, just before the Janquar looked in his direction.

Way too close. That was not smart, Rhom.

The suspicious Janquar hesitated, but after a few seconds, he joined the chase. Relieved, Rhom rolled back toward the door, letting go of the quantum hold to return the light warriors to the present.

Rhom noticed the Janquar that had pulled away from

the crowd earlier had drawn his weapon and was trying to cut Zreyas off. Rhom flicked his hand to help his mind concentrate on the weapon the Janquar was holding. Though moving his hand didn't help directly, he sent the weapon to the future for just one second. It disappeared out of his hand as he ran, and appeared behind him a couple of steps back, falling to the ground. He realized he had dropped his weapon and went back to get it, buying Zreyas precious time.

Scratching his head over his ear as he watched, he lost sight of where Zreyas was in the crowd. However, he could tell where he was generally because the flow of warriors trying to catch him was moving toward a focal point. He hadn't got into the thick of them yet. But Rhom wanted to see if he was okay.

He worked with the quantum to temporarily create a clear path to see. To his relief, Zreyas was okay. He's almost to the fracture. Was he going to go in it?

Rhom watched with bated breath, but he felt something weird behind him. He turned around to peek at the room quickly, including the dark hall. Rhom saw nothing that stood out to him.

Turning back, he saw Zreyas almost to the fracture. Many weapons were raised by the Janquar. *He might be okay, but I can't take that chance.* He flicked his hand one more time, released a conservative amount of his energy, blinked out the weapons into the future a couple seconds in a large area around Zreyas, and released. All weapons appeared again in the air and fell to the ground. Some of them fell on warriors that were running into that location. Others slowed down because of the falling weapons, and some fell to the ground after being hit on the head by a falling weapon. A mass group of Janquar bent down, scrambling to pick up their weapons. Rhom saw Zreyas now, running strong. He reached the portal and blinked out of sight.

– Yes! The light warriors made silent cheering motions while Rhom heard the cheers in his mind.

Wonderful. He used the device I gave him.

That was when Rhom noticed the change in the other fracture. The left half of it was cut off by the border of the dying dimension now. "This dimension is shrinking faster now!"

Zreyas apparently saw what was going on, because when he returned to the present time, his speed quickened remarkably. The light warriors turned to see if Rhom saw what they were seeing, pointing. Rhom used his mind for communication. *I see them brothers, but I'm not sure if he is fast enough. That fracture is probably too far out for him to make it, even at his speed. I'm a little worried.*

Rhom worked on a few calculations in his mind. Then he moved Zreyas through the quantum from where he was to ten seconds in the past to the spot he was now. As soon as he did, Zreyas appeared ten seconds' worth of running ahead. Rhom sighed in relief that he had consented earlier or it couldn't have happened, and it put him ten seconds ahead in his running in present time, giving him a chance to make it.

It also gave him a lead on the Janquar on his tail. It was as much as Rhom could muster with his depleted condition. Zreyas never stopped and somehow sped up yet again, causing Rhom to hang his jaw slightly. *He's using the quantum, brothers!*

Rhom heard cheers in his mind from the warriors. Then he heard something behind him again. Rhom turned around. "Now is not the time for more shenanigans. Show yourself or leave me alone," he said out loud, talking more to himself than anyone else that might make noise. That was when he saw a face in the dark hallway, distorted and black, with red eyes. As fast as it appeared, it disappeared.

Rhom turned back to check Zreyas' progress, and he noted it would be too close. The Janquar warriors were hot on his tail because of the ones that were behind the first fracture. The portal was about one quarter the size it was and was almost gone. *He will make it. I have to trust he will make it. He has to make it!* He was almost there, but the portal was no longer as tall as Zreyas was anymore, and it was closing fast. Rhom held his breath and waited, because he didn't have the strength to help anymore.

He forced himself to yell, trying to get their attention. No one heard him except the light warriors. Rhom saw the portal was too small and almost gone. His heart fell. Zreyas was not yet through. Letting his head rest against the door frame, he let out a grief-filled, "No."

Then Zreyas threw himself into a dive, and his body warped and shrunk, blinking through the fracture. His feet disappeared just before it closed. Rhom jerked his head up, not believing what he just saw from the golden-horned warrior.

"Unbelievable!" Rhom raised his arm weakly in celebratory victory, hearing the warriors cheering with him.

Rhom let out his breath, relaxed, and slid down the wall, feeling a peace inside. He slid his body inside the room to look at the fire. "Well done, my boy. Well... done."

He found the room comforting and noted again that the fire had no warmth. The clock still had the time 1:11. *It doesn't seem too bad a place to spend your last minutes in life.*

He scratched his head just above his ear and used the last of his strength for something he loved to do more than anything else... science. He loved it, and he wanted to use the curiosity for it to pass the time. Rhom used his High Seer sight, looked at the fire and he was looking at some sort of created illusion or quantum placement.

"Why didn't I see this before?" He looked past the deception and saw a wall with nothing on it. On the floor, inside the fire illusion, there were two inset symbols.

Rhom rolled on his belly and started scooting himself across the floor, spent and fading. One symbol was gold, the other was pewter. The symbols on both were an ancient type of balance scales.

He looked at the gold one closer. His eyes picked up on slight movements, like the neutrinic-gleam brick they used for Viduri: floors, walkways, structures, and other weapons and tools. Sliding his body further so his face was close, he confirmed the movement as rhomboid fractal patterns, each tiny shape flipping back and forth, giving the illusion of a moving texture. A pile of larger rhomboid shapes were on one side of the gold scale. On the other side, there was nothing. Yet, the scale symbol was in a position of equal balance.

Rhom slid his gaze to the other pewter symbol. It had the same scale and fractal patterns. One side had a pile of powder on the scale and nothing on the other side, just as before. The scale tipped in favor of the side that had the powder on it. This symbol seemed correct concerning weight, but the powder seemed still.

Rhom was not sure what to think about those symbols, though. One looked correct, the other one didn't. However, there was something about the wrong one that seemed more... correct. Rhom stretched enough to lay his hand down on the gold one to see if it was solid. It was.

He laid his head down and closed his eyes, ready to transition. Rhom was drained and spent. He was pleased Zreyas made it, and Ayya had hope of being found by him now. Rhom felt his spirit darting around, ready to leave his body.

"Interesting..." he mumbled, so tired and ready to go. He thought about his wonderful life, and he had no regrets. It was enough for him. He looked at the gold symbol, his vision blurring. "Just because I don't see what is on the other side of the scale doesn't mean something isn't there."

As soon as the words came out of his mouth, the symbol under his fingers moved. He jerked his hand off the floor and saw the patterns turning in on themselves in a swirling, fluid fractal movement. Just ahead on the wall, a portal opened—not a fracture.

A human woman stood holding a golden, ancient scale in her hand, dressed in formal and elegant cream-white leather attire of some sort he couldn't identify. It had gold filigree adorning it and strips of thin leather that flowed like material hanging from her arms and sides.

The woman looked down at him and said, "I'm trying to be official looking, dear. It's rare I get to make a grand appearance. *Do* get up and come in before the portal closes. I don't want to put you all together from the pieces you are getting ready to create when they finish with you." She pointed past Rhom.

Rhom turned and saw two things: the inky black face with red eyes in the hall and a huge Janquar war band racing toward the structure only fifteen meters away with weapons raised.

"All in now!" she ordered. "I can't do it for you. It would interfere too much to keep balance."

Three light warriors moved between Rhom and facing the Janquar, ready to fight. Two of them picked Rhom up and jumped through the portal as fast as possible. The light warriors fought until they got to the portal, then jumped in. A Janquar threw a weapon just before the portal closed. It ripped through one of the light warriors inside, right in the chest. The warrior slumped to the floor and dissipated in sparkles of light.

Rhom felt the loss. It almost overwhelmed him. Another friend gone. He looked up, and there were two very etheric and opulent beings standing over them.

The large, plump, dark-skinned male held his hand over Rhom. “Not bad for an old man.”

When Rhom felt his strength return, he said, “You sound like Zreyas.”

He looked up to see a smile on the man’s face. “My thanks.”

Rhom struggled to stand. “Just in time! I thought we were goners. Did you plan this all along? You said you didn’t want to interfere when the portal opened.”

The woman chuffed. “We just put out the choices; you decided. Wise, to pick the gold one. I don’t want to think about what might have happened if you didn’t. Besides, these are desperate times. There’s much to do, so rest. You’ve got work to do.

18 Landing

ꝏ Zreyas ꝏ

Zreyas opened his pocket and pulled out the tryst that Rhom gave him, holding it out in front of him. Cocking his head, he was not sure how to activate it and wasn't sure if it needed to be. Shaking it a bit in frustration and seeing no reaction, he put the tryst back into his armor for safekeeping. *No time like the present to see where we ended up, Aaru.*

Poking his head up over the rocky ledge of the large hole he was in, he tried to get his bearings on where he landed. He heard ocean waves beating up against a shore nearby. Seeing nothing around him but rock and sky, he slowly turned around to look before he raised up any further. He saw nothing but rocky ground and sky all the way around. *This is odd. No foliage either.* Leery now, Zreyas put his armored hands on the edge of the rocks that were now at chest level.

"Well, I landed safely, at least," he whispered to himself. "Nothing is around."

Zreyas lifted himself up quietly with adept strength and agility, staying in a crouched position. He noticed there was an extensive set of branches lying in a clump in front of him, arranged in a messy bowl-like shape.

An uncomfortable feeling came over Zreyas. Feeling a little paranoid, but heeding the inner call of caution, he popped back into the hole. Just as he hit the floor, he heard a screech that nearly deafened him.

Lifting his head up just enough to see out, he spotted the largest predatory bird he had ever seen in his life. Zreyas lowered himself again when he realized it was large enough that he would be an easy small meal for it. The razor-sharp talons were almost as long as his body.

His breath caught. He was accustomed to war, not massive birds of prey. Calming himself, he slowly exhaled and breathed the stealthiest breath he could muster. Then he made himself face his fear and watched the bird.

The impressive creature had feathers on its head that looked like styled hair. He couldn't help but grin. The two-toned rust and white feathers looked like someone with long hair that hooked it over invisible ears and shoulder length on the side, but it merged with the color on the bird's back. When it turned sideways, it revealed its sharp and intimidating beak.

What kind of world did I land on? This is crazy! The beautiful bird had a white chest with dark rust and black wings. The tail and back were the same two-toned white and rust colors as the tuft. Zreyas noticed the bird arranging eggs in what he knew now was undoubtedly a nest.

After what seemed to be hours, the bird finally left.

Full noonday sun was now popping through the top of the hole. Zreyas looked around his immediate surroundings in the hole, rather than outside, and saw that it was actually a cave.

The hunter in him noticed the elongated claw and paw prints. *Great, I landed on a world of giants.* He stooped down and spotted fur on the floor and stuck to the walls of the cave. Zreyas immediately began gathering it up and putting it in a pile. He rubbed it all over himself, noticing the fur shafts were thick and long. It would be great for rope, one tool he always had for survival.

Mumbling out loud, he said to himself, *This is going to be fun trying to get off this crazy planet to the place Ayya is.* He had to fight the urge to call her Aaru. *I'm out of my mind thinking I could even do such a thing.* In his past, Zreyas knew he would have loved to be in this situation. It would have been fun, and he would have peace. Though technically he was thriving right now, in his heart, he was afraid because he had a lot to lose if he failed to find Ayya. His brother's sacrifice would have meant nothing then.

After Zreyas was satisfied he didn't smell like himself, and more like the... whatever lived there, he sat down against the wall in a crevice and started work on the rope. *Now I know why I saw only rock and sky. I ended up on the top of some mountain or tall rock formation. Birds of prey tend to dwell high. I need to make as much rope as I can. I'm working on it, Aaru and Ayya... I'll find you.*

His hands deftly put together and wove the hair into a continuous rope. It felt good to do something so simple again. He found a little peace in it, despite the dire situation. *I'm glad I loved doing the survival training most and taught it. It's going to come in handy now, I think. Aaru, you would love this too. You were so good at this. I didn't really need to teach you. You seemed to do it naturally.*

After a couple of hours, he decided to go a little deeper into the cave to gather more fur. It was dark now, but he had no problem seeing in the darker parts of the cave with his vision. The hair felt good in his hands. It was thick, soft, and pliable. He tested pulling the hair apart and was impressed with its strength. *It will be a good rope, it's not only strong, but silky and pliable, so he could easily store it.*

After gathering another armful of fur, he carefully walked back to where he'd left the rope he was working on. Sitting down, he crossed his legs with his feet under him and worked quickly. Zreyas made it thick enough so that he could hold it without cutting and still support the weight of several of his size, just in case he had a load of something with him.

When he was done using all the fur, he had a rope longer than he expected. He looked up and estimated it was almost dusk. Zreyas wrapped the rope in a coil large enough he could drape it over one shoulder across his chest like a diagonal sash. He found a small amount of fur that he missed, picked it up, and stuffed it in his inner vest, under his armor, to use when needed. Zreyas was well versed in survival and determined to use everything useful at his disposal.

Zreyas reached inside his armor and pulled out a thin leather pouch to take inventory of what he had with him, other than his weapons. He already knew, but he used it to focus and trigger his mind and body to be aware and survive. He had a rolled-up water pouch, tinder, striker, flint, and a tiny knife in a sheath.

Nodding, he placed it all back together and tucked it safely back in its place. He checked his swords on his back, the axe on his right hip, and the dagger on his left, to make sure they were all there and ready. Zreyas unsheathed the hooked axe in his right hand and the dagger in the left, holding the dagger's blade pointing behind him. Taking a deep breath, he crept down the steep decline of the cave.

More fur hung on the rock walls and on the floor. He saw feces in corners and crevices, not out in the open. *Whatever lives here is a neat and clean type of creature.* Noticing the cave getting larger, yet more steep, Zreyas grew more cautious.

This all felt a little weird to him, like tastes of sweet and sour together. *There is something soothing about this place.* Though there were birds of prey that could also eat his face off in one chomp, he realized it was probably the ocean waves he loved hearing. He noticed he could feel the waves, too. *That is the invisible magic... that feel part.*

He approached a triple fork in the cave. He crouched and looked left to see a larger dead end. It looked to be a bedding area of some sort with a lot of fur, torn up leaves and feathers about... but nothing in there alive. Zreyas looked at the right fork because he couldn't see down the middle one; it dropped straight down.

Leaning his right shoulder against the rough wall, he peered around it carefully. He saw a layered sediment patterns in the walls going upward with no sharp edges. The water, at some point in history, was high enough that it smoothed the rock out over many varSas. The cave was taller in that section, too.

Zreyas' eyes followed the wall upward until he saw a slight movement in the areas that were rougher with outcroppings. The movement slid down the wall and to the ground. When it reared up and a hood on each side of its neck flared, he could see past its camouflage and made out what it was. Sheer terror hit him.

The hooded slither, with one large dark spot on each

side, raised itself up higher. This was the largest slither he had ever seen. Zreyas froze and looked into its eyes. It did not have vertically slitted eyes. His heart raced because the only slither he knew without vertical slit eyes and had a hood was a garavu, and that bandhula was deadly. *I am not in my world. I'm in someone else's, so I could be wrong, but I'm not taking any chances.*

The slither rose up, *way* taller than Zreyas, and it looked straight at him. Its mouth opened with a hiss and malevolence that made Zreyas freeze. He didn't breathe. Just as Zreyas had enough mind to prepare for a fight, the hooded hunter darted at him with lightning speed, but uncharacteristically shot sideways to his left before he could even react. It shocked him. *I should be dead by now, again. All my life I have been at the top of the survival chain, and in the past day or two, I should have been dead four times now. Zrey, you have learned nothing much at all. You are way over your head.*

All Zreyas heard was struggle, spitting, hissing, purring, and screeching noises. It dawned on him that he was in no pain, and he was not involved. He adjusted his eyes and sharpened his mind to recognize there was a battle in the left corridor. Several furry animals with long bodies, sharp noses, and masked faces were hunting the slither as a family.

The garavu spit and bit one of the four furry, long-bodied creatures. Zreyas joined in the fight, stabbing his dagger down into a tail segment and pinning it. The slither's movements and quick actions did the work for him, slitting its body in that area in two long strips. Its tail now looked like it had a bloody, forked tongue.

The one that was bit fought with the garavu until he could no longer move, giving the rest of his hunting party time to gain an advantage on the slither. One of the furry warriors bit down on the garavu's face, clamping tight.

Its family took advantage of that bite and ripped at its hooded neck, though the coils of the slither were squeezing around them. Zreyas jumped toward the neck and slammed the dagger into the back of it between the hoods, and he used his axe hook to dig into its flesh to stay stable. Just as he tried to lock his legs around the slither's body, it jerked its face around, throwing Zreyas off. He hit the wall and dropped to the ground, hard. At least he didn't lose his weapons. But he had done enough damage that the furry warriors took over.

It wasn't long before they completely severed the neck. The slither released its grip on the two it had in its coils and fell to the floor in a spasmed death.

After the fight was over, the three family members that were left checked on their downed member. It struggled to breathe and spasmed periodically. The others nudged, purred, and chirped to him. One grabbed its front leg with his front paws and pulled it close, trying to help it up, but it no longer moved.

Zreyas took advantage of the distraction and got up as quietly as possible, then moved carefully forward to the fork that was straight ahead of him. He turned back to watch the family that lost their member one more time, empathizing with their loss.

When he turned back around, to his surprise, a nose and mouth were right in this face, sniffing him. Zreyas looked up to see masked eyes. Its head was just shy of being as big as he was. He froze so he wouldn't startle it. He instinctively spoke with it in his mind. *I don't want to hurt you; you have lost so much today already.* Then it occurred to him, for the first time in his life, to use the words that Rhom taught him. *Giving a thanking to you for saving my life.* He snapped out of his momentary weakness and admonished himself that this sentiment was going to get him killed if he didn't stop getting distracted with such things. But he couldn't help but feel for them.

The nose bumped his chest with the rope on it, then it opened its mouth wide.

19 Tulyata's Realm

Rhom

The woman with the scales sat down at her opulent desk. "You may not remember us yet. Till you do, introductions are in order. My name is Tulyata." Pointing toward the man on her right, "This specimen over here with his happy and abundant self, is Rtukaiah."

"Just call me Rtu, it's easier." The smiling man patted his belly. "This expresses abundance and happiness!" He laughed, then his bright-eyed face leaned forward, looking at Rhom with curiosity. "Do you remember us?"

Rhom studied the plump but powerful man. He took in more of his features. His black hair, just past shoulder-length, was wavy and transitioned into gentle curls at the ends. It hooked over his ears and was held in place by a headband that matched his arm and ankle bands. Rtu's dark brown skin seemed to glow in an etheric way. When he smiled, the large black freckles on his high pudgy cheeks accentuated his smile and dark eyes.

Not wanting to seem rude by staring at them, Rhom looked around the room. "I'm supposed to know you?" He shook his head. "I don't think I..."

Rtu sat back with another smile. "Take your time. Don't worry about being rude. Look at us and see if it prompts your memory."

Rhom nodded, relieved he could stare at them now without it being an issue. Rtu's attire fascinated Rhom as he took in every detail. It was as if he was being drawn in by a gentle force. Rtu's clothing was of a primitive style, but etheric, celebratory, ritualistic, and more nature-oriented. His form was plump, but it radiated strength. He had no shirt, but energetic tattoos adorned his chest and shoulders that seemed to move and flow. His lower attire, composed of a dark-green, almost black, multi-layered loincloth, was split on the sides for movement's sake. It hung down to just above his knees, sporting an extra-wide waistband of woven cream-colored grass of some sort. Between the waistband and his loincloth were green, flowing, thin feathers that resembled grass. The bands on the three parts of his body matched the loincloth.

Looking at Rtu's face, he shook his head. "You have a familiar *feel* to me, but I apologize, I don't remember you."

Rtu laughed. "It's okay! You will soon."

Rhom looked over to see if he remembered Tulyata. She stood and walked over to a shelf to pull down another scale. When she turned to move back to her desk, she paused and let Rhom study her.

Her cream and gold clothing were a refined, unique style. Though in the style of a modern version of primal attire, it looked like it was for a royal position. Tulyata's skin was light tan, setting off the elegance of the cream clothing. The ornate gold trim complimented her beautiful body form. Her sleeveless shirt was cut off at her ribs, trimmed in gold stitching and beading. The shoulder pieces flared slightly and were made of contrasting black and white down feathers. They portrayed contrast and what Rhom assumed was the black and white nature of balance on her shoulders.

Her long, silky, light brown hair was pulled back loosely, and it covered half her ears, flowing down her back. Her headband was sculpted with gold. At the temples, gold-threaded beads and crystals hung down like tassels to her chest. They seemed like an elaborate extension of her hair. The gold medallion in the front had an etched symbol of ancient scales.

Well, now I know who put those symbols out there for sure.

When she stretched her arms out, it revealed under her arms a set of long thin strips of cream leather that hung almost to the floor close to her body. Tulyata's armbands were like sleeves, covering from biceps to wrists, the underside sporting strips of thin leather as well. The asymmetrical high-low skirt was long and flowing in the back. It gradually shortened until it reached her hips in the front. It left the front completely open, revealing short leather shorts. She wore high cream boots that ran up to the middle of her thighs, adorned with gold filigree patterns. She looked and felt like a Prime Visage of some sort to Rhom.

Rhom tried hard to remember them, but all he could do was shake his head. "I apologize. I don't remember meeting either of you before, but you seem familiar. Are you a visage, Tulyata?"

"The official title dear is Prime Visage of Balance," she confirmed.

"And I am one of two visages of the natural elements of creation," explained Rtu. "I am the visage of earth and air. I have a slight amount of fire, water, and aether to keep me creating when my brother is not with me."

"Well, I apologize, visages, for not remembering you. It definitely isn't because you are not memorable."

Rtu laughed. "Just call me Rtu. I know I'm a visage, you don't have to remind me. I would rather keep it casual!"

Tulyata interjected, "Let's get down to business."

Rhom understood why she was a Prime Visage from her tone and the passion behind it.

Tulyata leaned on her elbow in Rhom's direction with a matter-of-fact expression. "We can't do anything about your memory of the past, so let's concentrate on the present. You have a lot to do, Rhom. We are in a mess and you committed to keeping balance, no?"

"Yes. I assume you know my complete life and what interests me."

"Well, we want to help. However, there is only so much we can do, or it will upset the balance."

"Pfft, there's no balance right now," Rhom spat bitterly, still grieving over the losses of Ayya, his people, and Aaru. His thoughts turned to Ayya's new father.

Rtu leaned forward with closely observant eyes. "What made you so bitter? This isn't like you."

Rhom sighed. "There was an image sliding around in that body of the father of Ayya. I didn't want to believe it, and I didn't tell anyone, because there was nothing we could do. But I think the new father of Ayya's is the Janquarian Commander that I call Scar-face. He fell through a fracture, and it might have been to the same place Ayya is in now." He paused and mumbled, "But it does seem a little coincidental, doesn't it?" Drifting off in thought for a moment, he looked up to the visages. "I have an excellent memory; though I don't remember you, I remember a lot of science, information, and... that Scar-face."

"That is indeed who it was." Rtu spouted. "We have a big problem. That commander is bound to the Janquar visage so they will track him. Though he is not yet conscious of his incarnation, that will not stop the Emperor from tracking him down."

"He just fell through that fracture a day ago. How did he get incarnated and older so fast there? Do you know where that dimension is and its time in history? The only reason I put her there was because it was the only thing I could think to do to keep her safe."

"The fractures are all not on the same time lines or dimensions. He fell through a fracture that had multiple time lines and dimensions. He was dying himself and saw someone that was to be born and Scar-face's desire to kill and dominate was so strong that he sucked the poor soul in and incarnated instead. We have been watching him a long time and his pattern of behavior is always the same, suck in and take over... basically consume. Thankfully, he had a clean slate when he was born. But unfortunately, his past was still an influence on his incarnated design."

Rtu spoke up cheerfully, "But, you actually did what we hoped you would. We nudged the portal that way. It was all we could do without directly interfering. You still had to make the choices—It was either that, or she died."

"I'm glad you did! Ayya has a chance now. Your information about Scar-face is consistent with what

Zreyas told me about him and what I observed myself. Though I don't know where he is now, he is a new player in the game of balance. It's funny though—It doesn't seem like it's a game he's built to play. I need to find him and warn him about all this. Do you know what is going on with the accelerations in all the unusual star activity and prophecies?"

"Of course we do. However, we cannot tell you much. We need to wake Ayya up over time in her life or we are all in trouble, even us."

Rhom nodded, wondering how she was doing in that alien body.

Tulyata must have been listening in on his thoughts because she waved her arm to bring up a screen out of thin air and said, "Look how precious she is." The screen activated, and a baby with wobbly legs stood next to a camel saddle the human species used for a footrest. She was in a room with furniture and an ancient TV with antennas, denoting their technology in that time period. Ayya was playing with the saddle cap she was holding and her mother was sitting in a chair, resting her feet on the saddle. Ayya made joyful gurgles and pulled at the rubber pants over her diaper.

"She's grown that fast?" Rhom asked.

Tulyata laid her forearm on the desk, a little exasperated. "You forget we are visages; we are not bound to time or distance."

Rhom pointed toward the screen. "Hey, that style of building is like where we came from, the dying dimension. Is it the same time period?"

Lifting her arm back up off the desk, Tulyata began more work with her scales of balance. "Yes, but it was the part that got caught in the anomaly across all time and space. The dying dimension you were in was a parallel dimension that doesn't exist anymore."

"Oh." Rhom scratched his head just over his right ear. "So, what do we need to help wake Ayya? I know we can't do it all at once, but how do you plan to do it?"

"We won't. All we can do is facilitate what you come up with, oh wise High Seer of the learned light people," Tulyata said with a half-mocking dry tone.

Rhom looked at her incredulously. "Why me? I can't be the only one in the multiverse that has a few skills and wants to help."

"Rhom, you are the only one who can help your people because you understand them. They've been hidden for so long and are now exposed." Tulyata plopped her arms down on the table. "You really don't remember us, do you? You are seriously slow to remember, for all the knowledge and talent you have."

Rhom sighed, "Isn't that the way incarnations work?" He rolled his eyes. "But you have a point. I'm getting old and I don't have the energy for something this big alone... literally. What we did down there was amazing. Though Zreyas helped a great deal, it depleted my life's essence."

"Well, we can help in that department because it won't be changing who you are. We can just help you energize and use what you have forgotten that is yours." Tulyata waved a hand and opened a doorway to a room that wasn't there before. It was empty in the room, except for a chamber in the middle. It looked like they created it from clear crystal light material with an entrance.

"It will regenerate who you are. That is your chamber from your dimensional home. I just opened a door to it."

"Are you saying if I go in there, my incarnation will end?" He stared at them like they had just turned green, totally confused.

"Slowly, yes, but you would have died back there had we not come, anyway."

Rhom scratched his head again. He stood and walked to the room and to the entrance of the chamber. He felt more energized just standing near it. It seemed familiar to him, but he couldn't quite put his finger on it. He stepped into the chamber and all went white for a few heartbeats.

Bits and pieces of memory came to him, but nothing that made any sense. When his energy returned, he stepped out of the chamber.

"Better, like a new kid, but I don't feel any different." He thought for a moment. "Do I remember things I knew? Yes, yes, I do, but not enough to make any sense of the fragments. Thank you for letting me use my own... uh, room?"

Tulyata and Rtu looked at each other and just shook their heads at him.

"I love my life, or at least did, so it might play a part in my not remembering before my life."

Tulyata turned back around. "You really enjoyed your incarnation, Rhom. You don't want to let it go yet." She paused a moment, then sat up straight. "Right, to work we go... We've got some planning to do."

"We can't tell you much, but I can tell you this. There will be several times in Ayya's life that she won't live through unless she wakes up past a certain threshold." Tulyata paused a moment, then her eyes brightened with an idea. "We need to set up little triggers for her to have that choice to wake up. If she doesn't wake up enough as she passes the thresholds of those markers in her life, we will have bigger problems. We will have a hard time fixing them. Honestly, this is hard enough. Our success ratio is probably ten thousand to one. But there will be zero chance if we don't try. If unsuccessful, we enter a dark age that we won't recover from until we all blink out of existence and start again."

"A ray of sunshine you are," Rhom retorted bitterly, feeling overwhelmed in areas he was not familiar with. He now understood how Zreyas might have felt. "No matter how much I have learned in my two thousand two hundred and ninety-nine varSas, no one can prepare for this kind of news." Rhom paused a moment, then asked, "What about those symbols you created for me to find. Can we do something like that for Ayya?" He looked over at the screen to watch her. That body seemed weird to him. He couldn't help but smile. "She is cute for an alien type."

"Hey, we might take offense to that, seeing as how the human form is what we are using to let you see us," Rtu interjected with a smile.

"Zreyas really needs to be here and see this," said Rhom.

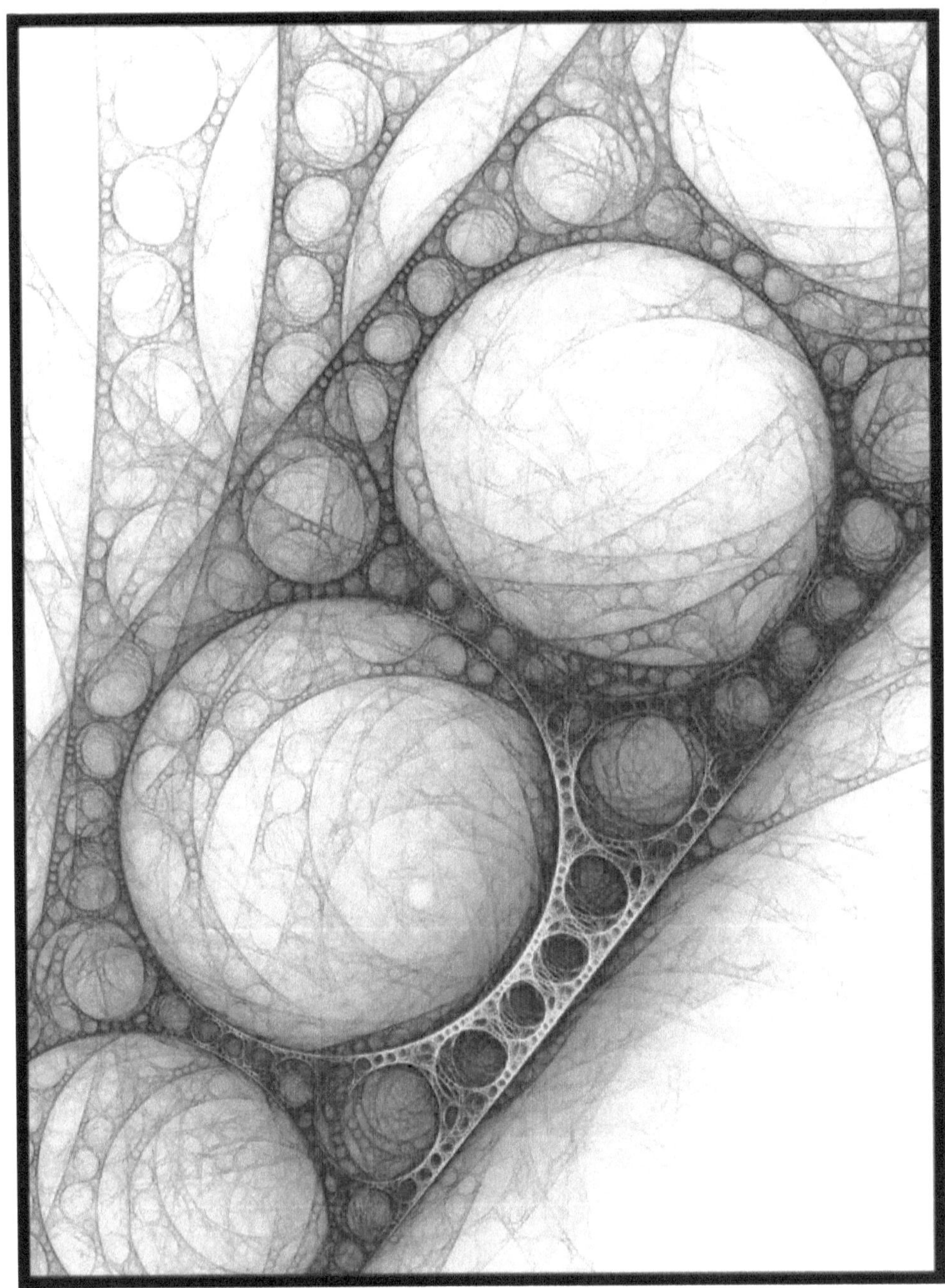

20 Fed

꩜꩜꩜ Zreyas ꩜꩜꩜

Though its mouth seemed huge to Zreyas, it didn't open quickly. It was all he could do to not slit its throat, but he felt no hostility. The animal picked him up by the horns. At first Zreyas struggled, but then he sighed and went limp, except for holding on to his horns to keep his neck from breaking from his body weight if it jerked him around. He wondered if he could find a way out of here through them. If nothing else, he figured he could always kill it later if it was a danger to him. *Do they think I am their family because of the rope of fur and were protecting me all along?*

It took Zreyas to the left corridor he had seen earlier with the bedding in it. It set him down, then laid down around him protectively. Zreyas loosened his grip on the weapons he was holding. The creature's underside had swollen bumps all up and down its stomach.

Zreyas noticed there was nothing between its legs. The creature had swollen spots that were pink looked to make it difficult for it to move. “Ticking-hell.” Zreyas startled himself. His voice sounded unfamiliar, higher than it used to be.

Not sure what to do, Zreyas thought back to his homeland. They didn’t have creatures because they lived on a sterile planet. They had to port in water and food and he never did that, the workers did. He had killed animals for meat, but never saw one with this kind of swelling problem. “Did you get bit?”

Another one of the long animals approached, looked at him with his dark masked eyes and nudged him, knocking him forward a little. Both of them purred and chirped.

The second creature watched him and nudged him again. It caused his pointing hand to bump into one of the swollen areas, making it leak a white substance with clear streaks. Zreyas stared at it and then looked back up at the two masked faces watching him.

“You have an infection! I got an infection on my arm once, and it leaked puss too!”

He sniffed the substance and added, “Hmm, it doesn’t smell like infection. But you are a different species. Well, I can help you.” Zreyas dropped his weapons and said, “I will repay you for saving me from that garavu.”

He put his fists on each side of the swollen infection and pushed in. It sprayed all over him. The creatures chirped. Zreyas pushed again, pushing out more.

“It hurts at first, but it will feel better soon.” The one he was helping licked him clean.

He stopped and looked up at it as he pushed again, “You really shouldn’t do that, puss is not something you should eat.” It kept licking him, but Zreyas wouldn’t stop, determined to help it and empty the sore.

He sat down, wondering how he was going to clean his armor. He picked up his weapons that he had let go of when the creature put him down and sheathed them. "Feel better?" Zreyas cleared his throat, not understanding what was wrong with his voice.

The animal licked herself, chirped affectionately, and got up. It gave him a couple of licks, knocking him over. It left him there and walked away, disappearing around the corner to the right.

Zreyas tried to wipe off the coating of the licks, but then figured he wouldn't bother. He sat alone in the dark. *That was ticking weird, but I hope she heals.* He stood and decided it would be the perfect time to get out of there and pulled his axe out again. Zreyas walked softly to the fork leg that went straight down. He felt all caked over with the film of that licking and wanted a bath.

Zreyas edged around the walls until he got to the opening of the fork. He looked back toward where the animal went and saw nothing but the fur from their family member. He noticed it had been drug away since he last saw. Then he saw what they left of the slither, nothing but the skin and head. They had eaten it. That was fast. There must be more of those masked creatures than he saw. *I hope that is who ate that meat, and not something else.*

Zreyas knew they could have done the same to him, but they didn't. They thought of him as offspring, or at least a friend. *These animals are expert hunters. Maybe Rhom can help heal that one if I ever see him again. He could learn a lot from them if he wasn't on an important mission.*

He turned and faced the downward tunnel. It grew much larger the further down it went. Zreyas put his weapon back on his hip and began his descent. Since the tunnel dropped straight down, he used the protruding rocks as grips and footholds to climb down, not wanting to use his rope if he didn't have to. He continued downward, struggling with the smoother, water-worn handholds. Just when he thought his strength would give out, he saw a small nook a little farther down he could rest in. It gave him motivation.

After a few minutes, he successfully entered the little alcove. He leaned up against the wall, shaking out his arms and legs while he looked down to assess his progress and what might be ahead. He noticed the distinctive light of the moon shining at an angle on the bottom.

Zreyas thought it might be best if he stayed where he was for the night. He used the small holes and rough small outcrops as rope holds to create a protective cage of sorts at the opening. Though it wouldn't hold anything of much weight, it would at least act as a warning for a possible escape or to ready himself for a fight. As he created a grid pattern. He was also ravenously hungry, and cold.

After he was satisfied with his warning system, he leaned back against the wall and thought about sitting with his brother, watching him. He had an epiphany that all these sentiments, emotions, and awareness of what they are was now comforting, and he didn't feel the shame of them anymore. *How did I get born into that, I wonder? And how did the old man's people get born into what they were born into? How did...*

Zreyas woke up with a jolt, seeing a large hairy face as big as his own head, two large black eyes with many lenses, and a pair of hairy fangs staring at him through his make-shift rope warning system.

"*Shit!*" Zreyas pulled his dagger out. He stabbed the

left eye hard with both hands, going deep.

"Why..." He stabbed again.

"... does everything..." He stabbed the other eye.

"... have to be so..." Zreyas stabbed it again.

"... big in this..." He pulled out his axe while he stabbed again, bringing it down between its eyes.

"... ticking place!"

The creature's eight legs struggled and curled. Zreyas helped the creature out, since it was still hanging onto his rope. He picked up his axe and slammed it across the leg, severing it neatly. The creature dropped. It scuttled and struggled to get away. It didn't get very far before it stopped, legs curled and spasming, save the missing leg. Zreyas shoved the severed leg away, watching it fall and join the rest of its body.

Zreyas sat down, breathing hard. He looked up at the woven warning system and saw it was still completely in place. Sheathing his weapons, he looked down to see how light or dark it was. It was still dark, and he realized he was exhausted and fell back against the wall, closing his eyes.

He thought about his new life and how surreal it seemed. *Just yesterday I was coming home from war in a culture that was cold, hard, but normal for me. Now, I have lost my home, my people, my rank, and I learned so much from Rhom and Aaru in a short time that it seems like my old life was all a bad dream.*

Rhom's words echoed in his head, 'There is good in you, Zreyas.'

Though it was more stressful and scarier as ticking-shit, his life meant something now. It didn't matter if he was alone. At least, in some warped way, it was peaceful. He couldn't help but wonder if they got to Rhom. *No, Rhom is too smart...* He tried to tell himself that his warriors would have found a way if he couldn't.

He decided he would settle into this new life like a new set of armor. It would take time to get used to, but it would feel better soon enough. *I may still be in a war, but at least it is for a good purpose; and for the first time, it is one I can believe in.*

Suddenly, he thought about the last time he saw Aaru alive, before going through the fracture. He remembered his face and how confused he was when he found out that who he saw was not the emperor. *I wonder who he saw?*

21 Testing

Rhom

"Now you are thinking, Rhom... If she gets the first one, then she will probably become inwardly aware of them in the future," Rtu said as he looked closer. He picked up his staff and pointed it at the screen. "There, we got the first one in for a test. If she doesn't get it, then we know to try something else. Would you like to be an observer, Rhom?"

"What do you mean 'observer'? I'm observing now."

Tulyata interjected, "Say 'yes,' because there will be times you will need to see things you can't see from a screen, and we will not be with you all the time. If it works, we could create a dimension for you to work from just for that purpose. And hopefully one day Ayya makes her way to it, eventually."

Tulyata placed something invisible to Rhom's sight

on her scale. The scale tipped. It tipped again the other way. Looking up, satisfied, she turned around and waved an arm. An extra dimension appeared.

To Rhom, it looked like a large dimensional room suspended in… nothing, attached to the one they were currently in. "What could we accomplish in an empty room, suspended in aether?"

"Don't judge. It would surprise you what that room will do. When we figure things out, this extra dimension could be attached to your own home. As you say, 'For science!' If our test doesn't work, then we will have to set up something different. I couldn't help it, I made it early because I am in a creative mood."

Rtu laughed, "She gets creative like that sometimes."

"Rhom," Tulyata said, "it will help you become more in tune with Ayya's new imprint and body if you observe from within her. You will feel what she feels as if it is you, yet you will be separate. It will help you find out if any of the elders that went with her during her imprinting are there, and conscious. That will be important to know."

Rtu added, "You know her better than anyone involved in the balance game. When you are ready, step up to the screen and use your wonderful quantum skill to observe, and I will teach you how to direct it correctly. That way, you can learn to do it yourself. We will keep you safe here."

Rhom nodded and stepped up to the screen. "Ready. Is there anything you need to do before I do this?"

"No, but we will watch with interest."

Rhom closed his eyes for a moment and noticed he had all his energy and talents back to normal, and then some. He was happy about that part, then scratched his head over his right ear as he looked at Ayya and used the quantum to concentrate on where he wanted to go. He felt and heard the familiar roar of the transition to the quantum and traveled. Rhom experienced the guidance of Rtu, helping him adjust on a molecular level. The sensation was indescribable and exhilarating. When he arrived at his destination, he settled into Ayya's head and connected to her mind.

He felt everything as if he was living in her body and watched her playing with a brass cap. It was interesting that he could feel it as if he was her. First things first though—He looked for the elders and felt relief that he felt the essence of most of them. He gently spoke with each elder to see if he could get a response. Treta signaled him first, then Gulloo, Vesana, and Dhi. He heard nothing from the others.

Then he focused fully on Ayya.

She picked up the camel saddle cap made of molded brass with a unique scene on the top. She lifted it up to her mouth and jabbered into the deep cap. It looked like a vessel that could hold water the way it was shaped. Rhom could feel the love she had for that object. She loved playing with it. Rhom felt how Ayya was drawn to the energetic history she felt when she held it in her hands.

As she picked it up and put it back on the horn repeatedly, Rhom thought about how amazing it was that she felt who made it and whose hands it had been in. Her brown-eyed mother laughed and talked sweetly to her, telling her she loved her.

As her mother stood, her short and styled brown hair shined in the light the window provided. Ayya watched her walk out of the room and into a kitchen to prepare food.

As Ayya put the cap back on the horn of the saddle

and stared at the scene molded in on the top, she stopped, loosing herself in it.

Rhom immediately noticed the fractal pieces flip and turn, making the scene appear to move and flow. The pyramid and camel in the picture came to life, and Rhom hoped Ayya would notice. Then he realized she already had, because he was seeing through her eyes.

Ayya jabbered at it, picked it up and immediately tried to shove it into her mouth, testing it, as babies do.

Her mother, as if in afterthought, walked back into the room and turned off the TV. Ayya observed with interest and watched it turn black from the outside going inward. A white dot remained at the center of the dark screen. Ayya ran awkwardly to it halfway, mesmerized. She cocked her head, looked at the cap in her hand, still moving and flipping, then awkwardly ran the rest of the way to the TV, wanting to go into that place. She smashed her face up against the glass TV screen, hard, and fell backward. A screaming cry ramped up and went to full capacity.

Ayya's mother came racing back into the room and scooped her into her arms, inspecting her face. "Aww, your little forehead has a huge, pretty red knot on it. Would you like me to kiss it and make it better?"

Ayya, still crying hard, nodded her head and waited for the kiss. Her mother gently kissed her head, then hugged and rocked her. Little Ayya tucked her head into her neck and heaved in sobs.

"Yep, she found it," Rtu said to Rhom, apparently watching. "You can come back now."

Rhom returned, then rubbed his forehead in empathy. "Well, that was an experience... powerful experiment, and a great way to assess how Ayya is doing internally. I felt the elders in there that went with her, but not all of them. I felt Dhi, Gulloo, Treta, and Vesana, but none of the others, yet. Will she even be what she was when this is all over so she can help our people?"

"It's not optimal, but it's a start. Have a little faith. At least she has most of them," encouraged Rtu.

"But Rhom, she isn't the same Ayya that left your home and never will be," said Tulyata pointedly. "Who knows, I think if she makes it through this, she might end up being better because of her experiences. Being incarnated in a body that low in frequency, especially imprinted with someone of the Janquar race, might prove to be an amazing journey of awareness that will help your people even more. Don't get your hopes up yet, but there is nothing to lament about at this point either, okay?"

Rhom looked through the screen at the little Ayya. "Do you know what they called her?"

"Consider it a mystery to keep up the fun factor," Rtu said, smiling brightly. "Part of this quest is for your benefit too, not just hers or your people's. There is a lot of poo-doo coming our way, and you will need all the wisdom and sharp mind of discovery you can get."

Tulyata looked exasperated. "Even I can't see it all because the choices of many have not yet been made, and I want to keep it that way. All we can do is to prepare you and help without making choices for you."

"Fair enough," Rhom said. "So, how are we going to scatter these... wake-up calls? I have one more question. I'm afraid to ask it, though."

"You mean the one that is all about how accessible she is to whoever hunts her and the boy, now also part of her?" Tulyata interjected.

Rhom nodded. "Just how likely is it they will find them?"

"You really want the truth?"

"No, but I need to know... so please tell me. Ticking-hell, I'm too old to be sitting around in denial." Pausing a moment, Rhom realized he had just used Zreyas' signature curse again and chuckled to himself. *He's rough around the edges, but I really like that boy.*

"They already know where she is, and they are working on a plan to finish their hunt. But they have gained aid. It is from a source that is here, way ahead of schedule."

"Don't tell me, the Dark One?"

"Okay, I won't tell you, but I don't have to, it seems. And there is more... and it is definitely not good. You had no way of knowing because he was never near Ayya before all this happened."

"Oh my, can this get worse?"

"Yes... yes, it can! Just hold on a second."

Slight visions of etheric fractals seemed to appear and disappear on her golden scales. Rhom realized he could see them this time. It seemed to toggle too far one way for too long to be comfortable knowing her commitment to balance. Finally, the scale balanced evenly, and his heart lifted with hope at the sight.

"Don't get too excited, because I can't tell you everything, and it won't be without a cost of balance that will have to be paid for by not knowing a few things later. Hopefully, you will have the girl in a better place by then, though."

"I understand. Please tell me what you feel is best for us all, Tulyata. I respect your vision and your commitment to balance." Rhom then turned to Rtu and acknowledged him with a nod as well.

Rtu smiled with sympathy in his eyes. "I will give my aid when the time comes. It is not important now, since my realm is more in nature, body, and environment, rather than the potentials of the quantum, though they do overlap."

Rhom nodded. "Thank you, Rtu."

"The Dark One is here... as in the one... as in... the Dark One. That much you probably guessed before we met up, but were too afraid to face it. You have been noticing accelerations for several varSas, but even I did not expect what happened."

Sitting down, she leaned back in thought for a moment. "When the anomaly started, the forever-banished dimensional prison got caught in the fractures and shearing. You will never guess where it showed up," she said casually, as if it was old news.

Rhom rubbed his forehead, scratched over his right ear, and groaned, "Wonderful... just wonderful. Let me guess, just because I can't think of any worse a place for it to show up... the Janquar dimension."

"Very intelligent guess... and... you are correct, unfortunately. But it isn't the worst of it. Shall I continue?"

Tulyata seemed to enjoy drawing this out, Rhom observed. *Visages must get bored knowing everything. They seem to relish when things get interesting*. Little things, like getting satisfaction out of being the informer, had to be what kept her interest peaked. *Now you are judging Rhom*, he said to himself.

Rhom felt himself getting frustrated, and he heard the light warriors in their internal communication.

— We think you are acting weird, High Seer. They may be visages, but do you really need to let her talk to you like you are not the High Seer of the Viduri? It is disturbing to see you doing so much cowering and lamenting.

Rhom replied to Tulyata, "Yes, Tulyata"

He looked up at the light warriors standing in his

chamber room. Rhom was so used to them being around that he knew he took them for granted. They must have been guarding him when he went into the chamber. *They are visages and I am not. But you are right; however, I need to be extra civil for Ayya's sake. They do not care what my station was.* Rhom paused for a moment, then added, *by the way, thank you for all you do to help and protect me. Thank you for saving my life. I don't say those things often enough.*

— It is our joy to live out our purpose and be successful at it. It gives us peace, even if it isn't always fun. You are our brother, and we love you. We love all you have done, and do, for the balance and our people. They might be visages of something, but we think you should be a visage too. We ask that when you transition, that you take us with you so we can give back to our people and the balance.

Your work and purpose are not yet done, my brothers. I need to get you back to the Viduri as soon as possible so that you can inform them what is going on and help prepare and protect our people.

— We would like that High Seer. Are you going to ask about going after Zreyas? We would like to help with that too. We decided we like him and he will be important in helping you.

22 Conquering Water

Zreyas

Zreyas drowsily sat up and remembered where he was. His senses sharpened. Peering through the webbed wall he had made the night before, he looked down to see that it was probably just past dawn, judging by the light.

He quickly unraveled the rope wall, coiled it up, and put it back on his shoulder diagonally again. He picked up his weapons and sheathed them back in place, ignoring the dried blue blood of the creature. Though a stickler for weapon care, cleaning weapons was not his priority right now.

Zreyas hopped down to the cave floor and investigated the spider. Cracked open and guts missing, he assumed... and hoped, that whoever gutted that spider was his new furry friends. He picked up a water-worn stick in the crack between the cave wall and floor.

Another tool for his journey. He looked at it and decided it would make a nice make-shift spear or stake. He gently tossed it slightly up out of his hand, testing its weight. It was heavy for something of that size.

"Nice, it's petrified. Well, onward to a new day in survival paradise," he said sarcastically rolling his eyes. He loved survival but this bloody-ticking-mag-shit of a place had him on edge.

He walked to the opening where the light was coming through and immediately crouched. Zreyas cursed in a harsh whisper. "Ticking-hell!" He closed his eyes a moment to gather himself before looking back around the edge of the cave opening.

The cave ended and dropped off a good thirty meters to rocks and surf below. Above him, on a nearby cliff to his left, was another one of those birds looking around for its next meal. To his right, on the shore, were thousands of Janquar camped and ready for a hunt.

To Zreyas, they seemed larger than normal, even at this distance. Then he remembered something that hit him smack in the face. Talking to himself softly, he said, "That slither was huge... the fur, those birds, the long furry animals, and the hairy creature with fangs; they were all huge!"

Leaning up against the mouth of the cave, he closed his eyes a moment, whispering to himself, "Ticking hell... somehow I have shrunk."

He breathed a moment, sliding down the wall to sit, wondering what he was going to do. Despite his predicament, the scenery was peaceful in the morning sun. He decided to take it in and enjoy it because the future didn't look great.

"Wait." He lifted his head erect again. "Those long, masked fur balls got up here somehow."

Zreyas looked around the cave. Sure enough, there was another exit with a downward slope almost hidden. He drew the axe on his right side and started the unknown trek down, holding the new smooth spear in the other hand. Zreyas knew there were much more advanced weapons in the Janquar race, but he had an affinity for old style melee and bow. He missed having his bow strapped to his back, but he never expected to have to need it when they went to see the emperor—Lesson learned.

The cave was a steady but a fairly steep slope. *Don't give up on me, Aaru. I won't let you down. I made you a promise.*

When the cave finally evened out, he heard an odd howl of wind and roaring echoes of water. The cave continued straight ahead and ended at the rough waters rushing in from somewhere to the left. It smelled salty. He reached down to scoop up some water in his hand and tasted it. *Yep, salt water for sure, not brackish.*

He stood up and noticed for the first time how beautiful this part of the cave was. It was more open with openings, rather than solid stone, so the light shone in, creating a beautiful, surreal effect, despite the fact that it was filled with... water.

Zreyas pulled the water-skin out of his armor and emptied it out into the fluctuating saltwater, rinsed it out, and then filled it with a small amount of water for nutrients later to go into his drinking water. *I need fresh water, and soon.* He rolled it back up and put it in his pocket. Zreyas held out the end of his rope and created a slip-loop at the end. He slipped it over one of the protruding rock edges.

Zreyas took the time to look through the water to see how far down it went. *This could be bad if I'm not careful.* Continuing to scope out water lines while he waded, he was now up to his armpits in water, but holding steady with his footing. He stayed close to the cave wall. The edges of the rock became coral reef. He knew as beautiful as it was, it could be razor sharp and deadly if he wasn't careful.

Zreyas composed himself as he faced his largest obstacle in life, water. He could see in the darkness, but he couldn't open his eyes under water. It was an odd trait of the Janquar race, an involuntary reaction that shut the eyes and sealed them, no matter how hard they tried to open them. It was a self-preservation mechanism because their eyes were not suited to be wet with foreign fluids. If exposed somehow, they disintegrated quickly. *Time to see what you are made of, Zrey.*

Zreyas used the new makeshift spear to poke downward to test how deep the water was. As he progressed, he noticed yellow coral, made up of long tubes. He had never seen anything like this before since he had never spent any time near water and found it interesting. He looked up, realizing it was pushing stupid limits to go any deeper with all this armor on, but he was close to an opening in the wall.

He grabbed his rope and jerked it up sharply, pulling it away from the rock it was looped around. He slipped it around one beside him, tugging it to test the grip. Once satisfied, he waded out far enough to see through the opening of the cave.

There was an empty beach about one hundred meters away. He paused to think, letting the swells of water break around his shoulders. It would be dusk in a few hours and he couldn't swim that far with armor.

An idea hit him. Zreyas grabbed the rope and whipped it up and to the side a few times to free the rope from the rock. He backed up to a safer depth, but still near the opening. He started taking off his armor and weapons.

With each piece Zreyas took off, he strung the rope through it or tied it on securely. When all of his garb was off, except his boots, he stepped back carefully and looked around for that coral that was shaped like tubes. Finally seeing it, he lined himself up with it and dipped down into the water, immediately causing his eyes to close and seal. He felt for the longest one he had his eye on and used his booted foot to break it at the base. He stood up again and waited for the water to drain enough so his eyes would open, facing the breeze as much as he could.

Finally, they opened, and Zreyas checked the coral and spotted a small creature in it. He held it under water and it jetted out, wanting no part of Zreyas' endeavors. He looked through it again, making sure nothing else was blocking the tube. Satisfied, he carefully held the rope in his mouth while he took off one boot at a time and added them to the rest of the armor and weapons.

It felt odd. The Janquar slept in armor, and now there was nothing between his skin and the water. The sharp coral didn't bother his feet because of his thick and hardened skin. However, Zreyas noticed he felt it more than he should have. He guessed it was because of the changes in his skin color, also meaning it wasn't as hard and thick.

He took one more step forward, just before it got too deep. Zreyas dropped the armor and weapons under water on the sand just ahead, outside the cavern mouth.

He needed a free hand to swim with and thought about how he was going to do that while he took several deep breaths, hanging on to the rope in one hand and the coral tube in the other. After he finished his preparation breaths, he put the coral in his mouth sideways between his teeth and let his lips rest against it. He breathed in through his nose and held his breath.

Lowering his head into the water, Zreyas swam as quietly as he could, just under the surface so he wouldn't be noticed by all the Janquar on the beach. Panic made him want to surface when his eyes sealed and he had nothing to hold on to anymore to make himself feel safe. His training belied his panic going on, though, and he kept swimming. He swam harder, thinking about how he had made a promise to Aaru, and he aimed to keep it. He felt himself shake in both determination and fear.

About a minute in, he needed air. He rolled belly up and used the coral to breathe, clearing the tube with his old air. He made himself use the breathing to calm down and talk to himself. *You are all right, Zrey. Look, you are doing what the other Janquar would never think about doing. You are strong and look at your ingenuity. Just breathe and use the fear to fill your war aura. Just don't let it out. It's all going to be okay.*

He repeated the process until he was about halfway to shore, where he bumped into an outcropping of smooth rock just under the surface. Zreyas grabbed the rock and held on, letting the water drain from his face until his eyes opened.

There was an opening in the cliff. The Janquar Nation camped on the other side. He looked around to judge his path. Turning his body in the chosen direction, accounting for the tide's current, he breathed deep.

Zreyas ducked his head under, eyes sealing again. He swam as fast as he could under the surface, hanging onto the rope wrapped around his wrist. In a short time, he noticed he was dragging his armor, making his progress a little slower.

He stopped to breathe as little as possible. Zreyas was

patient with his body's needs, and he finally got to the point where he could put his feet down on the sand and walk. The first thing he noticed when he could open his eyes again was that the foam seemed large to him. He turned and scanned what was going on around him to the right as slowly as possible so he wouldn't attract attention, crouching for safe measure.

Zreyas realized with horror just how small he was. The Janquar on the beach were giants to him. *What the ticking hell?* They would likely never him even if they were to look his way at first. However, they always seemed to know where he was all his life due to the leadership tag in their communication network. Their race had an attuning mechanism to the leaders, so they would always know where they were. Now that they were hunting him, it would be easy for them to find him. He had too much of an imprint on them.

If the emperor was with them, Zreyas knew it wouldn't be long till they found him. He sat down in the surf and pulled the line that held his armor and weapons hard and fast so he could get to a more hidden spot. Zreyas tried to channel his energy like Rhom taught him to make this task go faster, but it didn't work. He didn't have enough instruction on the matter, much less practice on that kind of thing. It was something to think about, though.

Suddenly, Zreyas jerked forward and face-planted into the water. He kept his grip on the rope, confused and blind, again. Struggling to stay with the rope, Zreyas braced his feet on what he could feel as a piece of porous rock, barely breaking the surface of the water. His right foot slipped on the sharp rock and cut it, but he used his war aura to keep himself going. It helped him ignore the pain.

His strength grew, and the old days of training came into play. He felt the line of rope jerk back and forth. It dawned on him that he had something living on the other end, trying to eat his armor and weapons. As the struggle continued, he went into calculation mode, something he did when he was at war.

Zreyas thought clearly now and time seemed to slow. All kinds of things about his situation started flooding his mind. He guessed he was now approximately one-fifteenth the size he used to be, in his estimation. This made him about fifteen centimeters tall. His jumbled armor and weapons at the end of the rope probably seemed like food to whatever was on the other end.

Zreyas had one thing on his side, though. He felt as strong as he was at full size. The problem was he didn't have the anchoring weight he had relied on before to go *with* the strength.

Zreyas pulled harder, using his body against the rock as the fulcrum. He turned slowly, wrapping the rope around his body like a rope spool to wind in whatever was on the other end. Zreyas was almost laying backwards, head barely above the water. He pulled the rope and shook his head to help the water get off his face. The sun helped too, since he was lying back almost horizontally. He kept feeling the pull and walked around the rock to compensate as he needed to, so he could keep his body as the fulcrum in place.

His eyes finally opened, and he looked at his feet and the rock he was working with. It amazed Zreyas at what he had been able to do blind. He could feel the struggle from the other end lessen slightly, but that wasn't saying much. *You are getting tired.* Zreyas was getting tired too, so he relaxed into his fulcrum position for endurance's sake, rather than fighting it. He almost lost his footing altogether once, but regained it by bracing a heel in one of the divots in the rock.

Finally, he spotted what was on the other end of the line. It was flat and had pointed leathery wings it used for swimming. Its mouth was on the underside of its body, and eyes on the upper side. It jerked its head around, trying to pull what it thought was food off the line. Zreyas' weapons began to cut the creature's mouth, and the water clouded red around the creature. It thrashed, and he noticed the creature had a long thin spike of a tail with barbs half as tall as his body. He let his war aura go, but without the sound to stay stealthy as possible. He knew it still might gain attention, but he was dead without his armor and weapons, anyway. It seemed to affect the creature, and it decreased the strength of its thrashes.

Zreyas pulled hard and slowly reined it in. *Now I will at least have food when I can get it close enough.* It wasn't long, though, until he realized that its mouth was a lot more intimidating than he thought from a distance, but he could see the armor half in and half out of its mouth.
Taking advantage of the creature's attention on food rather than him, he reached toward the bunched-up gear to grab one of his weapons from its sheath. He couldn't get to either of them because they were tangled up tight, so he backed up slightly, bracing himself against the rock. He could really use one of the old man's lessons right about now.

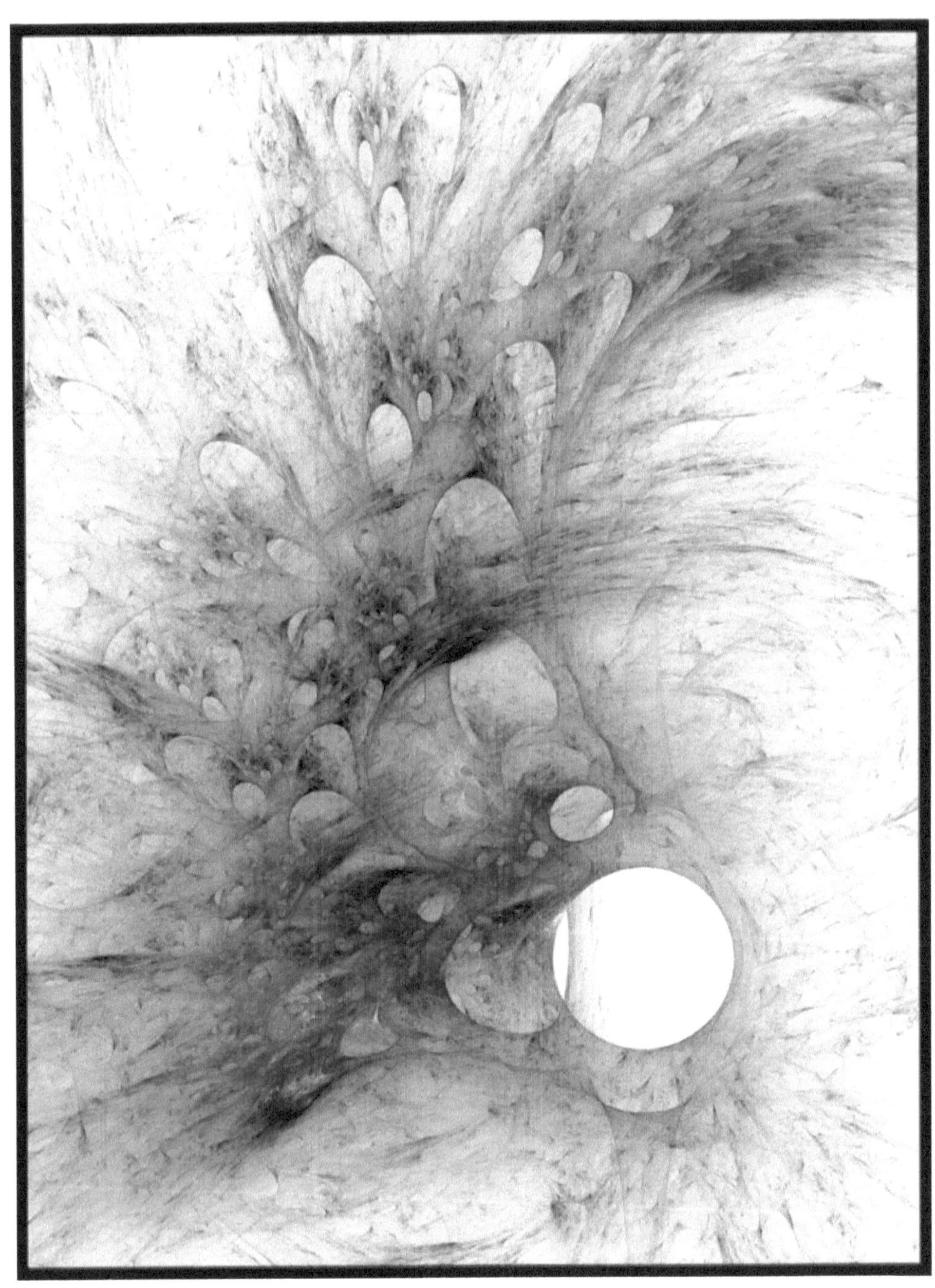

23 Breaking the News

Rhom

Tulyata leaned forward, her face lit up like she was almost excited to give the next piece of news. “The fracture that exposed the Dark One’s dimension showed up in, none other than, their emperor’s chambers.”

Rhom blurted out in an exasperated tone, “So the emperor discovered the Dark One!”

“No, not exactly. He didn’t discover him at first.”

“Well?” showing exasperation.

“Rhom, Rhom, Rhom, now don’t get that tone with me. I’m trying to help.” she winked, then relented. “Very well, the emperor didn’t discover him, nor did he initiate his release.”

“You will LOVE this next part. Get ready.” Rtu chuckled sardonically.

“Oh, wonderful,” Rhom said dryly.

"They were ordering Aaru to go on a suicide mission because they thought the boy was weak."

"Zreyas, his brother, mentioned this briefly; which reminds me, where..."

Tulyata held up a finger and shook her head. "One thing at a time and nothing without checks and balances. Are you ready to listen?"

Rhom nodded and bowed slightly. "I apologize, Tulyata"

"So." She sat up, leaning forward. "The one that found him first was none other than..." she pointed to Rtu.

Rtu picked up a tribal chanting drum beside him that Rhom hadn't noticed before, and began drumming. With a final thump of the drum, he yelled, "Yes, you got it! Aaru!"

Rhom flopped back against a console behind him, feeling suddenly weak from hearing the confirmation of what Zreyas suspected.

"And, yes!" Tulyata said unexpectedly.

"Yes, what?" Rhom said, lifting his head up, apprehension growing.

"Yes, that wasn't the worst part."

Rhom palmed his forehead. "Wait, so let me get this straight... The Dark One shows up in his banished dimensional prison that is not supposed to be accessible from any dimension in the multiverse. Then, not only did he get caught up in the whole fracturing the universe in two, he got discovered by Aaru, who is now bound with Ayya for eternity being chased by the Dark One?" He took in a deep breath, having run out of wind.

"Ding, ding, ding! And the winner is!" Rtu spouted, holding both arms up in victory.

Rhom stared at Rtu and Tulyata, completely dazed by

their lack of seriousness. "You are having way too much fun, as grave as this situation is." Then he realized they were probably just as nervous as he was. He looked at Tulyata, joining in on the sarcasm. "Oh, please go on, I'm dying for more fun here!"

Pausing a moment, Tulyata cleared her throat painfully and forced out, "Aaru was told to go see the emperor for this... suicide mission. Basically, it was their way to kill off a prodigy that had given the Rittak line glory."

"Why would they want to kill a prodigy that gave their line glory?"

Tulyata held up a finger. "Why does anyone do anything stupid or that harms someone?"

Rhom's mouth parted a moment in stall then he shook his head. "Fear."

Tulyata flicked a finger and gave a single nod before continuing. "He was told he would help with something in their minor war over territory, however, they were going to just kill him. Instead of finding the emperor, the Dark One was in there. Aaru never noticed the fracture because it was inside the wall. Trust me, this was not fun to observe. Oddly enough, he found the edges of it, but he didn't think it was the edge of a fracture. He thought it was its design because he had never seen the emperor or his chambers until that time, ever."

Rtu continued, "Therefore, he thought nothing was amiss. He walked in and immediately said he pledged himself to this mission, even if it meant his death. We were aware he was sick and tired of living a life not meant for him. He knew it was a suicide mission and welcomed it. Smart boy, that one. So, they chatted a bit."

"But he never did a full pledge commitment, right? He didn't commit three times, did he? And he was unaware of things," Rhom said hopefully.

Tulyata looked stern. "His innocence of the true motivation will never excuse a commitment. That first pledge was valid, and it held to the laws of the universe."

"Well, at least he didn't fully commit the full number of times to be unchangeable." Rhom sighed, relieved.

"Well..." Rtu gently said, with a little more sensitivity.

Rhom looked at him incredulously, then back to Tulyata.

"As Rtu said, they chatted a bit, and he committed again; but, when the Dark One repeated the commitment to get him to recite it, he included the commitment to say 'pledging to *him*', not to the mission. Aaru caught it, and asked him, 'to *you*?' The Dark One strategically aggravated him to be clear, and there, the third and last commitment was made."

Rhom put his face in his hands. "Oh, what have I done?"

"Rhom, don't be so melodramatic. All is not lost. You, of all people, know there is always hope. He didn't commit *himself* to the Dark One for life, he committed to one *mission*. Had Aaru not been so aware, he could have easily done worse, but he didn't. He committed to a mission, to do it with everything he had, even to his death."

"Why doesn't that make me feel better? What if he decides to not do this act... until his death?"

"It doesn't mean he has to die, though, to get it done. We only need to find out what this mission will be or prevent it from being declared. He was never told what it was. If we can keep Ayya away from the Dark One, Aaru can't get the mission, much less do one, or die for one."

"Oh, thank goodness, there is hope. Thank you for the information." Rhom slumped in relief. "So now what? Is there anything else I should know?"

"Well, that depends on you and how much your little ol' heart can take," laughed Rtu.

"Well, I think we have an enormous problem, though," Rhom said as he scratched his head above his ear.

"What would that be?"

"Scar-face? Her new father?"

Tulyata turned to Rhom and said, "We have been over this, but just to confirm, did you notice a limp?"

"I did, but I figured he was trying to get around the bed."

"Well, we didn't have time to look into it right away. It wasn't urgent at the time. Rtu, if you would verify, it just makes me feel better about the balances."

"Righto," Rtu said enthusiastically. "He was born with a foot problem; so yes, Scar-face is the man, though he has no scar in this new body."

"How can we keep him away from Ayya?"

Tulyata bored down her pointed gaze on the High Seer. "Rhom, he isn't her worst problem, the Dark One, the emperor, and who he has enlisted *is*. That is the part we have yet to tell you."

"Well, please tell me this more important information. I know I keep getting sidetracked thinking about Ayya. I have to get all these facts in my mind straight before I can even attempt to do what I feel is best, especially since I will not have your aid in the future."

"Now, now, don't be like that." Rtu said. "Life gives us things we don't expect. Here is the part you might want to know. After Zreyas slid into Aaru at the ceremony, shoving him in the portal, the Janquar emperor declared that there was to be a hunt. And he walked to his chambers for a rest and to think."

Rhom's expression didn't change, still waiting for the next part. Then the realization hit him. His eyes grew wide. "You mean..."

"Yes dear..., he means," interjected Tulyata.

"Oh, what have I done to my lady Ayya? I was only trying to help save her and my people."

Tulyata pointed to Rhom's body. "Rhom! Look at you! You are festering! Stop it, or you will end up like the rest! We can't afford to lose you too!"

Rhom looked down at himself and saw the dark conditioning caused by the guilt and anguish... Rhom understood that the lower frequencies were turning his body dark in spots and caused them to condense into warped, scarred, and dark areas in his body.

Catching himself, he closed his eyes and breathed. His intent was clear to the visages, and they waited expectantly. He opened his eyes and examined himself to make sure he was back to normal. "Thank you."

"You are welcome! As you can see, we are in a bit of a festering bind, due to who is on her heels. The Dark One is likely almost free, if not already. I won't check because it will tip the balance. He is after Ayya because he knows Aaru is within her and part of her now. He will use their innocence, power, and unique talents to conquer parts of the multiverse that he has never touched yet."

"She is now in an alternative universe and galaxy he never knew of, and he sees opportunity because they are much weaker," said Tulyata. "He has a *lot* of motivation to get to her... and Aaru. He will use that emperor. He likely possesses or shares a body with him now, and his resources, including all these people, to get everything he wants. There are billions of them at his disposal. There is no way he won't use that to his advantage."

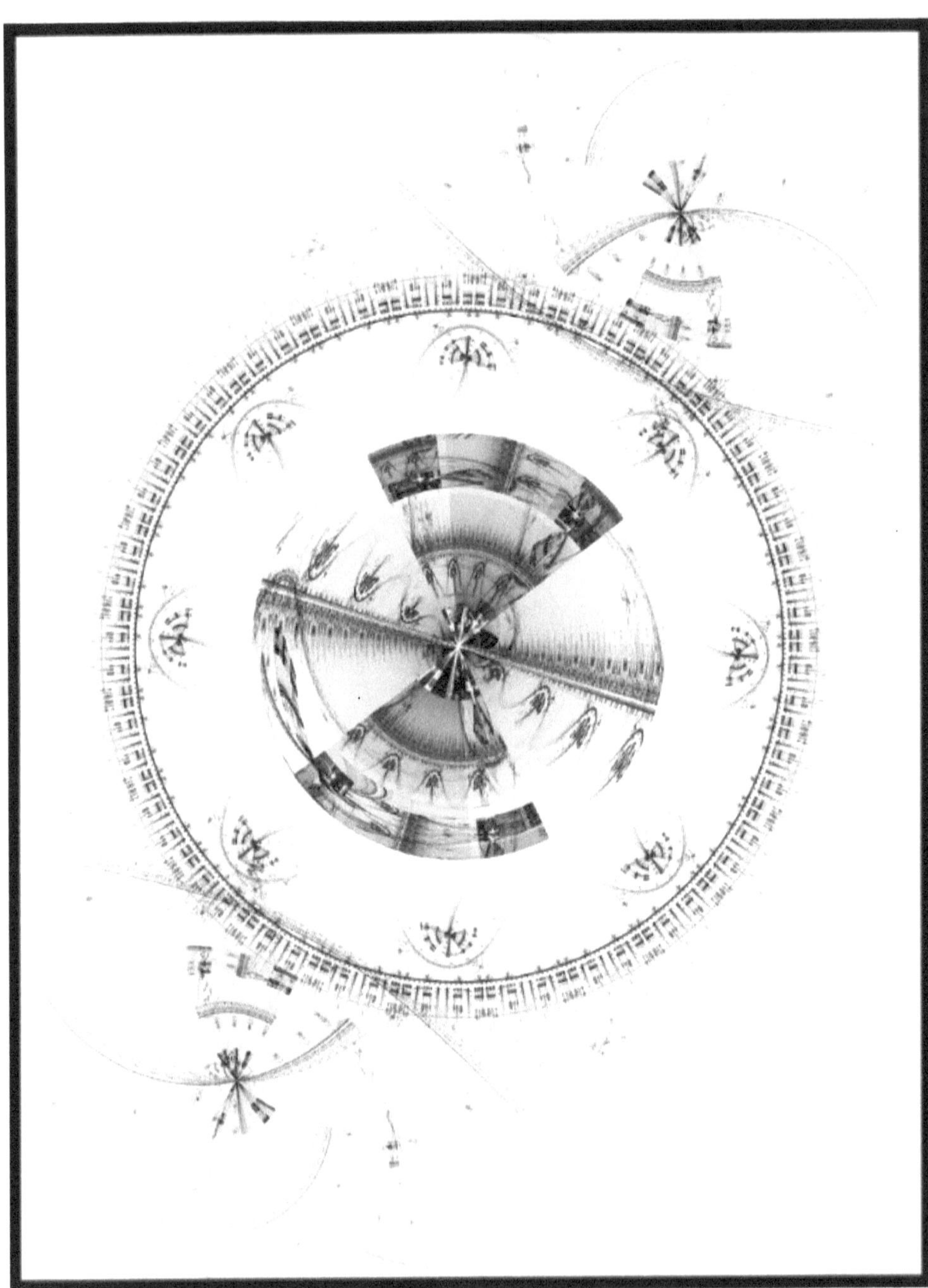

24 Where's Zreyas

Rhom

"There is one other problem," Rhom said. "We don't know where Zreyas is. My brothers and I watched him access the quantum, and he would be an amazing ally. Is there any way we can find out where he ended up and go get him? We have a lot at stake here."

"Hmm, let me check...," Rtu said, personality bubbling over. "It impressed us how fast he learned from you. It seems you have grown fond of the boy, and I can't blame you. I like him a lot!" He looked over at Tulyata. "Dear mother, be so kind as to look it up for us since you have hogged all the devices in your own realm."

Tulyata looked at him, incredulous. Rtu laughed as she started her typical busy work.

Rhom chuckled and Rtu let out a loud belly laugh that shocked Rhom so much he jumped.

Tulyata interrupted their laugh. “There, we have him. Well, this is interesting, he’s in one of the new galaxies... Oh my.”

“Don’t tell me, he’s in a bad spot.” Rhom said, groaning.

“You are correct. Two galaxies in that universe split. One of them is your home system, Rhom, Vela Eubeleus System. The other one is the Zagreus System.” Tulyata looked at Rtu, then back to the information. “You already gave the new sibling galaxies names.”

“Of course!” said Rtu proudly.

“Rhom, your home world galaxy of Vela has a new sister named Proioxis. And now it is heavily populated by the Janquar, and that... is where Zreyas is. I’m not sure how, though. Something weird is going on here because I should be able to get this information, balance or no balance, but it is not accessible for me.”

“So, I’m assuming Zreyas is on the same planet as those Janquar?” Rhom asked, trying to keep her on track and not get any more aggravated than he felt already.

“Correct. There is only one viable planet they can live on because the galaxy was just...” Tulyata paused and leaned forward. Her expression was as if she couldn’t believe she was seeing. “These two galaxies didn’t split.” She looked at Rtu, who nodded his head no to confirm they didn’t. “It’s like these two galaxies gave birth. Both new ones are very early-stage galaxies. The one that Vela birthed has a single umbilical-like connection.”

Rtu looked at her, head propped up on his hand and elbow on the arm of his chair. “Your assessment is correct, mother. However, it is reaching out in a few more areas trying to make connections to three other galaxies.”

Tulyata looked closer at the galaxy on her screen.

"You are right, that's interesting. We know energy has intelligence and transmits information, but these galaxies seem like they are more... sentient."

"Fascinating! I can't wait till I can get some time to do some research on this event! I need a lab to..." Rhom stopped for a moment.

Rtu and Tulyata looked almost excited, watching him as if they expected something.

"Why did I think about a lab?" Rhom couldn't help but think he was on the verge of remembering something, like trying to remember a dream, but couldn't put a finger on it. "I only have a library tower and observatory. I think I'm getting old and losing my mind. Anyway, I watched the fracture close behind him... maybe there was another one."

Tulyata shrugged, "Anyway, it doesn't matter how they got there, but they are both there now."

"The name is appropriate for the galaxy too, don't you think? Rtu sat up with pride. Proioxis, it means onrush pursuit in battle."

Tulyata rolled her eyes. "Your people are no longer hidden, Rhom. The Janquar and the Dark One know where they are now because Proioxis is the connected child. However, on the upside, they are not interested in your people at the moment. They are way over confident and riled up from the hunt. It's just a matter of time before they find Zreyas and kill him. It would be in our best interest to go get him, but that is going to be up to you."

"We can get you there, and we can give you a way off. That is all we can do," Rtu piped up.

Tulyata looked over at him sternly.

"This is in *my* realm, dear Tulyata. I have my own checks and balances in nature and they are far from being balanced, especially now that the Janquar are there. Our side has a lot of favors before they are balanced, since they are not naturally there as part of the local life. They also have help they shouldn't have."

Rtu looked at Rhom with a serious expression. "However, my aid is not limitless. You must make sure you use each piece of aid efficiently and spread it out as best you can, because you are going to need it."

"I understand, and thank you. And thank you, Tulyata, for your aid in getting me there and us off. I will not waste your assistance."

Everyone seemed in a thoughtful mode. Rhom considered this as well.

He looked at Tulyata's desk, screens, and scales, and an idea came to him. "Is there a way we can see what is going on there before I go? Can I choose where I go based on the plan I come up with? Or do I need to just randomly drop on the planet?"

"You can choose, Rhom," said Tulyata. "This is critical for all of us and the balance. You are only one man against billions at this point. However, with our aid, the chances of success go up a little."

"Do you have anything of his? or vise verse?" Rtu interjected.

"Hmm... trying to remember, he has nothing of mine, I don't think. Oh, wait. I made him a tryst device. He gave me a piece of hair. I had a gift from Ayya, and I made it from myself. I'm not sure that counts, but I wanted to make something for him with the ability to find Ayya to protect her."

"I want to adjust the tryst... so that it can be stronger and incorruptible in case he, or you, get caught with it. Also, the distance will increase."

"Good idea... Can you do that from here?" Tulyata

asked.

"Balance wise, no, but I can do it through Rhom when he is close to him. I will charge it with amplified natural elements. Think of it as a currency. Once its charge is used up, then it will return to normal ranges, but still protected."

"So basically, I need to get myself down there, find Zreyas, and get close to him in order for you to do it?"

"Smart you are!" exclaimed Rtu.

Tulyata's scales tipped with a clink, then it went into a balance. "See, you have a chance. All will work out, dear."

"We just have to get you there first. The Dark One has a massive range, and as soon as you land on the planet Zreyas is on, he will know you are there. Whoever he's likely trying to possess, if he hasn't already, is the strongest of them all, so it only amplifies his skills. We are up against one hell of a set of odds because there are things going on that we can't track. It perplexes me because we should be able to. I love games, but this game is not fun anymore."

"That is the power of the Dark One, don't forget. The hopelessness. And he just happened to land on a race he is most attuned to, unfortunately. We will need to be diligent in keeping ourselves in check," Rtu said matter-of-factly, as if he dealt with it all the time.

Rhom took in a breath and let it go. "Well, at least we have a general plan. Let's see the layout of what is going on there, if you please. I am eager to find Zreyas and decide where to land. However, I will need more instruction from you on the tryst exchange."

"Gladly. There isn't much to tell, really. I will give you this for the time being." Rtu pulled out a light crystal that was intertwined with miniature trees, lakes, waterfalls and vines. All of all the elements were included. Wrapping around the crystal was a life-filled scene, all of it back-lit by the white energy of life.

"Whoa!" Rhom reached out reverently to take the crystal. "What do I do with this?"

"Just make sure you don't lose it. You need to carry this on your person. It will allow me to do the work remotely. So, you need to wear appropriate clothes, especially if you are going to deal with the alternative universe Ayya is in. Because you are created with light, it's important that you have pockets that are external so that you don't change the energy of the object; otherwise, energy that is not yours will condition you, and you will condition it. Make sense?"

"Of course, it does! Ahem..." Rhom smiled weakly. "Yes, it does. I'm just not sure whether or not to joke with you two."

"Only when we are in a good mood, and that is rare." Tulyata winked.

Rtu let out a belly laugh and slapped Rhom on the back, almost knocking him over. "Of course you can! If we don't like it, we will just kill you and be done with it all!"

Rhom couldn't help but feel a little intimidated for a short period until he looked at the light warriors. The reminder of their earlier shared thoughts pulled him out of it. He found himself laughing in no time, then said, "Thank you for that permission, patience, and help."

"Yes, yes, we are worthy of your reverence." Rtu began laughing again. "But no need for permission from this point on. We are now brothers in cause and balance more than ever before, and I give you permission to be as rude and humorous as you want... I think." Rtu looked at Rhom, enjoying the banter. He sobered from the fun enough to tell him, "Seriously, lighten up. I have much respect for you and what you have done over the varSas, and your decision to incarnate."

Tulyata shot him a glare to shut him up.

Rtu ignored her. "You have done much to keep balance while waiting for the next Tantra, and I thank you for that, too. Anyway, now that we got that out of the way... That crystal, put it in a pocket."

Rtu waved a nature staff in his hand. Clothes of specially woven thick white silks with gold-leaf trim appeared on the desk. Rhom gasped at the workmanship. The hooded robes had wide gold trim at the bottom and sleeves, and embroidery of intricate elemental symbols up and down the front panels of the robes and on the sleeves. The fire, water, and aether elemental symbols were larger than the earth and air symbols, giving it variety and a sculptured look in the trim.

"They are simple, classy, scholarly, and practical. Thank you," Rhom said, mesmerized. He immediately stood and walked over to put them on.

"You have many pockets on the inside of the garment, as well as the outside. I recommend the inside ones for safe keeping. There is one pocket on the inside that is small but will hold just about anything, no matter how big or small. You just need to use your quantum skills to put it in there. It will also reduce the weight of the object to zero."

"This is amazing! I can't help but wonder how you pulled that off. I suppose if you..."

"... recorded the molecular structure." Rtu continued his sentence and chuckled, slapping his knee.

Rhom began pointing into the air as he thought it out, not realizing that Rtu had spoken. "... And then changed the structure to something that has no weight. But when it is pulled out, it remembers and changes it back!"

"Yes! You have the general concept of it! However, it will only hold three things at once. So, use it wisely. If someone takes the garment off you, they will not be able to access the pocket, even if they rip it to shreds. All you need to do is come to me or ask me to retrieve them for you. It will be at great balance cost though, so be careful."

"Thank you! These robes are very comfortable and seem to rejuvenate my energy as well."

"You noticed! Consider it a gift for all you have done in the past. Gifts are something I love to give. You incarnates all give me so much to watch and experience. It entertains me and makes me better. It is only right that it should be reciprocated."

"Really, Rtu?" said Tulyata. "You are way too sentimental for a visage that most think is a little man holding a judgment rod. You give us a bad reputation."

Rtu chuckled. "Good. I'm happy to mess that reputation up. Besides, as your son, it's my duty to make sure you are aware you are holding that judgment rod, so double the satisfaction."

Rhom couldn't help but laugh at Rtu's comment, at least until he saw Tulyata's gaze turn on him. His laughter trailed off, and he found himself a little uncomfortable.

"I like him," Rtu exclaimed.

"You are all right, Rhom, if a little stressed out," Tulyata admitted.

"Thanks." He scratched his head just above his right ear and looked at the crystal. He decided to put it in the special pocket. "What do you call this kind of pocket?"

"Pocket dimension!" Rtu burst out in a roaring laugh that rumbled the entire room.

Tulyata shot a glare at Rtu, “Corny, though accurate.” As Rtu laughed, she grew more agitated. “And you laugh because you know it drives me crazy!”

Rhom laughed, despite Tulyata’s intimidation, but quit as soon as he could. Rhom wiped his eyes down.

Ignoring Tulyata, Rtu spoke to Rhom. “Feels good to laugh! It’s healthy, no?”

“Indeed, it does, Rtu. Thank you for the laugh.” Rhom shot his eyes to Tulyata and held out a hand. “No disrespect to you, Tulyata.” Then he looked at the console that betrayed his intention to get on with finding Zreyas. “So, how do we view the planet he is on and see what kind of mess he is in?”

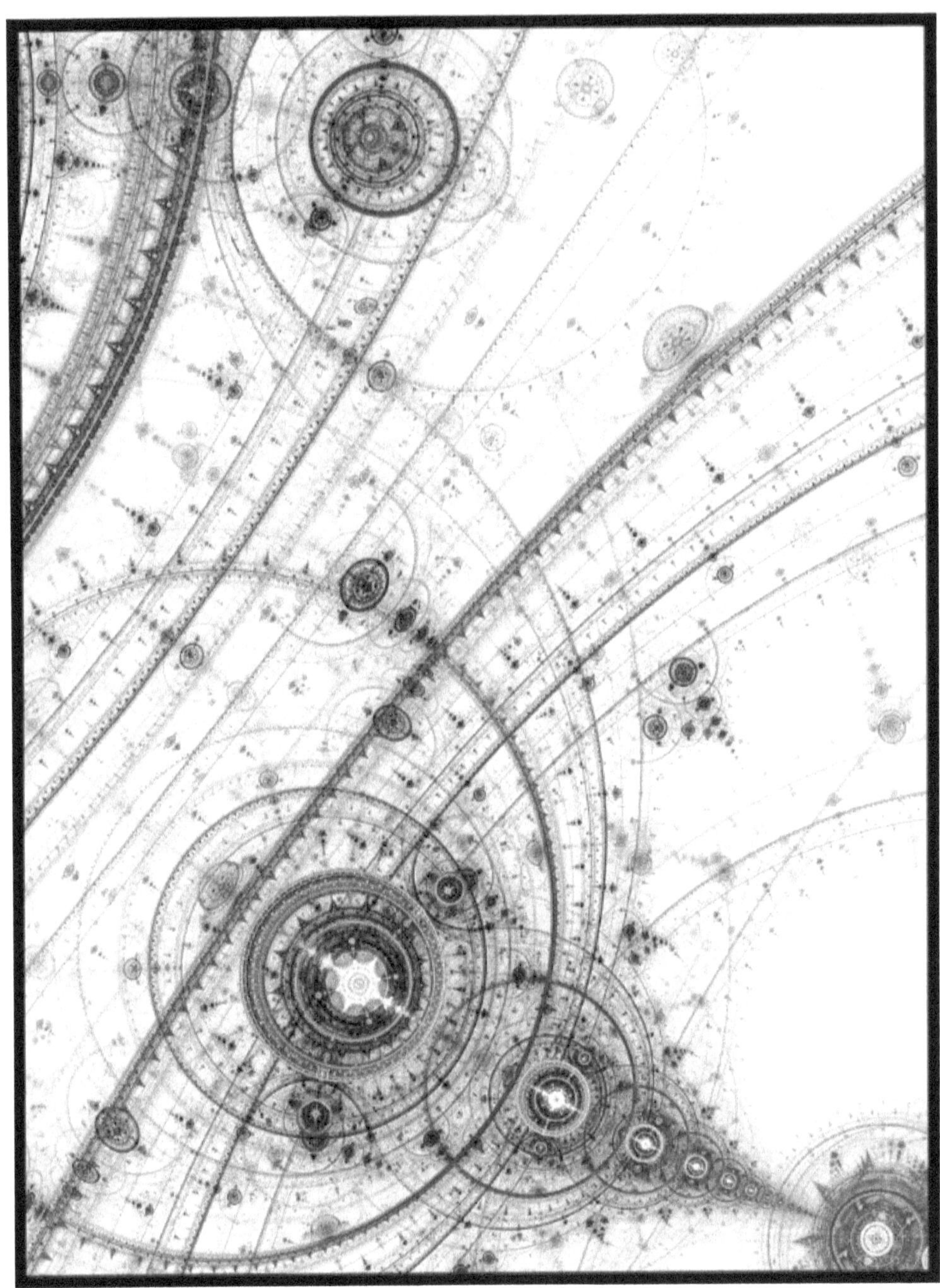

25 The Catch

꩜꩜꩜ Zreyas ꩜꩜꩜

Zreyas' mind reeled as he watched the rope fray from the creature's teeth. "Think, Zrey, think! I am dead if I lose my armor and weapons!" He prompted himself into a rage aura that would weaken the hungry creature further. He thought about how the coral tube was screwing up his grip on the rope, and that gave him an idea.

Zreyas struggled to pull the creature in closer until it was within striking distance. He held the coral at one end like a dagger, assassin style, with his thumb at the smoother end. He twisted his body with the rope, using his fulcrum position as leverage. Zreyas plunged the jagged end of the coral into the eye, toward where he thought the brain might be. The creature violently thrashed, jerking Zreyas off balance and into the water with it. His eyes sealed again, but he refused to let go.

Zreyas let out a war aura using the new transformation technique that the old man taught him and pulled the creature up close and personal while it dove, fought, and drifted. Because his eyes were sealed, he listened. His world seemed to open up in a way he never expected. He heard the armor and weapons clink, so he stabbed it blindly in the general direction of the creature's eyes, using his expanded war aura to weaken it. Without his sight, his world expanded in his hearing sense. He heard the surf in detail all around him. Zreyas even noticed what he did not hear... footsteps. All his life he was accustomed to hearing footsteps, no matter where he went and no matter what surface. He was almost never alone. Footsteps were like ambient nature sounds to him. Not having eyesight made him pay attention to what he heard, and he didn't hear any footsteps.

He continued to stab the creature until it went limp, with a few twitches periodically. He dropped the coral, now broken to almost nothing. Zreyas grabbed the rope near the bundle of armor, blindly feeling around the creature that was still holding on to it. He would assess why the armor didn't come loose after it died and after he got to shore. Swimming to the surface, he followed the sound of the surf until he could stand and get his head out of the water.

It was fortunate he did, because his war aura had attracted attention. He couldn't see, but he could hear and feel the footsteps at a distance. The giant Janquarian warriors were searching the beach. Zreyas shook his head violently to get the water away from his eyes. As soon as they opened, he looked around quickly, taking in all the details.

Down the shore, further away from the Janquar, there was a rock that broke the surface a good meter out of the water. He faced it and aimed. He took a breath and submerged, walking along the floor of the ocean, using the weight of the armor inside the creature over his head to both hide him and stay deep, away from the waves. Just when he thought he would have to surface due to needing air, he bumped into the rock formation.

Zreyas scaled the side of the rock. He put his face above the surface as much as possible to breathe, keeping the creature's body on top of him for concealment.

Once he could see again, he turned around and scanned his surroundings. He saw the Janquar scouting on the beach, but they never looked to the water. He knew why. The Janquar assumed he would not be *in* the water. Their fear and aversion to the water was now an advantage for him.

Zreyas hid behind the rock, using the rope to help him stick to it in the ebb and flow of the ocean wave currents. He was grateful it was low tide; had it been high tide, he would have probably been smashed by now inside the cave and never gotten this far. He hung on and waited for them to give up. He felt all the scratches, cuts, and bruises all over him.

Soothed by being in the water, in the sun, and listening to the waves, it almost rocked him to sleep once. To keep himself alert, he played back all the things he had learned from Rhom and his brother over the past few days. He revisited the experiences, new knowledge, and realizations. After each experience, he thought tactically about how it might be used in the future in different situations. Zreyas tried to think of advantages and disadvantages each would bring, and what opportunities they might open up.

When night fell and the stars peeked out, the Janquar still combed the area, although most of them were headed back toward the camps. Zreyas prepared to use nighttime as his advantage. Looking at another rock formation further down, he decided to swim toward it; but this time, he would not submerge himself. The tide was beginning to get pretty rough, and he was about to lose the safety he had obtained earlier, anyway. He reminded himself that he was also small now; even if they spotted him, they wouldn't see him as the Zreyas they knew. In addition, he had the extra advantage to use the creature as a disguise to redirect their attention.

He swam as fast as he could without causing too much splash to be heard past the wave sound. He reached the next rock over and looked at the beach again, illuminated by the moonlight. They were still scouting.

"Ticking hell, go back already." He knew the surf was his friend, both in sound and activity. As he looked up to the stars, Zreyas wondered if Rhom was okay. He spotted a star fall through the sky, and it seemed close.

Zreyas talked to the creature as if it would hear him. "There's some weird shit going on." To his left, further down, he saw another set of tall rock formations, like what he had landed on, and he decided to go for it. He couldn't stay here all night, and he was getting cold and dehydrated. It wouldn't be long till he passed out from exhaustion. He had an idea to wrap the rope around his shoulders like backpack straps and let the armor and creature trail behind him a good few meters to give him room.

Zreyas rolled up the rest of the rope around his waist so it wouldn't get caught on anything below him. He faced the formation, compensated for the tide, and swam hard, working with the waves. *Don't worry Aaru, I won't give up.*

He loved and hated the part of himself that was always pushing the limits, yet it had served him well in the past, and did so now. Zreyas swam harder, feeling an urgency from something he was not sure of, but he obeyed it and pushed his body to the limit. He felt light tugs on the rope behind him, and it almost freaked him out. The thought of having to fight something else that wanted a meal was not something he relished. *No one is going to eat my armor and weapons!*

Zreyas poured on the focus and lathered up the determination. His aura flowed, but with no sound, just enough to give him the energy he needed. He could tell his speed was almost unnatural, and remembered Aaru's speed.

It wasn't long before he gripped a rock in the formation and crawled on it. He rushed to pull everything from the water. Zreyas watched a large fish with a lot of teeth pop up out of the water, going for his kill he had just laid beside him. It scared Zreyas so badly he fell backwards, but he never let go of the rope. He scrambled to pull it away further and partially on top of him.

The Janquar on the beach looked toward the water. Zreyas leaned back, feeling the exhaustion, pulling the creature up over him further to get hold of his weapons and armor, quiet as possible. He assessed the situation and found that when it jerked to grab what it thought was food; it caused the two swords to shift. They acted as hooks, so he *couldn't* let go.

"No ticking wonder."

After several minutes of struggling to get the dagger

loose, he used it to get the other weapons free by cutting around its mouth. He had to break a few bones to give enough room to free them without cutting the rope.

Now that everything was loose and sitting on the rocks, he cut strips of the creature's flesh, still unsure yet if it was edible for him or not. Zreyas deftly sliced the strips and began eating; he was starving. He sat back and moaned at how good it tasted to get something in him, even raw. After eating his fill, he turned the creature over on the sunbaked rocks to keep flies from landing on his future meal until he could properly do something with it.

The rocks felt warm in the cool night air. Holding his bundle of gear, he laid his head back and, despite the stings of his wounds, he welcomed sleep.

26 Beam

ᘎᘎᘎ *Zreyas* ᘎᘎᘎ

Zreyas woke with a jolt of horror, tingling heat ran up the sides of his neck to the top of his head. He started scrambling for his armor, more specifically, for his vest. Had he lost the tryst that would help him find Ayya and Aaru? He was thankful it was daylight now, so he could see easier.

He was so frantic about trying to get to it that his hands shook. Zreyas had a vague and distant feel of his body hurting badly all over, but he rushed to untangle his things as carefully as he could. He told himself that rushing would only make things worse, so he calmed himself.

The tryst might have fallen from his under-vest, and he didn't want to accidentally dump it in the water.

Zreyas either set the armor aside or put it on,

depending on if he was ready for that piece or not. As soon as he got to his chest piece, he separated it from the under-vest and put it aside. He picked up the vest, freed it, and checked the inside pockets. One had his pouch still rolled up, but soggy.

His shaking hand reached into the other one. Zreyas felt the tryst, sat back relieved as he pulled it out to look at it. He got rid of the residual stress by telling it, “Ticking hell, you scared me.” It was still intact, dormant as ever. The white swirling material of the skewed diamond shape still fascinated him. The cyan triangle was unlit except for one point. It glowed, and he assumed it represented him. The other two probably represented Ayya and Rhom. It felt good to hold it. It seemed to hum with an ever so slight vibration. He couldn’t hear it, but it felt like a hum. *Our day is full of fortune today, Aaru. We have the tryst, food, and the Janquar have not found me yet.*

He wiped his armor off the best he could and put it all back on. Zreyas knew his gear would be a corroded mess soon if he didn’t get his armor and weapons cleaned off with fresh water and some sort of protective oil. After it was all on, he made sure the tryst was in his inside vest pocket again, safe and sound.

Zreyas peered around the rock formation to check how many Janquar were still scouting. To his surprise, there was no one all the way up and down the beach. He could hardly believe his fortune. Not wanting to get wet again, he traversed the rock formation to get to shore. Once he set his feet on the sand, he immediately started looking around at his surroundings.

The beach was wide here, and at the edge were sand dunes and sea grass. Past that, he could barely see a tree line off in the distance. He hadn’t planned to come here, but he was glad the Janquar were here. That would give him a chance to get some good old-fashioned sabotage done. He might be only one person, little at that, but that didn't mean he couldn't burn their supplies or create havoc to hinder their progress until he could find out how to get off this planet. Careful was key though, because they could track him. That was a dilemma he didn't know how to get around just yet.

Zreyas sighed and thought about Aaru and how much he missed him. He didn't know how he was going to find Ayya, but knew he had to. He knew he had no hope of ever seeing Aaru again, but he thought his sacrifice was worth it, so he was going to do his best to keep his promise to him to help him help her. If Ayya was killed, then whatever she was supposed to do couldn't happen and Aaru said it was important for everyone... so did Rhom. There was a lot he didn't know, but he trusted Aaru.

He sat down in the shade of the rocks and pulled out the last of the strips he had taken from his catch. Zreyas stuffed them in his mouth hungrily as he looked at the beach sand, seeing large footprints all over the place. He decided it might be wiser to head west for now, in the opposite direction of the Janquar that were camping east from there.

After he was done eating, he stood and turned west toward the grassy area just past the dunes. That would be good cover; however, it would be difficult for him to see through. *I think I'm glad about the size situation I'm in... for now. It will be easier to hide and scout.*

Zreyas walked, almost feeling like humming. He didn't because it was too odd for him; besides, Zreyas never tried it before, and he was a little stunned he thought about feeling like doing it. He had heard the blue camp members do it, but he had never been inclined to do so himself. It wasn't long before he was in a very large plains area. Suddenly, he felt something warm under his armor. Zreyas froze in his tracks and reached into his armor where the warmth was. It was the tryst, and he pulled it out.

Once out of his pocket, he opened his hand and let it sit in his palm. The familiar skewed diamond shape and cyan triangle were there as before, but a lot more brilliant. It seeped out through the cyan cracks of the intricate spiraling white crystal-like structure. The glowing dot he saw before was now connected to another glowing dot. That whole side glowed. It had strange shapes moving and flipping within themselves on that side. Light emanated from the openings, and the light rays joined together and merged. It turned purple and shot a gentle, flowing beam of light ahead of him toward the west.

"Aaru! I'm coming, little brother!"

Zreyas ran in the direction the light beam was moving toward. He placed the tryst in an outside fold of his armor to not attract attention. Every once in a while, he took it out to double check his position and direction. He ran inland, and the ground became more treacherous to traverse, but he pressed on until he came to a freshwater source. He pulled out his water skin and filled it, drank the entire contents, and filled it again.

Exhaustion hit him hard when he stopped that few moments to drink. He wanted to get to his brother as soon as possible, but his voice of reason kicked in from so many varSas of training. He would do no good for Aaru if he was too tired to be aware or have no energy to fight if he had to. Zreyas rested for a few hours while he washed off his armor and weapons.

There was no sign of the Janquar directly, though he saw a faint light from their fires, more inland, and that was enough presence to be wary as far as he was concerned. *That's why I didn't see them. They moved inland. They hate water. It's funny, I find I like water now that I'm not so afraid of my eyes closing. I can see in other ways.*

"I guess they set up something more permanent." He felt alone and assumed it was because he was on a mission pressed for time with no help. He was used to having help any time he wanted it. All he had to do was bark out orders, something he took for granted at his station. That life was over, and he needed to pull himself together. It was time for some straight talk with himself.

"But, Zrey, you are alive against all odds. You just need to find Aaru... I mean, Ayya." Pangs of grief filled him, and he sighed. Keeping himself as calm as possible, he decided he could still talk with Aaru as he put his armor back on.

"I'm sorry Nat tried to hurt you, bro. He was always jealous of you. In a way, I am too, but not like that. I just wish I had caught him, and what he was intending to do earlier than I did. I can't do anything about it now, but I can help your Ayya, I hope. If you are around, it would be great to get a little help, because I don't really know what I'm doing here."

Zreyas stood up, checked the tryst in his hand to get the direction he needed, then checked the surrounding environment. He put the tryst away and ran at a slow, steady pace to regulate his endurance. He knew days of running might be in store for him.

After several hours, Zreyas saw a light ahead for a short period. He pulled out the tryst to check his direction, and he realized he was, indeed, going in the direction of that light.

"Finally, something good is happening!" Zreyas poured on the speed and noticed the light going a little higher off the ground. "I wonder what that was?"

He channeled his anger and transformed it into the peace he felt watching Aaru. He looked ahead and imagined himself already there in his mind. Zreyas thought about how much he cared for his brother and allowed the transformed wave patterns to pull him ahead to the place his mind was thinking about while he ran. He guessed it was like wishing away the rest of the run, but at least it kept his mind occupied.

Abruptly, the sound that he had heard when Rhom moved them in the quantum to hide them surrounded him. Though startled, he kept running. After hearing it the third time, he realized he moved through the quantum a short distance that time. "Whoa!"

The grass was really tall for him now, but he fought it. It was like running through a crop field with no rows. He pushed harder, and he consciously tried to repeat the quantum leap again to practice. Again, Zreyas appeared where he placed himself in his mind, just like before, this time on purpose. "Ticking hell!"

Before he could get his bearings, he crashed into something and barely saw movement just before everything went black.

Rhom

Rhom saw an abrupt halt in seeing the signal beam. The more powerful crystal that Rtu had given him flickered out like its job was done. The life had left it. He sensed Zreyas nearby, but didn't see him. Though he was not an expert on tracking, he crouched down to look for footprints and realized he saw more than that.

"Oh my, look what we found here!" Rhom said quietly, astonished.

He gently picked up a tiny unconscious Zreyas who had just ran into his foot. The light warriors gathered around to see as well, curious.

"How did you get so small, my boy? I'm so glad I didn't step on you!" Rhom held Zreyas up, only about fifteen centimeters tall, he estimated. It amazed him how tiny he was. He wondered what happened. Placing his hand over the top of him to detect how he was doing, he sighed, relieved to find Zreyas okay. Just knocked out.

Rhom looked up and spoke upward. "Tulyata, we have found him."

He looked around, seeing a large group of Janquar walking their way. They had not seen them yet, but he could tell they were looking for Zreyas. It was too coincidental they were coming to their exact position.

Rhom crouched and walked toward a strand of trees to hide until they could get off the planet. The warriors climbed the trees to watch, dimming their natural light to match the sky like chameleons.

Rhom saw through their sight as if it was his own eyes. They had built the framing of a new fort, probably because they couldn't get back home.

"They are making the best of things for an invasion, it seems." Finding himself disgusted and in a wee bit of panic for his people, he decided it was not productive and just let it go. It would be much more valuable to think about what he could do something about. Rhom remembered what Tulyata told him earlier about the Janquar being more distracted with the hunt and conquest than his people. He hoped she was right.

"Tulyata, they are all over the place, and we don't have much time before they find us. If we move, they will find us immediately, and Zreyas won't be of any help if I don't get him aid."

27 Janquar-Fearing

Rhom

Safely in Tulyata's realm, with a smiling Rtu and a discerning Prime Visage of balance looking at him, Rhom sighed in relief. "Whew, that was close."

Both visages slid their gazes down to Zreyas in Rhom's hands.

"Woo, he shrunk! I think that is the best size for a Janquar, ever!" Rtu smacked his hands together, then rubbed them with excitement.

Tulyata looked interested, but went back to her calculations and balances, glancing up from time to time to study Zreyas.

It must be a bright spot in their existence to have so many new and unusual things going on, Rhom guessed. It made sense, after all.

"Put him here," Rtu commanded, pointing toward a

table near the wall.

Rhom carried Zreyas over and laid him down.

Rtu almost pushed him aside to get a closer look at him lying there.

He backed up and asked, "Do you have any idea why he is tiny?"

Rtu scrunched his face up in contemplation as he looked at Zreyas. "This is odd... I can understand why his body is smaller, but I'm surprised his armor is also small. He was just starting to learn about quantum from you."

"I should have watched closer. However, if I were to assume he did it, he would have been at a very high frequency when he used the quantum. I have to admit, it was amazing to witness him popping through that fracture."

Scratching his head over his right ear, he considered. "Aaru and Ayya were tiny, but almost dead... It's like the fracture sapped the life force out of them. But Aaru confirmed in a nod that something tried to hurt Ayya. Were they not so vibrant, I am not sure they would have been so lucky. Although, I think if Ayya had not been so vulnerable with the unfinished ceremony and part of her being ripped apart before she entered, things might have been different. Had it not been for Aaru, she would have died."

"You have the right of it, dear broth—uh, Rhom." Rtu examined Zreyas while he continued. "If we look at it on the surface, it seems like the first one through the fractures into the dimension are sapped of energy to the point there is nothing left. But she was attacked, and you did say that the Dark One was in that structure you were in. And I think that was who tried to attack them."

"You have a point. If Zreyas was using quantum, it

would account for his armor size. We can't assume that just because he was just learning, that he couldn't use it at a high level under pressure. After all, he spent approximately ten hours converting energy for me as practice."

Rtu scratched his freckled cheek. "What was he doing when he went through? I was not watching, we were too busy being Visages, hoping you would find the bread crumbs, not following Zreyas."

"When he left, I told him I would help him with quantum work if he ran into trouble. But it turns out, he figured out how to quantum leap on his own. He did it in a unique way I never really thought about before, using his unusual anatomy. It was fascinating to watch. As he got to the fracture, it was too small to walk into. He dove and did a quantum-leap at the same time and hit the target spot on. It was small, and the fracture closed less than a second after his... small feet went in. Oh my, he—"

Rtu raised a finger. "Shrunk himself! It makes sense that his armor would shrink with him because it was in the quantum more than in the dimension he was jumping from, just like his body. Ha! Simple, really, but not so much when you don't obtain all the details. I love discovering things I didn't know!" Rtu broke out into a full bellied laugh that seemed to rumble the entire area.

"Really Rtu, seriously... I'm busy here with the balances," Tulyata said, irritated.

Rtu paid her no mind and seemed to laugh harder. After a few minutes, he evened out into his normal happy-go-lucky attitude and looked at Zreyas again. "His armor is beginning to corrode. Where did you find him?"

"Inland near the shore. I wonder if he landed in the water. That must have been interesting."

Look at this... He's got a rope. Did he have that before?"

Rhom propped his elbow up on his fist against his torso and put a finger to his chin. "Not that I can remember. No..." He dropped his hand down to his side in realization. "In fact, I *know* he didn't!"

Rtu unwrapped the rope slightly and cut a piece off, then waved a hand over the top of it and enlarged it. "Bugger me batty! The boy made a rope out of fur! But this fur is not from a dead body, or I would feel the death on him *and* the rope. Color me in bright colors of impressed!"

"Seriously? What else can you find?" Rhom felt a growing concern rise up inside him. "Shouldn't he be awake by now?"

"He'll wake up. I have prolonged his sleep for two reasons. He needs it to replenish himself, and he is easier to examine and poke without him being awake. Janquar are not known for being pussycats. I'm quite literally afraid of them."

Rhom laughed. "Well, judging by that crowd before he went through the fracture, I would have to agree with you. But I will have to say, Zreyas and Aaru are not your typical Janquar."

Rtu magnified the air around Zreyas with his hand. "All the more reason to be afraid. The boy did a quantum leap and survived the fracture." Rtu lifted part of his armor. "He still has the tryst!"

"That must be how he found me! I didn't see him, but he must have seen me, or at least going toward me."

One of the light warriors made a silent gesture of height to Rhom.

Rhom's memory lit up. "That's right! Thank you! We were in a plains area with the grass quite tall for Zreyas.

He might not have seen us either, which is why he ran into my foot, and also why I never saw him coming," said Rhom, fascinated.

"Interesting... He has a skin of water and a piece of meat in his pocket! He killed this one. Resourceful..."

Rtu's hands were so huge compared to Zreyas that Rhom couldn't help but be amused watching him work on the boy. He wondered how he was able to do it.

"I've just traced the energy signatures still around him and looked into his past. It seems he had run into a kuravy, garavu, a shinit family, a lutari, and an aramzu! Being small, that must have been something to experience! I like this guy! He is one with nature." Rtu turned and put a hand on his heart, looking all teary-eyed. "He has made my varSa the happiest one in a long time."

Tulyata rolled her eyes, putting on a pair of half glasses, only to look over them. "It doesn't take much to do that." She rolled her eyes and shook her head. She then took the glasses off and put them down.

"You will never have an appreciation of my domain, dear mother, more the pity," Rtu said defiantly.

Rhom looked down at the peaceful Zreyas sleeping. "If he wasn't so ferocious, he would be a cute pet." Rhom slapped his own face. "What has gotten into me? What a horrible thing to think!"

"Don't feel bad," Tulyata said. "Rtu says the same thing sometimes. Surprised he hasn't yet."

Rtu looked at Rhom and started waggling a finger at him. "You are a man after my own heart! What's life without a pet here and there to cuddle with!"

Rhom felt the light in his face dim slightly, not sure whether to be happy about that or not, then he attempted a distraction. "So now what do we do? Do we have to leave him that size, or can we make him normal size again? Well, normal for him... which is rather large."

Rtu looked leery as he studied the tiny Janquar, but then seemed to do some calculations, "Hefty cost it would be to do that." His hesitation about the little version of a Janquar showed again. "He might actually be useful small, if you think about it."

Rhom got tickled at how afraid he was of Zreyas and did his best not to chuckle. "Oh, I don't know. How can he protect Ayya like that?"

"As resourceful as he is? He might just surprise us. Let me think and do some balance checking."

Rtu closed his eyes and held on to his two staffs.

Rhom took the chance to look at the staffs in Rtu's grasp. One seemed to have the element of earth, and the other, air. He also noticed no others around the room.

Rhom considered. *He's the visage of elements and natural balance... but why not the other 3 elements? He did say he had a little of the others when his brother was not around. I'm assuming his brother has the other three. There must be a reason the split is uneven.* Rhom scratched his head over his right ear again, and he decided that he should take the time to replenish himself too, while Rtu and Tulyata were busy. Rhom closed his eyes and slipped into a deep meditation and recovery session.

Rtu's good natured voice happily filled the entire room with a resounding, "Wake up, slacker! It's time to play! We need to figure out what to do now that I have done all the checking and balancing!"

Rhom woke from his sleeping meditation a little rattled. He rubbed his face and stroked his wilted horns. "So, what is your plan?"

"Well, all I did was do the checks and balances. I can

give you options, but you have to do all the work and make the choices... as well as him," Rtu said, pointing at the sleeping Zreyas.

Rhom instantly became overwhelmed. "How am I going to be able to do much here in a realm I have no control over? You give me way too much credit. I'm at a loss. I'm actually a bit frustrated. It's like I should know, but I don't. I feel helpless. So please lay it out for me as simply as you can. I'm used to working from my little hidden realm in the sky, trying to get a very unhappy Ayya to see she is not as confined and fixed in destiny as much as she thought she was. She got her wish though; she is now in a body where she doesn't have to be fixed and destined to an exact science. I am sorry she got her wish *this* way, though."

The larger-than-life visage looked at Rhom with sincere empathy in his face, but said nothing.

Rhom finally noticed it and was surprised that a visage would take the time to be... empathetic. "I've never felt so helpless or felt like I had no resources to research what might be there to do, or even how to get to Ayya to help wake her up. I've doomed her to be in that body, totally not ready for that race's design. She will still have her own essence, not for her current world, but for another she is no longer part of. She will not understand their ways, even if she grows up in their world. Ayya doesn't have the same frequencies. She—"

"Shh. It will be okay, Rhom. Do you want a hug?" Rtu held his arm out wide. "Come 'ere and give me a hug!" The large visage reached over, scooped Rhom up, and hugged him like a rag doll. After a few seconds, he put him back down. "Now doesn't that feel better?"

Trying to pull himself together again, Rhom softly chuckled. "Thank you, Rtu, of course I do. Who wouldn't feel better if the visage of nature hugged the... uh... hugged him really tight with so much love?"

Laughing heartily, Rtu patted him on the back, knocking him forward. He reached over quickly and straightened him up. "I apologize. Sometimes I don't know my own strength."

Rhom nodded and chuckled, "Ah, the love of a visage." He grinned, and then he thought it safer to sit down. "I'm supposed to protect her and guide her Rtu... how am I going to do that now? I spent my whole life preparing for this, and my life is no small span of time!"

Rtu sighed. "If you only knew the half of it."

Tulyata jerked her head toward Rtu and gave him a pointed glare.

28 Waking Up

ꙮꙮꙮ Rhom ꙮꙮꙮ

"Hmm?" Rhom was a little confused about Tulyata's look. Rtu's comment seemed straightforward enough.

"Nothing, I just understand," said Tulyata. "I see why you might be a little overwhelmed—well... a lot overwhelmed. Just how much are your warriors willing to help?"

All the light warriors immediately stepped forward, silent and sure.

"I guess you don't have to ask. They are as dedicated to her as I am," said Rhom.

Rtu turned. "How much do you think Zreyas is a player in this game of balance, Tulyata?"

She looked up from her scales and smiled uncharacteristically. "I've already been going over that. I would surpass important and say quite critical, though much is fuzzy and not written yet because of choices he has not yet made. He writes his own destiny, not us. Wake him up."

"If you are willing to take the risk of him going on a rampage, sure," Rtu said nervously.

"I'll hold him and wake him. He knows me, and I'll take the risk. Zreyas is quite an amazing man, honestly." Rhom stood and moved over to Zreyas.

"Let me put him in a cage," offered Rtu apprehensively, looking at Zreyas.

"Please don't. That would not be good because no one likes a lack of freedom and trust. It would just antagonize him. In addition, if he is a critical player in this whole thing, it needs to start with trust." Rhom picked him up gently and sat down with his back to the wall so Zreyas faced away from the nervous Rtu. "Okay, I'm ready."

Rtu, tentative in motion, waved a hand across his body.

Zreyas' eyes fluttered, and his body spasmed slightly due to his wilder nature.

The visage backed up to the other side of the room, where the light warriors were.

Tulyata looked at him and rolled her eyes. "You make us look very bad, Rtukaiah."

Rhom focused solely on Zreyas and smiled at the sleeping Janquar in the hope that he would know things were okay. "Zreyas... this is Rhom," he said in a soft voice. "Don't be alarmed, I am with you, and you are safe. I made it out of the dying dimension, too."

Drowsily sitting up in Rhom's hands, Zreyas rubbed his head.

"You will probably have a pretty colossal headache with as hard as you hit my foot, but you are okay, no permanent damage." Rhom gave him a few seconds, then gently added, "But things will seem a little different. Just don't freak out before you talk with me. It's a hell of a thing to wake up to."

Zreyas moaned slightly. "Mmm, okay." He rubbed his face before opening his eyes. He blinked several times. At first, he looked at Rhom's chest, and then Zreyas looked up where the voice was coming from and saw his face. "Hey, old man! I thought it would be a while bef—"

Suddenly, he jerked in surprise and crab-crawled backward, quick as lightning, too fast for Rhom to catch him before flying off his hands and onto the floor, rolling backward. He stood quickly and drew his weapons.

Rtu ran into Rhom's room and hid, though not very well, behind the doorway. "Told you!"

Ignoring Rtu and focusing on Zreyas, Rhom persisted in trying to calm him down. "It's really me, my boy. You just shrunk when you went into that portal."

Zreyas whirled around, hearing the loud, strange voice coming from behind him.

Rhom could tell that what he had said still didn't get to the part of his mind that could comprehend more than one or two words at a time.

Already in a full war aura, Zreyas said, "Ticking hell! What have you done, Rhom!"

Rhom jerked his head back at Zreyas' new voice.

Rtu must have been as shocked as he was because he started laughing from behind the doorway he was standing behind.

Rhom could tell Zreyas was still disoriented because he asked him why he was laughing, not Rtu. The more he tried to console him, the angrier and squeakier he got.

Rtu totally lost it and went into a booming fit of laughter that startled Zreyas.

Rhom quickly said, "Don't hurt him, Zreyas. He's one of the visages of natural elements. I wouldn't suggest it. Please calm down, my boy!" Then he thought to add, "... for Aaru's sake."

That did it. Zreyas froze and turned toward him, looking at Rhom's foot right in front of him. "I remember now. I ran into your foot right after I did a leap."

Rhom breathed out a sigh of relief.

"That explains the other animals I ran into. I thought I landed on a world of giants. Even the ocean foam was large to me." Zreyas walked up to Rhom. "You found me, though I am not sure what kind of help I will be in this condition." Zreyas sheathed his weapons while he still scanned his surroundings.

"It seems like that part is up to you. By the way..." Holding his hand toward the visage of balance to his right, "This is Prime Visage Tulyata." Then he pointed toward the doorway. "And this is Rtu, a visage of natural elements. His elements are primarily earth and air."

Coming from around the doorway, back to his bright calmer personality, Rtu said, "It's good to know you are awake, and not hostile! You are entertaining when you are small."

Rhom, Zreyas, and Tulyata stared at Rtu.

Tulyata said dryly, "Don't mind him. He never grew out of childish behavior. It is nice to meet you."

"It's... okay to meet you," Zreyas said.

Rhom could tell he was trying to follow the unfamiliar etiquette, shown and new to him.

Zreyas turned to face Rhom. "How... how did you find them? I thought you were..."

"Dead? I should have been. I didn't have to use my remaining strength to help you because you figured out how to do your own version of a quantum leap. You were fast enough on your own. It quite impressed me, my boy! All I needed to do was delay some weapons here and there. The rest was all you."

"I wondered what happened with all that! I thought I was going to have to fight on the run. My promise to you and Aaru kept me going."

"After that, I found two tiles that had symbols on them. I picked the right one to touch, and these two came to help just as a band of your people came."

"They are no longer my people," Zreyas barked bitterly.

Rtu said happily, "Yes, we saved his bacon, as they say in some dimensions, especially the one that your Ayya is in now. And before you ask, we have recently seen her in her tiny state as a human. Would you like to see her?"

Hearing this, Zreyas' face, still wild in nature, not yet tamed, said, "Yes! Now!"

Rtu jumped, Tulyata raised an eyebrow, and Rhom chuckled.

Rhom could tell that Rtu's jump humored Tulyata, paused only enough to decide to let it go, waved a hand, and a screen appeared. Ayya was less than two varSas old now, walking up to a rope hanging from a tree with a rubber tire on the end. Zreyas cocked his head, trying to see better.

Rhom picked him up to give him a better view and watched Zreyas' perplexed face, grinning.

Ayya was wearing little red tennis shoes with white toes and a flower-patterned dress. She climbed up on the black tire. Her dress got caught by her knee and it hindered her climb. Her face became red with rage.

Zreyas lifted his eyebrows, and Rhom couldn't help but grin.

She hopped down and took her dress off. She now had no shirt, but wearing underwear and shoes. Ayya climbed back into the rubber tire and started swinging and climbing to the top of the black ring, awkwardly hanging on to the rope.

"Yeah! Look at Ayya and Aaru working together!" yelled Zreyas. "It is female, yes?"

"Yes, my boy. Females are 'she,' like males are 'he,'" instructed Rhom.

Her mother came running out of the house with a very upset look on her face. Zreyas pulled a weapon in response.

"Whoa there! Watch her, you cannot go there," Rhom said.

Zreyas seemed to calm down and watched as he sheathed his weapon.

Ayya's mother picked up the dress and shook it out. "Well, at least you didn't rip this one up this time." The woman looked as if she was at her wit's end and sighed. "Ayya, what am I going to do with you?"

"Pway wit me, Momma! That's what you do wif me! Pway wif me, Momma!"

Ayya's mother laughed at her and began pushing the tire swing. Zreyas again jerked protectively before catching himself. Ayya began squealing in laughter. She turned her face to what seemed like the four of them watching through the screen, as if she noticed them for a moment before squealing again in delight.

Tulyata turned off the screen and made it go away. "From what I can gather, Ayya's mother's name is Lanna. But it is odd. I can't find out what they call her father, probably due to the influence of the Dark One."

Rtu faced Zreyas and quickly said to redirect the conversation. "See, she is okay and doing well at ripping off her clothing."

"They are really okay! Aaru always hated clothing too, at least until he found that weird armor when he was young," Zreyas reminisced.

"And Ayya never wore clothing in her life. We tried to get her to wear her ceremonial robe once, and she wouldn't have anything to do with it. Good match those two," Rhom said, chuckling. A sudden overwhelming gut feeling came over him to ask Zreyas, "Wait, what weird armor?"

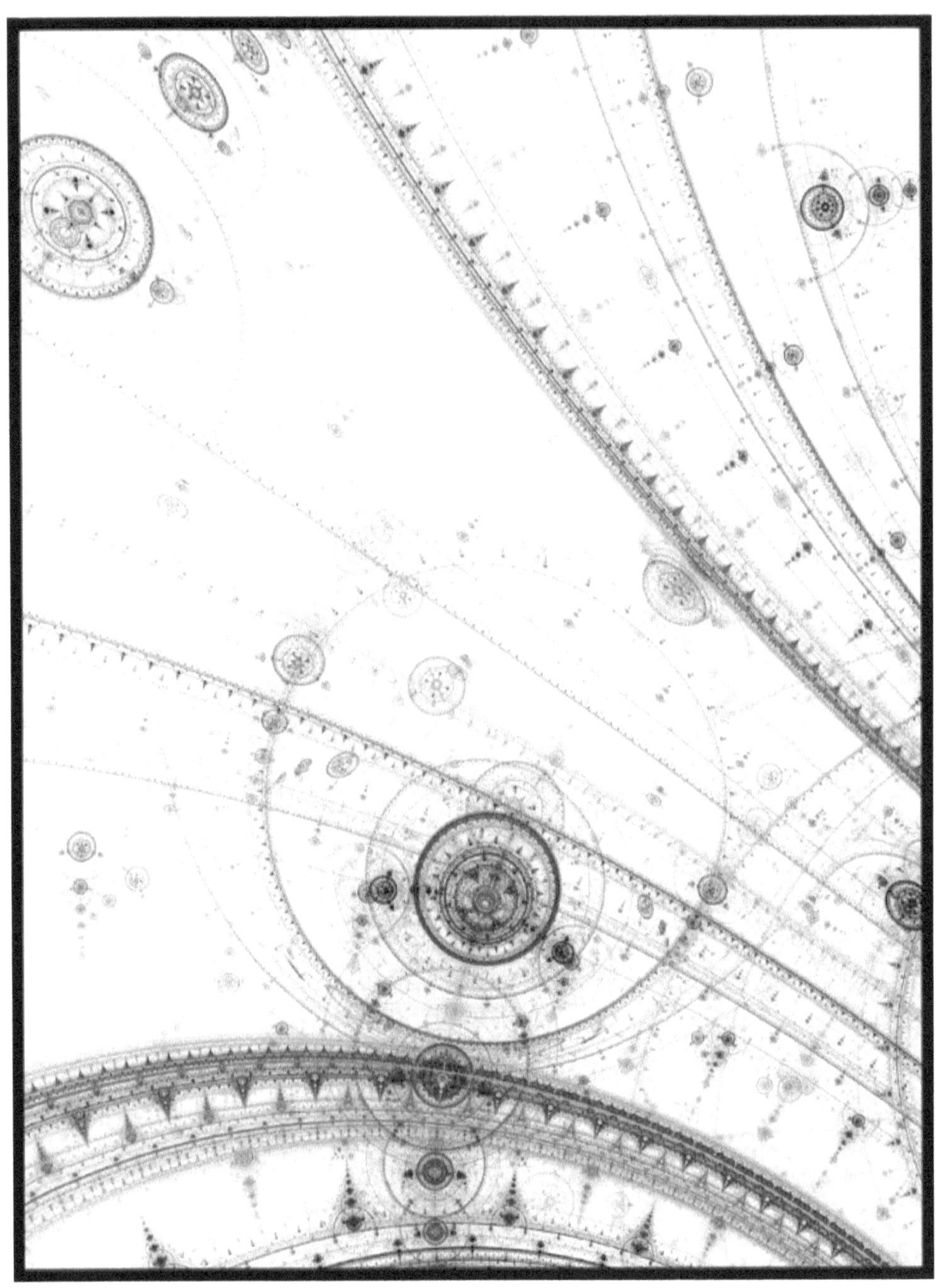

29 Armor

Zreyas

Zreyas scratched his cheek. “Remember when I told you about his first fight at the trader?”

“Yes, I do,” said Rhom.

“Oh, this will be fun to hear from your perspective. This is a significant event for both you and Aaru.” said Rtu.

Zreyas stalled and hung his jaw slightly, wondering what the ticking-hell he was talking about and who the hell this piece of mag-shit was.

“My boy, I would like to hear about this.”

Facing the old man again, Zreyas said, “While he plundered, he found this odd set of armor, unlike anything I had ever seen before. None of the Rittak line knew the style or where it might have come from. He found the helmet first. It had thin, stylized horns on it.

They stuck straight up, and the helmet had a flared bottom in the back, made for allowing motion, but it still protected the neck from behind. He put it on and never took it off. He turned around after putting it on and had this look on his face like you do sometimes with your mouth bent upward."

Rtu sat down and lifted a finger. "And that is where knowing his perspective would give you something extra special, Zreyas."

He looked at the visage, irritated at this ticking piece of mag-shit that kept interfering. "Would you shut the ticking hell up? Who are you and why would I listen to you?"

Rtu pulled his head back and looked incredibly uncomfortable. Zreyas grunted in satisfaction. The other Visage raised an eyebrow and put a pair of glasses on, looking down at him, completely looking over the glasses themselves.

Rhom held a hand out toward him and said, "It's called a smile. So, he turned around with a smiling face. Unusual for Janquar."

Zreyas nodded and turned back toward the old man again and pushed his mouth corners upward with his fingers for a moment, then let go with a shrug. "He found the matching armor, made with hand woven linked metal and pieces of wood. There were many pieces to be tied on with leather strings, each layering on top of others for protection and mobility. It looked so odd, but extremely intimidating."

Rhom looked as if he was trying to figure it out by the description. "I'm not well versed in armor styles and their cultural origins."

"It was an armor from an ancient human culture way before the time Ayya is living now," added Rtu. "I know my creations and their histories."

"Oh, that is fascinating," said Rhom.

Not knowing what Rtu meant by knowing his creations, he continued anyway. "Here is the interesting part; there were *many* pieces, but he put it all on like he knew the armor! He never hesitated. The boots were not normal closed boots, it was only a sole with strings that he threaded between toes and around the side of the foot."

"They were sandals," said Rtu

"What are these sandals?"

Tulyata answered, "They are a type of open-toed shoe used by many ancient races and cultures."

Zreyas nodded. "That is what these were, then. I always knew he was coming, unless he was being stealthy, because they made a sound, *flip... flop... flip... flop*. I finally helped him to put something on them to stabilize them so he wouldn't make noise. It annoyed the rest of the line. They liked nothing that didn't sound like a stomping foot. He didn't want to alter them, but I wanted nothing to set him apart anymore. When I told him why and that it was for his protection, he looked at my face, cocked his head, and agreed. He said it was for my sake he allowed it. When we got back that day, crowds greeted and cheered us, including our father. They took much pride in him and treated him like the prodigy he was. But, they had high expectations."

"Sounds like things improved," Rhom said.

Zreyas sighed and shook his head. "Not for long. After that day, he never did it again, no matter what we told him. If it came from the commanders, it was never a good reason. Though his horns grew, they never emerged. Until he outgrew that armor, no one ever knew. When the helmet finally split, everyone saw his lack of festering. That was when all the trouble started again."

Zreyas shifted his weight and rubbed the back of his neck under his horns.

Rtu smiled, then said, "Finish your story. There is more to tell that will play a part in your development."

Anger surged up through Zreyas' gut and his compartment filled. "Are you my commander? Hell ticking-no! Stop giving me orders!"

Tulyata looked over her glasses at him again. Something about that visage made him stall his words.

Rtu sat back quick. His face full of apprehension and he held his hands up in a warding gesture. He squeaked out a word, "Peace."

Rhom interjected, "My boy, he was giving instruction for your benefit. He wasn't trying to dominate you. Remember, you are no longer in the Janquar Nation."

Zreyas grunted and looked at Rtu and nodded. "When he was alone, he would do the most amazing fighting techniques. The anger fueling his abilities beyond anything any of us could have ever done, at least nothing I saw in my lifetime. He created new techniques I had never seen before and he moved like lightning."

"Remarkable..." Rhom muttered.

"Then there was the other extreme thing he would do alone. Just sit, for hours. He would sometimes look around, but mostly, he just looked straight ahead. I felt no waves of his war energy, no aura of communication, no... nothing. Well, at least anything I was familiar with that I could put a name to. But I did feel something almost undetectable, and breathing was easier for me near him. I would sneak away from my duties, sit down, and watch him. He didn't seem to mind. Aaru thought it was because I was there to help teach him, but it was not for that reason. He fascinated me, and I wanted to learn from him and watch what he would do next."

"The 'nothing' that made you breathe better being around it is called peace," Rhom said gently. "It sounds like your brother was a much higher being than your culture thought."

"What do you mean?"

"You said it yourself. He never found a reason for war... or his purpose. He is not designed for mindless war, or at least not war for the reasons that your people gave him. You said he is very instinctive. That denotes that he is also intuitive, like you, I might add." Rhom scratched his head just above his ear.

Rtu leaned forward and added, "To him, something that didn't feel right within him wasn't a good reason to go to war or fight for. Everyone has it, it's just a matter of if we listen to it or not."

Rhom nodded. "It sounds like Aaru listened to his inner authority and took his inner guidance seriously. Most ignore it to fit in with others. Your species is not the only one to fall into that trap. Members of mine have times like that. I've done my share of ignoring it in the past, too. Different cultures and environments, however, make it easier or harder to do."

"Humans, like the species that Ayya is now, fall into that trap easily too," said Rtu.

Zreyas felt excited to hear things that made sense for a change, yet it still overwhelmed him he could have been so ignorant to not catch on. He felt a little uncomfortable with this subject, so he shifted to his next question. "Hu-man, you say?" Zreyas looked at Rhom. "Do we know much about them?"

"Oh, he gets right down to business. Not that we can tell you," replied Tulyata, taking off her glasses.

"Always keeping the balance, that one," Rtu said, chuckling and pointing at Tulyata. "And I am, too, just in another realm of things. We all play our parts in the game of balance... even you, Zreyas."

Growing suspicious, Zreyas gestured to his own body, "Me? How will I do anything like... *this*?"

Rhom smiled. "Sometimes we have to adjust our view on our strengths, tactics, and way of thinking in whatever situation we might be in. You, of all people, should know that, my boy! It is always changing. It is just changing a little more extreme in your case at this time."

Zreyas reached down to look for his food he had put into his pouch and found it missing. "How can I get back? I need to hunt for food."

Rtu cheerfully said, "I can help with giving you some food."

Rhom smiled at him and asked, "While you eat something, would you like to tell us what happened to you when you went through the fracture?"

"Food? I'm starved! Yes! Food! I will tell you what happened, but you might not believe me."

Rtu said, "You might be surprised. I saw the energy signatures in your aura and your rope of fur. How did your armor corrode so fast? Did you land in the water?"

"Let him tell the story, Rtu," Tulyata said, irritated, "And you might not have so many questions." She sat up straighter and stared at him, daring him to say anything else.

Rtu shut up, conjured up food out of thin air and gave Zreyas a plate full.

Zreyas took the food quickly, and Rtu jerked his hand back defensively. He sat down and crossed his legs and laid the food on his legs. He ate and told his story between bites. Zreyas told them all about how he didn't land in the water, but ended up in it anyway, and every detail he could remember from the time he landed till he ran into Rhom's foot while he shoved food in his mouth.

Rhom

Rhom said, "Interesting, my boy. And by the way, the female didn't have an infection."

Zreyas stopped eating and looked up at him with a questioning expression.

"She was trying to feed you. It was milk. It's the way they feed their young."

"Ticking hell, no wonder she kept licking it. I never saw that kind of thing before, and I never had this... milk before."

Rhom grinned admiringly at how he wasn't embarrassed at all. It was a freedom many never experienced. He didn't care what others thought, because he knew who he was and accepted it, so there was no need to be ashamed. He chose natural self-empowerment, rather than fear of the thoughts or judgments of others.

He looked at the two visages and asked. "You have helped us all so much already; but I must ask, is it possible to restore Zreyas to his former state if we were to leave now?" gesturing to Zreyas. "How will we know where she is and what we can do to spread those prompts for her to awaken?"

"What do you mean, awaken her? What is wrong? You are even more serious now than you were in that dying dimension."

"The little ferret doesn't miss much, I'll give him that," Tulyata said with an impressed expression, holding her lips tight together and nodding.

They explained to Zreyas all they had discovered. To Rhom, it seemed to alarm him.

"I knew about the Dark One, at least some, but I didn't think he could get to her world so fast!" Zreyas stood up and paced, gripping the hilts of his weapons, but leaving them in their sheathes.

Rhom noticed his war aura flare, but didn't say a word. He had gotten to know him and knew when he was ready to pull them and when he was just simmering in the anger.

Rtu said with a thoughtful expression, "We can't change his size now. Some things need to happen before that is even possible with balances at the moment."

"That doesn't sound very promising, Rtu," Tulyata said.

"No, it doesn't," added Rhom. "There have to be more options or a better way of thinking about it. You are so used to being visages you don't have the—"

Abruptly, Rhom froze.

30 Light-blue

ꟾꟾꟾ Zreyas ꟾꟾꟾ

Zreyas and the two visages were gawking at Rhom's frozen body.

Tulyata broke the silence. "It was just a matter of time." She watched her scales for a moment. "With the release of the Dark One, Rhom's spirit is being called forth. He will be upset because he loved his life, but at least the balance will even out."

Zreyas stood there stunned, not understanding anything going on at the moment. "What did you do to him? Is he dying?" he said, incredulous. He freaked out internally and let the rage come. "I have lost everyone in my life, including my own body, and now him?"

Rtu did a warding gesture, then held a hand out to quiet him for explanation's sake, looking a little nervous. "Rhom is really my other half... my twin. You notice I am the visage of natural elements, but I hold mostly only earth and air elements with a small part of water, fire, and the fifth element... aether. My brother, on the other hand, is the visage of elemental balance, but of the elements of fire, water, and aether with a little earth and air to do him when I'm not around."

Zreyas' mood darkened. But Tulyata nodded to confirm Rtu's words.

Rtu continued. "He made the ultimate sacrifice and incarnated as a Viduri, to balance things out when the Dark One was banished. He wanted to make sure that Ayya was okay when she came as a living leader and protector of her people. An incarnation of a Tantra is rare and only comes in extreme need."

"Very extreme, which has me worried," said Tulyata. Rhom is in a... state right now just before emerging."

Zreyas' confusion caused him to grow restless and his body twitched, trying to keep calm.

Rtu leaned forward, looking straight at him. "He all but perished in that dimension, getting Ayya to the body she is in now. The only thing keeping him going was making sure you made it through the fracture. He thought you might just be Ayya's only hope to survive, even though he didn't know how you could help yet." Rtu leaned back again with a serious face.

"He doesn't remember his decision to incarnate, though, in that body. By the time he came through the fracture to us, there was too little of his incarnation energy left. We had to bring his chamber here to give him a little energy until he was ready to transition. When you got here and he knew you were safe, that was enough to trigger it," Tulyata said with a distant look.

"He is about ready to become my other half again now that he is in my presence. It's too much to resist.

Since he came here, he has been awakening quickly," Rtu said.

Tulyata frantically worked with the moving shapes in the scales, causing it to tip back and forth both erratically. "We need him back for balance," she said with a seriousness that was shocking to Zreyas. "I need to show you something. We have a rare opportunity to see things we shouldn't, only because the other side is seeing this too. And this scares the light out of me."

Rtu leaned forward again, looking at Rhom with a serious expression. "But something isn't right about him. It's like he isn't all here, suddenly."

"The good news first, or the bad?"

Rtu and Zreyas looked at each other, shrugging. Then both said in unison, "The bad first."

Tulyata put on her half glasses and looked over them, not through them, then took them off again. Zreyas wondered why she put them on to begin with.

"You two aren't right, way too much synchronization."

Rtu laughed hard, bouncing all over, rolling around in his seat, and bending over. Zreyas cocked his head and mouthed the word, "Ha."

"Pipe down, we've got serious issues. Look at this." She waved a hand over her scales, which were now balanced. "First, the bad news." She looked at a dark pattern on the screen with a background of open nothingness. The screen seemed to jump to different scenes that showed waves of black vibration. "I'm tracing this now to its origin, the old-fashioned way. It's the only way to keep the balance, so the process actually takes time."

Zreyas wasn't used to technology like this and wasn't sure what he was seeing. On the screen, they watched the black waves of energy and waited. Everyone in the room seemed to hold their breath. Zreyas noticed even Rtu was not smiling, and that made him a little nervous.

Finally, they saw Tulyata point to a small galaxy, partially exposed and half missing. Tulyata somehow controlled the screen view, and it zoomed in quickly. There were ruins around a fracture that seemed to be remnants of a strongly built fortress.

"There is the Dark One, still bound to his prison pedestal chamber. His upper half seems unbound," Tulyata narrated.

His face looked exactly like Aaru had described. It had red eyes and a haunting open mouth that black vibrations emanated from in all directions.

"Oh no," said Zreyas, "I hope this isn't what I think it is."

"Do tell, because to keep balance, I can't tell you. The information has to come from you. You must inform; besides, you are designed to manifest just like your brother."

Zreyas' questions started popping up in his head, but he was too zoned into what he was seeing to let himself get distracted. "Is there sound to this?"

"If I were to emulate the waves in space to sound... Yes, I can."

Interrupting, due to sudden recognition, Zreyas said, "That is our galaxy! That ruined part is, or was, the Tempest Tower, the place we were when the fracture to the light people showed up." Zreyas gawked at how his entire planet was just floating in pieces there. "No wonder there were so many Janquar on that planet you picked me up from. They all left when that happened. There must have been another fracture there other than what I went through."

"There was," Tulyata chimed in. "Go on."

"If this is what I think it is, then this is a bad omen. I was just going through commander training and learned about it. It is only something that the emperor knows how to do; I mean, our real emperor, not that thing. I don't know much, but here is what I know..."

"Here, pull up a chair and get comfortable. I think we will be here discussing things for a while." Tulyata waved a hand, created a chair small enough for Zreyas on her desk near the screen, and gestured toward it.

Zreyas looked up at her incredulously, wondering how he would get up there without help. Then he looked at Rtu.

Rtu had a mocking expression on his face. "Didn't you just learn how to do some quantum leaping? Try a q-leap, but silently this time, like you are infiltrating some place in one of your hunts. Take it to the next level while you are at it."

"That is kind of hard to do without the commander's war cry. It was easy in the dying dimension because they were constantly doing them there."

"Sounds like a closed mind to me. What do you say, Tulyata?"

"Wimpy closed mind," Tulyata prodded.

Not getting the game they were playing, Zreyas immediately turned angry like a flare in a second. He focused on the chair. Then a realization passed through him at how he might do it. With determination, he concentrated. A soft crack of energy sounded, gently reverberating through the room. Zreyas disappeared and reappeared at the same instant, right in the chair's space, knocking it over and off the table.

"The aim will get better with practice," Tulyata encouraged as she manifested the chair back where it was supposed to be, and then she gestured at it. “Not bad for a little ferret.”

Zreyas looked at her, feeling manipulated and angry.

“When you decide to go back into peace mode again, we will continue. Until then, steam all you like. But you just learned something about some of your potential by being prodded like a herd animal. You should thank us.”

She looked to Rtu. “Why is it that people ask for help from the visages, and then when they are given the tension situation they need in order to get it, they feel like they are being tortured, manipulated, deserted, or think we must not exist at all? But they asked for it to begin with!”

“Well, you aren’t any dif—”

“Shut up, Rtu.”

Zreyas let out the first laugh of his life. “Ha!”

“Watch it, little ferret. Unless you want to find yourself rolling on the floor without a chair.”

Rtu started laughing hard. “You got her number, Zreyas!”

Zreyas looked at Rtu, feeling the laugh but not sure how to express it like him. “Ha!”

Tulyata couldn’t help but half grin, then caught herself. “Would you like to tell us what you know now while we are still breathing?”

“Well, it’s called the Dark Song, and only the emperor knows it. When he trains a successor, he teaches them about the specifics of it just before he fights them in mortal combat. If the Emperor kills the challenger, then the secret is safe and so is the song. If the rising leader kills the emperor, he takes his place, and the song is still safe with the new leader. When they do all this, they are in a sealed place that they can neither escape from nor use the song itself when the combat starts.” Zreyas took a deep breath and let it out.

"Go on… uh… please, could you continue?" Rtu said with pure curiosity.

Zreyas wondered why he acted like he didn't know any of this. He shrugged. "As legend supposedly dictates, when the emperor sings this song, it devastates the area and anyone within a specific distance. But, this song also a call for all ancestors to come to the call and rejoin the ancient legion for a conquest for the history books."

Zreyas looked at each of them, then continued. "Everyone attuned to that sound is compelled to come join, and they will do anything they can to get to where they are being called to. But I'm not sure that is right because look at that place. How is anyone going to get there other than on a ship? Where would they stand? Why is he making the call if that is indeed what he is doing because he is not the emperor? I don't see our flesh and blood emperor. Is he dead? If so, they wouldn't have something to go to because, from what I understand, it has to be an incarnated soul that leads the people. That is all I know."

"Well, bugger me britches!" Rtu breathed out. "You bring up a good point. Did you happen to see if the emperor was with all your people on that planet you were on?"

Zreyas thought for a moment, then shook his head. "No, but I was concentrating more on getting away from them, not infiltrating them. But if he is there now, then that is where they will go, because he had the dark song in his heart. How far is that from where the Dark One is?"

"About nine universes away, so pretty far." Tulyata answered.

"How far is that place Ayya is in from the planet I was

on?" Zreyas continued with questions.

"About seven times that distance of the first. But don't let that make you think she is safe. There are fractures everywhere now, plus with technology, they can get there by ship in... let's say twenty to thirty of their varSas without fractures."

"Is there any way I can hear this song without having to succumb to its effects?"

"I can do an analysis on you to see if you would resonate with the frequencies first to get at least a general guess," Rtu offered. "This is more my realm since it has to do with your body frequencies and it is elemental." He waved his earth staff slowly around Zreyas.

"You don't really need that staff, do you?" Zreyas asked with a tone that had a knowing in it more than a question.

"Well, visages like to feel flamboyant every once in a while, just like everyone else. Just let me have my fun, and you can critique how believable it is then." He started laughing.

Zreyas leaned back, unused to laughter.

Rtu finally stopped, and his face contorted slightly. "You don't have the same frequency as your Janquar people. It is close, but It's still not the same. Though you will hear it, I don't think it will affect you. But if it does, I'm not sure I have the balance currency to pull you out. Your skin is much lighter than theirs, too, which indicates the frequency difference for your species. For your information, it doesn't work like that for all species. Some species just have different color skins but are no different in frequencies."

"My skin used to be an almost black navy blue," said Zreyas. He sighed, looking down at his armorless hands.

"In fact, none of the Janquar warriors are the color you are that I can remember," said Rtu.

"There are a few that are. The cooks, workers, and artisans have light-blue skin that were deemed too weak to be warriors."

"Interesting... In fact, your frequency is much higher than even theirs, though. Did you notice if your skin was different, other than the color?" Rtu asked.

Zreyas almost felt on the verge of panic as he pinched his skin, pulled on his horns, and felt his forehead. Finally, he spoke. "My horns have shrunk." He attempted to hide his anguish, but he could tell it revealed itself through the tone of his voice. "And my skin has less armor and thickness. What is happening to me?"

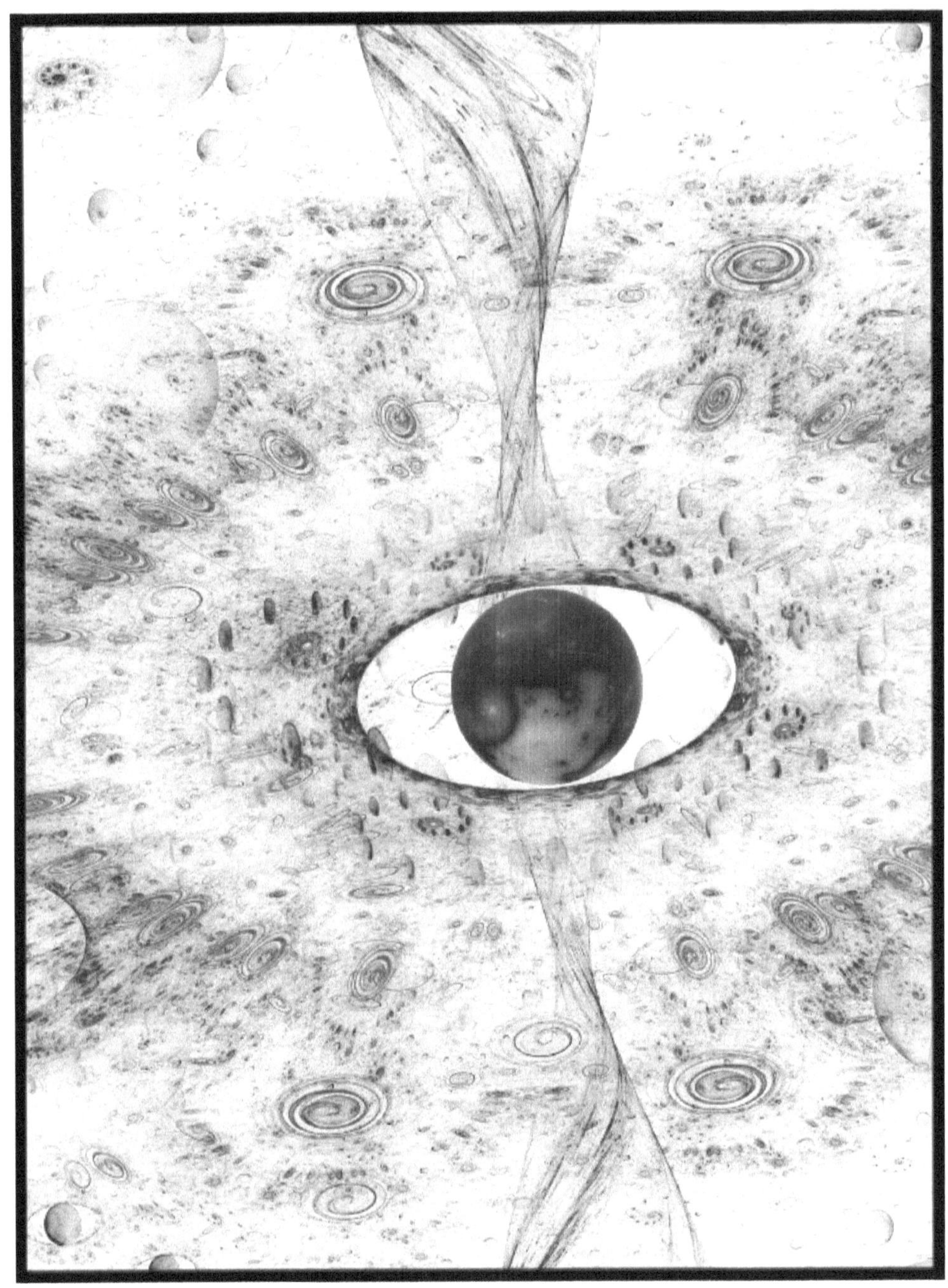

31 The Dark Song

Zreyas

Rtu smiled gently and leaned forward. “It’s not a bad thing. Your body is just changing to adapt to who you are inside. Your frequency has changed, and you are not even the same race anymore in a way. It typically takes many thousands of varSas for species to evolve into another species, but you have almost done it in less than a week.”

Zreyas turned his face toward Rtu’s smile. He couldn’t help it. “Is this what happened to my brother?”

Tulyata put her half glasses on, looked over them at him and leaned on her elbow. “Yes, and no. It is why his skin never turned dark and why his horns didn’t emerge, but it is not why things happened to him going through the fracture.” She took the half glasses back off and put them down.

Zreyas couldn't understand why she never looked *through* the glasses. It almost distracted him. "This is just... weird. How will I be able to protect anyone, much less myself, with the skills of a warrior and this little body?"

"You'll adapt, little buddy, you will adapt! Look what you did to get up onto the table. And look what you did from the time you landed on that planet till you found Rhom! You can change yourself back on your own if you want to. You just need to figure out how." He laughed with a happiness that still shocked Zreyas. "Even as a visage and at your size, I wouldn't want to go up against you if I didn't have to!"

Zreyas chest puffed slightly and his expression evened. "Now I understand what my brother must have felt like... the little secret you can't explain and don't understand. I have decided—I want to try to hear that song to make sure we know what we are dealing with. If I'm not too far gone from being Janquar, at least I will be able to tell you if this is what it is." He looked straight at Tulyata with an unwavering look.

"I hoped you would say that. Here's to science!" She turned the screen so they could see. "Now it's in an atmosphere."

Zreyas heard, and his eyes went wide and distant. It felt like dark overused oil flowing through his ears and into his body. It smelled like it, too. But how could a song have odor? He didn't speak at first, but once he adjusted, he nodded. "I know this is the song. I feel it in my bones and in my breath. I can even smell it. But I can also tell I don't have that compulsion to immediately go find a way there. Something bugs me, though. Did the Dark One used to be a Janquar emperor?"

"Smart little street rat, and the answer is no."

"Then the Janquar emperor taught it to him, so he is either dead or somewhere else, like on that planet. Wait, I feel the direction... You can follow that direction. Maybe we can find out exactly who it is that is holding the focal point." Zreyas suddenly realized he was almost giving orders, "I mean... if you feel like it."

He turned back toward Tulyata, and she had those half glasses on again, looking over them with an expression of 'you're pushing it.'

Zreyas didn't flinch and looked up with a straight face, waiting for a reply. "I might be turning colors and changing but that doesn't mean I have to cower to you... visages."

"I honestly think it is a good idea," said Rtu. "Let's do it. It won't bend balances."

Tulyata looked at Rtu and winked on the side Zreyas supposedly couldn't see, but did. She then looked directly at Zreyas. "Face the way you would want to go if you were compelled, both direction and angle. It's primitive, but effective."

Zreyas turned to the right until he passed the strongest waves, then adjusted left to hone in on the signal.

Tulyata sized up Zreyas' position and connected her navigation to him somehow because the screen in front of her reflected his movements. Then she put things in forward motion.

Rtu waved his staff and made the waves appear as if they were in the room. The entire room disappeared, and it looked like they were there virtually in space, following the waves.

To Zreyas, it no longer seemed like he was in a room at all, but out in space. It was invigorating, because nothing was around him and he felt freedom. There were stars and lots of dark space between them. When he traveled before, he never saw out of the hold. He was always in some metal cargo or passenger hold with wall-to-wall warriors.

Tulyata navigated and Zreyas kept turning toward the signal. Every once in a while, when Tulyata went into a new universe, the direction changed. Sometimes it was drastic, and they both had to adjust.

"A little further, I think," she said as she made another adjustment. "Yep, there the signal stops, on that planet in Proioxis where you were playing with shinits, lutari, and garavu. You can turn back around now. I have the signal target."

The room changed back into its normal state. All three leaned forward to watch as she zoomed in so close they could see the faces of each Janquar. She finally stopped at a very large Janquar with horns. He was so large and horn bound, he couldn't help but wonder how he could even move, much less fight.

"Oh man, that is Emperor Rok Phaar! But look at him." Zreyas pointed to his face. "Look at the inky black mist flowing in and out of his eyes! I've seen him many times, and that's not normal. If Rhom was... awake, he could confirm too."

"This isn't good, not good at all," Tulyata said. "No wonder so much is happening at once. The Dark One possesses the emperor and is acting through him from his own prison."

"He wasn't like this when Aaru went into the chambers and came out. Could it be possible he already did this then?" Zreyas asked as he watched the mist flow in and out of the Emperor's eyes.

"I don't know, to be frank." Tulyata squinted one eye.

Rtu grinned. "You are always frank, Tulyata," he said,

poking fun at her.

"I think it is about time to hear the good news, wouldn't you say?" a voice said, coming from another part of the room.

Everyone turned, and there was a large white watery mist that swirled in a clockwise direction. it had flecks of red flame that showed themselves periodically. Zreyas observed the cyan and white luminescence around it. It looked like churning and flipping water and a flame would drift up from time to time. Zreyas thought it was the most amazing thing he had ever seen. If he stared too close for too long, he felt vertigo.

"Bro! It's about time! But you don't look very... solid. Where is your fire and aether?"

"I have some, but let me get my bearings before getting all technical."

"Welcome back, Rhom. I bet that was a trip and a half you took," Tulyata said with a smirk.

"Yes, I think it was. So... I'm not liking the bad news at all." The watery mist turned more toward Zreyas. "Hello, my boy. You look even smaller now that I've gotten bigger. Thank you for your help, dear friend."

Zreyas was doubtful. "Is that really you, Rhom? And not some other weirdo visage I have to get to know all over again? If it is you, it's good to have you not frozen and useless. Now your... watery and useless!"

Rtu busted out laughing right along with Rhom. "That disrespect will get you everywhere, little buddy!"

Even Tulyata joined in.

Zreyas felt a light feeling in his chest and one single, "Ha!" managed to escape.

After the laughter died down, everyone started to ask in unison what happened to Rhom.

He shook his head. "I just kept a promise is all. We

can talk about it later. Now I want to hear the good news. But first, let me get into a form that is a little more familiar to us all."

Rhom morphed back into the form Zreyas knew, with a little more watery glow on his skin. This made Zreyas sigh in relief. Then he put the robes on that had been laying on the floor.

Rhom walked to the desk beside Zreyas. "We need good news."

"This is almost never possible for balance, but the multiverse seems to think we need to see this. I just hope the Dark One doesn't see it." She gestured at the screen and then said, "I can also take us there so we can be there in her mind."

Tulyata brought up a screen with Ayya playing in the grass in the sunshine with a ball and bucket. Tulyata zoomed in on Ayya's active mind and simulated the scene of Ayya's experience. "I'll translate the conversation to make things easier because she is speaking internally within her mind, and toddler mind talk is annoying."

An essence of Ayya was sitting in the center of her head. It seemed fleshy in nature to Zreyas. She was playing just as vividly in her head as she would externally in the world. It didn't take long to see that she wasn't just playing.

"Dhi, Dhi, I know you are there, Dhi. Gulloo, I know you are there I can feel youuuu. You are happy. Vesana, I can tell you are there cause you are doing things for me! And Master Rhom I know you are there too even though you feel different."

"I wish it were true, little phoenix, I wish it were true," Rhom said. "I'm so sorry I had to break my promise, but Treta will do fine in my stead. I just made my promise in a new way."

The sadness was palpable to Zreyas, but he didn't say a word.

Ayya paused. "I see you too, but I don't know your name. Come out, come out!"

Another essence steamed up through the floor, came over, and sat down with her, bold and confident. Zreyas felt his chest crack inside from the emotions swelling up. His breath caught.

"What's your name?" asked Ayya.

"Aaru, and I'm sorry ahead of time." He betrayed the confidence he had earlier.

"You didn't do anything wrong. Aaru... Aaru... I like that name, and I like you too! Have you met Master Rhom, Dhi, Gulloo, and Vesana yet?"

"No."

"It's okay, they are here to help me."

"Me too. You are my new purpose."

"What are you supposed to do?"

"I don't know. But I can fight good as long as it is for a reason I believe in. I feel good about helping you."

"You helped me once, but can't remember how."

"I don't either, but I remember doing it. What are you doing there?"

"Just playing with my bucket and ball. Momma won't let me bring my favorite toy outside, without her, because it is part of the furniture."

"You are weirder than me. I like you."

"I like me too! And I like you! You can stay here if you want since you don't have a momma."

"How did you know? I have a brother, though. I think he is way better than a momma I could have had. He taught me everything, and he didn't mind that I was different. I remember him clearly."

"What is a brother?"

"I don't know really, someone bigger than me that teaches me, maybe. I promise I will not try to hurt you."

"Okay."

With that, Tulyata whisked them back to their dimension and not a visage or changing Zreyas had a dry eye. No one said a word for a very long time.

Finally, Rhom broke the silence. "Very good news indeed."

32 Transition

Zreyas

Zreyas couldn't believe what he saw and heard the past several minutes. *All this time... Rhom was an incarnated visage of elemental natural balance? I thought they were ticking, messing with me.* "Wait so, if you are like twins with different elements, did you used to be one visage together?"

"The smart little ferret strikes again," Tulyata chimed in as she was working on her scales furiously. She glanced over to Rhom for a moment, then back again.

Rtu winced and then nodded. "Yes, it was a painful separation. We decided to separate for balances. We were too powerful to keep a balance with other things going on at the time. We became too powerful as one entity, and different events began as a result that caused things to grow unstable. Though we didn't do anything wrong, it still messed balance up in other ways. Too much of a monopoly of power anywhere, in any situation, is not good for incarnates and nature."

Rhom nodded. "It didn't use to be so hard though... there weren't as many places with incarnated souls in bodies and when more nature got created to handle it all, it caused us to grow, too. So, I have earth, but only enough to ground me. And he has a little aether and water, just enough to communicate, flow, and create."

"So... yeah, ticking hell. Am I asleep and in a dream?" said Zreyas, more as a statement than an actual question.

Rtu sat up and smiled. "Let's test it out!" He leaned forward and let out a puff of air. It knocked Zreyas on his ass, and he slid off the desk and across the floor. "What do you think? Did you like the soft landing I provided for you?"

Zreyas hopped up on his feet, quick and alert, then visibly relaxed. "I guess I'm not dreaming, but you enjoyed doing the test!" He narrowed his eyes at Rtu. Then he let out a single, "Ha!"

Rtu was totally triggered by Zreyas' laugh, and laughed so hard he cried.

Tulyata palmed her forehead, shook her head, and continued her calculations with a sigh. "Am I the only one serious around here?"

"You are serious enough for all of us, Tulyata!" said Rtu and Rhom together, then Rtu began howling in another fit of laughter.

Zreyas laughed harder. "Ha... ha!" He tried to let himself laugh. "This is a wild feeling! I never laughed like this before! Ha!"

Tulyata turned to look at both of them and looked like she was going to burst from aggravation, her face red and eyes narrowing. "Argh, wonderful! Another pathetic laugh fanatic around me."

Suddenly Rhom's body began to emit a high-pitched ring.

"Uh-oh, here he comes. There is that aether sound. Zreyas, you better get behind something," Rtu warned, uncharacteristically serious. He stood up and went down to his knees behind a console.

"Wimp," Tulyata said as she stood up with her scales and shoved them in front of Rhom's face as he began to morph larger and airier.

Confused, Zreyas turned to Rtu. "I thought you were air. And I thought he already changed back!" Zreyas moved and made sure he was well behind the desk, peeking around to watch Rhom. "Ticking hell."

"His water awareness came forth first. That is aether emerging from a dense form. Shh," Tulyata said in a sharp whisper.

Zreyas watched the form of a very pale, loose, flowing humanoid.

Making sure he saw only the scales first, Tulyata held them closer. "Look at the scales of balance and remember."

Zreyas found himself overwhelmed by what was going on. His friend wasn't what he thought he was. The energy in the room was strong and overwhelming. He felt like nothing in his life was stable anymore. Just when Rhom was back, he found out that was only part of him. How could he trust his own sanity, going through fractures, merging souls, standing before visages.

Rhom, if that was still him, seemed to morph and transform into something bigger as each element that was part of him joined. It started with the water part of him growing into that large swirling thing again. At different times he saw fire and earth-colored flame-like shapes join into the vertigo-causing swirl. Then the high-pitched ringing sound grew louder. Zreyas put his hands over his ears and watched as a steamy mist filled the room, getting sucked into the swirl. He didn't resemble a person anymore and filled the entire half of the room.

"See the scales of balance and remember!" Tulyata yelled more firmly, her hair and tassels flying all over the place like whips.

A low boom rattled the room.

Zreyas jerked and felt like he was to a point that he would explode out of both fear and grief. His friend was no longer... a person, but now a bunch of water, mist and fire. He wasn't sure he wanted to watch anymore, but he couldn't help but watch. "Ticking hell, Rhom. You are scary."

"You shouldn't even be seeing this, you little weasel. Be grateful and shut up," Tulyata snapped.

"Tulyata, that was mean. It's not his fault he is here, and he is actually helping," Rtu said, watching Rhom.

Tulyata moved her arm to stay with what she must have known was the face of the visage, though Zreyas couldn't make it out.

"Look at the scales of balance and remember," Tulyata repeated.

Zreyas looked over at the groaning Rtu, seeing apprehension growing in his face next to him. "Yeah, ticking hell, remember! You're scaring Rtu!"

"He's not the same! He doesn't feel like my twin."

"It's that promise he said he was following through with... He's given two-thirds of his fire for a cause for balance. But I couldn't say what that cause is." Tulyata demanded, "All right, Rhom, remember and pull yourself together!"

Rtu stood and looked at his brother. "He's rearranging because he is missing part of himself."

Zreyas narrowed his eyes and stared up at the visage of earth and air. "Rtu, I don't think you are being fair to Rhom."

All three visages turned to look at Zreyas with surprise and indignation in their eyes.

"I've changed a lot in the past forty-eight hours and it wasn't my fault, but now you are judging him because he helped someone balance things out? Just because he doesn't look the same doesn't mean he isn't a good part of you, Rtu. It would be like me rejecting my little brother because he got shrunk trying to save Ayya."

Rtu looked at Zreyas, stood taller, turned around, and walked forward slowly. Tulyata moved aside, still holding the scales out. Rtu stood right in front of the huge mass of swirling elements that filled the entire half of the room, and way past the walls. They didn't seem to be restricted to walls and physical objects.

Rtu held his arms out wide and his body began to change into a mish-mash of flowing earth and air.

Tulyata rolled her eyes. "Children will be children."

For once, Tulyata's cynical comments made Zreyas feel better because she was not alarmed. He knew they were okay now. Zreyas stood and q-leaped to the desk, sat down, turned his chair, and watched. He was now totally fascinated by what was going on.

Zreyas heard Rtu's voice, "My dear brother, I accept you as *we* are." All of their elements began mixing into one vast mass of power.

Wait, what did he say? How can he accept him as they both are? Hmm... oh, they were part of a whole, originally. He whispered to himself, "Rtu didn't accept him before because he was different than he was previously, so... Ah, I get what he meant now!"

"There is hope for you yet, little ferret. Hurry and figure it out, you two, we've got a lot to do."

Zreyas watched the display. The elements began separating and forming the familiar visages again. But they had an extra little something that he couldn't put his finger on. *Apparently, acceptance is powerful.*

It wasn't long and Rtu was as he was before, but a little more glowing and happier. "It's good to have you back, brother!"

Rhom coalesced into a humanoid form, but he didn't look anything like before. Zreyas supposed it was because he was no longer Viduri. He saw two faces in the mist near his shoulders. One was watery and one was fiery, though much smaller. Zreyas assumed the white mist all around him was probably the aether part of him.

His hair was shoulder length and white, and he had a long white goatee beard. In addition, it had a few beaded braids on each side. Rhom's attire was tribal, but the most simple of the three in the room. His loincloth was white with his hips exposed. There was a white cloth on his right shoulder that draped straight down on his right side in the front. It draped around his back and laid over the inside of the elbow on the other side.

"Whoa! Rhom, you are so... so..." Frustrated at his lack of good vocabulary, he finished with a simple ending. "Well, you look good now!" Zreyas' jaw hung as he stared at the visage manifest himself before his eyes more solidly.

Rhom's body was powerful and had multiple skin color tones that mixed with each other. His left arm and shoulder, along with the right leg and hip, were blue tinted tan skin. The opposite of his arms and legs was red. Both sides had flecks of purple mixed in with it, subduing the vibrancy into something pleasant to look at. His torso was a subdued dusty purple that blended gently into the other parts.

Zreyas wanted so badly to go over and touch Rhom's skin. It drew him in. He didn't seem painted; it appeared almost like its own dimension.

Rhom was someone he didn't even know anymore. Zreyas had nothing to say. He wondered what would happen to him now.

The leather pouch on Rhom's hip was simple worn leather with a thin strap that went diagonally across his chest. Zreyas loved the simple necklace he wore. As shiny as Rhom was, Zreyas wasn't sure if it was made of shell or bone, but each fragment was separated by leather knots. Rhom's body had iridescent white tattoos all over it, but they stopped at the middle of his thighs and his elbows; none past those points. They moved and lived on his skin.

He wore a simple headband and wristbands of leather that seemed long used and dirty, a contrast to the opulence of everything else about him. After Zreyas thought about it, he realized it was like the earth part of Rhom that grounded him.

Once Rhom coalesced into a firmer fleshy form, the misty faces at each shoulder and the surrounding mist disappeared into his body. He stood there in all his glory.

Rhom slowly turned his face toward Zreyas. That was when Zreyas noticed the brilliant light-blue irises. Rhom's eyes seemed to pierce through him.

"I'm still here, my boy! You are safe." And then he smiled that very Rhom-like smile that always shined in any form.

33 Two-Animal Reference

ꟷꟷ *Zreyas* ꟷꟷ

"So... the song, how long until we are dealing with legions of trouble?" Zreyas asked.

Rhom sat down in a chair. "Not sure, my boy, not sure. Though there are fractures now, they are not stable and most all of them don't last that long."

"You are the science geek, Rhom," Tulyata said. "We don't do science, and you have been incarnated for a couple thousand varSas. That means you have not been doing your weird science developments to figure all this stuff out."

"Well, I feel helpless. We've been sitting around talking a while, and so much has happened." Zreyas paced around in a circle in front of his little chair, thinking.

Rtu spoke up, "No worries, little buddy, we got time.

That is one thing we have on our side. None of that can happen overnight or even in a week or varSa. But we really do need to think about a plan."

Zreyas doubted they had that much time, but decided not to say anything.

Rhom looked up, his attention on something distant in his mind.

"Uh-oh, there he goes again," said Rtu, warily. "It didn't take long, did it?"

Tulyata chuffed, "It took longer than I expected it would."

Zreyas felt like he didn't know Rhom at all and wondered if this changing was shocking to him in any way. "What is wrong with him this time?"

"While he's... gone, I think I have an idea what is wrong with him. He was so dedicated to Ayya, and with the state she was in, maybe he gave a part of himself to her." Rtu cocked his head at his brother and looked closer.

"Well, I saw fire in him, it just seemed distant," Zreyas added.

"He's definitely more water than fire. It's not balanced like you are with earth and air," Tulyata said, her gaze on Rtu.

Rtu got up and walked over to Rhom. "You are correct. Though it is still there. I'll be buggered, Zreyas is right. It's there, but it is distant and active... Something else is going on."

"Do you think he is going to Ayya?" Zreyas inquired.

"Hmm, let me look at something here." Rtu seemed to go into a trance. After a time, he came out and nodded his head. "Hmm, there is a name I see within him... Samsara. I see a vague symbol of a phoenix. But my brother is being very elusive, I can't see anything else.

We may not have as much time as we think we do. There is a lot going on in the aether, and that is *not* my realm."

Rhom focused his eyes, making Rtu jump. "No privacy! And no, I didn't go to, or give, part of myself to Ayya—that would only be a short-term solution and would mess up the balances badly. That symbol is part of Ayya and part of her purpose and role of bringing in the new age. It's *always* been there because she has always been aware of her purpose... until now. I saw it long ago before all this mess started."

Tulyata nodded. "That explains a lot. What else do you know?"

"There is more than one major player in this game. It's part of the accelerations. One I know about now, though the source of it is elusive." Rhom stood and slowly walked in a circle while he explained further. "Ayya had these... cycles. It's like a lurching awareness. When she learned all she could from something, that new awareness would go dormant inside her. A similar example would be that of a phoenix. It dies and turns to ashes. And just like the phoenix, she used that dormancy to wait to respond for the right time to spawn forth another cycle, using what she learned to gain new insight and strategy. It's like she took the information and lessons from something, crumbled it to the base form of dust, and rested on it until it became part of her fundamental make-up."

"Ticking hell, that is an excellent strategy!"

"Agreed," Tulyata said, uncharacteristically focused on something other than her scales.

"It's like she burned up knowledge to fuel the birth of a new awareness, then went dormant and recuperated. Even in her recuperation, she was still in motion. This little phoenix is unique. It's the most beautiful process I have witnessed in all my varSas."

"I bet everyone thought she was a visage! I know I would," said Zreyas.

"No, unfortunately they thought she was the most heretical, short-sighted, Tantra we had yet."

"Wha-at?"

"Most thought she was fanatical, young, and stupid with ideas that didn't make sense. She had this tendency to announce things three varSas ahead of when the world was ready for it."

"Wow, no wonder Aaru was drawn to her, and me, for that matter. When I was watching the ceremony, I was drawn to her, just like Aaru was. But I was more concerned with watching over Aaru protectively than getting sucked up in it."

Rtu held a hand up in the air in a thankful gesture. "I'm glad you did; had you not, we all would likely be dead right now at the Dark One's hand, little buddy."

"As far as what you were examining while I was away, I keep my promise to her through a... donation. So technically, I fulfilled my promise. Don't bother asking me about it further, because I won't tell you. That is information that, if it reaches the wrong ears, would doom us all. But the phoenix is a key to her purpose, yet part of the future of us too."

Rhom threw up his hands, clapping his hands together, and smiled. "We have important things to do and places to go. We must stop that Dark One, the Janquar emperor, and keep them all from Ayya long enough to wake her up. She must ascend and save our... *her* people and the balance. That is quite the responsibility to put on her. She can't do it alone. She is not meant to wage war, but to ensure that the light race survives."

Zreyas narrowed his eyes. “So, what you are saying is, she is meant to just have babies? You told me many times her only purpose was to make sure your race survived by giving offspring. Are you saying that my brother sacrificed himself for a purpose of creating babies? This seems... flat,” Zreyas said, appalled, growing angrier every second. “Even *our* people didn’t put that much emphasis on procreation, even though it still eludes me how it is done for the Janquar. I’ve been paying attention. You just put her in the category of an animal mating for reproduction the way you explained it!”

He continued, completely and utterly annoyed, forgetting how small he was now. “If that was all my worth was to the world, I would just kill myself. No wonder she was unhappy with things being defined for her.” The fluctuating war aura energy showed around his body without him even thinking about it. “And you guys think Janquar are archaic! I think I would rather answer that Dark Song than help you make her into a light baby factory!”

Rtu observed with humor, unaffected by Zreyas’ growing anger, “Well, we know he has not lost that war ability, even if his skin is lightening up.”

Rhom stared at him in his observing way. He was completely unaffected by Zreyas and his growing fury. “Yes, fascinating isn’t it.” He leaned forward and closed in, face to face with Zreyas, close enough that he could hit him.

“No, my boy, that is not what she is all about. I sincerely thank you for putting that on the table. I think we forget that there is more to life than numbers in the balance. I think the ways of her people are long overdue to change, and she will find another way to keep her people alive and flourish. Even as a child, she would say things like, 'A fixed way of doing things for thousands of varSas doesn't necessarily mean it is the best way, it just means we were desperate to settle for a way for that long.' She had many sayings like that."

Zreyas crossed his arms, but listened closely. He wanted to give his friend a chance, but so far, he wasn't impressed. He was more impressed with Ayya than Rhom.

"She has always been my teacher, but she never knew it. Others just saw her as being young and rebellious of the traditions. I'll admit, I had those spurts when I judged her by it, too. But then it changed somewhere along the way. She would say things that were heretical to many races, not just the Viduri."

"So, did you tell her about her teaching you so much?"

Rhom's eyes filled. "No, not in those words, unfortunately. We all think we have time, and we never expect the unexpected to take our loved ones away so soon. There is nothing I can do about it now, though." Water spilled from his eyes and streamed down his cheeks.

Zreyas started to say something, but he changed his mind. The fall of tears was growing into something more on the lines of young waterfalls, a bit unnatural for any type of being in Zreyas' mind. *Well, he is the Visage of Water.* He never took his eyes from Rhom. "I'm listening." His face feeling the heartbeats of his fury.

Rhom's eyes twitched with a grief and love that Zreyas could see was so eternally deep that he could barely speak. Rhom's voice cracked. "And here is the kicker. I couldn't come up with any evidence that she was wrong in anything she said! It made me curious, my boy. It made me a better being, and I will never forget what she has given me—that is why I'm so dedicated to her, even now. She has made me a better visage. I want nothing else but to help her succeed in whatever she chooses to do in any incarnation. I promised her I would be there for her no matter what, so I am now one of her guardian angels, so to speak. So, to answer your question, Zreyas, I don't think your brother gave his life for a baby factory. He gave his life for a cause beyond all of us, beyond all races, ages, and genders, even if she, or we, don't understand it."

Rhom still looked straight at Zreyas, keeping his sincere face close to him more emphatically. "I don't care if she fails in what she wants to do, because she never failed me just by being who she is. I know your brother will help her and also play out his life's purpose, which he claimed back in the dying dimension. I aim to help him too because he no longer exists as himself but as part of her. You could say I'm as dedicated to him as I am to her because he paid a debt he didn't have to pay. We would all be lost if it weren't for him. I will say this, even if he was not part of Ayya, I would be as dedicated to him as I am to her. He has done more than many visages ever thought about doing. He has my respect and eternal dedication."

Rhom paused a few moments, and with the heart of a caring visage, made a plea to Zreyas. "Pray forgive us. We forget your whole world has turned upside down. You have lost everything you knew in life. You lost your new friend, Rhom, as you knew him, and you even lost the body that you knew. I want you to know, you now have me. Though our paths may part in the future for periods of time, I'll always be there to help you if I can. You... are *not*... alone."

That broke Zreyas. His eyes stung so sharply it made his stomach sick as the tears filled his eyes right along with Rhom now. Zreyas melted in his stance and leaned forward, resting his forehead against Rhom's nose. He released a choked, "I'm giving you the thanking. I'm not sorry about what I said. I only know one thing well—how to fight. It wasn't my fault up till now. But I'm also not sorry I want to learn more, so that I don't have to be sorry that fighting is all I know in the future. The thankings too for helping me."

After a few moments, Zreyas lifted his head, grinned, and looked at Tulyata, then to Rtu. "Speaking of wanting to learn more about your kids, Tulyata..."

Tulyata put those half glasses on again and looked over them at Zreyas. "I know what you are thinking, and yes, I'm a mother... but don't ask the question churning in your weasel brain, because if you do, you will regret it, you little ferret."

Rtu laughed and looked at Zreyas. "You just won a medal, two animal comparisons in one sentence. You'll get used to her nosing in your brain. I swear mothers can naturally read minds, Visage or not." He then turned to look at his brother admiringly. "It's good to have Rhom back. It's all about the balance of what is needed for the age; but for me personally, I missed you, bro!"

Rhom continued the conversation. "Even as balanced as we are, we still make mistakes as Visages. We don't see all things ahead of time and don't do all things right. We have our challenges, just like you. So cut us some slack too, my boy! We are in this together."

"So." Zreyas worked out his thoughts as he talked. "Let me get this straight. You two were once one, then split for the purposes of balance at the time, and to help see in the new Tantra because she is critical. Now that you are a Visage again, it is for the purposes of balance to offset the Dark One. These accelerations are from a higher visage-like entity that you haven't met yet?"

"You have the general right of it, my boy!"

Suddenly, a violent rumble shook the entire domain. It threw everyone around. It surprised Zreyas that even Tulyata ended up on the floor, too.

He rolled off the desk and grabbed the edge just in time to keep from falling.

Rhom fell into the wall, hitting the floor ass first.

Tulyata scrambled, trying to get up as quickly as she could, fighting the quaking room. She reached out to grab her scales before they fell, catching them just as they tipped.

Rtu, still sitting in his comfortable chair, propped his fist up against his face, waiting patiently. His full, large-freckled cheeks jiggled along with his body as the room shook.

Just as suddenly as the rumbling started, all went silent.

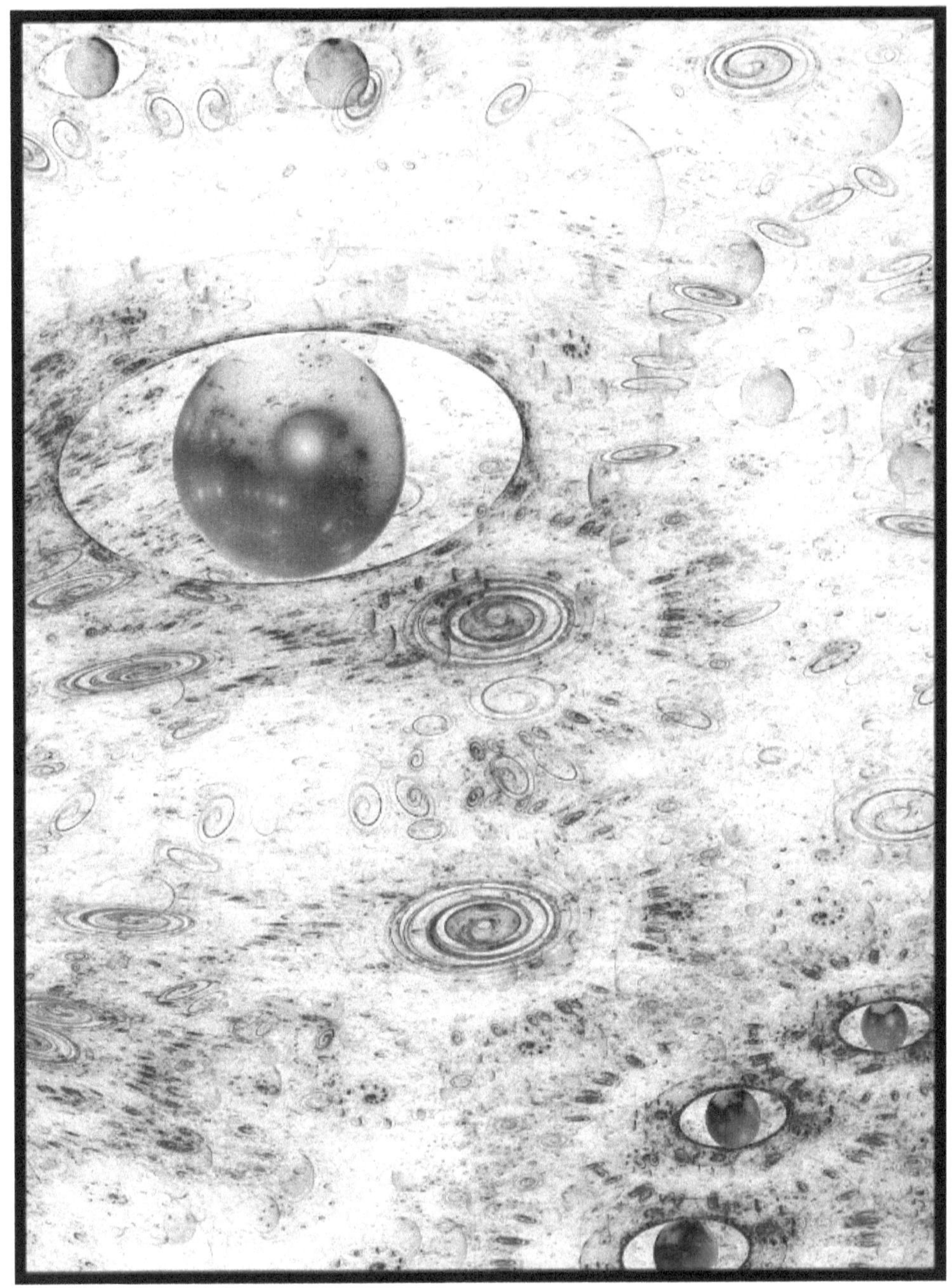

34 Dark One's Challenge

Zreyas

"This is not good," Tulyata grunted out as she got up and stared at the scales. "The challenge dimension has been evoked and created! The Dark One has been thinking and planning a long time it seems, but even I didn't expect this."

Zreyas still hung from the edge of the desk. He grunted and pulled himself back up onto the surface. "What is this challenge dimension?"

Rhom slid himself back upright as if rewinding time, causing Zreyas to look twice. "It's a dimension that is like an interstellar challenge for whatever it is they set it up for. The participants summoned must take part, like it or not. Anyone can ask for a challenge to be created as long as they are not in a dimensional prison. Someone created this dimension for the Dark One. And we didn't set up the challenge."

"Do you think he got the emperor Rok Phaar to do it for him?" Zreyas asked.

"So that is his name. Could be, if he's possessed him to the point of no will, then it wouldn't be valid, though. However, if he still has his free will, and basically has the Dark One as a *roommate*, then that would be legal," Tulyata said in a distracted tone.

"I don't see much difference."

"I'm checking this theory by dropping in on this Rok emperor." She paused a moment and continued. "Well, the Dark One is still imprisoned. Now to find the Rok Phaar emperor again. Yes, there he is. He is not possessed; it looks like the leader has a roommate."

Rtu, weirdly calm to Zreyas, said, "Damn, and I wanted to laugh a little. So where is the challenge dimension? I'm a little afraid to ask."

"It looks like..." Tulyata quietly talked to herself out-loud staring intently at her console. "Well, I'll be a witch's ass."

In unison, everyone said, "What!?"

"It's in the dimension of the Dark One's prison. He can't intervene or hurt anyone directly unless they are within his touch range; however, it *is* within his influence range! It is the Dark One's participation in the challenge." Tulyata blurted out a string of expletives that paled even the other two visages.

Zreyas opened his mouth to ask a question, but just couldn't find the words yet. His jaw hung as he cocked his head. Finally, he broke the silence with the first of many questions pummeling his mind. "Why did he do this? What is he challenging for? And what are the rules?"

"Those are good questions." Rtu said.

Tulyata stared upward and out into the open room.

It seemed to Zreyas that she was almost stunned at all the influx of information. “Uh, she’s processing something, I think.” Zreyas leaped on to her face, feet on her cheeks, and lifted her eyebrow a little, turning his head to look back at the other two, “See?”

When he turned back to look at her again, her eyes turned toward him, perched on her face. “Uh oh.” Zreyas executed a speedy quantum leap off her face on Rtu’s shoulder, shocking them all.

Tulyata picked her half glasses up, put them on her face, and looked over the lenses, looking ticking-pissed as hell. She looked at Zreyas, now hiding behind Rtu’s bountiful neck, “It’s a good thing I’ve got a lot more important things on my mind, little ferret, or you would be a marshmallow on a stick for me.”

“What’s a marshmallow?”

“Delicious, sweet food!” Tulyata said, as soon as Zreyas hid behind Rtu’s neck again. She turned and hid her face for a moment. It confused Zreyas when her body bounced a few times. Then she turned back to look at Rtu with a scowl.

Zreyas could tell Rtu did that smiling thing because his vision became obstructed by his pudgy cheeks when they went wider. But then his face returned to normal and he could see her again. Then Rtu said with seriousness, “So, what information have you found for us?”

“The prize for the Dark One is the right to summon Aaru for his mission... and that would be why we are allowed to see the interactions between Ayya and Aaru, because he already knows where he is. And like we feared, it would mean summoning Ayya. He could make the mission lifelong. Honestly, Ayya is what he is really after, in my opinion. And we all know that would not be good at all... for anyone, especially if he used Aaru's commitment to control Ayya for an indefinite amount of time."

Zreyas popped back around Rtu's neck with instant fury. "What?"

"I'm with you there in sentiment, little buddy, except I want to say something a lot harsher!" Rtu said.

"But how did he know? We were the only ones there when Rhom put those two together," said Zreyas.

Zreyas judged by Rhom's expression that the newly re-birthed visage was calm but angry at the same time. Then Rhom's eyes went wide in realization. "I think I know how he knew..."

"Spill it, brother!"

"Zreyas, do you remember that black hall you told me was bad, to not go in there?"

"Oh yeah! That was some ticking dark-ass nasty mag-shitting air."

"Well, while you were running to the portal, I kept hearing strange sounds and looking back to see what it was. I saw a face in that darkness. The features were warped and haunted... and definitely not pleasant. Just after I uncovered the symbols and activated one of them, the light warrior also saw it and he grabbed me. We both saw it reach for me for a moment. The light warrior turned his body to protect me before he dragged me into Tulyata's realm. He was also the one that was killed. Maybe it was who tried to attack Ayya because I think it tried to kill me. The question is, how did it know to sit in that one specific place. It had to have known we would be there."

"Bugger me britches, Rhom," Rtu said. "That would have given him dominion over all your elements! He would have claimed them since he is now considered a visage with all his followers, willing or not. And if he would have succeeded, that means he would have had access to me!"

Zreyas shivered. "I knew that hall was bad, it still makes my neck prickle." Zreyas cocked his head, "You said what the Dark One's reward would be, but what is the other side's reward?"

Rhom quickly added, "And who is to take part in the challenge? Is it specific? And what are other stakes besides calling Aaru for his mission? There has to be a benefit for all sides."

Totally frustrated, Tulyata pounded the desk with her fist. "Normally, when something happens like this, it is already out in the open for all to know. It seems we need to wait for the 'powers that be,' whoever they are, to make the proper calculations of balance and check the viability of the challenge itself. Since so much has happened multiverse-wide, it is taking longer than normal. So, we get to wait until it is all in."

"Well, that is a little annoying," Rtu said, then propped his face on his fist resting on the arm of his chair.

"Here is something interesting as well. All time and events of the multiverse have been suspended, and no one knows the difference until this information comes in."

"I could be wrong, but that doesn't bode well. It means the stakes are rather steep. It makes sense for the Dark One to get this challenge going, though. The Dark One has nothing to lose and everything to gain," observed Rhom.

"I think... hmm. I think... I'm actually stressed a little," Rtu admitted. "Well, slap me on the face and put my britches on backward, so that is what that feels like!"

"Well, you seemed stressed when Rhom was—"

Rtu gave a warding gesture with his right hand and turned his face sideways to the left. "That was different."

Zreyas said in a tone as if instructing young warriors again. "It's a power, use it."

All three visages turned to look at him, interested. Whether it was because they were just humored or offended, Zreyas didn't know.

"What? I'm not sure why you think it's such a new thing to remind you of. I've lived and grown up being trained to use stress and anger as power. I still have it, even though I'm turning blue; though I have to say, using anger to fuel anger or other lower emotions isn't nearly as powerful or productive as burning it away to fuel the higher frequency things like good purpose and that strong word for like."

"Love," said Rhom.

"Yeah, that word. They are too dense and heavy by themselves, but if you—"

Zreyas stopped talking, a little unsure of why what he was saying was so interesting to them. He looked at Tulyata and then to Rtu. "You haven't ever been in a body before, have you?"

Rhom sat up and distantly said, "I have, obviously. I know what he is talking about. I still remember what it was like to be an incarnate, albeit it was in a lighter form. It's still fresh for me. I used the quantum to leap and travel and bring things to me in life without cheating it because it is the science of the multiverse. You do it a different way, Zreyas. Knowing your anatomy and culture now, I understand what you mean. Thank you for the reminder and the lesson. The conversion from the lower to the higher is incredibly powerful compared to equal-to-equal frequencies."

"You should know, remember You taught me how to convert it to help you with energy."

"Oh, I remember, yes. The light warriors had to help mitigate it because it was too much, and they knew it. I was blind to its power. I mean, I had you do it on theory, but the results were so much more than I imagined."

"It's all because of you it worked. Why didn't you know for sure?"

"Because I did it differently. Being the species I was, it was easier and several steps less. I am in awe that you figured out how to do that from what little I told you. That gives me an idea about a ship I have been working on—"

A rumble shook the entire room again. The occupants, including the light warriors still standing in Rhom's chamber room, were starting to get accomplished at adjusting to the sudden rumbles.

"Oh boy, here we go, again," Zreyas said as he laid flat on the desk.

Tulyata leaned forward as she held onto the edges of the desk. "Hey, the information is in, and we have three hours before time starts again."

35 The Mechanics

꩜꩜꩜ Zreyas ꩜꩜꩜

After the rumbling stopped, one wall of Tulyata's dimension disintegrated as another room emerged.

Tulyata raised her voice and said, "Who is changing my realm? This isn't supposed to happen, *ever*!"

Zreyas watched her face intently. Tulyata's face was angry, but it also seemed like she wasn't that surprised, either. *She's hiding something. I can't shake that nagging feeling.*

"Seems we have a challenge node manifesting," Rhom observed.

"What is that?" Zreyas gripped the hilts of his weapons involuntarily at the unusual activity. "Does that mean we are part of this challenge? Is that how we enter this challenge to participate, and is it like an arena?"

"It looks like we are part of it. It is how we take part,

but I highly doubt it will be an arena. The Dark One is imprisoned and is too devious for something so straight up and honest, my boy."

Zreyas watched the completion of the forming node, having never seen anything like it before. He couldn't help but squint from the light that glowed from the material of the node itself. It looked like it was made from a strong glass material. "What is that clear material, old man? It looks like glass in the structure that you blew up with your bad singing in the dying dimension, but this seems more... thick and alive."

"This is not glass. We wouldn't be able to break this very easily. In fact, I don't know what it is, my boy. It's not a material I have ever identified. What about you, Rtu? This is weird."

Rtu leaned forward in his seat, looking carefully. "Nnoo, I don't know it, and I should."

Both Tulyata and Rhom just shrugged, but Rhom started assessing it.

Zreyas assumed Rhom's science mind couldn't pass that up. The challenge node attached to the room looked like a half-circle with a flat top and bottom. The floor, ceiling, and walls were also a vessel that housed a churning white luminescent liquid of some sort inside it.

When Rhom touched it, the material inside it reacted, turning purple.

Strange symbols of cyan and royal blue were stamped on the floor in a triangle pattern. The entire node seemed to be one solid, self-contained, molded unit with the liquid inside it.

There were five pillars sticking out of the walls that looked like clear tubes. They were spaced out evenly on the walls. Zreyas examined closer and the entire room had no seams or moving parts anywhere. There were blue symbols at intervals up the height of the pillars. The clear pipes ran up the walls and bent toward the center of the ceiling. The closer they got to the center, the narrower they got. They met at the center where they looped back into themselves. They looked like five flower petals made of clear pipes.

"Ticking-hell, this structure is odd," said Zreyas. "Is the other half of this room somewhere else?"

Tulyata leaned on her elbow. "This little ferret is annoyingly smart. It is indeed half of a whole. In fact, according to this, there are four full sets for entering and exiting the challenge. There are also an unknown number of challenge node halves inside the challenge to bind to our node that we can use to teleport between. However, they aren't just for us. Whoever discovers them first can bind them for quick transport. After bound, the other teams cannot access or use them."

Zreyas mumbled the information to himself to put it to memory.

Tulyata nodded at what she saw on her screen. "And the half-nodes may have areas nearby where portals can be created to go to Earth. Two sets are discovered, one of them is ours, and I assume the other one is known by the Janquar Nation because it is on Tarq, the planet you were on, Zreyas. The others, both outside and inside, must be discovered during the challenge, because at this time, there are only two sides to this challenge."

Zreyas persisted with the question he never got answered twice before. "What are the winnings of our side if we succeed? Is there a time limit? You never said that part either."

Tulyata turned back to her screen. She scanned for the information and her expression slowly got more and more confused and agitated the longer she looked.

"Uh oh," said Rtu.

Zreyas nodded. "Yeah, I think it's taking her too long to find the answer."

After several minutes, Tulyata looked up. "That information is not here. I have submitted a query to get it in before the challenge officially starts. Something is off about this whole thing."

Rhom pointed at the small screen to the right of the open node. "Looks like there is a screen for observation of the participants we send in."

Rtu said as he squinted to see what it showed. "Wow, this challenge is on a massive scale to have that benefit. I don't think I have ever seen a challenge setup like that. But it is small."

They all looked at the screen to see a dark mountain and a black lake right beside it. There, in the middle of the lake, amongst the many sidewalks of white brick, was the Dark One.

Shooting out a pointed finger at the screen, Zreyas informed them, "That is what my brother was talking about when he tried to tell us what he saw in the emperor's chamber! He mentioned a mountain, mist, and a black lake. So, he *was* there! And by the way, old man, that was the thing you told me to remind you to tell you about."

"Interesting!" Rhom responded.

"Indeed," said Tulyata. "It looks like from the information I am receiving here; the goal is to enter the challenge and find one of the portal rooms to gain access to the planet where Ayya lives. The idea is to get to her and hurt, capture, or protect and wake her, depending on which side you are on. Poor girl, she will probably see some nasty shit."

"I'm sorry, little phoenix. I'm so sorry, but I will be

there for you," promised Rhom.

"Yeah, I hope Aaru helps her like he promised," Rtu said to remind Rhom. "She's going to need it more than ever now. I'm glad he is there with her."

"Oh, he will," Zreyas chimed in. "I believe that more than I would ever believe anything in my entire life, now and in the future. That is how well I know my brother."

Tulyata said, half distracted. "First, let me set up a very large screen that amplifies that little one." She stood and held her arms out as if she was conducting. With a wave and gesture, all the rooms expanded to a much longer room.

Zreyas was still on the desk, but it was now in the back of the massive long room. The challenge node was in the center of the left long wall, a door was located at the midpoint of the right wall, and one more door stood at the back of the room.

Straight ahead, the end of the long room started bending into a wraparound wall. Then it morphed into a huge screen from floor to ceiling, extending till it hit either the challenge node or a door.

Zreyas had never seen anything like it. Tulyata moved the desk, Zreyas still on it, into almost the center of the room, leaving enough room for a walkway she created from the challenge node to the door across from it on the other wall.

"Now for some comfort," said Tulyata as she grinned with the happiest expression Zreyas had ever seen on her.

The entire room's floor was covered in a fuzzy flooring that Zreyas could only cock his head at. It looked like short, but thick, golden grass to him. It stopped at the walkway at the center of the room between the door and challenge node. The walkway morphed into a black and gold-veined, shiny stone.

"Whoa! I like that! What is that kind of stone?"

With a smirk, Tulyata said happily, "Marble, a special kind."

In the fuzzy floor part of the room, a set of plush chairs and couches appeared, arranged in a way that they could observe but still chat with Tulyata, with a table in the center between the furniture.

"I can get into this!" He bumbled over happily, plopped down on one of the fluffy chairs, and turned it so he could easily see both the screen and the node.

"Yes, well, don't forget you've got work to do, too," Tulyata said, looking at Rtu.

"I know, I know, but there is no harm in being happy about what we are given, is there?" Rtu retorted.

"No harm at all," said Rhom as he went over to sit in a chair as well.

Tulyata turned and created shelves along the entirety of the walls on the desk side of the long room. The material was a black and gold wood that seemed natural, but nothing like Zreyas had ever seen before.

"I like that wood. Is it real? I've never seen anything so beautiful."

"Well, the little ferret has an appreciation for quality, it seems. It's a wood that is from Earth that I've always liked. It's called Pale Moon Ebony. There is a scientific name they have there for it, but I can't be bothered to remember it."

"Well, I like that name, but I like the wood even better. It's very shiny too."

"It's had a coating put on it, my boy, to make it look like that. It makes it nice and protects it."

"Now for the floor."

Zreyas walked to the edge of her desk and watched

as Tulyata transformed the floor surface into shiny black marble tiles with sculpted edges.

Tulyata sat back down at her desk as Zreyas leaped over to the arm of the chair Rhom sat in.

"I like this place now," said Zreyas.

Tulyata got right down to business, ignoring his comment. "The challenge has not started yet. It says here that if we measure teams before the start of the challenge, there will be benefits."

"What teams?" Zreyas asked, confused.

Rhom looked at him. "Teams of people go into the node. The system will measure their aptitude, strengths, and weaknesses to make sure they are not over a threshold of a rating. It helps keep the challenge even and fair. Though, I am not sure what the benefits are in this challenge's case."

Zreyas and Rhom were the first team to try. They walked into the node and a mechanical voice said their names and asked if there were any other additions. Rhom said no. The liquid under their feet turned purple, starting at the floor where they stood. It rose evenly in the pillars on the walls. Every time it passed a blue indicator, it would light up. It filled up to the top of the walls and started creeping into the ceiling toward the middle. It stopped just shy of the center point.

"—The team of Rhom and Zreyas has been approved and locked in. It is noted that we established the team before the beginning of the challenge."

"Stay here, my boy, let's see how you measure up alone," Rhom instructed.

The purple started rising again. It stopped one-third the way up.

"—The team of Zreyas has been approved and locked in. It is noted that we established the team before the beginning of the challenge."

"Hey, I'm impressed! See, you are very powerful for fifteen centimeters in height." Rhom winked.

Over the course of the next hour, they all got into the node with different combinations to register teams. Tulyata was the only one that couldn't go in by herself. She went just over the threshold. She didn't seem to upset by it.

Tulyata said, "Teams."

"—The following teams have been approved and locked in before the start of the challenge:

"Rhom
"Rhom and two light-warriors
"Rhom and Zreyas
"Rtu
"Rtu and three light-warriors
"Rtu and Zreyas
"Zreyas
"Zreyas and four light-warriors"

Rhom thought for a moment. "Since we can see what is going on, why don't we send out the light-warriors and Zreyas. Please hear me out. Zreyas is small and fast. The light-warriors are strong in case something is sitting right down there at the drop off. I'm not opposed to going in; however, I'm not the old Rhom anymore, and my signature is quite beastly in energy radius. It might not be a great idea to go in first, that close to the Dark One, without knowing what is in store in general. He's already tried once to kill me for power reasons."

"You have a point," said Tulyata.

"I'll go," said Zreyas.

"My boy, you guys better hurry and find out what you

can, as quickly as possible. Remember, you have trained all your life for something like this. I have faith in you," encouraged Rhom.

"Maybe I should go by myself. I'm not wanting to be a hero or anything, but the warriors are a little... bright and big," Zreyas pointed out.

"We could fix the bright part, but maybe you are right. They are rather large these days. They can drop in with you, camouflaged, just to make sure things are okay down there, then leave."

Rhom squared his shoulders, facing Zreyas. "Remember, the quantum can be used for far more than just speed and warping around. You can change matter itself. Just remember, your mind sends the signal out and your heart sends out the waves to draw in whatever the similar wave potential is. You have to figure out the rest. It will take time, but it is something important to know. It will come, now that you have it in your awareness. You have done some amazing things with the quantum so far. I would love to have you as an apprentice one day."

Tulyata put on her half glasses, looking over them toward Rhom, and Rtu raised his eyebrows.

"Little buddy, you don't know what a compliment that was."

Zreyas nodded seriously, looking into Rhom's face. "I will remember that, I hope. Just in case. Thankings for everything. Aaru and Ayya taught me to not take anything for granted."

Rhom reached over to Zreyas, picked him up, and put his cheek on Zreyas for a make-shift embrace. "I have grown to love you, my boy. Please be careful."

Zreyas felt Rhom's energy permeate through his body as he spoke. He awkwardly reached around Rhom's cheek to hug him. It occurred to Zreyas that it was the first time he had ever hugged anyone.

Rhom put him down on the floor and Zreyas walked into the challenge node. The light warriors changed themselves into a camouflage mode of some sort once they stood inside the node. Zreyas was amazed that he could hardly tell they were there.

He put a fist to his chest. The determined ex-Janquar straightened his little body into a more confident posture, more for himself than anything else. He closed his eyes a moment and softly said, "Wartok."

"—Transmitting the approved team, in five, four, three, two, one. Transmission initiated."

36 Violent Whip

Zreyas

Zreyas felt an electric tingle down through the middle of his body and everything flickered for a moment. After a couple of seconds, he saw nothing but particles. The feeling was weird watching pieces of himself floating in front of him. Some of the particles seemed to be screaming, and others moaning in bliss. Zreyas found the two an odd contradiction, but they both resonated.

After it subsided, his vision cleared. He could move his body again and immediately crouched out of instinct, being in a strange place he knew nothing about or where the threats were. Nothing here could be nice if he was in the Dark One's prison realm.

Scanning his surroundings, nothing caught his eye at first. Zreyas absorbed the details of his surroundings, taking his time. When it came to strategy, he was patient. He found himself on a black sand beach. To his right, there was the lake with the black shore straight ahead. It slightly curved to the right until it disappeared in the dark mist.

The air here was dark, as if it were polluted with soot. There was no real detail in the environment right now, but general shapes and landscape were easily discernible. Still standing inside the challenge node platform, he noticed it was the mate of the one he left from. Zreyas realized there was an energy here that made it difficult to feel good about anything.

"Remember, this is the Dark One's prison dimension, not a normal dimension."

The voice startled Zreyas. He'd forgotten he had the light warriors with him. He breathed a sigh of relief. "Do you know if they can hear me back in Tulyata's place?"

The light warriors shook their heads. Then they sparkled and disappeared.

Zreyas took a deep breath and let it out, and then he stepped out of the challenge node. He immediately stepped back again, thinking he better get his weapons ready. As soon as his foot left the sand, black tendrils whipped the sand violently where his foot had been.

Zreyas whirled around to the right to see black tendrils racing toward him. They whipped and snapped violently where he was just standing a moment ago.

"Whoa! That was close! I *felt* that hate."

He looked out over the water and saw a pathway from the other side where there were ruins of what used to be the Tempest Tower. The small bit of familiarity, though ravaged, made Zreyas feel a little better at having a point of reference. Looking out at the pathways, he saw the Dark One, just as Aaru had said, except even with his description, it didn't prepare him for what this thing looked and felt like. He supposed that it was worse in person because of the icky feel he got being near him.

Anger surged at this creature that screwed up his brother's life, as well as many others. He kept the anger in his war aura compartment, observing it within himself to keep it in check. He allowed the container to grow full, but only observed it. *It's only a tool, it doesn't have to make me into something like that thing.*

He looked at the demented remnant of what used to be a normal, respectable person of whatever race. Its haunting open mouth and glowing red eyes made Zreyas think there was nothing left but anger. *Aaru, you knew this wasn't the emperor, right? Maybe he looked different then. But, by the visages, how did you get through that meeting?*

Zreyas' thoughts began to paralyze him when he thought about how horrible this creature was. He felt the alluring call lulling him. He suddenly straightened, remembering what Tulyata said about it being within the reach of influence. "Ticking-hell," he whispered to himself.

Moving to the opposite side of the node, he kept that compartment of anger ready. He hopped down off the node and took a step closer toward the black stone cliff to the left of the node. Seeing the Dark One's tentacles lash out violently, falling short of him by a couple of meters this time, he looked at the ground where the first tentacle snapped. He saw a faint gradual circular line on the black sand that seemed to surround the Dark creature's central place.

"That must be his range of touch." Zreyas coached himself in a mumbled whisper, "Okay, Zrey, you have trained all your life for stuff like this. You might be small and simple, but that doesn't mean your will, energy, and purpose are small. Let's do this!"

Finishing his pep talk, he stepped around the circle.

Just in case he was not correct, he looked toward the water for anything that might dart out again. Nothing came, but he noticed those red eyes staring at him menacingly.

Zreyas stood up straight and looked ahead at him in challenge. “For all you have done, and will do, to hurt others for your own selfish reasons, I will make sure you never get away with it, even if it is the last thing I do.” Squaring his body toward the staring Dark One, he gave him an upward fist movement. “Eat that, you ticking mag-shit!” He let the anger push a wave of war aura like he had never released before to the Dark One.

“Bah! Get it together, Zrey. We got business to take care of.”

He began assessing the area to the left of the beach. There resided a huge mountain that seemed to disappear into the sky. Without going all the way around, it seemed clear to Zreyas that there was only one way to go, and that was up.

Careful to stay out of the Dark One’s range of touch, he walked ahead and to the left, toward the mountain. More details came into view the closer he got. It didn’t seem totally natural. He moved right up to the base and realized it was a towering four-sided pyramid temple the size of a mountain. The angles weren’t harsh enough to be three-sided. It was so tall it disappeared into a strange mist.

Touching the material of the rough temple, it felt... alive. Zreyas shivered, feeling the energy of something cold. It didn’t feel bad, just... empty, but alive. This must be the mountain Aaru spoke of. He could almost feel the history just by touching the side of it, but his mind couldn’t grasp details.

An energy pushed at him, different from the Dark

One. It was almost like a strong nudge. Zreyas narrowed his eyes and had an impulse to talk to whatever pushed him. "If you have good intentions for me, then you are welcome. If you want to hurt me, then get the ticking hell away from me." The energy didn't push anymore, but he felt it crawl all over him for a few minutes, though he saw nothing around him.

He shook the feeling off him, "Here we go."

Zreyas looked up at the looming dark structure and made his way along the bottom edge of the base. He noticed growth on the sides. Despite the darkness of the surrounding air, life still seemed to prevail on some level. There was weird plant growth all around the temple base. Zreyas observed what seemed to be a stone step poking out from the base of the temple.

The Dark One's eyes were still laser focused on him. "You've made your creation, now go away, there is nothing more you can do." He knew it was futile and the Dark One was still half imprisoned, preventing him from going anywhere, but he was feeling very defiant right now. Zreyas turned toward the temple again. The stone coming out past the wall was indeed a step, but it was a rather gigantic step for Zreyas.

When he got to the step, he looked up the endless staircase of stone. Rather than traverse them as small as he was, he did a q-leap up to the stone slab rail, higher than the rest of the steps. That would be much easier to walk on for him, though it *was* steep.

The higher view also gave him a chance to take a better look around to get an idea of what might be on both sides. Though it was easy to slide on, he could keep traction. It was leg intensive, though. He shrugged and decided it would be excellent exercise and practice.

"Don't take anything for granted, Zrey. You can

conquer this!"

Looking upward, he began the trek up. The walk was steep and tiring. He could easily slip if he was not careful, and did a few times. Every few minutes, he stopped to rest and look around for any details he might have missed. The Dark One looked a lot smaller now.

"Yeah, that's right, rot-snot... enjoy your hell!" Zreyas shook his head at himself, wondering if he had gone mad or he was just doing all he could to distract himself from his own fear. Either way, he decided it was productive for him, even if it might not help the situation. He looked up, still not seeing the top, and made the decision to q-leap to get to the top quicker. He needed the practice anyway.

Every few jumps, he stopped and looked around, taking nothing for granted. He noticed that if he thought 'quiet' or 'peace' when he jumped, the jump was more quiet or peaceful when he landed. Then he started thinking of other words like 'anger' and 'war aura'. When he landed, he seemed to be in those states of mind. He didn't always do it perfectly, but he found the practice fascinating and fun, making time go faster.

After many small q-leaps over time, he realized there was no sound anymore. He turned around, and Zreyas no longer saw the eyes of the Dark One. Though he knew it was still there, he felt relief at being out of its sight.

Several hours of climbing the temple passed, and he wondered if he had missed something. Was there no end to this infernal pyramid? It seemed like it was getting smaller as he went up, though.

He looked down and saw an entrance, back where he came from. *There is no way in ticking hell that was there before.*

Zreyas realized it had to be the influence and illusion of the place. "Think... think," he told himself while looking around. It dawned on him what Rhom had told him about the thought being the signal. He looked up and got ready to q-leap. He thought about the top of the steps of the temple, and there was an entrance. He filled his anger chamber, picturing himself already there at the top. Zreyas released and converted the energy to a high frequency, letting the wave pattern of the future be attracted to him in the present moment. He leaped but didn't feel any different.

Recognition hit his mind, and he let out a quiet, "Yes!" when he saw he was standing on the top of the steps at an entrance of the temple. Zreyas didn't walk or move. He slowly crouched, just in case. He took his time to scan what was around him, taking in as much detail as he could.

The entrance was dark, and he could hear some stones grinding and shuffling against each other at regular intervals. To his left, just inside the outer wall, he barely saw a challenge node, unlit.

Zreyas walked toward it with caution. He stepped on it and the node lit up. It was similar to the one he had entered from, but with different symbols and colors. The colors of these symbols were purple and yellow.

"—You have discovered a new challenge node. You may now choose one of the following:

One, travel back to the original landing node.

Status: Open to all home node members.

Two, you may now exit to the paired entry node.

Advisory: Because you didn't enter from this node, if you leave the area, the exit might be impeded, have a hostile environment, be uninhabitable for your species, or submerged in unbreathable material. These factors may result in exposure to danger or death.

> Three, travel back to the original landing node.
> Status: Open to all home node members.
> Four," –

"Remain here," interrupted Zreyas.

"—We have registered Your choice for the unclaimed node."

"What do you mean, unclaimed node?"

"—For future reference, Zreyas of <redacted>, interrupted options may be detrimental to your progress.

> Four, claim this node—"

Growing impatient, he interrupted again. "Why would I want to claim it if I already have one?"

"—The request for answers to Zreyas of <redacted> is granted: Claiming this node will give you the following advantages:

> One, no one can use this node if it is found within the challenge dimension unless they are registered on your home node or according to given permissions.
>
> Two, no one from an outside node can use it to teleport into the challenge dimension unless they have killed the claimer or are registered members of your home teams.

Would you like to claim this node? Yes or No."

"Are there any disadvantages to claiming it?" asked

Zreyas.

"—The disadvantages to claiming this node are... none. Would you like to claim this node? Yes, or No."

"Then, yes, I would like to claim it." Something came over Zreyas to say, "Between you and me, something is nagging at me and I would also like to lock it to everyone, except for me, until I find the other outside node. Is that possible?"

"—Your request is accepted. The node is now locked to everyone except for Zreyas of <redacted>... And between you and me, that was wise.

Zreyas blinked. "Who *are* you?"

No answer came from the node.

"Well, I guess you are done talking." Zreyas stepped off the node, but it remained lit, illuminating a short way down the entry hall. "Ticking hell, I don't like this hall. What is it about dark halls lately?"

Before he continued, he wanted to get a good look at the walls themselves. The hall was about three meters wide at the bottom and only one meter wide at the top. To Zreyas, it looked like the corners of the walls and ceiling didn't join solidly and the side walls could slide. He looked closer at the seams, and they were rounded, as if they could rotate.

"Whoa, hey now! Don't get any ideas sliding in and crushing me. You stay where you are!"

A click sounded and echoed down and back out of the hall.

Zreyas jumped back, squatted, and watched closely around him for anything that might be dangerous. Strange symbols lit up on the walls of the hall in the cyan and blue color scheme of his home challenge node.

"Trap found by participant Zreyas. Trap disarmed by participant Zreyas. Would you like to disarm this trap for the other participants of your home challenge node?"

"If you mean Rhom, Rtu, and Tulyata, then yes."

"The trap has now been disabled for the duration of the challenge for Zreyas, Rhom, Rtu, and Tulyata."

Zreyas thought for a moment. "I didn't think Tulyata could enter."

Silence filled the air, and Zreyas couldn't help but wonder how he disarmed the trap. *Perhaps just talking to it and acknowledging it? This place really does feel alive. Maybe it is like a person.*

Keeping his back to the wall, he slid down the hall, taking full advantage of his new size, and stayed as close to that bottom corner as possible. The blackness eventually turned into what looked like an intersection with a statue at the end of the hall against a wall. He could only go left or right from what he could see.

Upon reaching the intersection, Zreyas didn't cross the hall. He stayed where he was, sat on his heels, and watched with the calculating eye of his life's training. He entered his zone of assessment and forgot time.

Straight ahead of him, against the wall across the hallway, was a large statue of a warrior holding his weapons. When the grinding began again, the statue slid to Zreyas' left, against the wall opposite him. There was a long line of those statues on that wall, ending in an open exit that seemed to have the lighting of a brighter outdoor area than the sooty looking air he came from. As the statue slid, another statue moved forward to take its place. He noticed that the wall on his side of the hall had nothing on it all the way down.

He turned to look down the hall to his right and saw the same thing as the left hall, except for the end. That end was black and he couldn't see through the darkness. *No ticking way I'm going down there.* As he turned his head away from the right hall, he noticed there was a hall behind the statue. There were more statues behind, sliding forward.

So, this hall straight ahead continues. What is it about me and finding triple forks? The cave had one too... a coincidence, I guess. He tried to look down the hall, but it was pitch black, though it seemed like a natural blackness. All he saw in it were statues coming his way.

As soon as the sliding stopped, a wave of sound and energy pulsed down the hall of statues. Though he had not stepped into that hall, it filled Zreyas with fear and wafted through him with a crash. He immediately went into a war stance, emitting his aura out of reaction, but he stayed put. He willed himself to concentrate on breathing as he looked at the new statue that took the first one's place. The wave of energy stopped.

Zreyas breathed a sigh of relief. *It's a good thing I didn't step into the hall yet.* He watched another warrior statue of a different race, stance, and weapons. This time, when the grinding started, all the statues continued on their way in both right and left halls. However, this time, the one in the center slid down the right hall, rather than the left. *So, they alternate halls.* As before, a wave of energy flowed through the corridor with force; but this time, it filled Zreyas with a feeling of excitement. Though it was much easier to handle and more welcome, it was overwhelmingly strong. Zreyas enjoyed the wave, but he stayed put. When the center one came in to take its predecessor's place, the wave stopped, just as before.

Zreyas watched through several cycles that took place with different energy and sounds whirling through the corridor. Each time, a different statue of a warrior took its place in the center position. The first statue he had seen still had not gotten to the end. He kept watching.

After several more cycles, the first statue he saw when he arrived slid out of sight at the end of the hall.

The wave that came through was smooth, gentle, and had no emotion.

He heard a weird short echoing high tone waft up the corridor, coming from where the statue had disappeared, and stood.

Zreyas heard words but felt the whisper of it. It was the oddest experience. He heard and felt them as if time warped or he was in the quantum. He watched and felt it move down the corridor as if it was inside him, too. It rushed through him, making his skin tingle, and traveled down the other side of the corridor.

"Patience in observing the waves is power, and it always reveals the right situation and right moment," a female voice said.

That voice didn't sound creepy at all. It sounded genuine, smooth, and calm. *I think that is Tulyata, but I'm not sure.*

The next time the statues slid forward to take the center spot, Zreyas saw a slight faint green glow back in the distance past the center statue. He continued to watch everything, not just down the center. He was determined not to let a momentary distraction get him killed. He was not about to do anything until his instincts kicked in—too much was at stake.

37 Body Language

Zreyas

Propping his chin on his hand and his elbow on his knee, he sat on his heels, continuing his vigil of acute observation. He watched the green light getting a little brighter each time a warrior slid forward.

Nothing else changed except the type of warrior. There were no more waves of weird energy and emotions. Just before the light seemed like it would reveal it to him, it went out. Zreyas looked around briefly and stayed still.

He fell back on the floor when he noticed something that made his skin crawl. The statue in the front now looked like a perfect replica of himself. It stunned him. He knew it was him, but there were differences that put fear into him. He was much larger than even his previous form. His horns were so large and long they wrapped around himself and on beyond that. The horns flowed up behind him and twisted and twirled upward in coils. What alarmed him was that the eyes were red, like the Dark One's eyes.

"No, this is just the influence of the Dark One. This is not me," he told himself as he closed his eyes. "This is *not* me. I can't let this statue of anger and hate influence me. This is not me anymore, and no one will make me be anything I don't want to be. That is my pledge to myself and to those I'm trying to help. I also hope I remember what I just committed to, *always*."

Zreyas opened his eyes. The statue was there, but the eyes were stone, not red and glowing anymore. He sighed in relief, and the statue began to slide down the right hall, toward the dark end.

He shivered as he watched the next one slide forward. The new one was again his own image. He knew it was him because of the face, but the body...

The entire body was in pieces on the floor, like someone chopped it up into parts. Its mouth was open in a scream, as if it died a horrible death.

Zreyas looked past the crumbled statue to see blackness in the hall. Then the walls behind the crumbled statue started sliding into themselves, closing. It stopped at half the original opening size. A green orb appeared and floated in the opening.

It began singing tones that were very nice to the ears and soul. Zreyas stood and walked across the hall over to the pile of stone body parts. Then he made his way to the mouth of the closing hall, where the orb floated. It moved away, then stopped as if to invite him to follow it.

Zreyas couldn't help but look at the statue of himself in parts just behind him. He heard a different kind of stone-sliding noise and looked up a little higher. Something more than a little alarming came to his attention. The hallway from which he had come was... gone. There was nothing but a solid wall there now. Zreyas had a choice to move forward or take his chances left or right. He looked at the orb and simply said, "No, this does not feel calm and even. It feels obvious, easy, and wrong to follow you."

A piercing screech ripped through Zreyas' body. The wall finished closing with a loud thump that echoed everywhere, and he now stood there alone in a long hall of statues. The screech continued, and it filled Zreyas. His body shuddered and part of himself felt like it was going to rip apart.

He focused on the statue while he was readying his mind to prepare for what he thought might be inevitable. Giving in was not something he would do, but fighting it was ephemeral. Zreyas knew that influence now when he felt it. It was conditioning him slowly, but surely. He now realized he might have made a mistake. Maybe he should have gone. All he knew was that his body was filling up with such anger and hatred that he couldn't hold it all.

Zreyas thought about Aaru and couldn't help but feel his love for him. It was the one thought he would like to think about as he left this life. Zreyas realized the energy ripping through him changed slightly, almost like a super charged transfer of anger to joy when he did a q-leap.

He was sweating as this screech pierced and ripped through his body. Then he remembered Rhom's lesson about the sound and glass. *I am the glass right now.*

Zreyas could barely think, but he rested his mind on his new friends; how Rtu called him 'little buddy', Rhom called him 'my boy', and even Tulyata called him a 'ferret'.

In the pain he closed his eyes and truly, fully smiled for the first time in his life. He felt himself swell, and it felt like he grew past his body. He opened his eyes. Symbols in the tunnel were starting to light up, slowly fading in. He didn't understand it and didn't care.

Zreyas' eyes watered as he switched his focus to tolerating the pain. As soon as he did, he felt himself condense, and the pain consumed and ripped through him again with such vengeance that he almost passed out.

He arched his back and felt his shoulder begin to sever from the inside. Veins popped out all over him. He barely got out the words through gritted teeth. "I love you, Aaru. I am sorry I couldn't keep my promise. I did try, though. Tell Ayya, I have found I love her too, because you are part of her now and I know she is important to us all, even if I don't understand the reasons." Thinking about all his new friends, his eyes watered. "I am sending the loving to you."

The screeching stopped abruptly, and Zreyas fell to the floor. Absence of the pain and torture ripping through his body became total bliss. The sudden absence of pain was so intense that it almost seemed torturous.

Zreyas realized he was lying in the statue's mouth, but he didn't care. He was forever thankful that there was no more screeching and pain. He breathed heavily, sweat running off his body. Zreyas closed his eyes and lost consciousness.

When he woke, the other tunnel he came in from was still blocked off. He was laying in the mouth of his own statue, like a hammock on the tongue lapped out of its mouth. He looked at it and said, "I'm so sorry you had to die that horrible death. I understand now how it might have felt and why."

Zreyas put his hands on both sides of his statue's mouth to lift himself up to stand on the back of the throat. His eyes caught a purple dim light out of the corner of his eye. He looked down the hall and didn't see a thing. Then he looked the other way and still saw nothing but blackness. He turned to look at the wall behind him where the statues came from. Nothing there but the wall. Then he saw it again, out of the peripheral of his left eye. He slowly turned his head and looked over the nose of the statue... nothing.

The next instant he saw a slow pulse of a purple light coming through the nostrils of the statue's nose. Crouching down a little to see up the nostrils, he saw a purple globe of swirling light, similar to the purple mist in the challenge node that rose up to measure him. He reached inside, but the swirling light moved to the other nostril.

"Well, nothing like picking your own nose for all the visages to see! This is for you, Rtu!" Zreyas reached in with both hands, one in each nostril, and felt the warm globe of light. He grabbed it, but the membrane between the nostrils was blocking the ability to pull it out.

He knew it was stupid, but he reasoned he was a creature of curiosity. "For science, Rhom!"

Zreyas tried to pull it out anyway, using both hands. Something clicked, the nose broke loose toward him, and the throat he was standing on gave way under his feet. He fell, nose and all, sliding through his own statue's throat. "Ticking hell, this is crazy!"

Zreyas hung on to the globe for dear life, the nose of the stone statue hitting his horns and head because he wouldn't let go. He saw stars, even with the protective horns, as he slid down its ribbed esophagus. Zreyas looked down. The tunnel went straight down and widened out.

"Yep, there's the stomach. I've gutted enough bodies that I know what this is and I'm glad it is empty!" Taking advantage of that, Zreyas gripped the orb with his left hand, pulled his right hand out of the nose and grabbed the orb by reaching around to the back side of the broken nose. Then he let go with this left and let the nose fall away. He gripped the orb with both hands, pulling it close to his chest for safety.

He realized he was in big trouble when the orb allowed him to see his surroundings, because it lit up the area better than his dark vision. Below him at the bottom was a pool of acid. And there was a cave opening, higher up, in the side of the wall.

"Ticking hell!" Zreyas did his best to flatten his body out and steer toward the tunnel, coming fast. He reasoned the curved opening of the tunnel might redirect the energy of his fall.

"Shit, this is going to hurt!"

Using the orb and his body to steer his fall, working with the resistance of the air, he moved closer toward his target. Zreyas hit hard, but he was true to his target and landed in the tunnel opening. Knocking the wind out of himself, the pain ripped through him from the jolt. He gasped for breath with difficulty while he slid down the bumpy tunnel full of ninety and one hundred eighty-degree curves. It seemed to go on forever and his body was being beaten to hell. Just as he got himself straightened, he ran into an extreme turn in the tunnel and dropped, just to keep going again.

After catching his breath, it dawned on him where he was in the statue. "A stone intestine! Ticking hell, I am technically my own piece of shit. I guess you were right after all, Commander!"

After quite a long bout of sliding, he realized what came next after the intestine. "Ticking mag-shit, now I'm literally going to shit myself!"

... and then he saw the light.

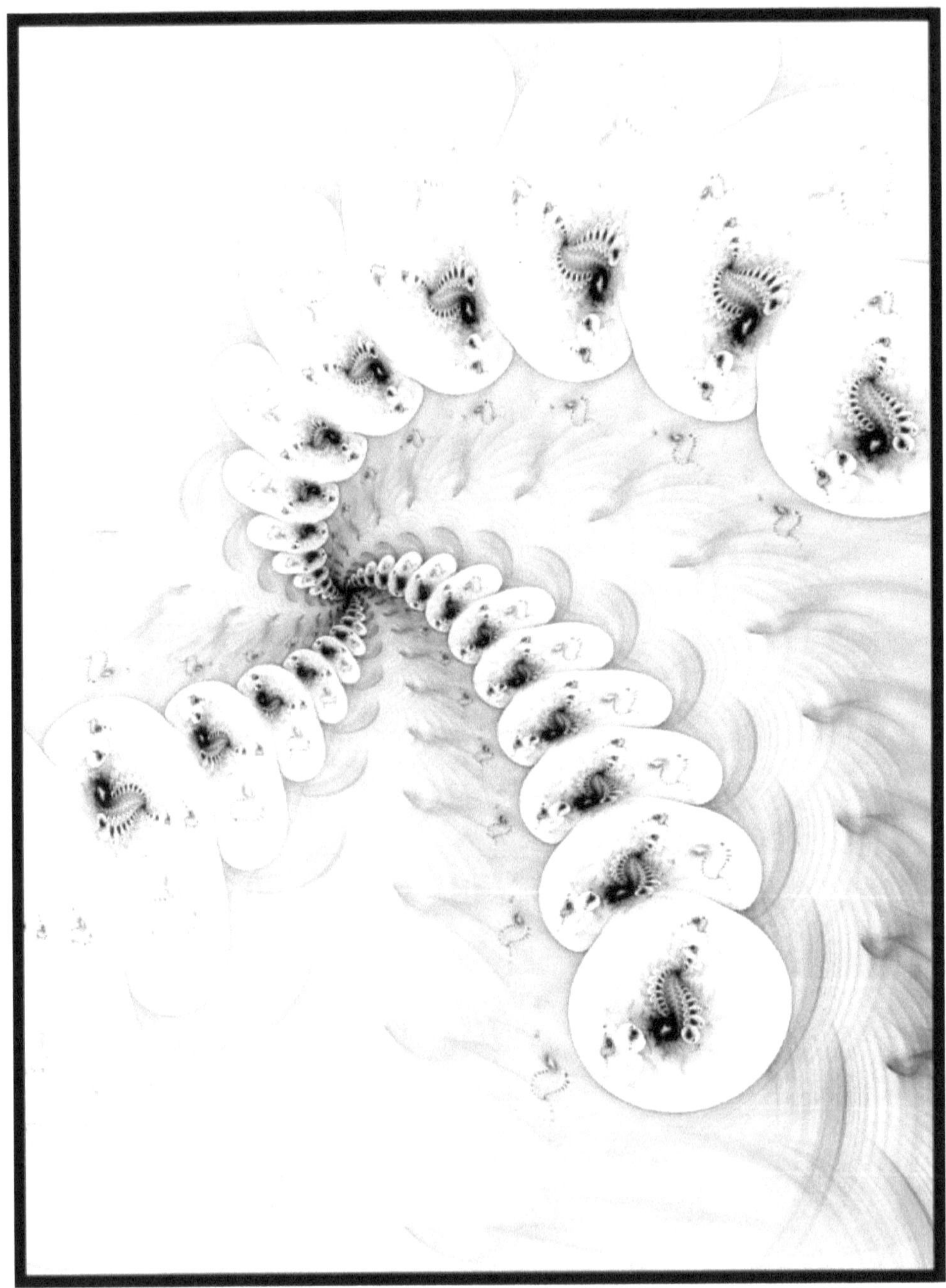

38 Redacted

Zreyas

Zreyas shook his head at the irony of it all and said, “Enjoy this, Rtu!”

Holding on to the globe for dear life, he saw nothing but white mist for a long time. But then he realized it didn’t feel like he was falling anymore. It was more like... floating. The floor came into view below, black and shiny. It was a large square floor with all the edges obscured by mist.

He gently landed on the floor, and he felt the weight of his body again. As he looked around, he turned and slid the globe around in his hands. The mist began receding and a challenge node appeared on his left. Breathing a sigh of relief, he continued his watch and meandered down the walkway.

On his right, there was a console, and ahead was a

large floor. Zreyas walked a little way towards the open space in the floor and the mist receded more, revealing a runway with occasional incoming walkway at a ninety-degree angle on the left.

There were three of them. At the end of each walkway was a square platform, larger than the width of the short runways. He did, however, see a small square crack in the floor. Looking to the right, he saw nothing but blackness. In fact, anywhere there was not a walkway or floor, there was nothing but space.

Zreyas walked back to the node in order to go back and speak with the others before he got himself into any more trouble. He was exhausted, hurting, and hungry. Walking back, he noticed the globe glow as he passed the first runway he discovered, just past the node.

Zreyas turned and walked down the short little runway a couple of steps near the platform. The globe made an electric cracking sound and zipped from his hand to the platform. It expanded and flattened into a large purple portal. It seemed stable. Zreyas looked back and saw that the other two had no portal.

"I hope you are all getting this because this is going to be one hell of an adventure to retell." Zreyas headed to the node quickly and stepped on the large floor. It lit up and came to life. Then he had an idea to ask the node that he was about to step on.

He stepped on the node and didn't wait for the mechanical voice to give him options. "Can anyone hear our conversation?"

"—Your request for an answer to this question has been granted."

— Yes, and No. Sensitive information is only said in communication through your mind, like how we are doing it right now. No one will hear that. Notice it sounds a little different.

Zreyas nodded. It had its own voice, but it had the

same tinny edge to the sound like when he spoke, with Aaru in his mind in the dying dimension.

"—Zreyas of the Atra, you have activated a new challenge node. Would you like to claim this node and link it to your home node? Yes or No."

That was odd. Zreyas heard 'redacted' in his ears and 'Atra' in his... mind. *What the ticking hell? I must be exhausted.* "Yes, I would. Hey, what did you say about an atra?"

"—You may now choose one of the following:

> One, travel to the original landing node.
> Status: Open to all home node members.

Zreyas interjected, "Did you hear me? Hello?" but the challenge node continued.

> Two, travel to entry node number three.
> Discovered by: Zreyas of the Atra.
> Status: locked.
> Three, set this node for future landing.
> Four, stay at this location.
> Five, return."
> — Six, Claim the Rsi Torana.

Zreyas was so tired he could barely think. *Atra... atra...* He had no idea what an atra was. He just wanted to go lay down after eating something. "Retur—" *Wait, what? Can you explain option six? I don't know what that is.*

— Zreyas of the Atra, you have constructed the unique Rsi Torana. There is only one of its kind in the challenge world. Challenge participants had a point-zero-seven chance to find it and point-zero-zero-zero-two-five chance to successfully obtain it without perishing. Would you like detailed information of the Rsi Torana if claimed verses not claimed?

Zreyas nodded and sat on his heels. He concentrated

and felt clearer in that position. "Yes."

— Zreyas of the Atra, if you claim the Rsi Torana, the following apply:

> One, no one else will be able to claim it.
> Two, if Zreyas of the Atra perishes, so will the Rsi Torana.
> Three, only those attuned or of synchronizing frequency may use the Rsi Torana.
> Four, no matter where the Rsi is, the Torana will take you to that dimension. Note: Challenge portals that can only take a participant to a specific location.
> Five, the Rsi Torana is indestructible and eternal as long as its master is alive.
> Six, the Rsi Torana may only be relocated by Zreyas of the Atra.
> Seven, if Zreyas of the Atra does not claim the Rsi Torana within fifteen minutes of activation, it will die. However, your team may still access the Earth dimension with another portal found made for the challenge.

There are seven minutes and thirty-seven seconds remaining until the Rsi Torana expires. Would you like to claim the Rsi Torana? Yes, or No?

Zreyas thought for a moment. Questions pummeled his mind. "Can you put up a timer for the expiration so I can watch it while I ask you questions?"

"—We approve the request for a visible timer without a balance cost."

Zreyas looked around the node but didn't see it. He stood and turned toward the portal and there it was, a large hour glass hologram that he couldn't miss if he wanted to. "Appreciation to you," Zreyas said.

He sat back down on his heels and took out the tryst and held it. When he brooded or strategized over something, he had normally taken out his small knife and whittled. That wasn't an option right now, so he just stared at the portal... he repeated the name of that portal in his mind that he heard. *The rru-shee tor-ana.*

Zreyas stared at purple swirling light. *What do the names mean? Short version.*

— Your request for a short version of your question has been approved and answered simply so that you will understand:

> Rsi means ancient singer of songs.
> Torana has several definitions; however, the applicable definitions are:
>
> > Portal
> > Arched doorway
> > Triangle that supports a large balance.

Silence filled the air and his mind, and the answer made sense to Zreyas because Ayya was to sing songs for her people, and that was a portal.

Three minutes and forty-nine seconds remaining.

Zreyas considered a moment, then asked, *If this portal is... unique and needs to be attuned to Ayya to use it, how the ticking-hell did it get into the challenge dimension? Because there is no way that pile of mag-shit Dark One is attuned to her, or anywhere near her frequency. I'm actually surprised I am remotely near it. There's some weird shit going on here.*

— We have denied your request to answer that question fully. However, we can say the challenge creator had nothing to do with getting the Rsi Torana into the challenge dimension.

It was the answer Zreyas expected, but someone had skirted the rules... somehow. He thought for a moment as he stared at the portal, then asked, *who made the Rsi Torana?*

— The request to answer your question has been granted: Zreyas of Atra.

Zreyas waited for the rest of the answer, but it never

came.

One minute, thirteen seconds remaining.

"I can't make a sound decision if I don't get all my answers. What am I supposed to do?" *And why do you keep calling me Zreyas of Atra?*

— Would you like to claim the Rsi Torana? Yes or No.

"Well, I don't want it to die unnecessarily. One more question. If I want to move it after claiming it, do I need to come here to do it? And will it come with the console or tools to use it properly?"

Forty-two seconds remaining.

— Your request for answers to the two questions has been granted: You only need to use your skills to make it portable and come to you. Zreyas of Atra does not need to be in its physical presence.

I will ask again... why do you keep calling me Zreyas of Atra?

Twenty-eight seconds remaining.

— Because you are Zreyas of Atra.

"Okay, I deserved that." *Yes, I will claim the portal.*

— There is no portal to claim.

Nineteen seconds remaining.

"Ticking hell!" Standing abruptly in a panic, watching the timer, "What are my options?"

"—You may now choose one of the following:

One, travel back to the original landing node.
Status: Open to all home node members.
Two, travel to entry node number three.
Discovered by: Zreyas of the Atra.
Status: locked.
Three, claim this node for your future
landing node.
Four, Stay at this location.
Five, return."
— Six, Claim the Rsi Torana.

Two seconds remaining.

Zreyas stared at the purple portal, hoping like hell he would say it right, and quickly said, *I claim the rrushi torana!*

— Zreyas of the Atra has claimed the Rsi Torana, and is now the master caretaker of said entity.

He watched the purple portal's timer disappear. Beside the portal on each side, pillars rose up and it created an archway over the top of it.

— Zreyas of the Atra may customize the Rsi Torana any time he wishes.

"—You may now choose one of the following," the node said aloud:

> One, travel back to the original landing node.
>
> Status: Open to all home node members.
>
> Two, travel to entry node number three.
>
> Discovered by: Zreyas of the Atra
>
> Status: locked.
>
> Three, claim this node for your future landing node.
>
> Four, stay at this location.
>
> Five, return."

"Make this node my future landing node, and return."

The challenge node's appearance turned into the home node colors of blue and cyan and symbols filled up with purple mist starting from the floor. Zreyas' mind was reeling, utterly confused about what just took place. Zreyas watched the particles and heard the sounds of the quantum transport.

Zreyas appeared back in Tulyata's domain to find them all arguing back and forth. He couldn't tell what they were arguing about because it was in a language of strange sounds he didn't understand, even with his translator. The language was like hearing and feeling the whinnies and nays of energy. Finally, after a few minutes of watching, Zreyas sat on the edge of the challenge node. When there wasn't a sign that it was going to stop any time soon, he laid on his side and immediately fell asleep, exhausted.

39 Voices

Rtu

A few hours later, Rtu stood and walked over near Zreyas, bent over, and propped himself up on his knees. "I can't stand it anymore." He sent a light puff of air toward Zreyas and said, "Oh, little buddeee! Wake up, little buddy! You have to shit yourself again!"

Zreyas didn't move and continued snoring like a growl.

"He's been through a lot for days and has never really rested well in peace that I know of," Rhom said with empathy clear in his voice. "If he slept, it couldn't have been long, and it had to have been on that island in between the creature interactions and making rope. I forget he is not one of us. Honestly, I'm surprised you let him in here Tulyata."

"Me too!" Rtu echoed.

"Well, I had little choice." Tulyata cleared her throat. "And yes, he has been through a lot for a carbon body."

"Pfft, no choice?" Rtu slammed his arm down on the chair arm and glared at her. "You are always 'finding balance' for your choices. Like you say, 'There is always time or circumstance if you want it badly enough, even more than excuses.'"

Rhom leaned forward slowly with a grin, looking at her face. "You actually *like* him!"

Tulyata whirled around in her chair and pointed at Rhom. "That will be enough of that from you! I've never liked anyone except you two, and even *that* is pushing it!"

"Until now," both Rhom and Rtu said at the same time. They looked at each other and busted out in fits of laughter, pointing at her.

Tulyata straightened back and raised her chin. "Don't you two have something to do?"

"We are!" both exclaimed with howls of laughter.

"I'm warning you..."

The two kept howling so hard in laughter they were crying. Tulyata smiled, despite herself, but Rtu could tell it was making her angry. Tulyata chuckled... then her face grew red in fury. She gave in and started laughing. "I hate you two!"

"Ah, pfft. I don't believe it," Zreyas said sleepily.

Tulyata whirled around. "How much of our conversation did you hear?"

Zreyas shrugged, "None, except all three of you laughing. That is something different to wake up to. I can't say I have ever woken up to laughter before."

They all looked at each other, and Rtu, Rhom, and Tulyata looked at Zreyas and started laughing again. They all yelled out exclamations about him being a piece of shit, shitting himself, and being a mouthful. Rtu watched Zreyas narrow his eyes and cross his arms, waiting.

After a bit, Rtu finally said, "Aww, come on, little buddy, we loved your show, and all you did."

"I hate to admit it, but I would have done something different and not ended up near as well as you did, I think." Tulyata interjected.

"Same here," Rhom admitted. "I think I would have followed that orb."

Rtu said, "I think I might have been dead from the start and bumbled in and got whacked by the eternal gloom tentacles. Well, maybe not. The point is, I'm impressed, *and* it was entertaining."

"Well, I touched a challenge node and one binder," Zreyas added.

Rtu looked at Zreyas, relieved he made it through. He wasn't sure what he meant and asked, "What do you mean by two challenge nodes?"

"There was an external challenge node at the top of the temple and a binder node at the portal area."

Rtu looked at his brother, then at Tulyata. He noticed Tulyata's face was just as confused as he was. "I saw nothing at the top of the temple. We saw you pause and assumed you were just testing something."

"Interesting... I saw it. I just assumed you both did too," Rhom said, scratching his head just over his ear.

"Well, it mostly looked like the one I left and landed in, but the differences were the color and symbols. The symbols were different, and the colors were purple and yellow."

"Go on." Rtu sat up and listened, but wondered why he hadn't seen it. "I don't like being left out of information! I'm used to knowing almost everything."

"When I stepped on it, it told me I could leave from there, go to the one I came in on, or stay. But it advised me that if I left the challenge area from that point, that I might not know where I was, or be in a dangerous situation, since I had not discovered the entry half yet. Did you guys see any that I might have missed?"

Everyone shook their heads.

"I'm stumped we didn't see this node," said Tulyata. "That means we need to communicate more and we can't assume everything we see is the only thing there, and vice versa."

Zreyas walked up to where the two nature visages were, jumped up and grabbed Rhom's loincloth and climbed up Rhom's leg. He sat down beside him, looking extremely little in that scenario.

Rtu looked at Zreyas, surprised he didn't leap. "Tired?"

Zreyas looked at Rtu. "I've had enough quick motion for a little while."

Rtu felt obsessive about not seeing that node. *So, Tulyata and I couldn't see it, and Rhom and Zreyas did. I wonder if it has to do with... Nah, has to be something else.* He looked at the node and wondered if a few choices he had made in the past might have affected his ability to see that node. Tulyata was looking at the challenge node, too. He saw his brother smiling, looking down at Zreyas, as happy and carefree as he had ever seen him. Still, his face had contemplation on it. Then he couldn't help but wonder what Rhom's little donation was that would cause his fire to be two-thirds gone.

Zreyas looked at him.

Observant little bugger. Rtu redirected him with a question. "So, do any of you have any idea what that portal is?"

Zreyas shrugged. "Well, I think it was the portal Tulyata spoke about earlier when she told us about the way to Earth; you were there."

All semblance of laughter gone, Zreyas finally broke the deafening silence.

"Thanks for the nice whispers. Every time you did that, I felt like things were going in the right direction and knew I had done something right."

Tulyata put on her half glasses and looked over them at Zreyas. "What do you mean, whispers? I didn't whisper to you, and we didn't hear any whispers."

"I didn't hear anything either," Rtu responded with pure fascination. Then he looked at Rhom.

"I heard them. I just figured it was part of the challenge. When he disarmed the traps and in the tunnel of... emotions, for lack of a better term," Rhom added.

"I knew it sounded much more kind than Tulyata, but I just assumed it wasn't anyone but her, since I didn't know any other females. You know, you sound different from males."

Tulyata glared at him over her half glasses.

Rtu piped up, knowing her too well, "It was no offense to you! In fact, it is more of a compliment."

Tulyata narrowed her eyes and lowered her head at Zreyas.

Rtu chuckled, holding out a hand and feeling sorry for his little buddy. "Remember, he is not used to having ladies around. They all sound the same to him right now because he has only heard you before, and you never whisper."

Tulyata pointed at Zreyas several times without a word and backed off silently.

Rtu looked at Zreyas and noticed, though still small, he was larger than he was before. He reached over and picked up the little chair and held it near him. “You’ve grown! How did that happen?”

Zreyas’ eyes grew wide in excitement, touching the chair.

Rhom held his hand over him for a moment. “Yes, he’s grown double. It’s still small, but going from fifteen to thirty centimeters is quite the growth spurt! I knew something seemed different about you.”

“I don’t remember growing.”

Rhom said, “It might have been the screeching and you getting through it with transforming energy. I didn’t hear what you were thinking about, but I could see the energy.”

Zreyas rested his chin on his knee, wrapping his now very flexible horns around toward the front of his body, holding them around him like a comforting shawl.

Rtu couldn’t help but notice Zreyas rubbed them, felt his friend’s grief, and noticed the pliable nature of them now. “Getting used to the new horns, little buddy?”

“I miss my old body. I worked hard for it. Though I could do without the body size, I miss my horns the way they were. Nothing I can do about it now.”

Rtu felt empathy for him as he watched him look around the room, totally content with just... being.

Zreyas closed his eyes, then opened them again wide.

Rtu cocked his head, watching him as he felt his peace. “It’s called peace, little buddy. Just be with it and enjoy it.”

Zreyas looked up at him with a genuinely soft smile.

Rtu wasn’t sure he had ever seen him smile, even when he was doing his one-‘ha’ laughing. He always had to watch people transform from a distance, being a visage, so he felt blessed to witness a life transformation up close for a change.

"Aaru, now I understand how you felt that day you found your armor," Zreyas said softly as he closed his eyes.

Rtu watched water drip from his eyes. He could tell everyone in the room felt the peace Zreyas was radiating. He watched it push out of his body, glad he could see the magic of life and energy. Everyone in the room stared at Zreyas, stunned.

Tulyata said nothing in her grouchy wisdom.

Rhom looked at Zreyas with such love for the little guy.

Maybe I should incarnate next time it is needed. Rhom seems to have gained something I can't pinpoint. Rtu felt lucky to have met Zreyas in person. Incarnates grew too needy and expected him to fix everything to their whim if he did. But Zreyas was different. He never asked him for anything.

Rtu silently cried, feeling in his heart every bit of Zreyas' emotional peace. He felt peace often, but he didn't get a chance to really be with it like this. Zreyas' aura was amplifying it to him tenfold... Another one of Zreyas' gifts that he had not yet discovered for himself.

"There is that voice again," Rhom said gently.

Zreyas smiled and nodded, eyes still closed. "Yes, I understand now."

Curious, but too into the peace to care, Rtu heard Zreyas say after a few minutes, "Okay."

Rhom gently patted the little guy's leg.

Rtu felt a jolting and sudden snap, like he was just released from a stretched rubber band. He felt like he was no longer tethered to something. Startled but still in the peace, he said, "I'm guessing you two hear that voice again that we didn't hear."

Tulyata stopped looking at Zreyas. She turned to

work with balances furiously, darting her eyes back to Zreyas for a quick look from time to time, obviously disturbed, yet she didn't seem upset. "That place did something to him."

"I hear it too, and I wasn't in that place," Rhom reminded her.

Tulyata, working herself into a lather, continued, "I wonder if the Dark One is doing this? For crying out loud, we are visages, but we aren't seeing near as much as we are used to."

"Or we are opening our eyes to the fact we are not as big as we think we are," Rhom interjected.

"As soon as he is out of his... peaceful state, we need to update him on what we think we have figured out. I don't dare to think we know anything for sure now. There is way too much weirdness happening."

"I don't think I have ever seen anyone change their state of awareness so fast," said Rtu. "It goes to show you that when you have acceptance of yourself during the largest disasters and loss in life, that is when we have the most room and potential to change, and... to notice the good things we already have."

"He's one of the rare ones to see it, recognize it, and put it into motion—voices or no voices," Rhom added.

40 Aqum

Zreyas

"That was a crazy episodic journey you had just now Zreyas!" said Rtu. "I'm not complaining. It was nice to witness and feel. That pushing aura of energy you have is powerful. It does the same thing when you are in that war state of yours, but you emanate something totally different for different reasons. I can see why your opponents might not be at their full potential when they are fighting you inside that field of energy."

Rhom smiled and looked at Rtu. "What he did was incredibly amazing for a non-visage. Zreyas always does his best, making being incarnated almost seem to have no limits." Rhom leaned forward with elbows on his knees. "You aren't inferior, my boy, you are amazing, and a breath of fresh air to us."

"Okay." Zreyas looked at Rtu and then Tulyata

awkwardly, not used to praise like that. “So, what did you figure out? Surely, you saw it all and figured something out while I was off in the land of DO. I mean, you *are* visages.”

Rtu chuckled. “DO?”

“Dark One... You know the big D.O. He is shit... DO.”

They all laughed, except Tulyata, though she smirked.

“Visages with limitations, it seems.” Tulyata said directly to Zreyas, with both eyes throwing daggers along with a little admiration. “But we figured out that you took the quick route being digested by your stone self. I don’t think you missed anything productive. If someone else had gone through there, they would have had to go the long way around. You are probably the only one who could fit into that big mouth of yours.”

Zreyas felt himself smile a small bit, despite himself. “Well, at least I helped a little.” He looked at the screen. “What is that console for?”

Rtu looked at Zreyas, “We were hoping you could tell us, because we don’t know. If mother was able to get through, then maybe she could figure it out.”

Zreyas looked at Tulyata pointedly, knowing she could. Then he turned to Rtu. “Did you go through and try to find out?” He faced Rhom. “Old man?”

Rhom and Rtu looked at each other, and Rtu said, “Uh... no?”

“Why not? I paved the way there for you. Why didn’t you go look? Do I have to do everything?”

Tulyata grinned. “Told you!”

“Is that what you guys were arguing about when I came back?”

“One of the things, yes.”

“Ticking-hell,” Zreyas said, feeling antsy from

exasperation. Then he turned. "Old man, I will go through with you to see what you can figure out if you like. You are the smart type; I *know* you will figure it out."

"I don't think we can go through together anymore, my boy."

"Why?"

"I have grown into more of my power, and I doubt we will meet the requirements anymore."

"What requirements?"

"The balance threshold of who goes through there together, remember?"

"I distinctly heard it say they locked in and approved the teams. It didn't say with conditions," added Zreyas.

"He has a point!" Rtu exclaimed. "Try it! If Rhom won't, I will!"

Zreyas leaped off the cushy seats and walked over to the node. "Can I eat something when I get back? I'm starved."

"Eat something now... here." Tulyata placed a table, a small plate of food, and a new chair on her desk. "We don't know what will happen next, so eat."

Rhom and Rtu exchanged looks with raised eyebrows.

Zreyas q-leaped over and sat down to eat like he had not eaten in a varSa.

"We forget about that part of your needs as well as... maybe other needs you will need after you eat," Rtu chuckled.

Tulyata suddenly looked prudish, waved a hand, and a small door appeared in the wall between the node and Rhom's dimension. "You can use that room for *those* needs."

Zreyas nodded and shoved more food in his mouth.

In a few minutes, he walked through the small door and closed it. As he looked at the thing sitting on the floor, he cocked his head. “Um… wha—”

“Lift the lid and sit!” he heard Tulyata say sharply. He could almost hear her eyes roll.

“Oh!”

“And make sure those bits of yours are pointed downward!” she added. “Don’t forget to wash your hands!”

“Ha! Good idea!” He heard them all chuckling out there.

In a few minutes, he walked out of the room and toward the challenge node, ready to go with all those needs taken care of. “That room was *handy*!”

Everyone laughed.

Zreyas stepped in the node and turned around. The purple mist started filling up within the glass. “Come on, old man!”

“Well, he is back to his old self,” Rtu laughed.

Rhom got up and shrugged his shoulders. “Why not? The boy might be onto something. I might learn something for that ship I was working on too.”

Zreyas turned toward Rhom with a bouncy stance, looked up with an expression that was full of wonder. “What ship? Can I see it?”

“Maybe, my boy, in time.”

Rhom walked over and stepped on the node floor. Rtu leaned forward, and they all watched with keen interest. Zreyas didn’t expect a rejection.

The room filled up with the purple mist, way past the point in the ceiling that was the threshold.

“—The capacity of the node is over the allowed threshold.”

“Come on, you said you already approved the teams,”

nudged Zreyas.

They all waited several long seconds.

"—Thank you for your patience. We locked in and approved the teams before the start of the challenge. We apologize for the delay."

A toned chime progression sounded. He and Rhom looked up above them where they heard it come from.

"—There is a pending update."

Silence rang through the room, with everyone's expression seeming to say the same thing. "Update?"

"—Our records indicate Zreyas was the first to reach, install, and bind a portal to your node. We have granted him one boon that he can redeem at a later time. All teams approved before the start of the challenge have permanent access."

"Boon?" they all questioned in unison as Zreyas and Rhom flickered out of sight, leaving Rtu and Tulyata sitting there with gaping mouths.

Zreyas and Rhom teleported back into Tulyata's room. Once materialized, they both walked over to the seating area without a word. Zreyas' mind was reeling about what they had just found out and the anger simmered and grew slowly the more he thought about it.

"Well?" Rtu held his palms up, waiting.

"Though the challenge said there was no time limit, it was misleading," said Rhom.

Just as Tulyata and Rtu opened their mouths to ask questions, Rhom held a hand up to stall their interjections. "We think that the console and portal is the way to do the same thing Tulyata does with her screen... but in a real physical way, like mini-incarnations. If we go through, we are physically there in whatever form we choose to take."

"Interesting," said Rtu.

"The console does a couple things: One, it switches time periods and locations within a specific range of five thousand kilometers of where our particular orb is attuned. Other portals found have a random radius. Two, we choose how we appear when we go. It must be earth indigenous matter and energy, or something that Earth technology could make. It could be a living being, plant, animal, or material; however, it may *not* be a pure single element. Three, the form, or body, we choose cannot change once there."

Zreyas thought as Rhom explained what they discovered. He found it interesting that Rhom didn't discover it was this... rrishi torana, or however it was said. *I think that is a message to me to keep my mouth shut about it, for now.*

"What? That console is replacing me?" Tulyata flared.

"I don't think that could happen no matter what the challenge..." Rhom consoled. "But I do think it gives the people going to Earth a little power to make sure they can go in as they wish, since you can't go in. There is also a mini scale of balances at the portal from the way it looks. There is an invisible chamber, like the node here, to make sure nothing goes through too powerful to keep balance and team integrity is in place."

Rhom and Zreyas looked at each other with the gravity of what else they found out.

Tulyata pointed at Rhom. "I know that look. What is wrong?"

Zreyas couldn't help it, he blurted out with a seething anger, "Ayya's in trouble." Then he looked around the room and said, "We have to help her!"

"The problem is, the Dark One, or some of the Janquar, have just landed on earth. They have set events in motion and we can't stop it until it gets close to the 'too late' point," said Rhom.

Zreyas curled his finger around his chin, then let his hand drop. "Well, there are always two, or more, sides to events when it comes to strategy. What that mag-shit has set in motion for that side might be there, but there is nothing saying that we can't change things from her side with a little influence, so their trajectory misses. His strategy is set, but ours is not, and there is nothing saying that we can't make their target move... or something like that."

"Good thinking, my boy!" Rhom looked excited. "There is something to be said for having things too easy. I'm used to having the power to do what I want. I really never had to learn strategy at the level *you* know it. What have you got in mind?"

"We are timeless here, right? I have a few minutes to think?"

"You have, but at the cost of the timeline we can go back to. Remember, we found out that we can only wind it back so far. But we are also new to the controls. We only did a quick check of functionality."

"Well, better to take a few minutes to think than do something rash without a plan." Zreyas sat down a moment and it wasn't long before he needed to ask questions.

"Rtu, you are willing to help, yes?" Zreyas asked.

"Sure thing, little buddy! What are you thinking?"

"Don't you do visage kind of things in your creations directly, right?"

"Yes, but I don't interfere directly much because

people would expect too much from me and start whining about all the things they need me to do."

"I hadn't thought about that angle," Rhom said. "I like what I am hearing so far."

"Good, and good, what I'm thinking isn't about doing a lot for people." He turned toward Rhom. "Old man, this is pure gut instinct thinking. I know Aaru, but I know a little about Ayya. But I also know you better than Ayya. What do you think about you going to that fire station that Ayya and her mother walk to a few times a week when we checked their living patterns? Establish a relationship. Maybe you can get her to wake up a little so she can listen to Aaru, or at least this awareness you keep talking about. Aaru's instincts are top-notch. Or at least wake up enough to grow some survival instincts on her own."

Rhom scratched his head just over his right ear. "You know, that has potential. The Dark One and Janquar can't do a damn thing about the person changing and making different decisions based on their changes. It will also give me a chance to see how she is developing, too. That will help us figure out how best to help her wake up in the future too... hopefully.

The old visage made good points he hadn't thought about for the long term, if he was honest with himself. "There is where your Visage-ness comes into play, old man. See, you are strategic."

Rtu laughed, "Visage-ness... good word!"

"Hey Chuckles, can you split yourself in half temporarily? Like you and Rhom did?"

Everyone in the room looked shocked.

Zreyas hurried to explain, holding his hands up. "It would just be temporary. We need two of you. Ha!"

"I guess I could, little buddy, but why?"

"Strategy! We don't exactly have an army of volunteers and Tulyata won't go through the challenge node."

Tulyata put on her half glasses and looked over them at him, raising only one eyebrow. He had gotten to know her a little and that meant she had something to hide or she was impressed, but wanted to punch him. He found out what he needed to find out by her reaction and quickly re-directed the attention of the room.

"Part of yourself is weaker than the whole and the smaller part can make up the difference to go through the challenge node with Rhom. The balance changes affect that thing's measuring, right?"

"Yes, yes it does," Tulyata said, looking as if she was now interested in what he had to say.

"If you go with Rhom to the fire station, even if it was the weakest form of yourself to fill the balance threshold of that node entity. You can help cover for each other as you snoop around to watch Ayya and what's going on around there. You might recognize a pattern."

Tulyata took off her glasses, leaned on her forearms against the desktop and said evenly, "The little ferret has a point. We don't know what we are dealing with yet. One person could easily get duped because there is only so much one person can see, especially posing in an incarnate's body with limited vision. You two have always had each other's backs. Just like Aaru and Zreyas always did. Seems like a good time for teamwork again."

Everyone looked at Tulyata, a little shocked, but she never flinched or went off on an insult tangent. Zreyas felt himself grin, and it felt odd.

Tulyata seemed like she had a significant realization and had made her mind up about something. He could relate to that and had done it *a lot* in the past week. *She is hatching a plan of some sort, but I don't think it is with the Dark One or the Janquar.*

"Tulyata, umm."

"Just give me the order, ferret. I see the strategy."

"Well, just do what you do best. Gather data, find loopholes, and gaps we could use while we are going to do what we are going to do this round. Split yourself if you need to get in to get messages to them, or me. Put the data in a place that is safe and still accessible to us in case we need it where ever we all are. Even if Rtu and I don't understand it, make sure Rhom knows where to access it. At each stage, you can advise us. You said this affects us all. I just thought you might want to be involved."

She nodded, "I'll do that." Then she turned to her scales and screens and started working.

"Uh, okay... well." That shocked him a little that she was so compliant without insults.

Rhom nodded to him, "Go on, my boy."

"Rtu, as for your *major* half that remains here, you could do a little hands-on work when needed with your people... nothing saying it can't be Ayya as much as anyone else. Just because this... challenge is going on doesn't mean you can't be the visage you are. I mean, visages have to do their work in their realms, right? I don't know what you do, and I'm assuming it's a little healing, guidance, or whatever needs to be done." Zreyas grinned and winked.

The twin visages laughed hard together. Rtu patted his belly as expressions slid across his face as ideas seemed to ripple through his mind.

He finally said, "Little buddy, you are a genius. That is right! A Visage has to do their work." He winked back. "I think I like you!"

"Pfft, you ticking give the *loving* to me, and you know it. Ha!"

Rhom chuckled, and Rtu howled in laughter. The working Tulyata grinned, not missing a beat on her working hands.

Then Rhom asked, "So, what are *you* going to do?"

"What I do best, be myself, scout, use the quantum, and fight when needed." When the three visages just stared at him, he elaborated. "Look, when you guys do what you do, I will also be there on a different mission. That challenge node didn't say we couldn't take different teams in at the same time doing different things we put in motion, did it?"

Rhom's expression looked doubtful, and he cocked his head, "Eehh."

"Pfft, let's just ask." Zreyas got up, walked over to the node and stepped up.

The purple color rose, but he didn't wait.

"I am Zreyas, and I don't want to go anywhere right now, but I have a question I would like to ask."

All three visages leaned forward with a mix of interested and fascinated expressions on their faces. Tulyata even paused her work to watch.

"—We recognize you. Your request to ask questions is granted."

Zreyas gave a quick nod of expectation. He knew somehow they would let him ask questions. "Good, sending one of those thankings to you."

"Huh, well that's a first," said Rtu.

Zreyas cocked his head, "Have you ever asked a challenge node if you could ask a question before?"

"No, little buddy, I guess I haven't," said Rtu.

Rhom chuckled, "I haven't either."

Tulyata harrumphed and flicked her wrist for him to

carry on.

Zreyas couldn't help but ask first, "Do you have a name? Seems odd to call you 'one of the challenge nodes'."

"—The answer to your question has been granted. No."

"That's too bad. Everyone needs a name. Would you like one?"

"—The answer is granted - We are not sure. We are not accustomed to questions like that."

Rhom chuckled, "He is the question generator, get used to it."

"—We are adding to the conversation - We have noticed this tendency."

Zreyas grinned, "Well I will call you Aqum since you said yes by not saying you *didn't* want one."

Rhom cleared his throat and held up a finger. "Aqum? What does that mean?"

He shrugged and looked at Rhom, "Ask questions, understand more."

Rtu said, "What does that have to do with—"

Zreyas nodded and held a hand up, not sure of how to explain since he didn't really know how to read or make letters. He just knew sounds. "AAAsk Qquestions Uuunderstand Mmmore."

"Oh, that is clever!" said Rtu.

"It's a thing I do. Ha!" Everyone grinned, and he turned to the node, "Do you always sound robotic and... even-toned?"

"—The answer request: granted - We are saying with robotic sound as usual - yes."

"If that is who you are, it's good. I was just curious." Getting a feel for this... entity was interesting. He had to find out if this challenge node was a communication device for someone else, or an AI. "How do you like your new name, Aqum?"

"—The answer request: granted - We are saying with humor and perplexity - It is... acceptable."

"Good. You know my name; you can call me that if you want. Next question is about the challenge. Can multiple teams be on earth at the same time?"

"—The answer request: granted - We respond impressed - It is not a current feature of challenges.

> Status: It is not a feature that has been submitted, accepted, or rejected.
> Actionable: Check balances for the possibility of said additional feature.

We request that you to wait for this calculation."

"It's okay we can wait, Aqum," said Tulyata. "It is critical information for us to know."

Everyone turned to look at her and she waved a hand and shrugged, "Just doing my part."

Rhom chuckled. "What made you think to ask that, my boy?"

"Well, I got to thinking that everyone assumed it wasn't allowed because you had to have teams below a threshold. But that didn't exclude the ability to have more than one team dispatched at the same time." He turned slightly. "Aqum, do you listen to suggestions? I would like to give you information to think about before deciding."

"—The answer request: granted - Interruption response - Yes, we will listen.

Slowly walking in a circle inside Aqum, Zreyas brought his finger and thumb to his chin, propping his elbow on his fist. "The rules you have in place for challenges are locked in. I understand this. However, no rules in a certain area like the status you stated earlier is like having space... and space is potential."

He turned and pointed into the air, his strategic mind calculating everything he had learned up to this moment, both living his past with the Janquar and also what he had learned so far with the visages. "It's like a rule already in place that you have previously set up. It connects your other rules because there has to be space to live around the rules... They are guides but are dead with no space to live, which means no potential. I would like to propose that in those spaces like this one, that we are free to use those spaces as long as they don't break rules already set up." Zreyas shrugged. "I'm done."

"You should have been a politician, little buddy!"

"What's a politician?" Zreyas hesitated only a moment and said, "Never mind, I have enough problems being myself. I don't need to add something more right now."

Rhom chuckled, "Now if only politicians thought that way."

"—We have received and recorded the information submitted. Calculating..."

A long silence filled the room while everyone waited for the response.

41 Time to Go

Zreyas

"—We have calculated the validity of your submission in accordance with the challenge core rules. - We respond with space - We also set the rule that you need to communicate the space - Would you like to travel? Yes or No?"

Zreyas q-leaped several times, bouncing around the inside of the challenge node. "Yess!"

The next thing he saw were particles of travel. *Oops.* As soon as he arrived at the portal room, he said, "I would like to travel back. I responded incorrectly. I was celebrating your answer and forgot you asked a question."

Particles flooded his view again, and the visages faded into view. They were all laughing.

"Accidental travel," said Zreyas. "Ha!" He ran over, q-leaped up to his chair, sat, and clapped his hands together and rubbing them back and forth. "Now that we got all that out of the way, we can finish planning!"

"No, you can't," said Tulyata.

"Why not?"

"Because you didn't get a full answer. All Aqum said that they set the rule to communicate the space. The rest of it makes no sense legally," said Tulyata as she tipped her scales back and forth as she worked with invisible... whatever it is she used.

"It seems clear to me," said Zreyas.

Rhom grinned, "I actually understood exactly what it said, but to be fair, it's more on the level of aether and the quantum."

Tulyata and Rtu both said, "Ah!" Well, Tulyata's 'ah' was more like a grunted indignant version. Then they looked at Zreyas expectantly. Rhom grinned and nodded for him to do the honors.

"Basically, Aqum is allowing the multiple teams, but when we do something in the future that is... in the space between the rules, we need to run it by Aqum to record it, but it won't be announced to the opposite side. They could do the same thing, though, if they see that... space. But I doubt they will think to ask questions. They don't think past rules... unless someone *tells* them to, which could happen."

"You got all that out of that one sentence?" asked Tulyata. She turned to face her son. "Rhom?"

"The boy is correct. That is exactly what that response meant. Look forward to the day he can be my apprentice. He has... space!"

"Ha!"

Rtu looked at Tulyata, both of their jaws half hung.

"Okay, I would compliment the little ferret, but it would make me fall over dead, so I won't." Then Tulyata went back to her busy work.

"It's okay I read the spaces. I know it was a compliment."

Rhom laughed. "So what is the plan you are brewing in that brilliant head of yours?"

"Okay, I will go to earth as myself and just be me and do what I do closer to time. There are no rules that I can't go as me since I am organic. I hide well. I got no skills other than fighting and strategy."

Rtu added, "Be careful about getting too close to Ayya's father. It might awaken the old lifetime in him and put you and Ayya into a lot of trouble."

"Ayya's already in trouble," said Tulyata. "The Emperor found him and is now on the way to being enthralled, though he doesn't understand yet what is happening to him. He has brief moments where he has a roommate. To his credit, he is resistant to the influence because he is so strong willed."

Zreyas couldn't help but have second thoughts about his plan. He wasn't really confident about it because it came out of a whim gut feeling. It was more like he laid things out on the table to look at. "Well, anyone else have a better plan than what I said? Mine is a little sketchy, at best."

"Nope," said Rhom. "I think we should go with it. What you put forward is a great idea and involves many levels of engagement in case one goes wrong. We can roll back the time line a varSa or so and get to know her and give her the opportunity to move up in awareness enough to avoid what the Dark One plans to do."

Tulyata turned and asked with a hint of bitterness, "How is he supposed to get to her according to that useless console out there."

Rhom answered with a slight grin. "If he has his way, as ludicrous as it sounds, an enthralled bird, with a poisoned beak, pecks her will expose Ayya to the Dark One. When the poison lends to unconsciousness, that is when he will make his move to enthrall her. If he is successful, it's all over."

"Thank you, Rhom." Tulyata turned to her balances. "You guys best be getting out of my hair so I can do my job. Rtu, you can go with them, and do your divide out in the console room. Now that Aqum is allowing... *spaces*, they will know you aren't all three going at the same time."

They all grinned at her and headed over to the challenge node.

Rtu went through the process of making two of himself still standing inside Aqum's node, speaking with the entity as he worked things out.

Zreyas and Rhom walked up to the console. He q-leaped on top of it to see things clearer. They spent some time getting to know the controls better and how they affected each other. Every control seemed to affect the other controls' ranges and settings available.

"We need to dial the time line back for going to Earth as far as we can to give us the most chance of success. A small child will not have a lot of wiggle-room for waking her enough to change course because she is still under heavy influence of parents. She doesn't have the independence an adult would."

"She seems pretty helpless compared to when I came

out of that tunnel," said Zreyas.

"Precisely, my boy. So, Rtu and I need to go back that far, but you only need to go back the day before the event."

"I would rather go back three days before. Just because the attack doesn't happen till a date doesn't mean they are not there influencing things ahead of time. Maybe something is hiding around there that I can eliminate before."

"You are *good*, little buddy," Rtu said, walking up behind them.

Zreyas turned to see two of him. One seemed a little less solid than the other. "Will you look transparent like that when you go to Earth?"

Rtu shrugged, "I don't know, you two are the techies."

"I doubt it, because you choose a form to go in as, and a transformation takes place. I don't think there is anything to worry about," said Rhom.

The old man suddenly balled his fists up and dropped his head a moment in exasperation, his whole body looking tense.

It surprised Zreyas. He had never seen him like that before. "What's wrong?"

Rhom exhaled and looked back at the screen. "We need to be careful how far in the future we dial this control. It affects the distance back we can go. Checks and balances I guess. I just lost a month of the past by going ahead a month."

Zreyas felt bad for the old man. It was easy to tell it frustrated him. "Good thing you didn't experiment too far then. It's okay, we can do this!"

"Let's take a minute to find out a little more about what Ayya's family's habits are so we can all go in with the same information," said Rhom.

They all watched the screen as the fire station came into view two houses down from Ayya's home. It was on a beautiful island in the ocean off the coast of the mainland. They looked for any signs of questionable entities and tried to tune the console to detect them.

"Tulyata needs to be doing this stuff," said Rhom.

Zreyas couldn't help but wonder what Tulyata was hiding, but he didn't need to get sidetracked on her. "I don't know why she won't come down here."

"She can't, little buddy, remember she was over the threshold," said Rtu.

"Yes, she can." He turned to look at Rtu. "She's lost power or something because when I was in the challenge the node told me I could give her access to the node I discovered, so I did."

Both visages looked at Zreyas like he had turned green.

Zreyas shrugged. "There is something she isn't telling us, but it's okay, she's helping in her way. Maybe she is afraid to go out of her room or something."

He pointed to the incarnation control to redirect their focus. "So, what form are you going to take, old man?"

"Let's see... let's try something like this..." Rhom's picture showed up on the screen as member one. Rtu showed up as member two right beside him. He watched Rhom fiddle with the controls and his image turned into a light-skinned male human with short, blond hair. Then he turned another that was about professions and it landed on 'custom'.

Rhom said, "Fire fighter," and chose the location of the firehouse they had been talking about.

"Hmm," said Zreyas. "So, this might seem crazy, but how are we going to get back?"

As if on cue, ancient words appeared on the screen in front of them. Zreyas had no clue what it said since he couldn't read.

Thankfully, Rhom started reading it:

> When a participant chooses a form, we will grant a token. Use the token when a team member wants to come back to this current location. The following rules apply:
>
> 1. You can use the token as long as you are not in immediate danger.
> 2. You may not use the token to avoid any circumstances you have created by being there.
> 3. Once you commit to a path, you must live it fully.
>
> In summary, you must be in a full peaceful mode with no threats, directly or indirectly. It doesn't matter what type of threat—Examples would include, but not limited to: physical, mental, or someone targeting you.

The screen turned back to the images of Rhom and Rtu.

"Ah, fair enough," Rtu said, and stepped up to the console "My turn to choose my form."

Rtu changed into a human as well, but a little pudgier than Rhom's with a darker skin than he already had. "Paramedic at the same fire house."

"Don't forget your freckles!" Zreyas pointed to the picture. "No such thing as a Rtu without freckles."

They all laughed and Rtu said, "I hadn't gotten to that yet, little buddy. I'll have my freckles."

Sure enough, his freckles appeared and Zreyas couldn't help but smack his hands together. The texture of his hair went from smooth and wavy hair to short and spongy.

Rhom looked around for another control that he couldn't seem to find, then just said, "Our team is ready to transform. How—"

The twins shimmered a moment, then started changing into the exact likeness of the pictures on the screen.

Rhom gasped and almost fell over. Rtu caught him.

Zreyas almost panicked at the sudden change in the old man, not sure what to do.

"It's okay, my boy. I'm adjusting to the weight and density of my new body. It is far tougher than being in a Vidurian body. It feels dense and heavy... Interesting."

"Why didn't you feel that kind of change, Rtu?"

"Because a lot of my element is earth. I'm used to density, little buddy."

"Oh!" Then Zreyas noted Rtu's new hair. Curious and excited, he said, "Okay, that's ticking good!" Zreyas q-leaped to Rtu's earth form, landing on his shoulder and started pushing on his hair.

"Hey, hey, don't mess with the afro, it's perfect." Rtu laughed. "Now, shoo!"

"Ha! Well, I like it! But okay, okay." Zreyas q-leaped back over to the console just in time to see Rhom finish typing in a question on the machine, mumbling as he typed, "Who has access to enter this room?"

A message popped up, and Zreyas looked to Rhom, hoping he would read it. He didn't want to tell them he couldn't read.

"I wonder why she didn't say anything." Rhom waited, but there was no further response. "Well, it seems like she has a lot of secrets we don't know about." He looked over at his brother and Rtu.

Rtu seemed to be a little squeamish. “Don’t ask me, her business is for her to tell.”

“So now you have verified what I said,” said Zreyas as he sat down on the console, gently kicking his heels against the side of the machine. “She might have secrets but she is still helping.”

Almost as if it would make him feel better about not telling them he couldn’t read, he said, “Rhom has the secret about his fire, Rtu has secrets about stuff, and even I have a secret or two I haven’t told you. At least she is helping us by doing what she does best now.”

Rhom straightened, and both visages looked at Zreyas. “You have the right of it, my boy.” Then he looked at his human brother. “You ready to do this?”

“This should be fun! Incarnating without having to fully incarnate and lose memories is the best incarnation ever!”

The human pair lifted their left hands and opened them. There was a token in their palms, and they both sunk into their skin and eventually disappeared. Rhom moved his hand around and opened his mouth as if he was going to say something and the token reappeared.

“Well, that will make things much easier. All we have to do is think about coming back and the token appears.”

“Looks like it is time for us to go,” said Rtu.

Rhom looked at Zreyas with a curious look.

Rtu’s normal body said, “He will be okay brother, he knows the controls better than I do. Besides, I’m here and we can get word to you if there is a problem.”

“As soon as I get there, I will come let you know so you will feel better. But I will go in at night time. I hope the tryst can come with me, though. That would be handy.”

Rhom nodded and put his hand on his human

brother's shoulder and turned around. They walked over to the portal. Zreyas walked up on Rtu's offered arm to his shoulder and they followed the two.

Rtu said "This seems momentous in a way doesn't it?"

The human brothers nodded. Then the old man said, "Yes... yes it does!"

"Good luck to you both! Wartok!—uh, in a good way! I need to come up with another phrase for that."

"We got your meaning, my boy, and thank you! See you on the other side!" Then Rhom turned and Rtu's human form followed.

Zreyas and Rtu watched them warp in shape a little before disappearing.

Silence filled the room for a few moments, then Rtu turned back to walk toward the console.

Zreyas q-leaped to the console, rubbed his hands together and said, "Now it's *my* turn!"

42 Feature Creep

ᘓᘓᘓ Zreyas ᘓᘓᘓ

Zreyas finished readjusting the time-line so he could go back to the same place he had gone to last time. When he was there before, he had seen a few things he wanted to influence, talk to, or move, but couldn't, while other things he could. He had come back since he had done nothing to lock himself there in a set pattern that the challenge would have recorded. He wanted to ask Aqum about seeing if there was a way the things already in motion could be marked somehow.

Aqum had said that it was a space between the rules, but granted his suggested 'feature' and suggested using auras. Things that showed a red aura were things that were already influenced by the Dark One's side and influence was out of the question, so he wouldn't waste time on them. Orange auras were things that were affected heavily but could still be influenced or changed in some way, though it might be more difficult.

He planned to let Rhom and Rtu know first before he did anything else. Just before he went into the portal again, he turned to the smiling and waving Rtu and said, "Don't forget to watch over Lanna just before. No matter what we do, if you—"

"Don't worry, little buddy, I'll do my visage thing. As *you* say, 'It's what I do'. You be careful, you got the hardest part."

Zreyas nodded and traveled back again to the same spot he had traveled before, beside a tree at the firehouse three days and a few hours before the event. Now that Aqum had put the new auras into play, he hoped he could see more of what he was missing before.

Paul came out of the firehouse and walked down the driveway. "My boy, what are you doing here?"

"Don't you remember? Oh, you wouldn't. I came back one minute before the last time I came so... never mind. Listen, I got some ticking-shit to update you on."

"Wait, let me get Rtu." The old man ran into the firehouse and he came back out with a groggy Rtu in tow behind him.

Zreyas told the old man and Freckles about the Auras that were implemented and that he had been here before.

"So what is going on?" asked Rtu.

"Tomorrow, Lanna and Ayya will come here. If her mate comes with her, then all is lost. I will probably be dead, and you will have to fight. But if she comes, and her mate doesn't, then there is still hope and they will come down here again to visit one more time two days after that. That will be the last chance you have to awaken her a little. You should see auras now and that should help you see what can and can't be influenced."

Rhom scratched just over his right ear, then crossed his arms and nodded.

"Oh, do you have a box that I can fit in? You need to send me tonight to Ayya as a gift. I got to become a ticking-toy."

Rtu grinned, "A doll."

"If that is the term, I'm not sure how to be a doll, but I saw a lot of Ayya's things there, so I get the idea. If she comes tomorrow *without* that mate of hers, then you will know that part of the plan worked. Then the hard part comes for us two days after that."

"So Rtu and I have two more visits to get her to wake up enough for her to survive this bird encounter. Do you know where or when that bird comes into play?"

"Yes, on the two days. And No on the when and where. I couldn't stay longer and find out or I wouldn't be able to go back and get Aqum's aura feature put in. It won't be long and you won't have to be fire fighters anymore."

Rtu's hand went to one cheek, "I'm going to miss it, honestly. I've felt useful and still learned a lot even with all my memories intact."

"At least you know us incarnates are not so bad now," Zreyas said with a grin.

Rtu chuckled, "True, little buddy, and let me get a box."

The three worked together and put Zreyas into a box with a note inside it from Paul. Rtu and Paul then grinned, shut the box, and talked with him quietly as they walked down the street and put it on the porch.

"Good luck, my boy," whispered Rhom.

ꟾꟾ ꟾꟾ

Zreyas woke, startled, when someone picked up the box. He slid to one side of the box, but did his best to not struggle since he was supposed to be a limp toy. He heard Lanna's mate grumble. Zreyas felt the energy from the man and it felt familiar to him, but he also felt something dark was nearby hovering around. It made his skin prickle.

"Lanna! You have a package!"

He heard a faint, 'What is it?' coming from Lanna somewhere distant over him.

"You had better not be ordering shit you don't need! I'll be back in a couple hours for your... walk."

He felt himself being launched, cramming him to one side of the box. Then the weightlessness of being in the air. He reached out and braced himself against the walls of the box, but he knew it wouldn't do much good. Sure enough, the wind left him when he landed on the floor.

Ticking hell, what a piece of mag-shit. That is definitely my father.

Zreyas put his face down toward the bottom corner of the box so that when they opened the box, his eyes wouldn't squint or react. After a few minutes, Lanna opened the box, read the note, and she presented Zreyas, the toy, to Ayya.

She squealed in delight and picked him up, squeezing him hard, and gave him what he thought might be a thousand presses of her wet mouth to him. Whatever was in her mouth was sticky. He had to try real hard to keep his war aura down, already fed up with being a toy and had to talk to himself... a *lot*. *Remember, Zrey, this is a child with Aaru inside that just did the mouth touch thing to you. She supposed to be saving the multiverse somehow and I'm trying to do something good.*

He did his best to stay limp and let her do what little humans do with toys. She cooed and gurgled to him, but he didn't know what she was saying. Then she shoved his face into her mouth and sucked on it. His right eye sealed and felt like she would suck it out of the socket at any time.

Don't hit her, Zrey. She loves you. Don't rip her face off, she doesn't know I am real.

Zreyas spent the next couple of hours being carried around, choked, and turned upside down. When Ayya tried to take his clothes or weapons off, he would smack her hands out of the way and whisper, "No."

When Lanna was out of the room, he would whisper to Ayya. It thrilled her that her toy was talking to her.

"Tell Aaru that Zrey is here protecting you."

Ayya slipped right into a little chant, "Aawoo, Aawoo, bwudah heaw poteh you. Aawoo, Aawoo, bwudah heaw poteh you."

Zreyas shrugged and went limp again as Lanna came back in the room. Finally, Lanna's mate came in the door and slammed it.

"I'm home! Let's get this walk over with!"

It wasn't long before Ayya grabbed him up, holding him in a tight grip under one arm and across his neck at her side. He did his best to position himself so he could breathe while the adults weren't looking.

The incarnated commander was right next to him as

they walked through the yard.

He felt himself panic that Lanna's mate was going on the walk. He also noticed that there was an aura around him. It was a dark orange, almost red.

The anger filled him when he could feel the man's anger and hatred. He didn't have much time, so he focused on his inner self-made conversion gateway to convert the anger. It was desperately wanting out. Zreyas wanted to just kill Ayya's father and be done with it, but Ayya would have to see it, and he couldn't do that to her. Zreyas began converting the rage as he looked up toward her father's hand.

"Dammit! Hand is hurting," the man said.

Lanna responded and stopped walking. "What happened to it?"

"I don't know, come on. It seems okay now." The man put his arm around Lanna and she moved Ayya to the other side of her so she could be next to her mate.

Ticking hell. At least I know it bothers him. Zreyas renewed his effort to push out high frequencies. It seemed to energize Ayya and Lanna. What surprised him was that they seemed to absorb it and wondered if they needed it or something.

Was there something else going on? It didn't seem to work on Lanna's mate, but he kept trying to push his converted aura out further.

Zreyas almost gave up just when he noticed him fidget when Ayya and Lanna were no longer absorbing the frequencies. He concentrated hard to push out more. After about thirty more steps, Lanna's mate dropped his arm and stepped away, his body language clearly agitated. He balled his fists up and turned in a circle.

Focusing harder on his chest, Zreyas converted more. He had no problem keeping the anger and the conversion going. Zreyas willed himself to stay limp and looked up to his eyes, trying to keep them empty of life. He saw a dark mist hovering around him and realized it stopped at the edge of the man's aura.

He decided to do a little test. Zreyas renewed his effort to push the converted frequencies out further. Sure enough, the Dark One's mist moved away, staying at the border.

Ayya's father shifted his eyes down to look at Zreyas. The agitation and anger clear in his voice, he asked with a booming voice, "Who gave Ayya that toy?"

Lanna jumped, obviously startled. "A man named Paul at the firehouse we are walking to... the ones that bake cookies for us." Ayya wrapped her arm around her mother's leg, hid her face, and squeezed Zreyas closer to her chest.

Scaring Ayya *really* pissed Zreyas the ticking-hell off, so he converted more... and more.

The man took another step back and held his stomach.

"Aargh!! I'm going to go home and make more shotgun shells for skeet shooting tomorrow." Lanna's mate darted in, grabbed Ayya's toy, and hurled Zreyas into the trees.

Zreyas did his best to relax and stay limp while he flew through the air, then q-leaped just before hitting the ground up to a branch just over the three.

Ayya started crying and Lanna asked, "Why did you do *that*?"

"I don't know. I'm going home," her father said, storming back toward their home.

Lanna picked Ayya up to hold her close as she watched her mate walk away.

Zreyas slumped with relief that they weren't all

doomed and he didn't have to play as a doll anymore and could go back to being a warrior.

As he watched Lanna walk away, he felt sick as he watched the dark mist that had been hovering around the man absorb into his body. He couldn't help but wonder if there was something else he could have done.

He had a lot to do, but he had to be sharp to do it. And right now, his back was hurting badly from being thrown so suddenly. He laid belly down on a branch, legs and arms dangling, and took a nap.

43 I Did It

Lanna

Lanna and Ayya leisurely walked down the end of the road that their duplex apartment was on. She loved living on James Island, and their road that ran straight into the water at a boat ramp with a firehouse next to it. She looked ahead and thought, *If someone isn't careful, or unfamiliar with the area, they could drive right into the water.* Lanna laughed because it had probably happened before.

The road was beautiful, with massive, towering live oak trees on each side of the road. It created a serene canopy with Spanish moss hanging down as if to say, "We have been here for centuries, and we are watching."

She loved to get out and walk with Ayya three times a week, at least. It was a highlight for both her and her daughter. Ayya was still a little whiny about losing her new stuffed toy, but she would soon forget it when she saw Paul again. The firefighters always waved them into the building for conversation and treats. They loved giving Ayya cookies and letting her wear their fire hats, which covered her entire head and shoulders.

Lanna thought about how Ayya liked to search for the fish and feed them. She only let her do that once a week, though, because they both always ended up in soaked clothes with mud from head to toe before it was over. By some miracle, she caught a fish once and hugged it. She immediately got slapped in the face a few times by the tail. Lanna looked at her daughter and giggled at the memory.

As Lanna and Ayya walked up the short driveway just before the dock, many of the firemen threw up a welcoming wave and beckoned them to come in as usual.

"Lanna, you are one beautiful lady, as always!" one man washing the fire truck shouted.

She blushed. "Yeah, you say that to all the women."

"True, but you really are!"

Ayya brightly smiled and let out squeals of excitement.

Lanna knew she had found her target. She always looked for her favorite fireman, a middle-aged man with a blond crew cut and kind eyes. Ayya's internal radar spotted Paul already under the fire truck as he was sliding out from underneath it. She ran awkwardly straight for him, giving him an affectionate leg hug when he stood.

Paul picked her up and held her up over his head. She pushed her arms out like wings, and he happily exclaimed, "That's it, that's it! Look at you fly! You are a bird!"

Lanna laughed, holding her arms in a crossed position, smiling.

Paul put Ayya down and said, "I have a surprise for

you!"

"Tookie!" squealed Ayya.

Paul grinned and scratched his head above his right ear. "How did you guess?!"

"Momma says I smar!"

"Yes, you are! You know where they are! Go get one for you and your mom."

"Tank oouu!!" Ayya immediately toddled along excitedly with the other men to get her cookies.

Soon her mother and Paul heard, "You drive a hard bargain!" She knew that voice and it was Ayya's second favorite man at the firehouse.

Paul laughed, shaking his head affectionately. "How are you doing today, Lanna? Have you had better luck keeping Ayya's dresses on her this week?"

"No! She hates them! I can put shorts or pants on her and she will leave them on all day, but if I put a dress on her, it's off somehow in less than thirty minutes, even if it buttons up in the back!"

All the firefighters still outside with them chuckled.

Paul and Lanna talked while they waited for Ayya to bargain with the other men. Paul asked how Ayya was doing developmentally, as well as other odd questions most people wouldn't think to ask.

Lanna still felt at ease with the questions. When they first met, she felt as if she had known him for decades. Paul had told her he used to be involved in the development and education of royalty in another culture, but then chose another career when things got crazy. She had known him a year now and thought nothing about answering his questions in the hopes he could give her something helpful in raising a first child that was lovable, extra adventurous, and... hated dresses.

"She did something very odd this week." Lanna chuckled a moment, but with frustration.

"Oh? Do tell!" Paul said, as he sat down on the bumper of the firetruck behind him.

"We were watching TV up in my bedroom since my husband was out of town. She decided suddenly she had to go 'free some animals.' With the imagination that she has, I didn't think anything of it. She hopped down off the bed, humming. She is *always* humming, and it wavered as I heard her butt hitting each step on the way down."

Lanna laughed. "She loves to slide down those steps. She goes through pants like crazy!"

Paul chuckled with her for a few seconds, then said, "I would love to be a fly on the wall to see her in action by herself."

Then Lanna laughed. "I'm not sure I would. Anyway, she went quiet a little longer than I felt comfortable with, and I started to get suspicious. Just before I got up, I heard her coming up the steps humming and singing the words, 'I did it, I did it' in Ayya-speak. Relieved, I waited for her, and she crawled back into bed with me. When I hugged her, she felt all slimy. I looked at her and she had spots of slime on her!"

"What? I can't wait to hear this. Did she get into some oil?"

"That is what I thought at first, but no! I picked her up and went downstairs, getting slimed myself in the process. When I walked into the kitchen. There was a chair pushed up against the counter beside the refrigerator. She bust every single egg I had in the refrigerator all over the kitchen counters, dripping everywhere! I'll admit, I was pretty angry, but I couldn't help but be perplexed and humored at the same time."

Paul put his hand over his mouth, his other hand holding his elbow, looking to Lanna like he would burst out laughing any time.

She finally said, "Go ahead and laugh! Maybe it will make *me* feel better."

They both laughed hard, and Paul wiped his eyes.

"Then Ayya said, 'I fwee dem, Momma, I fwee dem! Dey happy now!'"

"Aw, I would start watching her when she hums. Maybe that is the trick," laughed Paul.

"She hums all the time!" Lanna said, as she shook her head. "She drives me crazy, but I love the little pip."

Ayya came through the door, opened by a fireman behind her, with one large cookie in each hand. They were as big as her face.

Lanna couldn't help but laugh. "You gentlemen spoil her!" She bent down slightly to talk with her.

"What have you got there, Ayya?"

"Tookies, Momma!" she exclaimed.

She replied excitedly for Ayya's benefit. "I see that! Wow, those are *big*!" She darted her head up to the dark-skinned fireman with a big grin and black freckles walking behind her. "This is your doing, Sir bakes-a-lot!"

"Guilty as charged! We made those two just for you," he said with a bright smile.

"You guys are getting her dental bills," Lanna said in jest.

Paul replied with a hearty laugh, "I will gladly pay! I don't have kids, and I will take that as part of the experience."

"Welcome to my life, then. I didn't realize how many bills kids mounted up getting into trouble and breaking things. My grocery bill just went up with the loss of eggs!"

Lanna paused a moment, feeling thankful for the fun diversion from all her worries. She knew it helped Ayya get distracted from her recent loss of her new favorite toy. “Thank you for being so good to us. I’ll keep praying for your safety in those fires you fight and lives you save. I just wish my husband would come down to meet you all. He started to, but he said half way here that he didn’t want to and left to go make more shotgun shells for his skeet shooting.” She shrugged and shook her head.

Ayya held up a cookie for her with delight.

Lanna took the cookie and thanked the men. They waved as Lanna turned around, held Ayya’s hand, and started walking down the drive. She realized she was half dragging Ayya, because apparently, eating a cookie and walking took too much brain power, and eating the cookie had priority. It waved around in the air as Ayya tried to catch a bite. All the men were laughing affectionately.

Suddenly, she heard a faint, “Thanks for making our day again, little phoenix!”

Ayya paused in her tracks, almost toppling over from Lanna walking. Lanna turned to see what was going on. Ayya had a distant look on her face. She knew the look well. She had gone into that imaginary world she went into often.

She saw Paul smile, give a wave, and walked back into the firehouse, out of sight.

Lanna had a nagging feeling in her gut that it would be the last time she ever saw him. *Now I’m imagining things. Where did that thought come from?*

44 You Feewl Bettah

Ayya

Ayya and her mother sat down on the front steps of their home to eat their cookies in the sun. She looked at the cookie, deciding it was the best thing she could think of at the moment. The raisins in it were her favorite part. Half of it broke off and landed on the ground. She pulled away from her mother and picked it back up and was now holding both halves. She ate the half that fell first so her mother wouldn't take it away, cramming in as much in as possible.

Ayya smiled and looked up at her mother to see her shaking her head.

Her mother smiled. "Go ahead and eat it. It's already in there now." Then she winked.

Ayya nodded brightly, looking up past her into the live oak trees and hanging moss. In the light, she noticed something moving that was dark and inky with red eyes. She tried to tell her mother that it was a bird, but it didn't come out well through her mouth full.

Holding her finger over Ayya's mouth, she said, "Don't talk with your mouth full unless you want to lose that cookie."

Ayya chewed while she watched the spot move around in the air. That thing made her feel uncomfortable, but she didn't understand why. It made her want her favorite thing in the world. She swallowed, then looked at her mother. "Cap pwease! Cap pwease!"

"You are lucky I want some water." Her mother walked in the house while she looked around the yard, taking a big bite of cookie.

Ayya's attention was drawn again to the inky blotch that now slid across the yard, zig-zagging closer. "I see ouu," Ayya said.

Her mother opened the door, and the inky thing darted away. She sat down and handed the cap to Ayya.

"Tank oou! I fewl bettah, Momma." Ayya consumed her cookie with grateful reverence, the cap in the other hand. She smiled and looked up at her mother and offered the cookie to her mother for a bite.

Her mother smiled and took a tiny bite, and Ayya felt sad that she didn't do the thing she normally did.

Her mother grinned and grabbed her cookie hand and took many bites and chewed the treat.

Ayya giggled so hard she almost fell back. It always made her wonder how she ate so much of her cookie, but it never got smaller. She stabilized herself and worked to finish devouring what was left of the face sized cookie she started with.

Once done, she gripped the cap and stood. Ayya held the rail with her left hand to climb down the one step she was standing on. She held the saddle cap and wandered around the yard, watching the symbols on the cap talk to her. She started talking to it and told the cap about her cookie and the new toy her daddy threw away. Then she asked it to help her find it.

A flash of something flew past her face that startled Ayya. She watched a bird crash into the chain-link fence nearby. It bounced and fell to the ground. She looked back up where the bird came from and saw her toy up in the tree with shiny sticks shaking its head no.

Ayya looked at the bird and felt the loss and watched it. “Bye-bye,” she said sadly and cried, dislodging large crocodile tears.

“Go over and pick it up for me and bring it here, sweetie. It might be okay and just sleeping,” her mother encouraged.

She waddled over slowly, holding her brass cap like a coveted security blanket, and looked down at the bird. The eyes were empty and open, its beak had green icky stuff on it, and it had a fuzzy black mist moving around it. Something in the middle of Ayya’s stomach felt like static with the message of ‘*no, wait*’. She looked down at her cap and waited. Then she looked at her mother.

Ayya felt an edge of exasperation on her mother’s still smiling face. She got up and walked over to retrieve the body.

Ayya looked back up to where she saw her toy in the tree and it wasn’t there.

“Let’s see...” her mother said.

Ayya watched her pick the bird up carefully with two hands. She rubbed the green icky stuff off with her finger as the black mist swirled around and went into her skin. Then she walked back over to the steps and sat down, casually putting her feet down on the last step.

Ayya’s sense of adventure and curiosity perked up and watched her mother’s every move. She wanted to cry when she saw the black mist move in and out of her. Ayya turned her body more to come closer but felt that static in her stomach again that seemed to tell her '*wait and watch*'. So, she watched her mother from where she was.

Ayya's mind got distracted and looked at her mother more than the bird. Her mother was more beautiful to her than normal. The white jeans and sleeveless shirt seemed to glow a little. Then her skin started to shine. Her mother's glowing appearance captivated her.

After a short time, a glowing light began materializing behind her mother while she watched the bird, held lovingly in her hands, stroking it. The light seemed to change to the shape of a large person with a happy belly. The person had no shirt and a leafy skirt. It smiled and seemed to laugh with no sound, then pointed toward her mother.

"Bootiful, Momma." Ayya cocked her head and held her hand up toward the light now growing wings.

"Hello," she said excitedly to the happy man light. It looked at her and gave her a big smile. She could now see long, wavy hair and freckles on the face. She watched as if stuck in time at the large human-shaped light that all but enveloped her mother. The being behind her mother bent slightly, putting something on her head that looked like a crown of light. It was different from the paper ones her mother made for her from time to time.

"Oou pwetty, Momma," she slurred out in her mesmerism.

The winged light man broke apart and swirled all around her, and then disappeared. Her mother smiled, lifted her hands, and opened them. The bird flew out of her hands and they both watched it fly off to a nearby tall tree, singing.

Ayya clapped wildly with the cap between her hands and ran as fast as her awkward balance could carry her to sit down. She imitated her mother and sat right beside her. Ayya looked up to her and blurted out, "You and Mither Angel maked a new bir. The bir is happy now and fwies."

"Ms. who?"

"When angel put dat crown on your head, Momma." She looked at her mother's face, still seeing remnants of the light. "You a queen now, Momma, and you maked a new bird. Goo job!"

"It was just asleep, and it woke up, nothing more," her mother said.

"Mmm, You Mith Angel Qween now, Momma," Ayya twittered as she fidgeted with the cap in her hands. She knew what she saw and disregarded what her mother said.

Her mother laughed and stood. "Time for you to put that cap back now and take a nap, Miss Imagination Princess."

With a white knuckled grip on the cap in her right hand, she grabbed her mother's hand with her left, cherishing each second she had that cap. She looked across the yard as she turned and saw her toy waving from behind a tree, then disappearing.

Zreyas

After waving to Ayya, he turned around and sighed, leaning against the tree. "Ticking-hell, I'm glad that is over. She's safe, for now."

"Is she?" a voice said, coming from above him.

Zreyas jerked his head up, only to realize it was the biggest mistake as a warrior he had ever made. What felt like a rope whipped around his neck and pinned him against the tree. VarSas of training kicked in and instinctively he lowered his chin and expanded his neck muscles, and grabbed the rope from the tree side with his left hand in an attempt to take up some space.

In front of him, three human males with bright orange and yellow clothes came out from around the surrounding trees holding the oddest looking spears he had ever seen. It looked like each of them had one and they held them in an odd position under their right arms and pointing it toward him. The ends were cut off and had holes in them. They looked ridiculous, but he was not in his world anymore. There was no telling what those things were.

"Who... are you?" Zreyas asked, as he concentrated on keeping his chin low and throat protected. Then he saw their feet and the black mist wafting in and out of them.

"It seems you are out-matched," the voice said from behind and higher than him. "Four against one, and you are not in a good position, and you are tiny."

"You... don't kn.. know me very well, do you?" Zreyas tried to q-leap, but he realized he was connected to entities that might not be willing to do that, so it didn't work. The tree for one, and indirectly to another. It was time to stall.

"Do I really need to?" said the man.

Zreyas felt the rope jiggle and jerk. *Good, they are tying it.* He dropped his hand down, feigning a tired arm flop, deliberately hitting his axe sheath latch. He also started pushing against the rope to work with any slack that might be in the knot they were tying. It was hard though because the rope was large to him.

The one that was behind him walked around from behind the tree, but he couldn't see their face. Protecting his neck and pushing was more important.

"We heard there was a new traitor beast in the woods here that would be good hunting. And hunters *love* to hunt game. Looks like after two days, we finally found it. It's not as formidable as we were told, though."

One of the three in front of him said, "You might have killed it already, just tying it to the tree, just in case. It looks fragile and *weak*."

Another of the men then said, "Hey, are those little weapons on his back? He's so weak he can't even get to them."

That did it. The anger flared and filled him up inside. Then he saw one of those shiny double cut-off spears come into his view. Just as it was about to touch his chest, he grabbed his axe, parried the spear up, hearing a clash of metal against the spear.

A deafening boom sounded, and he saw tree splinters and bark fly out. With a ringing in his ears, Zreyas used the hook on the back of his axe to jerk the man's spear down. The man didn't have a good grip on it because it went to the ground.

He used that opening to do two things. First, he converted the frequencies of his anger to something they would not like—at least the Dark One wouldn't like. When they immediately slumped slightly at the jolt, he dropped his left hand and whipped the axe upward across his body, cutting the rope most of the way through, loosening it. Then he ducked and pulled himself away as he twisted around.

"It's free, Landry, shoot it!" commanded the voice that had tied him up.

Zreyas saw, who he assumed was Landry, raise his spear to his eye and braced it against his shoulder.

Pulling his dagger, Zreyas q-leaped right in front of his face, standing on the metal spear.

The man's eyes went wide and a metal piece on the top of the weapon moved. As it snapped into place, the spear jerked back toward the man and tilted up with lightning speed. A loud boom deafened Zreyas and ringing ripped through his head.

The jolt threw Zreyas forward, feeling his back crack all the way up and down from the sudden whip motion that he wasn't ready for.

Zreyas q-leaped again just before hitting the tree behind the Landry man. He didn't q-leap far, just enough to turn his position and land feet first against the tree with less velocity. Launching himself with pure leg power toward Landry, he twisted for momentum as he hacked the man's neck from the side with his axe. Zreyas used the embedded axe to turn just enough before pulling it out to land on the ground in front of one man still standing.

Fire shot up Zreyas' back when he landed, but he focused and looked up to the man that said he was fragile and said, "I'm fragile, you say. I would spare you, but it seems you have a roommate that I have a problem with."

The two men in front of him turned to run.

Zreyas let out a converted frequency blast of his aura. The two men grunted and fell to the ground. With sadness in his heart, Zreyas quickly killed them both fairly easily. Then he turned to look for the last one, but he was already laying on the ground dead.

He approached the one he had not killed. The dead man had an enormous hole in his chest with small punctures around it. Zreyas looked at the spear and realized it wasn't a spear at all, but he didn't know what the ticking-hell it was. He knew he had gotten very lucky.

Zreyas looked up in time to see a car, a term he had learned recently, pulling into the driveway of Ayya's home. He backed up and watched the mist slide in and out of her father as he got out of the car. He wondered if the man knew who he was before. It was hard for Zreyas to wrap his mind around how that used to be his own father. *Commander, look at you now, someone's slave and all that bluster for nothing.*

Just as the man opened the door to the house, he stopped and turned around.

Zreyas ducked in behind the tree and watched him look around aimlessly, almost like he heard something. *Well, that was weird. It's not like he can read minds.*

"Well, she's *semi*-safe for now. Time to go. My back is killing me." Zreyas sheathed his weapons and opened his palm and the token activated.

ꟾꟾꟾ *Ayya* ꟾꟾꟾ

(15 minutes earlier)

After her nap, her mother got Ayya dressed up for a gathering with friends later, putting a dress and black patent leather shoes on her. Ayya was not happy with the clothes and fussed emphatically.

Lanna got her last shoe on and told her she could go outside in the backyard to play a little.

Ayya toddled outside, tugging on her dress.

"And don't you take that dress off Ayya, I will spank you."

Lanna headed back into the kitchen while Ayya picked up a stick to bang rhythms on the patio grill. She could see her mother through the low set windows. She waved at Lanna with the stick, then watched her for a moment.

She heard her mother say, "Your daddy should be home soon, Ayya!"

A few bangs of her stick on the grill and she heard her daddy come through the front door of the house. He said a grumpy hello to her mother and heard him stomp up the steps.

"Bad day?!" Lanna yelled up to him.

"Yes! But it will get better. The party will be fun. I will get to brag about my skeet shooting scores. Landry will regret last week!"

Ayya held a stick in her hand and began waving it around, bored with beating on the grill. She looked for the light angel again, but didn't see it.

Something caught her eye, though, coming out of the bedroom window upstairs. A dark swishy thing with red eyes slid down the brick wall whispering, "I see you Ayya."

"I thee ou too! But you not pwetty. Did thum one thcare

you?"

"Yesss," it hissed. "Someone scared me Ayya and almost pushed me away from you."

"Aw, I thorry."

"Do you see this Ayya?" as it moved around the grill, near a can sitting on the low windowsill.

"Mmmmm, uh huh, I thee it. oou can have it. you feewl betta."

"Oh no, Ayya, I can't drink it, see... no hands. But it will make me feel better if *you* drink it. It will make me feel *much* better."

"Otay. you feew bettah!" Ayya dropped the stick and reached up on her tiptoes to grab the can on the outside windowsill.

"That's it Ayya, it's already open and it will make me feel *so* much better. You are such a good girl," it hissed.

Ayya turned the open topped can up and drank the contents.

"That's it, I'm feeling better already, drink it all... yes, drink it *all,*" came the hiss as the black ink mist slowly slid back up the wall and into the bedroom window again.

Ayya drank as much as her tummy could handle. "You feewww... betta... now?" and looked up to see the black ink cloud, but didn't see it.

"Oh, I feel much better," she heard.

Ayya felt foaming bubbles forcing themselves up through her chest and past her throat. The bubbles streamed up and out of her mouth at a constant rate, and her eyes watered. She tried, but she couldn't breathe. Ayya wobbled up the two stairs to the door and ringing assaulted her ears. She saw her mother inside in the kitchen as her vision blurred. Then everything went dark

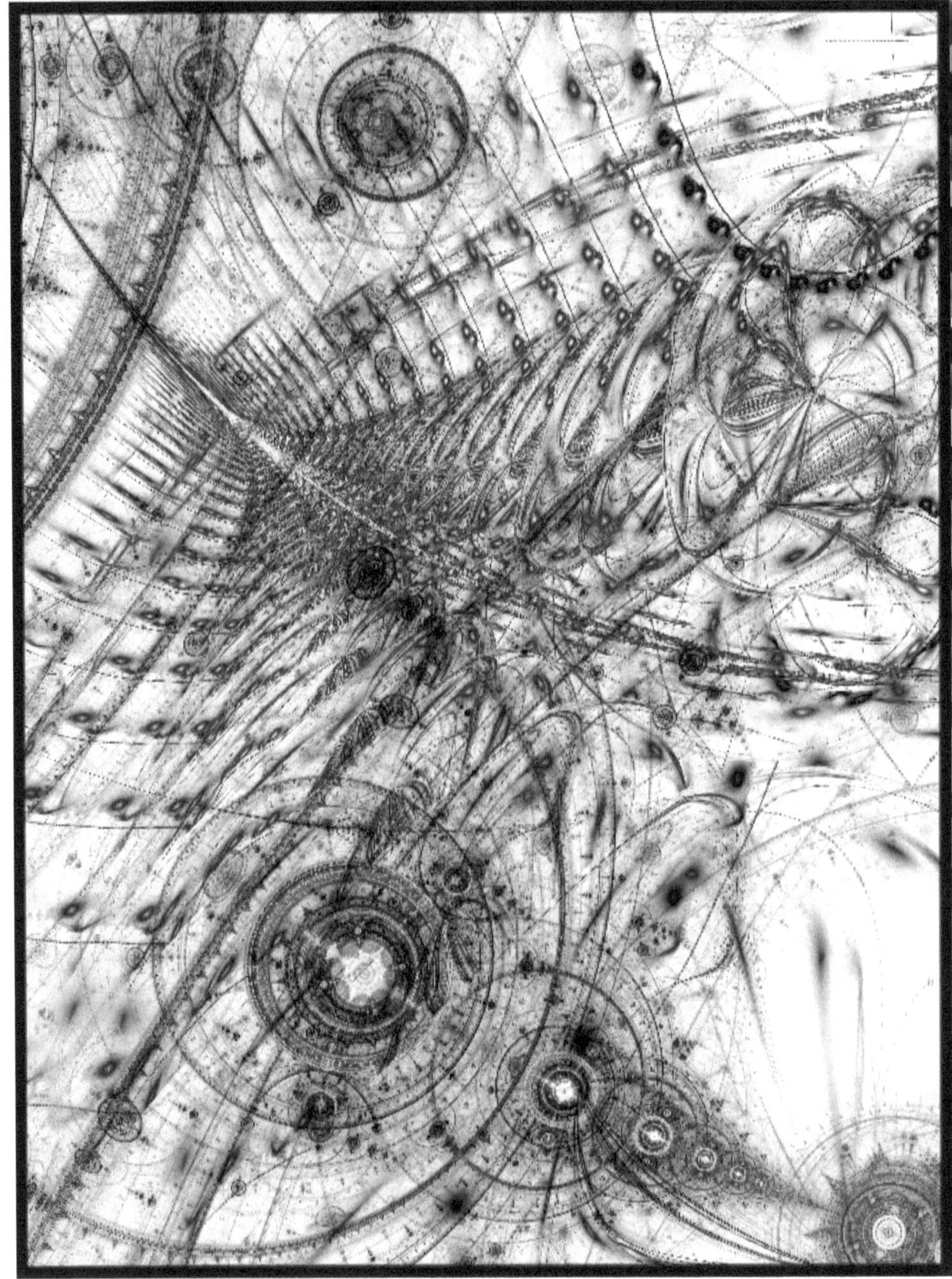

45 You'll Miss Me

Zreyas

Zreyas landed on his feet, pain shooting through his back and into his head. His legs felt numb and his head was spinning. He sat down a little hard. "What the ticking-hell did I do to myself?"

"My boy! Don't panic, you are going to be okay," Rhom encouraged.

He looked up and saw Rhom and Rtu running toward him. Even Tulyata was there, standing behind them on the Aqum's floor with her arms crossed.

"You did it, little buddy! Poisoned is much better than dead!"

"What do you mean, poisoned? After all that, I failed? I need to go back." Zreyas struggled to get up.

"No, no, no, she is okay, my boy. You didn't fail at all. We will tell you all about it if you will just allow us to help you."

Zreyas nodded as he winced again at the pain shooting up his back, causing tendrils of fire, cramps, and spasms in his ribs, arms, and legs.

Rtu gently scooped Zreyas up and as they walked toward Aqum, all three visages took turns telling him all about how the Dark One fooled Ayya into drinking charcoal starter. Then they explained to him what a hospital was and how they pumped her stomach.

"To pump a stomach seems... weird, but I can understand how it would help. So you were able to wake her up some, yeah?"

"Yes, my boy! And you helped her wake up a little more." Rhom told him about the visit and how he called her Little Phoenix.

The twins told him their stories about the fire house days and what they did for a varSa and their favorite calls while they worked on him. He knew it was to distract him from the pain, and he was grateful for that. But it also fascinated him they would make up a job for that specific thing, not to mention how they put their lives on the line for people they didn't even know. He decided he liked fire fighters on earth.

Tulyata stayed quiet and seemed to be recording, balancing, or whatever it was she did all the time.

Zreyas told them about what he had done as well and how he enjoyed sneaking around in that forest because the trees were so big. He also told them about how he was watching Ayya and her mother eat cookies from high in the trees and how he got lucky to spot the corrupted bird. "You know, birds are hard to throw a weapon at and hit! I almost missed it. The blade missed it, but the guard on the dagger hit."

Rtu conjured a table out of thin air and set him down on it.

Rhom and Rtu's smile seemed genuinely happy, judging by their expressions. He guessed they enjoyed being incarnated, in a way, for a time. They got to spend time with each other for a varSa on Earth. Though it was only moments here, it was still life that was lived.

"Well done, my boy! You should tell—"

Tulyata interrupted and said, "The little ferret doesn't have to tell his stories, we saw them all."

"Oh." Zreyas said. "I didn't know."

He knew right away that Rhom got upset, considering the rare frown on his face—and maybe the fact his face got red. "Tulyata! It's important to voice and have the fun of talking about experiences as an incarnate. Not everyone is a Visage! Now that I think of it, it's important even as a visage, it helps to integrate the lessons and let go the trash we don't need."

It shocked Zreyas that the old man blew up like that, but after he thought about it for a minute, what the old man said made sense to him.

Rhom turned to look at Zreyas, immediately going straight back to his genuinely cheerful mood, as if the anger had never happened. "Don't mind her, she is in a weird mood and upset about something that she is *not* telling."

"Yeah, I know," he said. "I would have to be dead in all senses to not see that." Zreyas winced again and put his head on his knee to stretch his back out.

The twins worked together to heal Zreyas' injuries while they explained to him he had a sprained back and a little torn cartilage. When he asked them what that meant, Rtu explained, and it fascinated him to understand more about his body.

Then Zreyas asked what those boom-spears were. They gave him a lesson on shotguns and how they worked.

"So *that's* what he meant when he said he was going back to make more shotgun shells when I was being carried around by Ayya down the road. If I'm honest, though, I was glad he threw me in the woods there. I was getting ticking-sick as hell of getting carried around by the neck and feet. She tried to take my clothes and weapons off!"

They all laughed—even Tulyata.

"I tried to feel Aaru, but... I didn't feel or recognize him." Zreyas felt sadness deep inside himself. Ayya was good and liked her, but he still missed his brother. He felt a gentle patting of Rhom's hand on his back. The old man always sensed his moods.

"Little buddy, had you not been so strong and in good shape, that might have broken your back. Your strength and flexibility are amazing. I got to see the status of your body when we first met, after you ran into Rhom's foot and were unconscious. It really paid off for you this time. You should be good as new, though." Rtu wiggled his fingers around like he was doing magic with a grin.

"Take it easy, stand up, and do a few easy stretches to make sure all is good, my boy."

As Zreyas did as instructed, he looked at all three of the visages and said, "We did great teamwork. It's the most fun I have had in my whole life doing this kind of work. Killing is not as fun to me anymore—but the *reason* I did it made me feel okay about it. Giving the thankings to you for checking on me when I got back." He pointedly looked at Tulyata and almost smiled.

"Pfft," Tulyata said. "I just wanted to make sure you didn't... mess up the portal is all." Then she looked at him and cocked her head... *almost* like a slight bow of acknowledgment.

That was about as much of a show of care as he would likely get out of Tulyata, but he was grateful. He smiled at her anyway.

She grunted like she was allergic to it and went back to work.

"I think it is time to celebrate, little buddy! How about a nice big festive dinner?"

"Don't celebrate too much. More things are brewing and you got work to do. I've got it all here, ready and waiting," said Tulyata.

"Always the killer of joy, dear mother!" said Rtu.

"Nice work, Tulyata," said Zreyas sincerely. "I knew you would be perfect for that!"

Tulyata turned, put her half glasses on, pointed at him a few times as she leaned back.

"I am sending the likings to you too," he said to her.

That seemed to horrify her. She took her glasses off and said, "Don't talk to me little ferret, or I just might turn you into a piece of—" She stumbled on trying to remember something, then turned to him and said, "ticking-mag-shit."

"Ha!" Zreyas looked at Rtu, "Sure! A feast sounds good!" He q-leaped up on Rhom's shoulder and sat down. While Rtu got the table and meal placed with a few waves of a hand, he bent down a little to whisper in Rhom's ear. "Now I understand how you must have felt dealing with a grouchy Janquar when we first met. She's up to something, but she's okay now… I think."

Rhom chuckled, "Agreed, my boy. And you definitely were quite the hostile handful then." He smiled, turned toward him, and winked, "And… you *still* are."

"Maybe so, old man, maybe so. But you will miss me when I'm dead and gone."

"That I will, my boy… that I will."

The End

From the Author

Thank you!

I hope you enjoyed the book, had fun, and maybe even learned a thing or two. I know I did!

I never thought in a million years I would be doing something like this. It is the most difficult thing I have ever done in my life. The fact that I can share it with incredible people like yourself makes all the *thousands* of hours worthwhile.

If you did enjoy it, please tell a friend and rate the book at the establishment that you bought it from. Your reviews and word-of-mouth recommendations are the lifeblood of an Indie author.

Until next time, I hope you create an amazing day for yourself!

~ ishKiia

And now, as a special surprise after the glossary, here is a sneak peek from Part II of The Sleeping Phoenix Series.

Glossary of Terms

All definitions are related to this story. Some definitions are fiction, some may have full or partial real-world application but may, or may not, be applied in a fictional way.

Atra - <redacted>

Aramzu - An ocean creature similar to Earth's stingray, but with larger mouth and the teeth to match. The barbs on its tail are much larger and more deadly.

Bandhula - Bastard

Festering - The process of conditioning one's self to a lower frequency. It manifests physically in the body as deterioration. Festering can also happen when doing, or being, something that is not natural for a person that is learned from those around them, with or without being aware of it.

Garavu - A deadly slither that resembles Earth's Cobra, but significantly more predatory. Unlike the cobra on earth, however, they ravenously eat much quicker, and the garavu's throat has hooked serrated bone blades with poison ducts. They slice the prey as it moves down through the body to enable faster digestion. The bone blades also prevent them from sliding back out.

Incarnates / you incarnates - Term the visages use referring to someone that is incarnated in a body.

Kuravy - Eagle-like predator. Description in the story text.

Lutari - A giant arachnid-like creature that has a leg span of a meter wide (approx. 39 inches) as an average adult. It bears two fangs that are 7.5 centimeters long (approx. 3 inches). It doesn't make webs like the smaller arachnids on Earth—it hunts and builds nests in small caves or crevices in rock. Its venom is potent and it uses its fangs to liquefy its prey from the inside. The lutari can carry quite a bit of weight back to its nest. Their downfall is they can't see very well at all.

Mag - A parasitic insect that thrives on low frequency species, like the Janquar. Its body is jelly-like. No matter how it spreads, or its shape, it can't attach itself to the host. The chemical make-up of the secretions of the body slowly eats away at the skin, though. The mag secretes its feces, creating a crust that attaches itself to the skin of its host. Its weak hair-like legs take a long time to attach to its host, however. It isn't until there is a firm grip of its feces that it is more stable to stay on the host, and eventually burying itself under it. The mag eats away the flesh and its feces replace the host's skin completely. It infiltrates the inner tissues, eventually rendering the victim unable to move because of its solidity of the feces. The host eventually dies a long and painful death. Depending on the host's health and lifespan of race they are, their death could take between fifty to two hundred and fifty varSas. The feces material is so hard, it takes high technology to crack or cut it. It is often taken from victims after death to use for prefabricated armor, or used with other materials to make high grade and incredibly difficult to crack technology for space technology tools and ships.

Mag-shit - An insult, referring to the feces of the mag that attach to a host's skin and gradually kill them. (*See* **Mag** *for more details*)

Neutrinic-gleam - Building blocks of the Viduri

Rsi - Singer of ancient songs.

Shinit - A meerkat-like species much larger than the species found on Earth. Found on many planets in the multiverse.

Slither - A family of creatures similar to an Earth's species called 'snake'.

Torana - Portal; arched doorway; Arch or a triangle supporting a large balance

varSa - One rotation around the sun. In Earth terminology, this would be equivalent to the word 'year.'

The Sleeping Phoenix
Part II

Sneak Peek of

NAGODARA

1 Your Path and Mine

ꜭꜭꜭ *Rtu* ꜭꜭꜭ

(one hour before executing the plan to save Ayya)

Rtu looked at the screen and saw Rhom and Zreyas walking off the node into the weirdly suspended area. Zreyas leaped over to the console, showing Rhom where it was, like a kid would show his father something he was excited about. Then he q-leaped up on Rhom's shoulder, startling Rhom visibly. Rhom chuckled and shook his head. He said something to Zreyas with smiling eyes. Then they both looked down at the console.

"Seems our new little buddy is very useful. What are we going to do with Rhom and Zreyas? Do you think they will win the challenge? I have to admit I like being on their side more than helping the Dark One."

"What's a war without turncoats, my dear son? I like this side better too, but we need to make the Dark One believe we are still on his side."

"Doesn't he know already if we are or not?"

"Does it matter? Besides, I think there are higher powers involved here. Plus, it would devastate Rhom. The Dark One approached us after we thought Rhom would be dead. All the pieces of the game have changed, and I am glad we are back where we belong and of our own minds again. Zreyas has no idea what he has done for us."

"I wouldn't want to be on the other side of his wrath, even if he isn't a visage." Rtu laughed and watched the two. "Besides, I like our little buddy. Can we keep him? You even like him." Rtu let out a mock gasp.

"Shut up, you," Tulyata said sourly.

Then they both laughed as they watched Rhom and Zreyas.

Rtu sighed at the relief of no more demented connection to the Dark One, feeling his power slowly heal and grow, glad to be free of that wretched entity.

"Who would have thought his aura of peace could break a bond of contract with the Dark One," Tulyata said with wonder. "I felt the recoil when it broke."

"I did too." Rtu propped his elbow up on the arm of the chair he was sitting in, his conscience getting the better of him. "If they ever find out without us telling them first, it will cause damage without the ability to repair it—It will forever shatter their trust. Do you think they will forgive us for showing the Dark One where Ayya is? Not that we had much choice at the time, even so, we are responsible for that."

"Let's not find out, because I don't know. Zreyas is not the type to forgive something like that, I don't think. He is likely to commit himself to revenge right now, even with his improvement. He was, after all, a Janquar all his life and very conditioned to be so."

"He isn't Janquar anymore, mother. He's morphed into something fascinating. What scares me about it is, I didn't foresee or create that variation of him."

"Let's just count ourselves lucky Zreyas' powerful peace aura broke the connection and released us. I just checked to make sure, we are no longer bound to him. The laws of balance say that since it was for balance we made it, someone else can break it for balance."

Tulyata rubbed her nose, slammed down her half-glasses, and continued. "That bastard Dark One is powerful! I'm terrified of that creature's potential to do things we never thought of. We lost a lot of power from that escapade. I can tell it in the checks and balances."

Rtu looked at his mother. "Don't worry about it. We are ourselves again, and it will all come back soon enough. I wonder though, can you check yourself with the challenge node again? I mean, you can get locked in maybe if you are under the max?"

"We can try. It is after the start of the challenge, though. So, if I grow in power later and go past the max, I just won't be able to go again. But it might come in handy until then."

She stood and moved into the node, and they watched the purple mist rise. It flowed up the walls and into the ceiling. It finally stopped a few hands from the center.

"—Tulyata is an approved team member. Would you like to travel now? Yes or No."

"No, but is this configuration locked in for the duration of the challenge?"

"—One moment, please... We are sorry, this team is not a permanently approved team.

Reason: It was not locked in before the beginning of the challenge.

"—Would you like to travel now? Yes or No."

"No, but do remember me for future travel, in case we are in a hurry," she grumbled as she walked to the desk.

"You don't want them to know you lost power, do you?"

"No, because I don't want it to lead up to having to tell them what happened."

"Wouldn't it be better to just tell them and let the news come from us?"

"I've checked the odds and balances; it would not be good now."

"It's never going to be a good time. You are using your purpose of balance as an excuse again."

"The percentage change we can awaken Ayya and out of there is much slimmer than if we don't tell them at this point in time."

"I'm not sure why you say they forced us into that decision to help when you made the choice to do it, Tulyata." Rtu sat up. "Just because you like balances, and living your life as a balance maker, doesn't mean that the odds can't change depending on someone's choice to grow or unexpected known circumstances that may or may not show up."

Growing more aggravated and sitting forward, he continued. "Have you thought about factoring in your own growth? I think it is important that we honor the mistakes we made. Perhaps we can at least tell them we made a mistake, but we can't tell them about at this at this point in time to help with the balances."

Rtu leaned back hard. "At least we would have our honor on the table, even if we cloak it for a time, which you are so fond of to begin with. Are you sure you were released from that dark and cursed connection? This doesn't seem like you. You are normally fearless when it comes to facing... Wait... That's it! You are *afraid*!"

Rtu sat straighter in astonishment at his own realization. "Honestly, I'm scared shit-less, but you... You aren't used to experiencing fear."

Tulyata froze and just stared ahead, saying nothing. He thought she might be trying her best to decide if she would lash out in her bitterness or listen to what Rtu had to say.

"Remember what Rhom said about it being rare to see the problem, acknowledge it, and then put something into motion to work past it? Now might be a fantastic time to go by Zreyas' example. If Zreyas can do it at such high improbability, then why not visages?"

Tulyata stared at him, incredulous.

"You are so good at objectively putting things from everyone else on the table to guide us throughout life's choices. Now is a great time to apply that to yourself. I'm putting it out on the table for you, dear Mother. I'm calling you out and inviting you to step up. If you don't, I think your valuable contribution will deteriorate." Rtu paused to see what his mother was going to say, if anything.

Tulyata lowered her gaze.

Rtu knew his mother all too well. She was feeling the conflict and fully expected and explosion. But he had to try to push this. "Mother, I'll put something else out there for you on the table you feel most comfortable with."

He paused and took a deep breath, feeling the fear of his thoughts travel through his body with a death grip. "I'm afraid if you don't face this, you will begin festering and fall. The multiverse needs you right now more than ever. I... need you. But I think there is more at stake this time around. It's not because of the Dark One, not because of me or Rhom, but because you actually like Zreyas. That is in the realm of the heart, and that is an amazing miracle by itself with it coming from you. If you—"

"Stop! You are right, my dear. I'm not used to having issues because I'm cooped up at a desk with my mechanical like design with only one friend—the scales. All I do is formulate strategies. I don't have to deal with real issues of living incarnate-life, in any capacity. I just don't know what to do. I feel... helpless."

A wave of shock ran through him, her saying those words. He just let her talk.

"There are some things about all the checks and balances I can't figure in, because it is all part of the quantum field. The factorable pieces from choices people make, no matter how hard I try to estimate, are almost never known until after the choices are made."

Hearing his mother's words made him realize he had no clue about what she was up against every day. He had his own problems in his role as a visage of earth and air, but he didn't want the problems of being a visage of balance. He felt compassion for her. "I do not understand what you are up against every day. I'm not sure I could take it. You do a phenomenal job at that though, and much better than anyone could."

Rtu turned his body, leaning on the arm of the chair to make sure she knew he was sincere and serious for a change. "I know I seem like I take things too lightly and laugh too much, but I say to you with all my heart that you have balanced things I never thought could be balanced. It's just mind blowing. You care." He paused a moment for emphasis. "But you are not used to showing it because you are not a caregiver. There is a difference. It's a new adventure for you. I invite you to take it. Factor in what you can and live the rest."

Tulyata broke loose suddenly. "Enough of this talk! I'm your mother and superior!"

And there was the explosion he expected. Rtu held his hand up as if to signify peace. "You have your path... and I have mine." Rtu stood, looked at the node feeling quite uncomfortable but excited. "Time for me to go to earth and try out a pseudo-incarnation as a paramedic."

An Author's Lifeblood

Request From the Author

Dear friends,

This is really me, ishKiia.

I would like to stop and explain how important you are to the survival of me, as an author, to write more books. This book is not traditionally published. I published it at my own expense to get this story to you in all formats, and with quality. It would really help me if you could take a couple of minutes of your busy day to review this book and tell friends and family about it. Here are a few reasons:

> 92% of consumers believe suggestions from friends and family more than advertising.
>
> Beyond friends and family, 88% of people trust online reviews written by other consumers as much as they trust recommendations from personal contacts.

You have the power to help make a book you enjoyed more successful. If you enjoyed it, please tell a friend and rate the book at the establishment that you bought it from. Until next time, I hope you create an amazing day for yourself!

~ ishKiia Paige

Keep in Touch

Scan the QR code with your smartphone

If you would like to support an indie author that cares about the community, visit **ishKiia's Patreon**:

https://www.patreon.com/ishKiiaPaige

The Sleeping Phoenix **Facebook Page:**

https://www.facebook.com/IshKiia-Paige-The-Sleeping-Phoenix-Series-107707978352041/

You can subscribe to **ishKiia's personal newsletter.** **NOTE:** She does this personally and promises to never sell or use your information except for this newsletter.

https://www.subscribepage.com/s9y6mo

Finally, if you would like to find out about all of ishKiia's Services, wander on down to her **website**.

https://ishkiiapaige.com

www.ingramcontent.com/pod-product-compliance
Lightning Source LLC
Chambersburg PA
CBHW030540310726
48979CB00010B/1983/J
9781956297201